What the hell have I walked into?

Adam stared at the closed door. He felt like an animal trapped in a cage.

He'd known this trip was going to be hard. And he refused to lie to himself—he'd felt edgy about meeting Carolyn Trent from the start. What sane man in his position wouldn't?

During the whole trip he'd hardened himself to face her. When he'd climbed the stairs to her home, his heart had pounded like a sledgehammer. He'd supposed she'd be polite—initially. After that, he'd been prepared for anything.

Except this. The woman he'd come to meet wasn't here. Instead, he'd been thrown off from the first moment by the strange, starchy Michele Nightingale. As haunting as he found her looks, her manner set his teeth on edge. She'd seemed snippy and stuck-up.

Or so he'd thought until the moment she'd burst into tears.

He swore aloud. What to do now? Everything had to be rethought. *Everything.*

Dear Reader,

This book exists because of four extraordinary people.

One is my husband, Dan, who learned that there were endangered wild horses in the Bahamas—and knew I'd love to find out more. He tracked them down and took me to see them. I was hooked by their story, and I hope you will be, too.

The second person is the all-too-modest Milanne Roher. Milanne has selflessly dedicated herself to these beautiful, mysterious and threatened creatures, the wild horses of Abaco.

I wanted a character who, like Milanne, could bring great passion to a cause, and that character turned out to be Adam Duran. Though he and the heroine, Mickey, have a volatile clash of loyalties, they find they also have deep and abiding similarities.

The two other people who influenced this story are my mother, Beatrice, who was orphaned at fourteen, and an older woman—a stranger, Frances—who took her in. What began as an act of charity turned into a lifelong friendship. Frances's kindness, warmth and generosity continue to echo through the generations of our family.

These women are the basis of the relationship between the characters of Mickey, the protagonist, and Carolyn Trent, who proves so important to both Mickey and Adam.

Please drop in and visit me at my Web site, www.bethanycampbell.com. You'll find more information about the horses there, a contest for you to enter, other goodies and a chance to get in touch. I'd love to hear from you!

Sincerely,

Bethany Campbell

P.S. To see the real horses that got this story off to its start, just check out the Web site for the Abaco Wild Horse Fund, Inc. There are photos, videos, a history and frequent updates. You'll find it at www.arkwild.org or you can simply type the words "Abaco Wild Horses" into your search engine.

BETHANY CAMPBELL

Wild Horses

HARLEQUIN®

TORONTO • NEW YORK • LONDON
AMSTERDAM • PARIS • SYDNEY • HAMBURG
STOCKHOLM • ATHENS • TOKYO • MILAN • MADRID
PRAGUE • WARSAW • BUDAPEST • AUCKLAND

ISBN 0-373-71261-8

WILD HORSES

Copyright © 2005 by Harlequin Books S.A.

Bethany Campbell is acknowledged as the author of this work.

This edition published by arrangement with Harlequin Books S.A.

® and TM are trademarks of the publisher. Trademarks indicated with ® are registered in the United States Patent and Trademark Office, the Canadian Trade Marks Office and in other countries.

www.eHarlequin.com

Printed in U.S.A.

To Bea and Aunt Frances, with love

Books by Bethany Campbell

HARLEQUIN SUPERROMANCE

837—THE GUARDIAN
931—P.S. LOVE YOU MADLY
1052—THE BABY GIFT
1129—A LITTLE TOWN IN TEXAS*
1181—HOME TO TEXAS*
1207—ONE TRUE SECRET

*Crystal Creek

Don't miss any of our special offers. Write to us at the
following address for information on our newest releases.

Harlequin Reader Service
U.S.: 3010 Walden Ave., P.O. Box 1325, Buffalo, NY 14269
Canadian: P.O. Box 609, Fort Erie, Ont. L2A 5X3

CHAPTER ONE

IN THEIR DAY, the Randolph brothers of Crystal Creek, Texas, had been famed for three things.

They were handsome as sin. They were rebellious to the point of recklessness. And they tended to drift off to faraway places and never return.

Enoch Randolph was no exception. He'd left Texas over thirty years ago for a life of ease in the Bahamas and never looked back. As time passed, the crankier he grew. He cut off his ties with all the people of Crystal Creek—except one.

That person was his niece, Carolyn. He stayed in touch, not out of love, but for money. Each spring Enoch mailed her a handwritten receipt. This receipt acknowledged that she'd sent him the yearly check for the range land that she leased from him.

Although Carolyn was Enoch's closest living relative, he never added any greeting or message, except this: "Mrs. Carolyn Randolph Trent: My will stands as per the agreement I made with your mother in 1968. Enoch Randolph."

So, in May when an envelope arrived with the Bahamian stamp, Carolyn's secretary, twenty-six-year-old Mickey Nightingale, opened it as a matter of course. She expected Enoch's usual statement in his usual, crabbed handwriting.

But instead of the receipt, Mickey found an entire letter. Unfolding it, she saw that it had been typed with an old-fashioned typewriter on a sheet of yellowing paper. As she read, anxiety tightened her chest and her heart raced ominously.

May 7
Box N-204 West Bay Street
Nassau, Bahamas

Mrs. Carolyn Trent
Circle T Ranch RR 1
Claro County, Texas 78624, USA
Dear Mrs. Trent:
I regret to inform you that your uncle, Enoch K. Randolph, died in his sleep one week ago on the night of April 30. It was peaceful.

As executor of his will, I am charged with settling the part of his estate involving his lands. Mr. Randolph left specific instructions that I am to do this in person.

I will arrive in Claro County on May 19, the Wednesday afternoon after next. Time is of the essence, and your full cooperation is necessary so matters can be settled by Friday. I can stay no longer.

Please reply immediately. You may leave a message at 424-555-1411.

Sincerely,
Adam Duran

P.S. Your uncle was cremated and his ashes scattered in the Caribbean without ceremony, as per his request.

"Uh-oh," Mickey murmured. Whoever Adam Duran was, he seemed to have the tact and sympathy of a constipated rhinoceros.

Not only that, his letter must have been delayed. Good grief, May 19th was the day after *tomorrow*. The rhinoceros was practically on their doorstep.

Mickey hoped that news of Enoch's death and the brusqueness of the message wouldn't upset Carolyn. Concerned, she rose from her desk and hurried to find her.

Mickey was brisk, efficient and fiercely loyal to her employers, Vern and Carolyn Trent. She kept their lives organized and running smoothly; she liked this job and excelled at it. Officially she was Carolyn's secretary; unofficially she was family, almost like a second daughter.

The Circle T was not only Mickey's workplace, but her home and sanctuary. To her, it was like dwelling in a castle at the heart of a benevolent kingdom. Her growing-up had been harsh, but here she felt privileged, fulfilled—and grateful.

So it pained her to bring bad news to Carolyn, especially since Carolyn was so happy of late. And she was due. Caro had traveled a long stretch of hard times. But now she was giddy, almost girlish, and blooming like a Texas rose.

Carolyn's only child, Beverly, who lived in Denver, was about to make her a grandmother. It was a miracle, pure and simple. Beverly and her husband, Sonny, had tried nine years for this baby. The baby was a girl and she would arrive in three weeks by C-section. She would be named for Carolyn and called Carrie.

As the due date neared, Carolyn's excitement had quickened into intoxication. She and Vern were to fly to Denver to welcome the baby like the little princess she was. The trip was eclipsing almost everything else at the ranch.

Mickey was certain where Carolyn would be—in the spare bedroom she was transforming into a nursery for the baby's visits. Mickey followed the scent of fresh paint down the hall.

She found Carolyn humming as she coated a window frame a rosier shade of pink. She was so intent on her work that she barely glanced up. "What do you think, Mick? Looks better than that pale pastel, doesn't it? Cheerier?"

It's the third time you've switched the color, Mickey wanted to tease. Carolyn had changed her mind about the wallpaper four times, the curtains three times, and the crib twice.

But the news of Enoch Randolph hung like a dark cloud

over Mickey, so she could make no joke. "Carolyn," she said uneasily. "You got a letter from Nassau this morning. I think you'd better read it."

Carolyn kept painting, a small, puzzled smile crossing her face. "I don't know anybody in Nassau." Then suddenly her smile died, and her brush went still. "Wait. Uncle Enoch—he could be there. Is it about him?"

"I'm afraid so."

Carolyn saw it then, the envelope in Mickey's grip. She set the brush aside, her face wary. *She knows,* Mickey thought. *She's guessed.*

Carolyn turned from the window frame, her face pale. "I don't think I want to read it here."

Mickey didn't blame her. The nursery was meant to be a happy room, a place to celebrate life, not think about death.

She took Carolyn's arm. "Maybe we should go into the den."

Carolyn nodded, her lips pressed together. Mickey led the way, and when Carolyn sat on the leather couch Mickey settled beside her and handed her the envelope.

For a moment Carolyn only gazed down at it. She smoothed her blond hair, a nervous gesture. "He's gone, isn't he?" She kept her face severely controlled. "He's dead."

"I'm sorry." Mickey felt the illogical guilt of the bearer of bad news.

Carolyn squared her shoulders, withdrew the letter and read it. Tears sprang to her eyes. She wiped them away. Mickey suspected they would be the only tears shed in the whole state of Texas for the old man, perhaps the only ones in the world.

"I'm glad he didn't suffer," Carolyn said in a shaky voice. "I'm glad it was peaceful."

Mickey nodded.

"He had a long life," Carolyn said in the same tone. "And he lived it the way he wanted. But I wish that this—this Duran man had phoned when it happened. This is so impersonal. Enoch and I didn't have much of a relationship. Oh, hell, to tell the truth, he didn't really even like me. But he *was* family."

Mickey put her arm around Carolyn's shoulder. "You always treated him well. You never forgot his birthday. You remembered him at Christmas. Whenever there was news about the land, you wrote him."

"And he never answered." Carolyn's sigh was rueful. "My God, it's the end of an era. He's the last of my father's generation of that family. And now I'm the last of *my* generation—the oldest living one. It gives me a shiver. Like a goose walking over my grave."

She waved the letter unhappily. "But this really *is* cold. Hard-hearted, almost." She frowned and reread it. "Who *is* this man?"

Mickey shrugged. "Nobody uses a typewriter like that anymore. He must be an old man, sticking to old ways."

"Why is *he* the executor? And why does he have to come *here?*"

"I don't know. Maybe your uncle wanted him to hand over the deed in person. That was the agreement, wasn't it? The lease land's yours now."

Carolyn stared at the dates, frowning harder still. "Yes…but he's coming tomorrow? Good God—tomorrow?"

"He wrote the letter more than a week ago," Mickey said, pointing to its date. "It must have got misrouted."

"Great. Just peachy. He doesn't sound like Mr. Charm, does he? But I should invite him to stay with us. Especially since he's coming all this way."

Inwardly Mickey flinched. Things were frantic enough without an unbidden houseguest, and a stranger at that. Carolyn was trying to be gracious, but Mickey could tell it cost her effort.

"Do you want me to phone him for you? I'll be glad to."

Carolyn grimaced. "I'd *love* you to. But no, it's something

I should do myself. He's probably wondering why I haven't answered."

She folded the letter, stood and handed it to Mickey. "Put it on my desk, will you, sweetie? I'll call him later. First I'm going into town. To the florist. Maybe Enoch didn't want any ceremony, but I can't stand not to do something. I'll order some flowers for the Sunday church service."

"But if he didn't want any ceremony—"

"They're not for him. They're for me," Carolyn said. "I won't even mention his name. I just need to do—*something*. Closure. A way to say goodbye. The Randolph men. Dead. All three."

Mickey knew Carolyn's heart churned with complex emotions. The old man had been eccentric, unfriendly and a loner. He had never married, he was basically shiftless, but he'd stuck to the bargain he'd made so long ago.

Carolyn had always been prompt with her checks, and over the years had raised her payments without being asked. She always saw that he got a fair price for the use of the land. And the money let him live as he chose, a free man.

Enoch had made the original agreement with Carolyn's mother. He didn't give a damn about his Texas land, which he'd won in a poker game. He'd gone to the Caribbean and bought a houseboat in the Bahamas, at Little Exuma. He'd never worked another day in his life.

Now Carolyn gazed down at her fingernails, speckled with rosy paint. "I'd better clean up to go to town." Her face was pensive.

But she was, after all, Carolyn Trent, and half an hour later, when she walked out the door, she held herself royally straight, and she looked like a million dollars. With pride, Mickey watched her go.

LEON VANEK, the new foreman, also watched as Carolyn left. He stood in the shadows just inside the stable door.

At fifty-six, Carolyn Trent was still glamorous. She came from a long line of strong and beautiful women who seemed born to rule. Her domain was the Circle T, twenty-one thousand acres of prime Hill Country.

It was Carolyn who had run the Circle T since the death of her first husband. Her second husband, Vern, was an affable fellow, kindly and intelligent, but no cattleman. He was the county J.P., not a rancher.

Vern presided over justice court, small claims court and administrative hearings, and Carolyn presided over the cattle business. She did it with a firm and expert hand. Generously, she claimed she couldn't handle the job without Mickey Nightingale.

Leon Vanek was new to his job, but he had long studied the Trents because they fascinated him. He was also interested in Mickey, for more than one reason. First, he liked the Circle T. It was the best job he'd ever had.

He'd been raised five counties away, and had worked his way up to assistant foreman at the old MacWhorter Ranch. Earl MacWhorter was a tightfisted old fogy, and both he and his ranch were in decay.

When Earl died, Leon forged glowing references for himself and snagged a series of jobs in Wyoming and Oklahoma. He was an abnormally proud man who had felt he was meant for finer things. With each job he left, he added to his doctored résumé. He didn't think of his false recommendations as counterfeit. In his mind, he deserved them.

When he'd heard of a foreman's position back near Crystal Creek, he lusted for it. He'd grown up looking jealously at the well-run ranches in Claro County. Two were so superior that they filled him with an almost aching covetousness.

J. T. McKinney's Double C was the biggest and best, but Carolyn Trent's was a close second.

It wasn't just these places he looked upon with envy, but

the people, as well. Hell, they were *aristocracy*. He burned to be one of them, so he typed a few more letters of praise for himself.

At the Circle T, he had found his place, and he intended to keep it. He was gentlemanly to Vernon Trent, courtly to Carolyn and unctuously polite to everyone more important than he was.

Now that Carolyn had left the ranch, he figured it the perfect time to call on Mickey. She was part of his plan.

Leon had been at the Circle T for four weeks now, and he saw that Carolyn was so fond of Mickey that she treated her like blood kin. Leon had quickly realized how to cement his relationship with the Trents permanently: he'd marry Mickey.

Then he'd practically be family. Carolyn was about to become a grandmother, with a brat to visit in far-off Colorado, and the Trents would travel more and more. Leon could see himself and Mickey running the place, running it smooth as silk, because Mickey was almost as capable as he was.

Hell, in a few years, the Trents could retire, and he'd reign over the whole shebang. It would be as if the Circle T belonged to him.

Now he knocked on the kitchen door. He used the back entrance out of deference to his position, but he didn't aim to always do so. When Mickey opened the door, he was struck by another reason she interested him.

She was easy on the eyes.

Her skin was perfect, with a natural golden cast, her high cheekbones burnished with health. Her hair was sun-streaked brown, and her eyes were hazel and coolly mysterious.

She greeted him politely, as always. She wore blue jeans, a plain white shirt and a navy blue blazer. A yellow pencil was thrust neatly behind one ear. Everything about her said "strictly business."

Except her hair. She wore it long, parted in the middle and

tucked behind her ears. But it was thick and always seemed slightly tousled. It hinted that she had a secret: *I'm not as prim as I act.*

Leon believed that her prissiness hid a nature that was hot and wild. She had a good body, and in his imagination he did things to it. And he imagined her doing many, many things to his.

"Can I help you?" Mickey asked. "I'm afraid Carolyn's gone."

She had to look up at him, because she was only of medium height, and he was a tall man, almost six and a half feet. He enjoyed the sense of power his height gave him.

"Could I come in?" he asked. "It's you I want to talk to."

She looked startled, but stepped aside to let him enter. Cowboys usually kept their hats on inside, but Leon never did. He liked to emphasize that he was a better sort. "Thanks," he said. "I hope I'm not interrupting."

"I was taking a break from the household accounts. I haven't got any coffee made, but I could offer you a glass of sweet tea."

"Sounds mighty fine." He watched as she moved briskly about, getting a glass, opening the fridge, pouring the tea— waiting on him.

She handed him the tea, but had poured none for herself. She gestured at the kitchen table. "Please have a seat."

He sat, settling his hat on one wide thigh. She remained standing. She crossed her arms as he sipped the tea. "You wanted to talk?"

She was deliberately keeping distance between them. He'd noticed that about her. She acted as if men didn't much interest her.

He'd asked some of the more talkative hands about her. They said if a guy put the move on her, she'd get standoffish and sometimes sharp-tongued. Well, she just hadn't found the man who could give it to her the way she needed.

He reached into the pocket of his green western-cut shirt. He drew out a short length of glittering gold, a bracelet. "I found this. It's the one you lost, isn't it?"

For the first time, real emotion lit her face. The polite smile became dazzling. "Oh! I was afraid it was gone for good. Thank you."

He held it toward her, dangling from his thick fingers. He made sure his hand brushed hers as she took the bracelet, but she didn't seem to notice.

"I saw you and Miz Trent looking for it down by Sabur's stall," Leon said. "She asked me to keep an eye out for it. I found it a few minutes ago."

She radiated happiness. "Carolyn and Vern gave it to me for my birthday. I was *sick* when I lost it."

She tried to fasten it in place, but had trouble doing so with only one hand. He stood and moved next to her. "Here. Let me."

He took the bracelet and slid the clasp in place. This time she couldn't help but be conscious of his big fingers against her bare wrist.

Her cheeks flushed. "I can't thank you enough."

"I know a way you could thank me. Go out with me. Get better acquainted. We work together. But we don't see much of each other." He said this with a smile he thought was charming and nonthreatening. He'd practiced it in the mirror until he thought he'd perfected it.

Yet she seemed disturbed by the suggestion. "That's very kind of you—" she began.

He cut her off smoothly. "There's a new Bavarian restaurant just opened over in Fredricksburg. I thought that maybe tomorrow night—"

She inched backward, her chin rising aloofly. "Sorry. Carolyn's having company from out of town. I have to help out."

He'd expected this refusal. So he gave her the same rehearsed smile. "Maybe some other time."

"Maybe. Things are awfully busy lately." She said it without enthusiasm, as if she meant to discourage him.

At that moment, Leon heard tires on the gravel drive. He stole a glance out the kitchen window. Damn. Vern Trent was home early. Leon should make an exit. But he had one more ploy.

"Jazmeen should be foaling in two weeks," he said. Jazmeen was Carolyn's Arabian mare, and she'd homebred her to her stallion, Sabur al Akmar.

"She's not showing signs yet, but I've seen the charts when she's due. You want to see the little critter when I got it cleaned up and on its feet?"

A look of pure pleasure brightened her face again. Mickey loved horses; he knew that. That's when he'd first taken real note of her, when he'd seen her riding. A woman who rode the way she did had a lot of passion bottled up inside. "I'd love to," she said.

"I'll come get you," he promised. "Then afterwards we'll have a drink, celebrate." He picked up his hat from the chair seat just as Vern came in the door.

Vern looked harried. "Oh, hello, Leon. Everything all right?"

"Everything's fine, Mr. Trent. Found Miss Nightingale's bracelet. Just dropped it off."

Vern glanced at Mickey, who held up her wrist and smiled.

Leon said, "Got to get back to work. Need to take some cotton-seed cake out to that herd by the creek. Thanks for the tea, Miss Nightingale."

He lifted the glass, finished the tea, then set it back on the table. "I'll be seeing you. You know. About Jazmeen and all." He tipped his hat toward both of them, then left.

He went out the back door, putting his hat back on, pulling the brim down hard. Well, he'd made his move, and his campaign was in gear. She really did play hard to get, this one. But she liked him, he was sure of it. She'd be lucky to get a man like him. Why, if Carolyn hadn't taken her in, she'd be no better than a guttersnipe. But she'd cleaned up real good, as the saying went.

The bracelet had given him points—he'd made her face light up, all right.

He'd seen the bracelet fall from her wrist yesterday morning when she'd dismounted Sabur. It had slipped into the straw in the stallion's stall. She hadn't noticed, and he'd said nothing. When she left the stable, he'd picked it up.

Later, when she and Carolyn came back to look, Mickey'd been near tears. She'd felt terrible about losing it; it was special. Leon pretended to help search. He didn't say a word about having found it.

Not then. He was too smart. He'd waited for a moment that was better—for him.

WHEN LEON was gone, Mickey said, "You're home early, Vern. A light schedule at the courthouse?"

"A couple cancellations." He squinted at Mickey with interest. "You're *blushing,* Mick. Carolyn's claimed that Leon Vanek's got his eye on you. She's never wrong about things like that. Asked you out, didn't he? Are you going?"

Mickey gave a defensive smile. "I don't think he's my type."

She wanted to escape back to her office, but Vern wasn't through with her. "What do you mean not your type? He seems like a nice fellow. Hardworking. Polite."

Mickey swallowed and glanced toward the sanctuary of her own rooms. "He's nice enough," she murmured. She hadn't had any say in Vanek's hiring. She'd been down with a killer case of flu, and Caro, who'd needed a foreman quickly, hadn't wanted to bother her.

Often, though, Mickey felt that Leon Vanek was *too* nice, almost groveling. But this was only an intuition, and she didn't want to say such a thing to Vern, who'd helped Caro pick him. Still, Vanek made her uncomfortable.

Her uneasiness must have shown because Vern took pity on her. He smiled kindly. "I'm sorry. I shouldn't play Cupid. Carolyn's all hearts and flowers and family-family-family now. It's contagious. Pay me no mind. I'm a doddering old man about to become a grandpa."

Mickey managed a smile. "You're not doddering, and you're not old. But I've got to get to back to the accounts."

Vern's face went serious. "Help me out first, will you? Caro called me on her car phone. Told me about Enoch. She took it harder than I thought she would. I suppose it brings back the other losses."

Mickey nodded, for death had taken most of Carolyn's family. Her father had deserted the family long ago and later died in Canada. Her mother and sister had both died of breast cancer. She had lost her first husband to a heart attack.

Now, both her uncles were gone, too. Beverly and the new baby were her only close blood relatives.

"I never knew Enoch," Vern said solemnly. "Carolyn always shrugged him off as just a loner, but he sounded like a kook to me. I hope he hasn't pulled any funny business with this will. Show me the letter, will you?"

Mickey led him into Carolyn's office. Vern read it and shook his head. "I wonder who the hell this guy is. Hope he didn't insinuate himself into the old coot's life to fleece him. Enoch was getting up in years. He might have been losing his grip on reality."

The thought was a grim one, and it had occurred to Mickey, too.

Vernon swung open the framed painting that hid the wall safe. "The original will's in here somewhere. I'm going to take it into town and show it to Martin Avery. I want a lawyer's opinion. I won't have Caro cheated out of what's rightfully hers."

"That makes two of us," Mickey said. There were eleven thousand acres of lease land, more than half the ranch. If Carolyn lost them, it would be ruinous to the Circle T. Next to her family, Carolyn loved the ranch more than anything in the world.

CAROLYN KNOCKED at Mickey's door.

"Come on in," Mickey called. She lay on the couch reading a library book. Carolyn entered, unceremoniously pushed aside Mickey's stocking feet and sat next to her. "Well, I finally got through to the number Adam Duran gave."

"And?" Mickey bit into an apple, her midevening snack.

"The number wasn't a personal phone. It was a marina of some kind. I talked to a man who sounded like he was reciting the lyrics to a Calypso song."

Mickey laughed. "So what did you learn?"

"Not much. I told him I was trying to find Duran to invite him to stay with us. He said he'd relay the message, that he'd see him later tonight."

"Did you ask him who Duran is? What he does?"

"No. Too much noise. Like there was a party going on in the background. Anyway, I left word."

"Hmm." Mickey shrugged. "So what did the lawyer tell Vern?"

"Martin? He knows the old will was valid—his father's the one who drew it up. If this Duran tries to pull something shady, Martin can handle him. He's going to look it over and get back to us. But at this point he doesn't think we have to worry."

"That's a relief," Mickey said. "Super Barrister on the job. Hooray for Mighty Martin."

Carolyn rumpled her hair playfully. From the front of the house, they heard the doorbell chime. A moment later, Vern knocked at Mickey's door, which stood ajar. "Carolyn? Mickey? Come on out here. Lynn's here. And she's got a surprise for you."

"Oops," said Mickey. "Shoes? Shoes?" She groped around

and slipped back into her moccasins, then followed Carolyn to the living room. Carolyn gave her niece's cheek a smacking kiss, and Mickey greeted her with a grin.

Petite and auburn-haired, Lynn was the daughter of J. T. McKinney and Pauline, Carolyn's late sister. In her thirties, Lynn looked young for her age, and her jeans and riding boots made her seem tomboyish. She was smiling like someone almost too joyful to contain herself.

"I just found out," Lynn bubbled, "and I had to ride straight over to tell you in person. Guess what?"

"You've got a new horse?" Carolyn asked. Horses were Lynn's passion.

"No," laughed Lynn, "much better! Tyler and Ruth sold the winery in Napa Valley. They're coming home! This time to *stay*."

Lynn threw her arms around her aunt. She and Carolyn hugged and laughed and cried at the same time. Mickey grinned. Carolyn's nephew—her late sister's firstborn—coming home! Tyler was Carolyn's favorite of Pauline's children, and the one about whom she'd worried most.

Tyler had brains, determination and an almost endless capacity for work. What he'd never had was luck. His younger brother, Cal, seemed to prosper without effort. Tyler struggled to run two wineries that were a thousand miles apart. He was deeply in debt, mostly to Cal.

Carolyn had feared Tyler and his family might stay in California forever. His wife had inherited the Napa Valley winery. But running it was not only expensive, but a backbreaking job. Tyler's heart belonged truly to the more humble winery he'd started in Claro County. He had sweat blood to keep both operations working.

"When did this happen?" Caro drew back to study Lynn's beaming face.

"He called this afternoon. Ruth said she couldn't watch Tyler work himself to death any longer. She decided she wanted to come back, and just this last weekend they put the winery up for sale. They didn't tell anybody here, because they thought it might take forever to sell—"

Vern nodded. "True, from what I've read lately about the California wine market. I'm glad for Tyler. He's had enough hard breaks."

Lynn was so excited, she practically bounced. "But this movie star decided he wanted a winery—and it was *theirs* he wanted. It was just the right size, he said. So, as soon as they close the deal, in two weeks, they'll move back."

"To the house they built," Carolyn said with satisfaction. "And the vineyards they planted here."

"I've missed them something terrible," Lynn admitted. Tears still glistened in her eyes.

"I know, honey," Carolyn said. "We all have. But they had to try."

Vern shook his head. "Two outfits, that far apart, that high maintenance—I was scared he'd work himself into an early grave trying to handle it all."

Or go broke trying, Mickey thought. She knew Carolyn had worried about that, too. Without Cal's help, Tyler would have failed long ago.

Carolyn took Lynn's face between her hands. "I'm glad good luck's finally come his way. He's long overdue, that big brother of yours."

"And Cal's coming next fall, too," Lynn said. "*Both* my brothers are moving home. I can't believe it. We'll all be together again."

"Well, this occasion calls for one thing," Vern announced. When the three women looked at him questioningly, he gave them a superior smile. "A toast. In wine. *Texas* wine."

Mickey laughed, and so did Carolyn. Lynn hugged her aunt again and said, "And Beverly's having a baby in less than a month. Nothing's more important than family. Everything's *perfect.*"

"Indeed, it is," agreed Vern.

And everything did seem perfect. So perfect that no further thought of Adam Duran crossed anyone's mind.

CHAPTER TWO

ON TUESDAY, Martin Avery came to the house to discuss Enoch's will. Martin, in his mid-sixties, had rosy pink skin and snow-white hair.

Mild, mannerly and tidy, he had practiced law longer than anyone in Claro County. He was a peaceful man who worked hard to bring about peaceful solutions.

He sat at the dining room table with Carolyn and Vern. Because Mickey handled so much of the ranch's business, Carolyn asked her to stay and listen to what Martin had to say.

Martin touched the two wills that lay before him. "These are simple documents. Enoch didn't like doing things in complicated ways."

Martin summed up the agreement Enoch had originally made with Carolyn's mother. As long as she paid the lease monies, she was heir to the land. When she'd died, Enoch had the will redrawn naming Carolyn as heir, but nothing else was changed.

He paused. "Did he ever express dissatisfaction with the arrangement?"

Although Carolyn's face showed concern, she shook her head no. "Every year he endorsed the check and wrote saying that the will stood according to agreement."

"And when's the last time he confirmed it?"

"A year ago." She frowned. "But last year's lease was legally up on April 21st, and he never cashed this year's check.

If he didn't cash it, technically, right now, I'm *not* leasing the land. Is that a problem?"

"Let's hope not. He probably didn't cash it because he was ill."

Vern spoke up. "It still worries me, and so does this executor. Who is he? Why's he coming here? I don't like the sound of it."

Martin laid a slim, pink hand on the older document. "A will has to name an executor. In the first one, he named my father. But my father was retired when Enoch made you heir, Carolyn. He didn't know or trust me—I was just a young whippersnapper to him."

He touched the more recent will. "The executor for this one's a judge in the Bahamas. If he retired or died, Enoch would have to name someone to replace him. Someone he trusted, and he didn't trust easily. He'd be hard to hoodwink."

Vern didn't seem convinced. "Wouldn't he have to rewrite the will to do that?"

"A handwritten codicil with witnesses should do it."

"I hope you're right." Vern muttered. "But it bothers me. Duran sounds like a crank."

Martin smiled and handed the two wills to Vernon. "Enoch was a crank himself. It figures he'd hook up with one of his own kind."

"I wonder why he wanted this man to come to Texas," Carolyn mused. "What's the point?"

Martin gave a good-natured shrug. "Maybe that's how he wanted it done. A friend to carry it out in person. Not to hand it off to some long-distance lawyer." He made a wry face. "We lawyers are reputed to be a shifty lot, you know."

Vern laughed, and Carolyn and Mickey both smiled. Carolyn said, "So I shouldn't expect any surprises?"

Martin's expression grew serious again. "There can *always* be surprises. If there are, we'll deal with them as they arise. In the meantime relax, Caro. You've got a blessed event coming up. Don't let some vague worry spoil it."

Bridget Blum, the cook, knocked at the door frame. "Carolyn, that antique dealer from Austin's on the phone. He wants to talk to you about the high chair from England. He can get it after all."

Carolyn whooped. "He can? Fabulous! I'll be right there—excuse me, everybody."

And she was dashing off, the will forgotten for the time, her thoughts happily centering again on the coming of little Carrie.

Vernon pretended to hold his head in despair. "Antique? From England? The shipping alone will break us. She's a woman possessed."

"But it's a good way to be possessed," said Martin.

Mickey and Vernon walked him to the front door. As they watched Martin climb into his car, Vern said, "She *has* been extravagant lately. Beef prices aren't what they used to be. It's harder for her every year to keep this ranch in the black."

Mickey knew. Every year she'd seen the profits wobble and sometimes shrink. "It's just that she's so excited right now. She'll come back to herself. You'll see."

Vern patted her shoulder. "You're exactly right. She's kept a tight budget for a long time. She ought to be able to indulge herself." He glanced at his watch. "I need to get back to the courthouse, but I'll be home as early as I can. Mick, are you ready for this Duran character to descend?"

"Ready as I can be."

Early that morning the man with the Caribbean accent had phoned and left a message on Carolyn's answering machine. He said that he'd told Duran of the invitation, and Duran sent word he would stay if she wanted him to. But only *if*.

Carolyn and Mickey had found the message cryptic and wondered why Duran hadn't phoned himself. Carolyn said maybe he was one of those people who didn't like phones, and Mickey guessed that he was deaf, and they'd spend the whole visit shouting into his ear.

"I'm sure Carolyn's delegated you the job of getting ready for Duran." Vern smiled. "She's too busy in Babyland."

Mickey shot him a grin. "Bingo."

She'd already seen to the guest room and given Bridget a supper menu. If Duran needed entertaining, she'd made a list of things that might amuse him. The Hill Country was in full spring bloom now, and if she had to, she'd drive him past every bluebonnet in the county.

Mickey spanked her hands together. "Don't worry," she said with total confidence. "I'll handle him."

THAT AFTERNOON Mickey was going over Carolyn's extensive lists of Things That Must Be Done For the Great Journey to Denver.

Round-trip first-class tickets from Austin to Denver. *Check.*

Rental car in Denver. *Check.*

Arrange to courier extra luggage. *Check.*

Get Vern's prescriptions refilled. *Check.*

Carolyn's travel wardrobe. Fifty-two items, stored in guest-room closet, ready to be packed. *Check, except two pairs of shoes.*

Vern's travel wardrobe (as if Vern cared). Twenty-one items. Stored with Carolyn's to be packed. *Check.*

Presents for Beverly, twelve items. *Check.*

Presents for Sonny, nine items. *Check.*

Presents for baby, thirty-seven items. *Check except locket to be picked up from jeweler in Austin.*

Regular camera. *Check.*

Digital camera. *Check.*

Video camera. *Check.*

Film. *Check.*

Videotape. *Check.*

Mickey was starting page two of the list, when Carolyn called her into the living room. She was once again obsessed with The Matter of the Panda. Vern had just got home from work, and Carolyn wanted to talk to him, too.

"I've decided *yes* on that pink panda from Saks," Carolyn announced. "But I don't want to send it, I want to take it. I'll have to carry it on the plane. See what the airline says, will you, Mickey? I'd hate to buy an extra seat for it. But I will if I have to."

"Good grief!" Vern said. "A seat for a panda? We'll be bankrupt."

"Oh, hush," Carolyn said. "When we come back home again, I'll behave. You know I will. But that panda's going to Denver."

"That thing's four feet tall," he protested. "How can you carry it on? It's big enough to carry *you*."

"I don't care," said Carolyn. "It's the most wonderful panda I've ever seen, and I want to give it to her myself."

"*Her?* She's a baby, Carolyn," Vern reasoned. "She won't even be able to see it."

But Carolyn wouldn't be budged. "I want to make Beverly laugh when she sees us deplane. It's the cutest panda in the world. It'll tickle her to pieces."

"It won't fit in the overhead."

"I'll hold it on my lap," Carolyn replied. "It's only a thousand miles or so."

Vern rolled his eyes heavenward in mock despair. But when he let his gaze rest again on Carolyn, he couldn't disguise his affection for her or his pleasure at her excitement.

Carolyn was thinking out loud. "But if I'm going to carry a pink panda, I can't wear the red suit. I'll wear the new pink one. But the shoes haven't come yet. Mickey, will you call the store? I ordered them three weeks ago. What's so hard about dying shoes pink?"

"Should be easy," Mickey agreed and wrote,

Call airline about panda.

Call about pink shoes.

Carolyn laid her finger against her chin thoughtfully. "I should make an appointment at Curly Sue's just before we go. This new tint she put on my hair isn't holding. I want my old brand. I don't want to go to Denver half blond and half gray…."

"I'll call her for you," Mickey promised, adding Curly Sue—old tint, to her list.

"You'd be gorgeous if your hair was green," Vern said and kissed his wife's forehead. "Settle down, honey. The baby isn't due for three weeks."

"Don't pay any attention to me," Carolyn said cheerfully. "I'm losing my mind, that's all."

"You need reality therapy," Vern said. "Go change into your jeans. Maybe we'll have time to take a little canter before this Duran fella comes."

"But—" Carolyn started to protest.

"Go change," Vern said firmly. "It'll do you good. I'm going to get a glass of tea." He ambled toward the kitchen.

Just as Carolyn headed for the master bedroom, the telephone jingled. Mickey reached for it, but Carolyn, brightening again, said, "I'll get it. Maybe the locket's ready."

But when she picked up the phone and listened to the voice at the other end, her expression changed, and her body tensed as if she'd been physically struck.

Mickey had been on her way to her office, but the transformation in Carolyn alarmed her. She halted, staring in concern.

Carolyn sank onto the sofa as if her knees no longer had strength to support her. Her shoulders sagged, and her hands shook so hard she had to use both to hold the receiver. Her face turned ashen, and suddenly she looked every one of her fifty-six years.

She hardly spoke. From time to time she stammered out a question. But mostly she listened. And listened. Tears welled in her eyes.

Mickey's heart went cold and clenched up like a fist. She had a sickening certainty: only one thing could hit Carolyn this hard. *Something's happened to Beverly. Or to the baby. Or to both.*

When Carolyn hung up, her hands shook worse, and tears streaked her cheeks. Mickey, frightened, hurried toward her just as Vern stepped back into the room.

"Sometimes Bridget puts too much sugar in that stuff," Vern grumbled, "Doesn't even taste like tea anymore. Tastes like—"

He stopped when he saw Carolyn's face. "Caro?" He went to her side and put his arm around her. "What's wrong, honey?"

Carolyn could hardly speak. She struggled to keep her chin from quivering, but her lips moved jerkily, and she had to choke out the news.

The caller had been Beverly's husband, Sonny. He'd had to rush Beverly to the emergency ward that morning just before dawn. Doctors had performed an emergency caesarian.

The baby was undersized, and her skin had a bluish cast. Her heart had a serious defect.

Carolyn started to cry harder, but forced herself to tell the rest. Sonny said that little Carrie had an obstruction of the right ventricle. She'd been put in a special neonatal unit. She needed open-heart surgery as soon as possible. Without surgery, she could not survive.

Then Carolyn lost control, and Vern drew her into his arms, holding her tightly.

Mickey, stunned and feeling helpless, put her hand on Carolyn's shoulder. Never before had she seen Carolyn break down completely. Never.

"They'll try to operate tomorrow," Carolyn sobbed. "But she's—she's so tiny. And Beverly doesn't know yet. They haven't told her how serious it is. Oh, Vern, I want to go to them *now*."

"Then we'll go." Vern held her tighter.

As he stroked her hair and rubbed her back, his troubled brown eyes settled on Mickey. "Mick, call the airport, will you? Get us on the first flight out of here."

"I want to get to Beverly," Carolyn said. "And my grand-baby. I've got to."

Mickey's mind raced, searching for the best way to meet this crisis. "What if I call J.T.? Maybe he could fly you."

J.T., Carolyn's brother-in-law, was a pilot, with his own small jet.

Vern looked at her gratefully. "Bless you, Mick. I didn't even think of J.T."

"I'll phone him," Mickey said. "Then I'll pack for you."

J.T. NOT ONLY AGREED to fly Caro and Vern to Denver; he insisted on it. He would be ready to take off in an hour, and urged Mickey to just get them to his place. And so Mickey packed only two suitcases instead of the dozens Carolyn had so painstakingly planned.

Carolyn refused, superstitiously, to take any of the presents, especially the baby gifts. If the worst happened, it would be too unbearable to have them there, each like a pulsing wound.

Mickey drove Carolyn and Vern to J.T.'s ranch. As Carolyn climbed into the plane, she looked dazed. She wasn't wearing her pink suit or pink shoes or carrying the big pink panda designed to make Beverly laugh.

Mickey noticed, sadly, that Carolyn had been right. Her hair was half gray and half blond. She had planned to get off the plane in Denver looking glamorous and confident, ready to buck up Beverly's spirits. Instead, she would arrive wan, disheveled and shaken.

Mickey brooded on the unfairness of it all the way back to the Circle T. Carolyn, Vern, Beverly and Sonny were good people, kind and generous. Carolyn had been like a second mother to Mickey—no, in truth, she'd treated Mickey far *better* than Mickey's own mother had. She had been Mickey's salvation. And so had Vern.

As for Sonny, he was himself a doctor, easing suffering and saving lives. Beverly was a hospital administrator. She, too, had worked to serve and heal people. Why was *their* child stricken? Life wasn't simply unjust, it was random and cruel.

Lost in these gloomy thoughts, it wasn't until late afternoon that Mickey realized she'd forgotten something. Worry and sorrow had driven all else from her mind.

She was puzzled when she heard an unfamiliar-sounding car come up the drive and stop. Its door slammed, and someone mounted the front porch steps. The doorbell rang, buzzing like an impatient wasp.

Mickey stifled a swearword. *Oh, no,* she thought. *Adam Duran.* Who needed him at a time like this? And Carolyn had invited him to stay.

The last thing Mickey wanted at this point was to guest-sit a stranger and pretend to be hospitable. She stamped to the entrance foyer, feeling anything but welcoming. But Carolyn would want her to be gracious, so she tried to hide her irritation as she swung open the door.

She saw the man standing there, and she blinked in amazement.

Good grief, he's gorgeous, she thought in confusion. *This can't be him.*

But it was. "I'm Adam Duran," he said. He had a low voice, slightly husky. "I'm here to see Carolyn Trent."

He held out his hand. She grasped it. It was warm and seemed to vibrate in hers, as if his gave off an electrical charge.

He was six feet tall with unfashionably long hair that fell past his ears and curved in a thick forelock across his brow. The hair was dark blond, and he was as tanned as a construction worker. His eyes were azure-blue.

He was dressed casually, almost insolently so for someone on a legal errand. His jeans were faded. The cotton shirt, too, was washed out, laundered so often the fabric was thin.

Yes, she thought, slightly awed, he looked like someone who lived on a sun-drenched island, who swam in the ocean every day, who was a different breed of man altogether from the land-bound cattlemen she knew.

The only thing that seemed out of place was that he had on cowboy boots, well-worn black ones, scuffed and down at the heels. In his left hand he carried a battered duffel bag.

A giddy, fluttery sensation filled her with bewilderment. He was a striking man, but handsome men didn't have this effect on her—ever.

The expression on her face must have gone odd. He looked at her more closely and frowned. "This *is* Carolyn Trent's place?"

Mickey, embarrassed by her reaction, tried to seize control of herself. She'd been carrying her reading glasses, and thrust them on as if donning a protective mask. The lenses blurred her vision. This helped her regain control of herself. Dimmed and out of focus, he was not as disturbing.

"Yes," she said in her crispest tone. "I'm Mrs. Trent's secretary. She said you'd be here. Come in."

He took a step closer then paused. The sea-blue eyes had a critical glint as he looked her up and down. "And your name is…?" he prompted.

Her smile felt stiff, forced. "Miss Nightingale. Michele Nightingale. Er, Mickey."

"Miss Nightingale," he repeated with an edge of sarcasm in his voice.

"Yes," she said, opening the door more widely. "Please, come in."

She stood well back so that his body wouldn't brush hers as he stepped inside. He stopped in the middle of the foyer and looked about. The living room was gracious, yet homey.

"Nice place," he said, but he had that same edge in his voice.

"I imagine you had a long trip," Mickey said, primly as an old-fashioned schoolmarm. "May I get you something to drink? We have coffee, soft drinks, sweet tea, juice, beer, wine—the wine's local. Made just down the road, in fact. Or water, if you'd prefer."

"Water's fine," Adam said. His eyes drifted to a painting over the fireplace and lingered there. Mickey stole a glimpse at him over the top of her glasses. Most men, seeing that painting for the first time, were bewitched.

Adam Duran also seemed struck by it, but his expression was critical.

"That's Beverly, Mrs. Trent's daughter," Mickey said, keeping her teacherlike tone. "She lives in Denver now."

He said nothing, just kept staring at the portrait. Beverly looked stunning; she was the sort of woman men could fall in love with at first sight—even if their first sight of her was only a picture.

Mickey turned away sadly from the image, for it made her wonder how Beverly and Sonny were, and if Caro and Vern had reached Denver yet. How was Caro holding up? If anything happened to this baby, Carolyn would be shattered, destroyed—Mickey could not bear to think of it.

Trying to push the fears from her mind, she went to the kitchen and poured a glass of ice water. Her job right now was to tend to Adam Duran. He should be told as soon as possible that Carolyn wasn't there.

Carolyn had invited him to stay at the ranch, but with her gone, there was no need for him to stay. Mickey hoped he'd have the good grace to know it. Who cared about the technicalities of the stupid lease land at a time like this?

She carried the glass back to the living room and handed it to Adam, who still gazed up at Beverly's likeness. "She looks like the sort that entered beauty contests," he said. "And ended up marrying a doctor."

Mickey didn't like his tone. "She was," she said coldly. "And she did."

He smiled, as if smug about his own power of observation. Resentment tore through Mickey's frayed nerves. Who was he to walk into Carolyn's home and make a snide remark about her suffering child?

She no longer needed defenses against such a man. And she forgot that Carolyn would want her to be cordial. Almost defiantly, she laid her reading glasses aside and gestured at the couch.

"Sit," she said, as much an order as an invitation. "I'm afraid I have some bad news for you."

He raised a brow questioningly. But he sat. He didn't sink back against the couch. He stayed on its edge, his posture alert, gazing at Mickey with narrowed eyes. "Okay. Bad news. What?"

She sat down in the chair opposite him. She crossed her ankles and clasped her hands in her lap. "Mrs. Trent and her husband were called away this afternoon. It's a family emergency. I don't know when they'll be back. It may be a few days. It may be longer."

He straightened his back and frowned. "I *have* to talk to her. As soon as possible. I can't hang around here waiting. I've got tickets back home for Friday—"

"Nobody foresaw this, Mr. Duran," she said. "It's unfortunate for everyone concerned."

He gave her a piercing look, almost intimidating. "You've got no idea how unfortunate. How can I get in touch with her?"

"I don't know. She's probably still en route."

He gritted his teeth and cast an angry glance toward the ceiling, as if demanding that heaven give him patience.

Mickey said, "She invited you to be a guest here, and she's not a woman to go back on her word. If you can't change your ticket to go back sooner, you're welcome to stay on until Friday or—"

"I can't go back sooner," he retorted. "The fare would be higher. I tried to get here as cheaply as I could."

Well, Mickey thought, that was *almost* a point in his favor. At least he didn't want to squander the estate money on travel expenses. But, still, his interest was only in himself. He hadn't even asked about Caro's troubles.

But then, though he still looked unhappy, he said, "What's the family emergency? If I can ask."

Mickey clasped her hands together more tightly. "Her daughter's just had her first child. A little girl. The baby has a serious heart condition. They're going to have to operate tomorrow."

He looked at her, frowning as if such a thing could not be, *should* not be.

"A serious condition? You mean the baby could…"

Die. He didn't say it, but the word hung in the air like a curse: *The baby could die.*

"Yes," she said, her throat tightening.

"That's lousy," he said. "That's terrible. I—I'm sorry." The sarcastic tinge had vanished from his voice.

Her throat clamped even harder. She couldn't speak. Only nod mutely.

He leaned toward her. "I really am sorry." He paused. "You said it's a little girl?"

"A little girl," Mickey managed to repeat. She thought of the dozens of pink outfits Carolyn had bought for the child. They were still wrapped and stacked in the closet.

Her gaze fell to the coffee table. The Saks catalog lay there, still turned to the page picturing the enormous pink-and-white panda with its huge, rosy bow.

Again it flashed through Mickey's mind: Carolyn's plan to get off the plane, dressed all in pink, holding that ridiculously large animal, just to make Beverly laugh and not be nervous about the birth…. But now…

Mickey couldn't help it. Tears welled in her eyes. She'd fought them ever since Sonny's call, and until now she'd won. Suddenly they overtook her, and she turned her face so Adam wouldn't see.

But he already had. "Are you all right? Miss Nightingale?"

She heaved a shaky sigh of anger at her own weakness. "I'll be fine," she managed to say. But memories cascaded madly through her head.

Carolyn had shopped so lovingly, had refused store gift wrap, because *every* purchase had to be brought home and shown to Vern and Mickey for approval. Then she and Mickey had wrapped them all, to make them more personal. Carolyn had gone through extravaganzas with paper and imaginative bows…she and Mickey had fussed and giggled and carried on, and Carolyn had been so *happy*….

Mickey swore to herself and covered her eyes. She'd never considered herself sentimental, but now she was coming apart over booties and ribbons and bows. She should be made of sterner stuff. But the tears spilled over and slipped down her cheeks.

Get hold of yourself, dammit.

Suddenly Adam Duran was before her, bending on one knee in front of her, putting a hand on each arm of the chair. "Miss Nightingale?" he said. "Michelle? Mickey—don't cry. Please don't cry."

Now chagrin compounded her grief and fear. How stupid to let a stranger see her like this—and his kindness made it worse. It had been easier to be steely when she'd thought him cold and smug.

She kept her eyes covered and bent her head lower, but she could feel more tears coursing down, and her body shook with suppressed sobs.

"Well, no," he said, sounding flummoxed, "Cry if you need to. Cry if it helps."

He dug into the pocket of his faded jeans and pulled out an equally faded blue bandana handkerchief. She'd balled her free hand into a fist. He took the clamped fingers in his hands and gently pried them open. He tucked the handkerchief into her palm then closed her fingers back over it.

"Take that," he said. "It's old—but it's clean. Really."

She raised the handkerchief to her face. It smelled of old-fashioned laundry, the kind that dried by sunlight and breezes. She scrubbed at the offending tears.

"I—don't—usually—do—this," she said.

He touched her arm, a surprisingly gentle gesture. "Can I get you something? You want my glass of water? Or a fresh one?"

The sensation of his hand against her flesh sent a strange, new frisson through her. She hazarded a glimpse of him over the handkerchief. His forehead was furrowed, and his eyes were filled with worry that seemed real.

She realized she would do better if he were not so near and so tensed with empathy. "I—I'd like a glass of water," she said, her voice thickened by crying. "There's a pitcher in the fridge. If you wouldn't mind."

"Sure thing," he said, patting her arm. "You bet."

He rose and went toward the kitchen. Perhaps he understood she needed to be alone awhile to pull herself together. He took his time.

She stopped crying. She dried the last of her tears, straightened up in her chair. Taking slow, deep breaths, she got up and went to the coffee table.

Without looking at the page, she slapped the catalog shut and thrust it deep into the magazine rack. She would not allow herself to look again at the picture of that damned panda. Not until she knew the baby was well.

And little Carrie Dekker would get well, she told herself. Doctors could do miracles these days, and Sonny knew the finest ones. *But still*, her mind nagged, *but still…*

Adam came into the room again, holding a blue glass misted with cold. He offered it to her. "Feel better?" he asked.

She took it. "Much better. Thank you."

The drink cooled her aching throat. He watched her, concern still etched on his face.

"I really don't usually do that," she apologized.

He nodded, hooking one thumb in his belt. "I didn't think so."

"I—I've been holding it in. I didn't want to break down in front of Caro. She didn't need that. She was having a tough enough time herself."

"I imagine she was."

"This is her first grandchild," Mickey said, feeling she owed him an explanation for her outburst. "She's been planning for months. This really blindsided her. Did I mention Beverly's her only child? She's worried about her, too. Beverly's wanted a baby for so long."

He cast another look at Beverly's portrait over the mantel. He no longer looked critical. "How long?"

"They've been married nine years."

"I hope it all works out for them."

"So do I," Mickey said with feeling. "They're good people. All of them."

He looked suddenly troubled. "I shouldn't impose on you at a time like this. I'll go. I noticed a motel when I came through town."

The motel, she thought dully. *Oh, Carolyn wouldn't want that.*

"No," Mickey said firmly. "You came all this way. You were invited to stay, and the invitation stands. Carolyn would be mortified if you checked into a motel."

He said nothing. He stared down at the carpet, rubbed it with the heel of his scuffed cowboy boot.

Mickey was starting to feel more like her usual, efficient self. Or at least she thought she was. "Everything's ready for you. The guest room's waiting. Bridget's got everything for supper…"

He looked up, meeting her gaze. Again she was startled by the vivid blue of his eyes. "Bridget?"

"She's the cook and housekeeper," Mickey said. "She lives here. We both do. And she *likes* company. She's been looking forward to your visit."

Mickey didn't add that Bridget was the only one who'd looked forward it. But now she herself was determined to show Adam that the Circle T was a hospitable place, even in crisis.

Adam still looked conflicted, his mouth twisted with doubt.

"It's a big house," Mickey said. "You can have all the privacy you want. There's a den with a TV and—things. And there're horses, if you ride. Can you ride?"

His chin went up, and he seemed to stand taller. Any aura of uncertainty vanished. "Yeah," he said. "I can ride."

"Then it's settled. Come with me. I'll show you the guest room."

A frown line appeared between his eyes, but he lifted the battered duffel bag and slung its strap over his shoulder. She led him down the hall, past Carolyn's open office and her own. She noticed that he glanced in both rooms. He seemed to be observing the house with unusual keenness.

The guest room was a large, airy room with an adjoining bath. The white curtains had been pushed open, and the windows overlooked a garden of native Texas wildflowers. It was May, and they bloomed in profusion, the delicate gold of the daisies, the bolder gold and scarlet of the Indian blankets and the deep, tender blue of the bluebonnets.

Mickey had set a white vase of the flowers on the antique oak dresser with its framed oval mirror. Matching the dresser was a four-poster bed. It had a long white skirt and was covered with a colorful patchwork quilt.

A bookcase was filled with volumes old and new, from classics with faded spines to recent best sellers, their covers still crisp and shiny. A television sat on a low oak bench across from a pair of chintz-covered armchairs. Framed Audubon prints of songbirds hung on the walls.

She said, "The den's next to the living room. There's a bigger TV there, videos, more books and a pool table. If you need me, I'll be right down the hall in my office."

She moved to the door and stepped into the hall. "Supper's at seven-thirty. Since there's just you and me, I thought we'd eat in the kitchen, if that's all right with you."

He looked her up and down, then nodded. "It's fine."

She had never before thought of the guest room as womanish. But in contrast to his masculinity, it suddenly seemed so. He looked out of place in the midst of the snowy curtains and polished furniture and delicately framed prints. He didn't seem a man suited for chintz and flower arrangements.

With his faded jeans and work shirt, and his skin so burnished by the sun, he would have looked far more at home on the deck of a boat on a lonely sea, tugging ropes and raising sails. As she closed the door, she had the uneasy feeling that he was the sort who wouldn't be comfortable shut up in any room. He gave off the air that he wasn't quite tame.

What sort of person *was* he, anyway? Who was this man, really, suddenly sharing the house with her and Bridget?

WHAT THE HELL *have I walked into?* Adam thought, staring at the closed door. He felt like an animal trapped in a cage.

He'd known this trip was going to be hard. And he refused to lie to himself; he'd felt edgy about meeting Carolyn Trent. What sane man in his position wouldn't?

During the whole trip, he'd hardened himself to face her. When he'd climbed the front stairs, his heart had pounded like a sledgehammer. He'd supposed she'd be polite—initially. After that, he'd been prepared for anything.

Except for *this*. The woman he'd come so far to meet was gone. Because of a sick, newborn baby. Maybe a *mortally* sick baby.

He swore under his breath and pitched his bag onto the bed to unpack it. He'd been thrown off from the first moment by the strange, starchy Mickey Nightingale.

When she'd first opened the door, she'd stared at him as if he were a freak. He supposed that in her eyes he was. She was neat as a pin. The creases in her jeans looked sharp as blades. Her long-sleeved white blouse was ironed to perfection. Almost everything about her radiated purity and order, except her tousled hair. And the wildly startled look in her eyes.

She'd even put on her glasses, as if to make sure of what she was seeing on Carolyn's respectable porch. He supposed he looked like a bum.

Before he'd come, he'd thought about getting a haircut. He'd thought about buying new jeans, even a dress shirt. Then he'd remembered the maxim: *Distrust any enterprise that requires new clothes.* To hell with upgrading his wardrobe.

He'd meant to show up as himself, not pretending to be anyone or anything else.

Yet he'd been immediately daunted by the Nightingale woman. She was *attractive* in an odd, unattainable way. In spite of her primness, there was something about her that was—only one word came to him—exquisite.

Her skin was so perfect he'd been tempted to reach out to

find if it could possibly feel as smooth as it looked. She wore no makeup except for a touch of pink on her lips. Could her face really be so flawless?

Her hazel eyes were a rich, brownish gold. Her hair was brown slightly tinged with dark gold—a color as mysterious to him as autumn, a season that never came to the Caribbean. Her curls were rumpled, the only slightly untidy thing about her. Yet that one touch of disorder became her. It made her seem human, after all.

Otherwise she was the very essence of a proper, civilized, well-bred young woman. The complete opposite of him.

But as haunting as he found her looks, her manner had set his teeth on edge. She'd seemed snippy and stuck-up.

Or so he'd thought until the moment she'd burst into tears.

He'd been confounded by her news about Carolyn Trent and the ailing baby. He hadn't noticed Mickey's growing distress in talking about it. He'd been bewildered, wondering what in hell *he* was going to do now.

Then, before he knew it, the facade of her primness broke. Who could have thought such storms of feeling could toss within her?

What alarmed him was how deeply grieved she seemed. Her body had heaved in the effort to control the sobs that threatened to break out of control. She said she was a secretary, but she obviously cared a great deal about Carolyn Trent and her family.

Adam was not cruel. When he saw suffering, his first impulse was to ease it. And her tears brought the reality home to him: Carolyn might well be a person worth caring about. And Carolyn, too, was suffering.

He swore aloud again. What to do now? Everything had to be rethought. Everything.

And as for the Nightingale woman, she'd gone from tempestuous sorrow back to cool efficiency so quickly that she'd thrown him off balance yet again. Well, he was stuck here with her until Friday. He supposed that having dropped her guard once she'd be careful not to do it again.

So be it. It'd be easier on both of them.

He hung his two spare shirts and other pair of jeans in the closet. He truly wasn't much for clothes. For him, living on his small boat, wearing more than a pair of ragged cutoffs was dressing up. What he had on now was like formal wear to him.

The rest of the contents of the duffel bag were books, photos, a videotape, a folder, two sealed manila envelopes with Enoch Randolph's legal papers and some documents. He put everything but his books into a dresser drawer.

He looked about the room, and homey as it was meant to be, he still felt trapped. He resisted the impulse to pace. He picked up one of his books and flopped down in a chair, draping one leg over the arm.

He opened the book and began to read, although he knew it nearly by heart. His eyes fell on one of the opening sentences.

"At present I am a sojourner in civilized life again."

That's me, he thought, more restless than before. *A sojourner in civilized life. I don't live here. I'm just here for a temporary stay.*

CHAPTER THREE

"VERN?" MICKEY HELD the receiver so tightly her knuckles paled. "Are you in Denver?"

"We got here about two hours ago." Vern sounded exhausted in body and soul. "We're at the hospital."

"How's the baby? How's Beverly?"

"The baby…" He paused, as if uncertain how to say it. "The baby's hanging in there. They—they say she's a fighter."

"She has to be," Mickey said, her throat tightening. "Look who her grandma is."

"Beverly's pretty much out of it," Vern said. "They've got her on morphine. She knows the baby has a problem. They haven't told her yet how serious."

"Does she know there'll be an operation?"

"Not yet. They're scheduling surgery for tomorrow. I'll call you as soon as I know anything."

"How's Sonny?"

"Sonny's Sonny. He's holding everything together. He's with Carolyn right now."

Mickey shifted in her chair and stared at the framed snapshots ranged along her bookshelves. From those frames smiled their faces, all of them—Carolyn, Vern, Beverly and Sonny. She herself was in some of the photos. Carolyn and Vern had taken her on the family vacations to Aspen. In one shot she stood in her rented skis, laughing between Beverly and Sonny.

She had to turn her gaze from the reminders of those happier times. "How's Carolyn?"

Again Vern paused. "She did just fine until she saw the baby. It's such a *little* thing. On a respirator, and all these tubes and wires running into her. Poor Caro just sort of—lost it. Sonny got her pulled together again. She asked him to prescribe her tranquilizers. She wants to stay calm as she can for Beverly's sake."

Mickey shook her head in sympathy, unable to speak.

"Listen, Mick," Vern said. "We took off from home like a pair of bats out of hell. There's a lot we didn't tend to. Carolyn had some signed checks in her desk drawer. I planned on depositing them when I went to the courthouse. Could you go to town and put them in the bank? Otherwise we'll have checks bouncing all over town. And some are paychecks."

"Of course. I'll do it right away. But, Vern?"

"Yes?"

She nipped at her lower lip. "Something else got lost in the shuffle."

She thought of the man with the azure eyes. The man who could look haughty as a king in spite of his shabby clothes, who could be either icy or kind.

Vern sighed. "I'm sure *dozens* of things got lost, Mick. What is it?"

She took a deep breath and said, "Adam Duran is here. The executor of Enoch's will."

"Oh, damn!" Vern almost moaned. "*Damn!* I never gave him a thought. Neither did Carolyn, I know. Hellfire, she doesn't need him on her mind, too. Why didn't I *think*—"

Mickey, feeling guilty for adding to his troubles, tried to reduce them. "Don't give it a moment's thought. He's here, he's comfortable, I'll see to him."

"I don't know why he couldn't have handled this damned

will business by mail," Vern grumbled. "What sort of guy is he? A lawyer? A banker? Or just a friend of Enoch's?"

Mickey remembered the untrimmed hair and faded clothes, and thought perhaps the less she said the better. "I don't think he's a lawyer or banker. Just a—an acquaintance."

"Well, God knows what kind of acquaintance that old coot would make. Be careful. But feel him out, will you? Maybe there are some strings tied to this lease-land deal. I hope not. I don't want any nasty surprises sprung on Carolyn. She's in no shape for it."

"I'll find out all I can," Mickey promised.

"Tell him you're Carolyn's most trusted agent. Anything he has to say to her, he can say to you. It's true, God knows."

A glow of pride warmed her, in spite of her anxiety. "I'll be glad to. So rest easy about this, Vern. And don't let Carolyn fret over it."

"I'm not even going to mention it to her. She's got enough on her mind, God knows. You should have seen that tiny child. All those tubes—Lord."

"Whatever you think is best," Mickey assured him. She told him to give her love to everyone. They said their goodbyes, and she hung up.

Feeling strangely agitated, she walked down the hall and knocked on the guest-room door. "Mr. Duran, I'm leaving. I have to go into town on an errand," she said through the door. "I'll be back in about an hour. Bridget should be along any minute. I'll call her and let her know you're here."

She waited, holding her breath. At last, from the other side of the door, he answered, "Fine."

That single word was apparently all the reply he was going to make.

She felt odd about leaving him alone in Carolyn's house, but she had no choice. And what she'd told him was true; Bridget would soon be there.

AS SOON AS Adam heard the car pull away, he opened the door and glanced down the deserted hall. The house had that eerie, empty feeling that houses get when their dwellers are gone, but a lone visitor stays. The place was still and silent with no sign of life—except for him. The unwanted guest.

He walked down the hall and saw that the office doors that had been open before were now closed. He tried the first one. Unlocked, it swung open easily.

Adam hesitated a moment, staring into the room. He wrestled with his conscience. His conscience lost. He stepped inside, not only an intruder, but a spy.

He told himself that he must do it, he had to learn as much about these people as he could. He needed to know their strengths. And even more, their weaknesses.

Once they knew who he really was, they could become his enemies—any or all of them—in a heartbeat.

BRIDGET BLUM, the cook and housekeeper at the Circle T, was one of seven children of an Irish mother and a German father. Her father, Dolph Blum had been the chief wrangler at the Double J, the old Kendell spread.

Dolph was a large man with a square jaw, a pug nose and a ready grin. His wife, Maeve, was tiny, as slender as a wand, but it was she who'd kept those seven children in order. Her voice could crack like a whip.

Bridget took after her father. She was almost six feet tall, and she had big hands, a big smile and a big heart. At forty-five she had never been married, and if she missed having a husband, she never let it show.

She seemed happy and busy with her own family: three married sisters, three married brothers and a whopping total of thirty-one nieces and nephews. Maeve had died four years ago, and Dolph was frail. Bridget, the eldest daughter, had become surrogate mother of the clan.

She had, as well, her adoptive family: Carolyn and Vern and the people of the Circle T. Yes, Bridget had plenty of people to care for and love; she did not know what an empty day felt like.

Because Carolyn and Vern were like kin, her heart filled with empathy for them over the ailing baby. But because, unlike either of them, she came from a large family, she was not as frightened as they were. In Bridget's sprawling brood, someone was always falling off a bicycle or crashing out of a tree or tumbling down the stairs.

So when a true emergency arose, Bridget did what she always did: she went to church, lit candles and said prayers. That's what she'd done today.

Just as she drove through the gates of the Circle T, her cell phone rang. This startled her, for she wasn't yet used to the contraption—it still seemed supernatural to her. She prayed its ringing didn't signal bad news about the baby.

She pulled over to the side of the drive, parked and rummaged through her purse for the chirping phone. "Hello?" she said breathlessly. "Hello?"

"Bridget, it's Mick. I called to tell you that the Duran man got here from the Caribbean. I need to get to town before the bank closes, and I'm on my way. I had to leave him alone at the house. Are you close to home?"

Bridget glanced down the lane. The house was just around the curve. "I'm good as there right now. I'm nearly to the gates."

"Good." Relief eased Mickey's voice. "I didn't like the idea of giving a stranger the run of the place. And I wanted to warn you he was there."

Bridget's heart skipped guiltily. "Tarnation! I truly meant to get straight back. I stopped in the parking lot to help Mary Gibson with a flat tire. I swear I forgot about what's his face—who?"

"Adam Duran. It's all right. I'd forgotten about him, too. Anyway I've only been gone ten minutes."

"Ah," said Bridget, relieved, "and I'll be there in two. What trouble could the man get up to in twelve minutes, I ask you?"

IF A MAN is determined and observant, he can discover a great deal in twelve minutes. Adam was determined, observant and quick to learn.

He was looking over Mickey Nightingale's office when he heard the crunch of tires on the gravel driveway. *The housekeeper—she must be back. I need to get out of here.*

He turned from the pictures arranged on Mickey's bookshelf. Her office was neat, almost Spartan, but like Carolyn, she enjoyed having framed snapshots about her while she worked. Adam had studied those snapshots with interest. Mickey's choice of pictures was revealing—and mystifying.

But he had no time to ponder the significance of the photographs. He slipped out of her office, shut the door and made his way to the den. He sat down in an armchair and snatched up a copy of *Western Horseman*. He swept his legs up onto the ottoman and opened the magazine just as he heard the front door swing open.

He waited, giving the woman time to enter. Tentative footsteps sounded on the tiles of the foyer. A female voice called out, "Yoo-hoo. Mister Duran? It's me, Bridget Blum. Mickey just phoned to tell me you were here. Mister Duran?"

Then she appeared, framed in the doorway, a tall woman, sturdy rather than plump. Adam sprang to his feet, holding the magazine in his left hand. He tried to seem friendly, comfortable and confident—as if he had every right to be sitting in the Trents' family room, as if he himself were like the Trents—someone of note and power.

He approached Bridget, stretching his right hand to her. "Hi. I'm Adam Duran. Miss Nightingale said it was okay to use this room."

The woman gripped his hand and shook it with surprising strength. But she had the same look of disbelief on her face that Mickey Nightingale had when she'd met him.

For the second time that day, he wished he'd sprung for new jeans, a more respectable shirt. But if his shabbiness caught her off guard, she quickly recovered.

She pumped his hand more vigorously, and friendly words began to spill from her as if she were a very cornucopia of hospitality.

"Welcome, Mr. Duran. I'm sorry you got left here rattling around alone. Everything is at sixes and sevens today. I don't know if Mickey told you, but we've had such sad news, well, I hope it doesn't stay sad, and that the ending is happy. Mrs. Trent's grandbaby came early. She's not well, poor tyke."

Adam nodded. Her warmth disarmed him in a way Mickey's chill could not. "She told me," he said, troubled anew at his mission here. "I'm sorry. I came at a bad time. I'll try to stay out of your way."

"You're not in my way at all." She dropped his hand but gave his shoulder a motherly squeeze. "Are you hungry? Why, I hear they hardly give you any food at all these days on an airplane. You're lucky if they toss you a pretzel. Did you have lunch?"

"No," he admitted. "But it's okay. I—"

The big woman seemed shocked. "Didn't Mick feed you anything?"

"No," he repeated, almost shyly. "But it's okay, really—"

"It's not okay," Bridget said firmly. "I made some cheese bread for you special. You come into the kitchen and have a little snack while I start whipping up supper. If Mickey didn't get some food into you—well, she's upset, is all. Carolyn Trent is as dear as a mother to her."

Before Adam could protest, she had him in the kitchen, seated at a round oak table. He watched as she bustled, plugging in the coffeemaker, putting the cheese bread into the oven to warm.

She was an attractive woman in her large-scale way. She had a broad, fair face with pink cheeks, a small nose and a generous jaw. Her dark red hair was so curly it was almost crinkly.

She asked all the polite questions about his flight, and he answered, but he didn't want to talk about himself. He guided the conversation in a different direction. "Have you worked for Mrs. Trent long?"

She set down a coffee mug, a plate and a fork before him. "Nine years," she said. "My aunt Consuela used to have this job. But she quit after the tornado, when the barn fell on Mr. Trent. *'No deseo más de este tiempo de Tejas,'* she said. 'No more of this Texas weather for me.' And she made my uncle Emil take a job in British Columbia. Well, maybe she had a point. Because, at least, she missed that accursed flood last fall."

Adam looked up, his interest piqued. "Tornado?" he said. "Flood?"

"Indeed." Bridget shook her head with feeling. "It's never dull around here. Now the tornado was an act of God, but that flood, it was another matter entirely…."

She took the conversational bit between her teeth, and she was off and running.

MICKEY STRETCHED out her trip to town. She went to the library, and Violet, the head librarian, had already heard about Beverly and the baby. News traveled fast in Crystal Creek.

"Bridget's sister told me," Violet said with a sad shake of her head. She led Mickey straight to the medical section and handed her the latest book about children with heart conditions. "It's a good book," she said. "Last winter, Dr. Purdy recommended it to Betsy Hutchinson when her little boy was diagnosed with a heart murmur. Betsy said it was a great comfort."

She patted Mickey's arm, and Mickey thanked her, touched by her concern.

Mickey went to the Long Horn Coffee Shop. Kasey, the manager, came right over and filled her a coffee cup. She nodded at the book on the red-and-white checkered tablecloth. "I heard about what happened. Nora Slattery was in here earlier. She was mighty upset."

Mickey nodded sadly. Nora was the wife of J.T.'s foreman and had lived on J.T.'s ranch for years. She had known Beverly since childhood.

Kasey said, "My cousin's baby had the same problem, Mick. She came through with flying colors. You'd look at her and never guess. I hope it's the same for this little gal. But Carolyn's devastated at this point, I imagine."

"More than devastated," Mickey said. "I—don't think I can talk about it." She didn't want to cry again.

"I understand, hon. Tell her hello, and that we're all pulling for her and the whole family. I'll leave you be. Read your book. Maybe you'll feel better."

She surprised Mickey by giving her a brisk kiss on the cheek. Then she vanished into the kitchen. It was an hour before the supper rush would begin, and Mickey was the lone customer. She nursed her coffee and tried to read, but the words danced senselessly before her eyes.

She finished her coffee and knew she couldn't put off returning to the Circle T forever. Reluctantly she drove home. Just as she pulled into the carport, Leon Vanek appeared. He stood at the carport's edge, shifting his weight, clenching and unclenching his big hands.

His expression was far from happy. She wondered uneasily what he wanted. She got out of the car and faced him. "Yes, Leon? Did you want to see me about something?"

He stared at the gravel in the drive, pulling his hat down

farther over his face. "Mr. and Mrs. Trent are in Denver. Because that child is sick."

I know that all too well, Mickey thought. "Yes. We're all concerned."

Leon said, "You should have notified me. I'm the foreman here. You should tell me these things. I heard it from Werner. Him a common hand, and he knew before I did."

Mickey knew Leon was a proud man and that his pride had been hurt. But she resented his accusatory tone. "I'm sorry. I just had a lot on my mind. We all did."

Leon didn't look placated. "I saw a man come today after they left. Come to the house."

Mickey stared at him in puzzlement. "Yes? It's the man Carolyn was expecting. He's come about the lease land."

Leon frowned. "Well, she isn't here. And neither's Mr. Trent."

"Right now their place is with Beverly and Sonny."

"You didn't have time to tell me Mrs. Trent's gone. That puts a lot of responsibility on my shoulders. But you had time to take him in and make him feel right at home."

"That's part of *my* responsibility," she shot back. "It's what Carolyn would want."

"That man isn't staying, is he?" Leon scowled and kicked the gravel.

"Carolyn invited him to stay. She couldn't know this would happen."

Leon raised his face, which was red with displeasure. "I saw him. He doesn't look respectable. He looks like one of those hippies."

Mickey almost smiled at the quaintness of the word "hippies," but Leon's disapproval seemed real. When she didn't answer, he frowned harder. "It's not fitting, a man like that to stay alone in the house with you. If you want me to ask him to leave, I will."

"I'm not alone with him. Bridget's with us. And if I wanted him to go, I'm capable of telling him myself."

He looked more aggravated than before. "I'm concerned about your reputation. It doesn't look good. Bridget or no. That's all I got to say."

"Thank you," she said coolly, "but I can watch out for my own reputation. Good day, Leon."

She started toward the house, but he put his hand on her wrist. It was a possessive move, and her resentment flared more hotly. He said, "I'll watch out for you. If he bothers you, you let me know. I'll take care of him."

She snatched her hand away. "I said *good day*." She turned her back on him and walked away in anger.

MICKEY FACED fresh exasperation when she found Bridget covering the dining room table with a white linen cloth. "Bridget, I want us to eat in the kitchen tonight. Didn't I tell you?"

"No, you did not," Bridget said righteously. "And this is what Carolyn would *want*. I aim to do it to the way she'd have it done herself. She'd snatch me bald, giving him supper in the kitchen."

Mickey rolled her eyes. "He doesn't exactly seemed the type for formal dining. The way he dresses, he'd probably be more comfortable on the back porch, eating beans out of a can."

"Humph." Bridget put her hand on her hip. "You sound high-and-mighty all of a sudden. It's not like you, Mick. He's a very nice young man. He has a nice way about him. Not uppity at all. And he's handsome, to boot. Lord, like a movie star. But he acts like he doesn't even know it."

Mickey gazed at her suspiciously. "Have you been talking to him?"

"I fed him—which *you* forgot to do. We chatted a wee bit. It seemed the polite thing to do, that's all."

Bridget would not hear another word about eating in the kitchen.

So Mickey, as Carolyn had intended, sat across the dining room table from Adam Duran, but she sat alone with him.

The good silver and china were set on the best linen. There were flowers—and candlelight. Carolyn was a great lover of flowers and candlelight.

From the kitchen came the succulent scents of Bridget's sauerbraten and dumplings. One of Carolyn's favorite albums played softly on the sound system, *The Ballad of the Irish Horse.*

Bridget had succeeded all too well; the atmosphere was pleasant, touched with elegance, even intimacy. *Drat,* thought Mickey, who didn't want to think of intimacy with this disturbing man. *Drat and double drat and triple drat.*

She hadn't dressed for supper. Neither had Adam. She wore the same denim slacks and high-necked white blouse. He wore the same washed-out jeans and faded work shirt.

He and she both bent, without speaking, over their salads. The music swelled, faded, then built again. The candlelight gleamed on the gold streaks in Adam's hair. It flashed from their silver forks and the crystal glasses.

On the way home, Mickey had mentally listed enough neutral subjects to get through the ordeal of supper. She would save her more pointed questions for dessert, when he might be warmed enough by wine and good food to be candid.

She trotted out her first innocuous remark. "I hope you got to enjoy the wildflowers on your drive here. It's a particularly nice spring."

He was supposed to say, *Yes, the drive was nice, the weather was nice, and the flowers were nice.* Then she'd ask, *Is it spring in the Caribbean, too? What's the weather like there? Is it already hot?*

But he instantly booby-trapped her plans. "I hear you had a fall that wasn't so fine last year. That some developer caused a helluva flash flood. Mrs. Trent was in a lawsuit against him. She and the other ranchers."

Mickey almost choked on her lettuce. She stole a quick sip of water. "Oh," she said, flustered. "That. Thank God it wasn't worse than it was."

"Which wasn't worse? The flood? Or the lawsuit?" Shadows played on the planes of his face, but even in the muted light she thought she saw a glint of challenge in his eyes.

"Neither. The flood didn't do any major damage, here at least."

"Really? I heard it wiped out a housing development."

He said it calmly, but his words hit a nerve, rousing her wariness.

"A *would-be* development," she corrected. "There were only five houses. None was finished. The developer put up this stupid dam—"

"—and the dam didn't hold," he finished for her. "So the developer pulled out. His name was Fabian, wasn't it?"

He was right, and two suspicions struck Mickey at once. He and Bridget must have had more than a wee chat. Bridget seemed taken with Adam. Had he charmed her into spilling out information the whole time Mickey was away?

But the more ominous one was the same fear that had haunted Caro when Fabian started buying up local land.

Mickey threw discretion to the wind. She said, "You seem to know a lot. Fabian wanted all the land he could get. Enoch Randolph had plenty of it. Did Fabian offer to buy it?"

Adam tilted his wineglass so the candlelight reflected in its red depths and studied it. "Oh, yeah," he said. "He offered."

Mickey held her breath. "Well?" she challenged.

Adam tipped the glass to another angle, watching the changing refraction. "Enoch wouldn't sell. Some fancy lawyer came to the Bahamas to try to talk him into it. Enoch laughed in his face."

Relief swept through her. "Caro always said Enoch was his own man."

Adam's gaze shifted to her eyes again. "He turned down a hell of a lot of money."

"So did Carolyn. So did most of the ranchers. It takes character to hold out against greed."

"Does it?" There was mockery in his voice. "With Enoch, all it took was cussedness."

Mickey looked at him questioningly.

"He knew he was dying," Adam said. "He said, 'This son-uvva bitch says I'll be rich. What good's money gonna do me? Buy me a gold coffin? Screw it.'"

The humor was dark, but Mickey smiled dutifully. "Good for him. Some men might find it tempting, to be rich for even a little while."

Adam shook his head. "He didn't like anything about the scheme."

"We didn't either. We've got a way of life here. Fabian threatened it."

"You're in favor of preservation?" Adam raised an eyebrow as if doubtful. "Protecting nature?"

"Yes, and so is Carolyn," she insisted. "She and the others worked hard for it. She'll be grateful to know Enoch helped."

"Grateful?" he echoed. "He didn't do it to help. He did it because he felt like doing it."

Bridget swept in, carrying plates of sauerbraten, dumplings and homemade applesauce. "Save room for dessert," she said cheerfully to Adam. "I made my special German chocolate cake."

He smiled at her, and Bridget beamed at him as indulgently as a fond aunt. Mickey shot Bridget a warning look that said *You and I are going to have a serious talk*. But Bridget didn't notice.

Gamely, Mickey raised her glass in a toast. "Here's to Enoch, for helping to protect the Hill Country, whatever his reasons."

"I'll drink to Enoch," he said, clicking his glass against hers. He did not mention the Hill Country.

They each sipped. He said, "You're very…close to Carolyn and Vern."

Good Lord, had Bridget talked about *that,* too? "Yes. I guess I am."

"Especially Carolyn."

Mickey felt unsettled by this turn in the conversation. "Well, it's Carolyn I work for," she said, trying to sound casual.

"Vern stays busy at the courthouse?"

"Very busy. He's the only justice of the peace in the county."

Adam gave a wry smile. He had a good smile, too good. It did odd, tickly things to the pit of her stomach. "I thought a justice of the peace was just a guy who could marry people."

Mickey fought to ignore the tickle. "No. He handles civil and criminal cases and small-claims court. And works with juveniles. He's got a lot of duties."

"So Carolyn runs the ranch."

"Yes." Mickey pushed at the applesauce with her spoon. "But let's talk about you. How did you come to know Enoch?"

"Let's save that for later," he said. "I'm staying in Carolyn's house, enjoying her hospitality. I'd like to know more about her. She's run this place a long time?"

Mickey's guard went up. "Yes," she said, not elaborating.

"How long?" he persisted.

"She inherited it from her mother. Almost twenty years ago."

"She's lived her whole life here?"

"Yes," was all Mickey would say.

But Adam wasn't put off by short answers. He pressed on. "Carolyn had a sister. She married a neighbor, J. T. McKinney. But she's been dead for years, hasn't she?"

"Yes." Mickey didn't know where these questions were leading, but they made her nervous.

"What happened to Carolyn's father?"

Mickey's body tensed. "He—deserted his family. The marriage was never very stable. One day he just disappeared. I don't feel comfortable talking about it."

Adam took another drink of wine. "It's not easy for a man to disappear completely. Does she even know if he's alive?"

Mickey squared her shoulders combatively. "She got word five years ago that he'd died in Canada. Now let's drop the subject. *Please*."

"Fine," he said with a shrug. "We'll talk about you. How long have you worked here?"

"Nine years," she said. "I sort of 'interned' here for two years while I finished high school. I started right after Beverly went to Denver."

"Hmm," he said. "Beverly's an only child. You must have become a sort of substitute daughter."

Mickey blinked in displeasure. "I'm an employee, that's all."

This was not the truth, but Mickey would be damned before she told him any more. Mickey and Carolyn had filled painful emotional gaps in each other's lives, and there was more than affection between them. There was love and the truest friendship Mickey had ever known.

"I didn't mean you replaced her daughter." Adam shrugged. "It just seems you're more like one of the family. What about your own family? Where are they?"

"I have no family." She said it sharply.

Suddenly his expression, so unreadable before, became sympathetic. "I'm sorry. Your parents are dead?"

"My mother died when I was sixteen." Mickey said it with such acrimony that she hoped it would stop his questions.

But he nodded, almost sadly. He had an unexpected gift for seeming concerned. "That's a hard age to lose a parent. And your father?"

She should lie. She should tell him none of this was his

business. But if he wanted the ugly truth, she would give it to him. "My father divorced my mother when I was seven. He moved to California and married another woman. He never communicated with us again. He made it clear he didn't want to."

He set down his fork. He whistled softly. He put his elbow on the table and his chin on his fist. He stared at her. "So you were sixteen years old, without parents? What did you do?"

"I became a ward of the court. Nobody wanted me for a foster child. So Vern and Carolyn became my guardians. They took me in."

He gazed at her with disconcerting steadiness. "Bridget said Carolyn put you through business school."

I'm going to kill Bridget, Mickey thought. *I'm going to put my hands around her neck and strangle her dead.*

"Can we please talk about something else? What about *your* family?"

He shook his head. "I see why you're close to Carolyn. You both had the same experience. The runaway father, the abandonment. She must seem like a second mother to you."

No. She feels like my only mother; the one who really counted, the one I could depend on, who never shamed me or scared me or made me feel bad about myself.

But Mickey didn't want to think about her real mother, a deeply troubled woman. Her appetite had fled, and she pushed her plate away. She struggled against the urge to excuse herself from the table and leave Adam sitting alone.

She must have looked as unhappy as she felt. He said, "I'm sorry. It's just that your relationship is unusual. I— glanced into your office. You have all these photographs. Of you and her and *her* family. None of you and anyone else."

Mickey's emotions, so off balance for so long with this man, tipped again. Anger seized her. "You looked in my office? You looked at my pictures? How *dare* you?"

"I'm a daring guy," he said. "I looked in hers, too."

His brazenness appalled her. "You went in our offices? Those doors were closed. I closed them on purpose."

"You didn't lock them," he said. He had the effrontery to smile.

"That's inexcusable," she accused. "I'm calling Vern. I'm telling him about this. And I hope he says to put you right out of this house. What right do you think you—"

He cut her off. "Look, I didn't commit a crime. I didn't go through the drawers or read the mail or move so much as a paper clip. I opened two doors, I looked at some pictures. That's all. And I didn't hide it from you. I told you."

"It's still a violation of trust," she said with the same indignation. "It's an invasion of privacy. Carolyn opened her house to you—even while she's going through this—this horrible thing. And you flout her generosity by poking and snooping and spying on us like a—a—"

Resentment crackled in his eyes. "Stop it. I came here expressly to see *her*. I didn't even know what she looked like. When you took me to the guest room, both those office doors were open. I saw the photos. I wanted to see close-up. I especially wanted to see *her*. It's not like I picked your locks and stole the damned silverware."

Mickey stood and roughly shoved her chair back in place. "You still had no right."

"I said I wanted to see her," he repeated, his lip curling in a sneer. "And I did. I figured out which one she is from the pictures of Beverly's wedding. She's a very lovely woman, Carolyn is."

"Yes, she is," Mickey snapped. "And you're a very ill-bred man. Good night."

She stalked from the room, her heart slamming so hard she could barely breathe. She *would* call Vern. She hoped he would tell her to throw Duran out of the house, executor or not, will or no will. Let Martin Avery handle it. And she *was* going to read Bridget the riot act.

But not now. Not yet. She was too upset. She threw open the French doors in the living room that led to the screened deck. She stepped outside into the gathering darkness, grateful for the coolness of the evening air on her heated skin.

She was so furious that she shook and her blood banged in her temples. Too much had happened today. She could stand no more. She forced herself to breathe deeply. She closed her eyes and covered them with her hands.

Perhaps she had overreacted to the man. But he really was the last straw. She started to count from one to a hundred, trying to calm herself.

But suddenly she realized she was not alone. She could feel another presence; feel *his* presence. She opened her eyes and whirled to face him.

She was about to order him to get away from her, but before she could speak, he laid his forefinger against her lips. The movement was full of such self-assurance, it shocked her wordless.

He pressed his finger against her mouth more firmly. "Shhh," he commanded in a low voice. "I only wanted to see what she looks like. What she seems like. And I *have* the right. I'm her brother. Her half brother. Enoch's my uncle, too. And he didn't leave the lease lands to her. He left them to me."

CHAPTER FOUR

MICKEY GAPED AT HIM, speechless. She felt as if she'd taken a punch to the stomach. Nausea and giddiness spun within her. She couldn't get her breath.

Carolyn's half brother? Impossible. He couldn't be. He was younger even than Carolyn's daughter.

Yet, *not* impossible.

Frantically, Mickey's eyes explored his moonlit features. He did resemble Carolyn. Even more, he looked like Carolyn's late sister, Pauline. She should have seen it from the first.

He had Pauline's square jaw and stubborn chin. He had her straight nose, her sculpted mouth. His eyes were blue, like Pauline's, but otherwise they were like Carolyn's eyes, too: deep-set, thick-lashed, intense.

But his age and masculinity had disguised the similarities. So Mickey stood transfixed, both believing and not believing. "No," she objected, as if that word could break the evil spell his words had cast.

"Yes," he whispered. He was so close she could feel his breath tickle her cheek, stir an errant lock of her hair.

She realized his callused fingertip still rested against her lips. She jerked her head away to break the contact, yet her mouth tingled as if rubbed with something spicy. She wanted to move farther from him, but shock paralyzed her.

He touched her jaw, gently forcing her to face him again. "My father was Steve Randolph, the same as Carolyn's."

His expression was hard, but paradoxically his touch was almost tender. He said, "I was born in Florida."

"Florida?" She didn't understand. "I thought Steve Randolph went to Canada. I never knew he'd married again."

"He didn't." A muscle twitched in Adam's cheek. "He moved on before I was born. He must have had a habit of moving on."

Mickey blinked in surprise, yet she felt an unexpected surge of sympathy.

Adam's upper lip curled slightly. "So if you want to call me a bastard, go ahead. The name fits."

She tensed. The news that he was Carolyn's half brother had so stunned her, she'd forgotten the other bombshell he'd dropped. The lease land was his, or so he claimed.

Her sympathy died; suspicion loomed up in its place. She pushed his hand aside and tried to jerk away. But her shoulder blades struck the barrier of the screened windows. He had her cornered.

She jerked her chin up. "How'd you hook up with Enoch? How'd you talk him out of the lease land? Suck up to him?"

His mouth twisted sardonically. "I tried to track down my father. I found out he died in Ontario. That he'd had two brothers. One was dead—"

"—Thom," Mickey said. She knew the story. Thom, the middle of the three Randolph brothers, had died in Thailand.

Adam cocked his head and leaned nearer. "But my father's obituary notice said he was survived by a brother in the Caribbean—Enoch. Enoch and I had lived near each other for God knows how long. I looked him up. Last year. Until then, he hadn't known I existed."

She used her suspicion militantly, like a protective shield. "United, at last. How touching. And what a nice bonus for you—to learn you had a rich uncle. Or did you know he had property *before* you found him?"

She wished her heart beat less violently. She wished her flesh didn't burn where he'd touched her.

His laugh was sarcastic. "I didn't know about any money or land. He told me that he had land, but I didn't know how much. I didn't ask, and he didn't tell. Until he was dying."

For some insane reason, she wanted to believe him. A dangerous impulse, she fought it as hard she could. "You went looking for him just because he was your uncle? Not because he was your *wealthy* uncle?"

"What's the problem?" He leaned one hand on the window frame next to her and bent nearer still. "The idea of wanting to meet your kin? Is that something ritzy Texans don't understand?"

Stung, she glared. And his arm, so near, made her feel more trapped than before. "What are you talking about? Say what you mean."

"I wanted to meet my father's people. I just wanted to *know*. That's all."

"Know what?" she demanded.

His frown was earnest. "Know about him. His people. My father was a part of me that was missing. I just wanted to understand. You know?"

"No, I don't," Mickey flung back. "You're talking about a man who—who ran out on your mother. Who deserted you before you were born. Whose family never lifted a finger to help you. Why would you want to have anything to do with him or them? It makes no sense to me."

His eyes narrowed. "You're calling me a liar?"

She wanted him to be a liar. She wanted it for Carolyn's sake and her own. If he was an imposter, nothing more than a con artist, they could be rid of him; he would get out of their lives and stay out. He couldn't hurt Carolyn, and he wouldn't confuse her so wildly.

She challenged him again. "Why go chasing after Enoch, of all people? I didn't know him, but—"

"—That's right. You didn't. Not at all."

"—but he's always sounded like a—a crank. A lazy, anti-social crank. My God, if you wanted to meet somebody in your family, why didn't you get in touch with Carolyn?"

"I didn't know she existed. Until Enoch told me."

"You must not have had a very good detective," she retorted.

"Steve Randolph covered his tracks well. Nobody in Ontario knew he had children in the States. Carolyn and Pauline didn't know about me. And I didn't know about them."

Mickey was dizzied by hurt and anger. "When you found out about Carolyn, why didn't you call her *then?* Why wait until now? It's only about the land, isn't it? Not about finding your people or a part of you that's missing."

He tensed with resentment. She didn't care. She knew how Enoch had treated Carolyn, taking her money and rebuffing her courtesy with an indifference that bordered on contempt. For years he'd lived on her fairness and generosity, acting like a shiftless old pirate.

Mickey had to strike out in defense of her friend and benefactor; she couldn't live with herself if she didn't. "I don't know why you'd be satisfied with finding only Enoch for family. Carolyn's respectable, at least."

"Respectable?" Adam mocked. "That's what's important? To you? To her? Is that how she felt about Enoch? He wasn't as good as she is? Because he didn't spend his life getting—stuff?"

He made a wide, disdainful sweep with his free hand to indicate the Circle T and everything on it. He radiated such disdain that Mickey's temper flared higher.

"Carolyn's worked hard for everything she's got. Which is more than *anybody* can say for Enoch. If you knew about her, why didn't you write her? Instead of cozying up to some eccentric old grouch who was probably losing his mind—"

He jerked his head in frustration, so that his hair fell over his forehead. "Why are you so judgmental? Before I met Enoch, I damn well didn't know Carolyn existed. It was Enoch who told me the whole story about my dad's first marriage. And that only Carolyn was left."

Mickey put her fist on her hip. "So why didn't you get in touch with her then? What happened to your burning urge to find your kinfolk? You waited until Enoch signed *her* inheritance over to *you*. And now you show up."

Adam raked his hand through his hair. "He warned me about you people. He said she looked down on our kind."

He dared to call Carolyn a snob? Carolyn, of all people? "Don't you criticize Carolyn," she warned. "You don't even know her."

"Then don't criticize me. Or Enoch. You don't know us, either."

Mickey shook her finger in his face. "For years and years he promised that land would be hers."

"Don't do that," Adam warned her, his voice flat.

But her dander was up, and she kept shaking her finger. If it annoyed him, she would shake it until doomsday. "But you come along like a thief in the night—"

"I said don't do that."

"I'll do as I please, and you can't stop me."

"Yes, I can," he said from between his teeth. He seized her wrist, and stepped even closer.

Her pulses drummed crazily. His body was too near hers, his face too close, his hand too strong, his anger growing as charged and heated as her own.

Mickey, who hardly ever lost control of herself, wanted to clench her fist and hit him in the stomach so hard that he'd double up in agony. Yet, paradoxically, she was swept by the dizzying and irrational wish that he'd kiss her. And just as irrationally, she knew he wanted it, too.

They stood glowering at each other, breathing hard. She saw a vein in his neck throbbing as fast and strong as her own heartbeat.

Just as she was about to either knee him in the groin or collapse into his arms, she heard Bridget's cheery voice.

"Hello? Where's everybody gone to? Are you out on the deck, Mickey? It's a lovely night, isn't it? Dessert is ready, and we have company come, just in time to share."

Mickey nearly swooned in bewilderment. Company?

Bridget added, "It's Reverend Blake and Reverend Casterleigh. Right this way, gentlemen!"

Mickey closed her eyes and thought, *What have I done wrong, Lord?* Guilt settled on her like a rough and heavy cloak.

Not one, but two ministers appearing at a moment like this?

SHE MET THE VISITORS in the dining room. Bridget had turned on the overhead lights, but the candles still flickered in their silver holders.

Reverend Howard Blake was an elderly man with an amazing head of white hair, full, lushly thick, and wavy. Although age had stooped his tall body, his cobalt-blue eyes still twinkled from behind his trifocals.

He had been the most respected minister in Crystal Creek for as long as Mickey could remember. But now he was getting ready to retire, and nobody envied the young man given the impossible task of replacing him.

Reverend Hugh Casterleigh was fresh out of divinity school. So lean he seemed gangling, he had an innocent, boyish face and a slight stammer. He was so sincere and goodhearted, he seemed like an awkward young angel being forced to serve time on Earth.

"Good evening, Mickey." Reverend Blake took Mickey's hand in his. "Forgive us for dropping in unannounced. We were driving by, and we just wanted to tell you that everyone is praying for Beverly and the baby. And dear Carolyn and Vern, as well."

Mickey's heart fairly shriveled with guilt. She hoped these two godly men could not see how bedeviled she'd just been, her heart torn by both anger and desire.

She bowed her head and murmured, "Thank you. I'll be sure to tell Caro and Vern."

He put his other hand on her shoulder. "I know this is hard on you, too, my dear. You're like her second daughter. Our prayers are with you, as well."

Her face burned with shame. "Thank you," she said, her voice even smaller than before.

Howard Blake clasped her shoulder more tightly. "This is a trying time for Carolyn. First losing her uncle, now this. She's lucky to have someone as steadfast as you to depend on."

"P-please give her my condolences about her uncle, t-too," Hugh Casterleigh said.

Howard stepped aside and let Casterleigh shake her hand. He pumped it as if he wished he could pump all sorrow out of the world.

"And you," Howard said to Adam, "must be the executor. I'm Howard Blake. I was sorry to hear about Enoch. I knew him when he was young."

Mickey fought not to wince. She became acutely conscious of Adam standing off to the side. "I'm sorry, I'm forgetting my manners," she apologized.

Hugh Casterleigh blushed in sympathy and didn't seem to know what to say. But Adam stepped up to Reverend Blake and offered his hand. "Thanks. I'm Adam Duran. From the Isabella Islands. I arrived at a bad time, I'm afraid."

Howard clasped his hand. "You couldn't know, my boy. But I'm sure that Mickey will take good care of you. Very capable girl, our Mickey."

Her cheeks flamed more hotly. She managed to say, "Reverend Casterleigh, Adam Duran. Mr. Duran, Reverend Casterleigh."

Casterleigh shambled over to Adam and engaged in another of his energetic handshakes. "S-sorry about Mr. Randolph," he stammered.

Mickey went limp with relief when Bridget came in bearing a tray of dessert plates. "Y'all sit down," she invited. "And I'll be right back with the coffee."

"Ah, Bridget," Howard said. "Is that your famous German chocolate cake? You're leading me into a temptation I can't resist."

"Oh, go on with you," Bridget said, her cheeks flushed with pleasure. She set down the dessert plates, cleared away the remains of supper, and bustled off.

"Please sit," Mickey said to the men. She sounded cordial and confident. *What a faker I am. What a phony.*

Howard Blake gallantly drew out her chair for her to be seated, and Hugh Casterleigh nearly tripped over a throw rug. Adam once again sat across from her, his face betraying nothing.

Howard asked what Mickey had heard from Denver, how everyone was getting on, and showed special concern for Carolyn. As Bridget poured the coffee, he turned to Adam. "This must complicate your travel plans, Mr. Duran. When did you plan on returning to the Isabellas?"

"Friday," Adam said shortly.

"Ah." Howard nodded. "So what shall you do now that Carolyn's not here?"

Adam shot Mickey an unreadable look. "I'll have to see. It depends on when Mrs. Trent can come back."

"Yes. Well, that's in God's hands. Perhaps before we partake of Bridget's talent, we should bow our heads and pray."

Mickey ducked her head but didn't shut her eyes. She

watched as Howard said his prayer and Casterleigh pressed his hands together, his eyes tightly closed.

She could not help but notice that Adam barely lowered his head, and that he watched the others at the table. He blinked as if displeased when Howard said, "And may the soul of our brother Enoch rest in peace."

He finished, said "Amen," then turned to Adam again.

"My wife and I have been to the Caribbean a few times. Just what part of the Isabellas are you from?"

"The island of Los Eremitas," Adam said.

"And what do you do there?" Howard's question did not seem prying, only courteous.

"This and that."

Adam said it in a way that blocked closer questioning. Mickey bristled inwardly, and Howard clearly noticed and changed the course of the conversation. "And what do you think of that cake, Hugh? Isn't it a wonder?"

Casterleigh had to swallow before he could answer. "Sure enough."

Howard Blake turned to Mickey. "Mick, I know everything's topsy-turvy. And I hesitate a bit to bring this up, but Vernon was going to teach Sunday school this weekend. I'm sure it's slipped his mind, and I wouldn't have him feel bad about it for the world."

"Oh," Mickey said, taken aback. Vern often volunteered to substitute teach the first and second grade class. And she was sure Howard was right; the crisis had knocked all thought of Vern's promise out of his mind.

"If Vernon never remembers, all the better," Howard said with feeling. "It's a small thing compared to Beverly's poor baby. But I was wondering if you'd replace him. You're the one he and Carolyn always count on, you know. And with good reason, I might say."

Mickey's eyes widened, and her skin went cold. "Me?" She'd never taught a Sunday-school class in her life.

"Yes, you." Howard smiled. "Who knows? You might like it. And Hugh here is going to need a long list of volunteers to count on. Aren't you, Hugh?"

Reverend Casterleigh blushed again and stared at her with eyes full of innocence and apology. "I would never want to p-put you out. Oh, no."

To refuse Hugh Casterleigh a favor would be like kicking a cocker spaniel puppy, Mickey thought helplessly. And Howard was right. Vern would want her to take over the duty to spare Howard from searching for another replacement.

"I...I haven't worked with children much," she confessed, "but I—well, I could give it a try."

"Bless you." Howard leaned over and patted her hand. "It won't be hard at all. The theme's already set for all the classes. It's 'Love Thy Enemy.'"

Mickey's spine straightened like a ramrod. Worse, she accidentally met Adam's gaze. He must have sensed the irony of her situation. The barest hint of a smirk touched the corner of his mouth.

"It's an important lesson," Howard mused. "And a difficult one. We can't start teaching it too early. What do you say, Hugh?"

Hugh Casterleigh's smooth face grew sad. "We n-need to remember it every day of our lives."

Howard sipped his coffee and nodded. "We're all one human family. All men are brothers."

Uneasily Mickey thought, *And then there are the half brothers*.

"Oops," Howard said with a laugh. "Showing my age. That was sexist. Sorry. We're all bound together, brother and sister."

"How true," Adam said. Only Mickey seemed to hear the mockery in his voice and see the glint of it in his eyes.

Howard's tone turned almost jovial. "So, Mickey, it won't

be hard. Just think of some examples that the little ones can understand. I'll drop off a teacher's book for you tomorrow. Unless you know where Vernon's copy is."

She shook her head. She was often in and out of Carolyn's office but seldom in Vern's. "I don't. I'd appreciate one. I'll need all the help I can get."

Howard patted her hand again, reassuring her. "My dear, you'll find it's easy to *talk* about loving an enemy. What's hard is putting it into practice."

Mickey smiled sickly.

ADAM STUDIED Mickey's reaction to the two ministers with a mixture of amusement and cynicism.

Her mood had been murderous when they'd arrived. She'd disguised it immediately, the little hypocrite. She'd wanted to seem like a nice girl.

Her fury had vanished like dew in the morning sun. Her manners became flawless, her ways welcoming, her temper mild. She was every inch the perfect lady.

Ha! He watched her nibble daintily at her cake. He remembered her tossing her hair in outrage, killer sparks in her eyes. Oh, yes, and the defiant jut of her chin, and how she'd spat the word *thief* at him.

Now she sat meekly listening to the old minister preach about loving thy enemy. It was more delicious to Adam than the cake, more stimulating than the strong kick of the coffee. Beneath her calm facade, she was squirming like hell.

He held his coffee cup in both hands and stared at her across its rim. Because what fascinated him most was that she really *was* a nice woman.

Both ministers treated her with affectionate respect. He thought the younger, the tongue-tied one, might even have a crush on her.

And why not? She had the kind of clean-cut prettiness that

grew on a man. It was growing on him. Everybody seemed
to hold her in high regard—Bridget, the cook, had gone on
and on: how hardworking Mickey was. How dependable.
How loyal. How *sweet*.

Yes, a very paragon of a woman, this Mickey Nightingale.
He lowered his lids slightly, appraising her.

Yet she wasn't completely what she seemed. For a few seconds on the deck, he had sensed something stronger than
anger in her. It was sexuality. He would have smiled at the
irony—she was so precise, so controlled—but somehow the
thought intrigued him.

He didn't want to be intrigued. It was the wrong time, the
wrong place. And she was, he could tell, by God, absolutely
the wrong woman.

MICKEY FELT DRAINED by the time the Reverends Blake and
Casterleigh took their leave.

She stood at the door, waving farewell as they climbed into
Hugh Casterleigh's humble compact. She could feel Adam behind her, as if he stood in the background emitting invisible
sexual rays.

When the car pulled away, she had no choice but to close
the door and face him. He looked her up and down, a smile
haunting his mouth. She knew what he was thinking, that she
was shamelessly two-faced.

She shot him a warning look that said *Don't yank my chain*.

But he only crossed his arms across his chest and nodded.
"Nice folks." She heard the edge of sarcasm in his voice.

"You didn't exactly knock yourself out being sociable,"
she said.

He shrugged one wide shoulder. "I'm not used to talking
to preachers."

"Why does this not surprise me?" she said, rolling her eyes
heavenward. "Listen. It's late. I have to talk to Bridget. And

then I'm going to bed. Stay up as late as you want. But breakfast is early. Seven o'clock."

His eyebrows rose quizzically. "You're not going to kick me out? I thought now that the God squad was gone, you'd revert to type."

She held up her hand, a gesture for him to stop. "Reverend Blake's right. I'm sorry for blowing up at you. What you said shocked me and I…and it seemed so unfair to Carolyn that I— Never mind. We'll talk about—"

"The lease land?" he supplied, staring from beneath his blond forelock.

She sighed. "Yes. We'll talk about it later."

He cocked his head and smiled. "The good reverend got to you? You're going to love your enemy?"

Oh, he was a maddening one, he was. And he liked being maddening. The way he said *love* had nothing to do with the kind of love that Howard Blake spoke of. Was he trying to annoy her—or flirt with her? Or both at once?

She wanted to forget that irrational moment of temptation that had jolted them on the moonlit porch. But he wasn't going to let her forget. To him, it was a weapon.

Did he know how handsome he was, standing there in his shabby clothes? How strong and vital and burnished by the sun?

Of course, he did. He was probably a seduction machine, finely tuned and well serviced. She needed to keep her distance, her scruples and her cool. He was out of her league.

But she smiled back, with the same false, taunting sweetness. "I think I'd better lock things up. For safety's sake."

She marched down the hall to Carolyn's office, feeling his gaze burning into her back. She ducked into the room and took the ring of keys from the big desk.

She backed out and locked the door with a flourish and a loud click. She went up and down the hall, locking all the doors but his, hers and Bridget's.

She walked back into the living room. He hadn't moved. He still stood, his arms crossed, watching her.

"I guess that's my cue to turn in," he said in a low voice. "Are you going to lock me in, too?"

Pretending he was invisible, she refused to meet his eyes. "Good night—Mr. Duran. If that's really your name."

"It's the name on my birth certificate. Sweet dreams, Miss Nightingale. And don't forget to say your prayers."

She didn't condescend to answer. He snagged an apple from the fruit bowl on the coffee table and swaggered down the hall, tossing the apple into the air and expertly catching it. He whistled something tuneless and jaunty.

She waited until he disappeared into his room. Then she squared her shoulders and headed purposefully toward the kitchen.

Bridget was loading the dishwasher, and when she saw Mickey, her broad face brightened. "Now wasn't that nice? Reverend Blake and Reverend Casterleigh dropping in? Where's Mr. Duran? Gone to bed? He said he was up at four this morning to catch his plane."

Mickey wasn't smiling, and her eyes narrowed menacingly. "Bridget, you and I need to have a talk. About our guest, *Mr.* Duran…"

ADAM AWOKE EARLY, feeling restless and disoriented from sleeping in a strange bed. The bed was too soft; it had been like trying to sleep on a giant marshmallow. It had multitudinous sheets and coverlets and ruffles to entangle, bind and smother him. He was used to a bunk with a single thin blanket or none at all.

He rose stiffly, and minutes later, felt his body return to normal under the blast of the shower—ah, that was nice. In the islands, he was used to showers that only dribbled.

But he mustn't be seduced by the comforts of civilization,

he told himself, wrapping a towel around his middle. He had duties back in Los Eremitas; he had lives depending on him. He lathered up and shaved with an old-fashioned straight razor.

He put on a pair of jeans, clean but threadbare, and donned another faded work shirt. He pulled on his boots and wondered if he was the first one up. It was just after half past five, and he smelled no aromas of breakfast. Maybe he'd go outside and find out what it was like being surrounded by land instead of water.

Yesterday, when he'd driven up in the rental car, he'd seen stables and a pregnant bay mare grazing in a separate paddock behind the larger one. Maybe he'd stroll over and get acquainted with the horses. God knew he was more used to talking to horses than people.

He walked quietly down the hall and let himself out the kitchen door—no sign of Bridget yet—that wonderfully chatty woman. But Bridget might no longer be talkative. Mickey Nightingale had probably hauled her over coals for saying too much.

The sun, large and red-gold, was just clearing the hilltops. As Adam crossed the yard, the wind brought him the rich scent of the stable, and he pushed Miss Mickey Priss from his mind.

Yesterday he'd started to think of her as attractive, which just proved how out of his element he was. He'd even flirted with her, and he'd tried to provoke her, too. He hadn't been himself, not at all. He didn't belong here, and he needed to get home.

He approached the paddock, where the bay mare stood, watching him warily.

He leaned over the top board of the fence and began to talk to her. Slow, nonsensical, musical talk, punctuated with chirps and *chuck-chuck* sounds made deep in his throat.

Her sensitive ears flicked back and forth, her dark eyes studied him. For a few moments she hesitated, then she came straight to him, as he'd known she would.

In another moment, she was letting him touch her, even on her velvety muzzle. She tossed her head and rubbed it against his arm. Then, just when he thought he had her attention completely, she thrust up her head, nostrils wide, ears set forward. She looked beyond him.

Idly, Adam craned his neck to look around the corner of the stable. He saw, being led out to the bridal path, a very vision of a horse, the most beautiful horse he'd ever seen, a black Arabian.

The horse was unsaddled, and Mickey was leading him. Then she leaped agilely onto the stallion's bare back. For a moment Adam thought he was still asleep and dreaming. He blinked, resisting the impulse to rub his eyes.

The spring dawn was spreading brightly, rose and golden. The woman kept the big horse reined in until he got all the capering out of his system. Then she urged him into a glorious trot that would have made most women—and many men—bounce helplessly. But Mickey didn't ride like most women or men. She rode with a kind of pagan grace.

He blinked again as she leaned low over the horse's neck and urged him into an earth-devouring canter. *This* was the prim woman who'd so coolly greeted him yesterday? How many layers to her character were there? Adam watched until she and the horse disappeared over the crest of a hill.

As he watched, a strange ache gripped his throat. It grew until it pressed the breath out of his chest and locked around his heart.

CHAPTER FIVE

WHEN CAROLYN couldn't exercise the Arabian, Mickey gladly did the job. She loved waking early and riding Sabur across the hills.

Most times she didn't bother with a saddle. She bridled Sabur and leaped to his bare back as nimbly as a trick rider. She would warm him up, taking time to soothe the mischievous quirks from his temper.

Mickey was only average-size, but the horse was large and powerful, seventeen hands high with sculpted muscles. His every step had dance to it, and he had a beautifully shaped head that he carried high and proud.

Always restless when they began, he sometimes pranced sideways, tossing his full mane until it fluttered like a flag. When she urged him into his high-stepping trot, her body moved with his, and she sat him light and sure and easy.

The trot flowed into a canter, and she bent lower to the streaming black veil of his mane. Then she crouched lower still, her heels pressing his great sides, and urged him into a gallop that seemed to shake the earth.

On Sabur Mickey felt strong and free. She had always loved horses. For all her father's flaws, he'd been a top-notch wrangler and rough-string rider. She could not remember a time when she could not ride.

And Sabur, beautiful Sabur, was the finest horse she'd ever handled. When she was astride him, the world changed. It became beautiful and unified, a meaningful place, and she lost herself in the joy of it.

But finally she knew it was time to turn back. Reluctantly, she reined him toward the stables, slowing the gallop to a canter. He tossed his beautiful head in protest, as if he wanted to play all day.

He protested even more, rearing slightly and prancing sideways when she slowed him as the stable came into sight. Mickey patted his neck, leaned forward and crooned into his ear, "Sabur is my honey. Sabur is the wind. Sabur gives me wings. Thank you, Sabur baby."

The words were nonsense, of course, but the Arabian seemed to like their sound. A pointed black ear swiveled toward her voice and twitched in recognition.

She laughed, and then both his ears twitched. She combed her fingers through his thick mane. Life seemed almost perfect, she thought, drinking in the cool spring air.

But then she saw Adam Duran standing in the stable doorway, watching her. Her perfect world vanished, she thudded back to reality, and troubles closed in on her like a pack of yapping hounds.

Carolyn and Vern were gone. Beverly was in the hospital, drugged with morphine. And little Carrie would soon go into surgery, her chest cut open and her tiny heart laid bare to scalpels.

The skin of Sabur's neck rippled, as if he sensed her anxiety. He snorted and stepped higher.

Adam leaned against the frame of the doorway as if he owned the place. *Which he claims he does—at least half of it,* Mickey thought resentfully.

He was a devil, threatening the very soul of the Circle T. Yes, he was attractive, but the most effective devils almost always were. She tried to ignore his lean body and handsome face. But he wasn't ignoring her. His eyes never left her.

She vaulted from Sabur's back and led him into the stable. She passed Adam with only a brusque nod for greeting.

"Where'd you learn to ride like that?" he asked. He straightened up, stuck his thumbs in his old leather belt and followed her to Sabur's stall.

"What are you doing here?" she asked, neither answering his question nor looking at him.

"I didn't think anybody was up. I came out to look at the horses."

She unbuckled Sabur's bridle. "Snooping again?" She knew she shouldn't use such a tone, but the man unsettled her badly.

"Not snooping. The door was open. I didn't come in until you got here. I just petted the one outside. The pregnant mare."

Mickey gave a small, disbelieving laugh. "Jazmeen? She's nervous. She won't let anybody she doesn't know touch her."

"She let me." He looked over Sabur appreciatively. "This is a beautiful animal. I'll help you rub him down. What's his name?"

"You'd better keep your distance," she said. "His name is Sabur, and he's more high-strung than she is. He can get aggressive."

Adam shrugged. Softly he said, "He won't with me."

Mickey picked up a feed sack and began to rub down Sabur's back. The horse's skin quivered at her touch.

She said nothing to Adam, hoping that would discourage him. She wanted to build a wall of silence against him that would be breached only when *she* willed it. She clamped her lips shut, picked up a brush, and began to work on Sabur's onyx-black neck.

But Adam picked up a curry comb. "I don't suppose you've heard anything from Carolyn. About the baby."

"No."

Vern had promised to phone if there was news of any sort.

She'd gone riding with her cell phone clipped to her belt. No call had come.

He tapped the oval comb against the palm of his other hand, as if familiar with the tool's feel. "I want to say I'm sorry. Sorry that I showed up at such a bad time. That I blurted things out the way I did. That I—acted the way I did."

She looked at him in surprise. Looking was a mistake; his eye color was so vivid it was as if she'd made contact with a live wire.

A frown line formed between his brows. "I'd give anything if what happened between us had gone differently."

She fought against being ensnared by his steady gaze, his tone of conciliation. Too much was at stake. "How about the lease land? Would you give that up?"

The line of his mouth hardened. "No. I wouldn't. I can't."

"I didn't think so. Your sympathy has limits." She picked up the dandy brush and began to rub against the hair of Sabur's neck.

He put aside the curry comb and crossed his arms again, an almost truculent gesture. "I need that land."

"Really?" She didn't try to keep the sarcasm out of her voice. "For what? Going to start your own herd of cattle? Be our neighbor? Won't you miss the beach?"

"I need the money."

"Ah," she said, brushing Sabur's back. "Money. The root of all evil."

"The *love* of money is the root of all evil," he corrected. "I don't love it. I need it."

"What for?" she challenged. "A yacht? Your own island? A nice, private Caribbean sanctuary?"

A strange expression crossed his face, a mixture of surprise and resentment. Her words had obviously stung him, and this gave her not only a perverse pleasure, but a feeling of safety. He would not soften her up or ingratiate himself; she wouldn't let him.

Suddenly she caught sight of another figure in the doorway. With the sun at his back Leon Vanek was a silhouette, tall and thick. Lately she'd been happy to avoid him, but this morning she was relieved to see him.

"Leon," she said, falsely cheerful. "Good to see you. This is Mr. Duran, Carolyn's houseguest. Mr. Duran, Leon Vanek, our foreman."

Leon ambled up to Adam, eyeing him suspiciously. Adam stared back without friendliness. But the two shook hands and muttered greetings.

"Everything all right here?" Leon asked Mickey.

"Pretty much," she said.

"Want me to take over for you?" Leon asked, nodding toward Sabur.

Normally Mickey liked grooming Sabur herself, but the big horse tolerated Leon, and she was eager to escape Adam's company. He filled her with simmering nervousness.

"I wouldn't mind at all," she said with a smile. "Oh, and when you're through, would you show Mr. Duran around the stable? He's says he's curious about the horses."

"Sure thing." Leon took the dandy brush from her. She wiped her palms on the thighs of her jeans. "I'd better go clean up. It's going to be a long day."

"Heard anything from Mrs. Trent?" Leon asked. "About her daughter or the baby?"

"Not yet. I'm hoping that no news is good news."

"Tell her not to worry about things at this end. Between the two of us, Mick, we'll keep things under control."

"That we will." She was conscious that the two of them were speaking as if Adam wasn't there.

She smiled again at Leon, with more warmth than she felt. "'Bye, Leon. Thanks. I'll talk to you later, about that windmill over in the Cutler Hill pasture."

"Take care, Mick." Leon spoke in a voice that hinted at intimacy.

She turned and left the stable. Behind her she sensed the two men checking each other out silently, mentally circling each other in a rivalry that was both instant and ancient.

This made her even more eager to escape to the house. She'd shower, change and eat breakfast alone in her study. She needed to martial her thoughts, and next time she confronted Adam, she'd be prepared.

She'd just stepped inside the sanctuary of the house, when her cell phone rang. A premonitory chill went through her. She hesitated before answering, only for a split second.

"Hello?"

It was Vern, sounding distant and fatigued. "It's me, Mick."

Mickey went cold. "Vern? What's happening?"

"They're going to operate early this afternoon. One o'clock." His voice was ragged with emotion.

Mickey threw a glance at the kitchen clock. It was a half past seven here, an hour earlier in Denver. Surgery would begin in six and a half hours. It seemed an intolerable stretch of time, not to be borne.

"How's the baby?" she managed to ask.

"She made it through the night. But not without—not without a struggle."

"Does Beverly know yet?"

"No. No. It's hard on Carolyn. She spent the night with her. Beverly's conscious, but…but she's in a fog."

"The morphine?"

"Yes. Thank God for that."

"Carolyn?" She could barely get the name out.

Vern sighed. "She's holding up. She'd rather die than not be there for Beverly. She's with her now."

"I'm so sorry." Words seemed pitiably feeble, close to useless.

"I don't know how Caro's going to make it through the operation. J.T.'s still here. And the family's been calling. That helps. Tyler's been especially good. He knows what Caro's going through. She can talk to him. The others don't really understand the fear and worry the way he does."

Mickey bit her lip. Tyler and his wife had lost their first-born. "Yes. Tyler knows all too well."

Vern said, "Carolyn's running on nothing but nerves now. But she'll do it—somehow."

"She's a champion," Mickey said.

"A champ. My Caro." Vern's voice broke slightly. "But she can't take much more, Mick."

Neither can you, Mickey thought.

Vern took a deep breath. "Sonny's talking optimistically. As if he's totally confident. I hope he means what he says."

"Sonny wouldn't sugarcoat the truth. He's not that kind of man."

"No. He's not. He spent the night with Beverly, too. I stayed at the house. Didn't sleep much. Sonny offered me a sleeping pill. I should have taken him up on it. But I wouldn't have felt right about it. If Caro had needed me…"

Mickey forced herself to sound confident. "Tonight, Vern. Tonight will be better."

"I hope to God so."

There was such fatigue in his voice that she knew she couldn't tell him about Adam Duran and his claim to the lease land. But that was the very matter he brought up next.

"That Duran guy," he said. "What's happening with him?"

Mickey could not lay more worries on Vern. She simply could not, so she lied. "Nothing really."

"God, I can't think straight. I suppose he'll be going back to Nassau. Just make him comfortable until he does, will you? Tell him we're sorry he made such a long trip for nothing."

She gritted her teeth. "Don't give it a moment's thought. I'll deal with him."

"You're a treasure, Mickey. I'd better go now. I see Sonny coming with coffee."

"Love to everyone," she said, fear and sympathy swelling in her chest.

"Same to you, Mick. I'll call as soon as I can."

He said goodbye and hung up. Mickey stared at her cell phone helplessly, as if it were an imp that had just whispered evil news in her ear.

"It was Vern?" Bridget asked, looking perilously close to tears.

Mickey braced herself. She refused to fall apart, and she didn't want Bridget to, either. She put her phone back in its holster. "They're going to operate on the baby at one this afternoon, Denver time. Sonny's very optimistic about the outcome. And he ought to know. He's a doctor."

"May he be right," Bridget said, crossing herself. "Jesus, Mary and Joseph, may he be right." Then she squared her shoulders. "How long does it take, an operation like that?"

"I don't know. A while, I suppose. It's complicated."

"And her such a little thing." Bridget looked downcast again.

"I told you," Mickey said briskly, "Sonny says the prognosis is good. In the meantime, the family's all there, pulling together. It's our job to keep things running at home. Mr. Duran will probably be here soon. Give him breakfast, will you?"

Bridget twisted the hem of her apron uneasily. "And you?"

"I'm going to clean up. Then if you'd bring me something to the office. Not much. I'm not very hungry."

This was an understatement. Her stomach pitched and ached.

"Fine." Bridget glanced out the window. "Ah. There he is now."

Time to escape! But Mickey paused long enough to give Bridget a stern look. "And don't go telling him things about the Circle T. Or any of us? Understand? This man is not a friend."

Bridget twisted her apron again, her face both guilty and puzzled. "I won't say a word."

Mickey walked slowly from the kitchen to hide the fact that she was fleeing for all she was worth.

ADAM HAD LET himself out the back door. Now he swung it open and looked inside. He saw Bridget Blum, her back to him, standing at the counter.

"Hi," he said. "Okay if I come in?"

"Come in, come in. Sit yourself down. I'll feed you. I'm just getting a start on lunch."

He detected a difference in her tone from yesterday. She didn't sound unfriendly so much as self-conscious. He doubted if she had it in her to be unfriendly; she was a good soul, and a warm one. Unlike that bastard Leon Vanek, who struck him as an arrogant son of a bitch.

"Smells good. What is it?" He came to her side to see.

"Onion cornbread. It's Mickey's favorite. I thought it'd cheer her up. She's so—"

He watched her stir sour cream into melted butter and sautéed onions. "She's so what?"

She looked at him in shame and wariness. "I shouldn't say any more. I talk too much."

So Mickey *had* read the poor woman the riot act. Her expression was so contrite that pity for her surged in him. "I'm sorry if I got you in trouble," he said. "I asked too many questions yesterday."

"I got myself in trouble. For answering them."

He peered at her more closely. Her eyes were red, her face mottled. He bent nearer in concern. "Bridget, have you been crying?"

"No," she said. "I've been trying not to."

Impulsively he put his hand on her shoulder. "About Mrs. Trent's daughter and grandchild?"

"I shouldn't be saying." She hung her head and poured shredded cheese into the bowl.

"Look," he said earnestly, "I'm not trying to pry. I know the baby's sick and everybody's concerned. It's not gossip. Has there been bad news? Because if there is, I'll pack up now and leave you alone—"

Bridget looked indecisive. He squeezed her shoulder, trying to comfort her. She hesitated, then burst out. "They operate today. But Sonny—"

"Mrs. Trent's son-in-law," he said, nodding.

"Sonny says the prog-prog-prog—"

"Prognosis?"

"Yes. That it's good. Surely, there's no harm in telling you that."

"No. I think there's no harm at all. And I hope he's right."

"Well, it'll be a tense day, and that's a fact. Now sit yourself down. I'll make you a Spanish omelet and some toast. Sit, sit. I'll pour your coffee. Would you like me to slice you a peach or orange or cut you a grapefruit?"

He sat, but he wasn't used to this sort of attention. "You don't have to wait on me."

She waved away the remark as if it was a pesky fly. "I need to keep busy. I want to."

She had set only one place. "Will Mickey join us?"

"No. She's taking a shower."

This created an instant fantasy in Adam's mind, a picture of Mickey naked, water streaming down her trim body. Her head was thrown back, her eyes closed, her untamed hair pulled back and shiny with water.

Stop, he warned himself. Resolutely, he pushed a mental shower curtain into place.

Bridget went on. "She'll eat in her office. She hasn't much appetite."

"Will you join me, then?"

"I've got no appetite myself."

Adam did, to his chagrin. He felt like an insensitive lout to be hungry when the women were upset and distracted. But he was ravenous, and the scents of the kitchen were so succulent they made him dizzy.

Flesh was weak, he thought darkly. He'd been in this house less than twenty-four hours and he was craving rich food and stoking lustful thoughts about Mickey Nightingale. *Was she out of the shower now? Drying herself, maybe? The towel moving over the damp curves of her body...*

He gritted his teeth and told himself to stop thinking of her. This was what happened to a man when he was surrounded by too much comfort, by a lifestyle too cushy. It made him soft, it weakened his will.

Friday he would go back home. He would confront Carolyn Trent another, better time. He would warn her ahead of time what was coming and explain his plan. In the meantime he would live on his boat, simply and without complications. And he would do what he had to do.

Bridget slipped the omelet onto a plate and set it before him. It looked so tempting, he wondered if he'd forfeit his soul by eating it. He couldn't help himself; he had to chance it. It tasted wonderful.

He heard the toaster pop up, heard the soft scrape of a knife. Bridget put a plate of buttered toast beside his omelet. She gave him juice and coffee. Then she sat down across from him, watching him with an expression of sad curiosity.

"Did you really do it?" she asked. "Go into Carolyn's office and Mickey's, too?"

The delicious omelet went suddenly tasteless in his mouth. He swallowed it with difficulty. "Yeah. I shouldn't have."

She shook her head, still looking sad. "Yes. It was wrong. Why did you do it?"

What's Mickey told her? he wondered. *Not the whole truth, not who I am.* Adam knew this instinctively. Mickey had a strong sense of duty, a stronger one yet of loyalty. She would break the news first to Carolyn or Vern. No one outside the family.

He didn't want to lie to Bridget, so he told a partial truth. "I was curious. About Enoch's family. I looked at snapshots, that's all."

"Mickey says you don't come here as a friend. Do you have something bad in store for Carolyn?"

Bridget was a kindly woman, but shrewd.

"I mean no harm to anyone," he said. That was the truth.

"Carolyn needs no more bad luck, she doesn't."

"I know that."

"Mickey knows why you're here. It troubles her. I don't ask her what it is because it's not my business. But I tell you, these are good people. The folks in this house are good folks."

Adam nodded moodily because he sensed she was right. He'd imagined Carolyn as spoiled and haughty, a rich Texas society bitch. That was the impression he'd gotten from Enoch, who said he came from hardscrabble folks. Carolyn, Enoch had mocked, had been born with a whole set of silverware in her mouth, not just the spoon.

Adam hadn't thought of her as a family woman, frantic with fear for her loved ones.

Bridget studied his face. She got to her feet, but leaned toward him. "I have to take a tray in to Mickey. And I'll say only this to you—I have the feeling you don't have a bad heart." She put her hand on his shoulder. It was gentle, but strong. "Be kind," she said.

She moved back to the counter. He said, "Bridget?"

She took another omelet from the heating pan. She didn't look up. "Yes?"

"Mickey..." he hesitated. "If I went to her office, would she talk to me?"

"Not now. Wait. Until after."

He understood. After the baby's surgery.

Until after. Morning light streamed steadily through the windows, but it was as if the words cast the room in shadow.

Bridget arranged plate, silverware and a napkin on a tray. He said, "You'll tell me, won't you? When it's over? How it's gone?"

She still didn't meet his eyes. "I'll tell you. Yes. As soon as we know."

She took up the tray and went down the hall, leaving him alone. He finished his food, no longer savoring it. His task had seemed simple when he'd come, even righteous.

Now his heart was full of conflict. He yearned for the isolation of an island, the elemental simplicity of the sea.

THE MORNING was the longest of Mickey's life. She should have been updating the breeding records for the cattle, but when she sat at the computer, her fingers fumbled, striking the wrong keys. She couldn't concentrate.

She weeded her files instead, dull work taking little thought. She kept glancing at her watch. The minute hand seemed stuck in slow, slow motion.

At nine, she sucked in her breath. They wouldn't be taking the baby into the operating room for another five hours. A few minutes later, Bridget, her face flushed, peered into the room. "Mickey, would you mind if I went to church?"

"I wouldn't mind at all. I think it's a fine idea."

"I'll be back in an hour and a half at most. And if you get any news, I've got my thingy—the cellar phone."

Mickey almost smiled. Bridget did not have an easy relationship with her cellular phone. Mickey could not live without hers; it was the only one she used.

Bridget leaned farther inside the room. "You won't mind me leaving you alone in the house—with him, I mean?"

Adam. She hadn't thought of that. The prospect didn't

please her, but she shook her head. "Not to worry, Bridget. I can handle him."

Bridget nodded, obviously relieved. "Then I'll be off. At times like this I do my best waiting on my knees."

"Say one for me."

"I always do."

TRUE TO HER WORD, Bridget was back before ten-thirty. By that time, Mickey was half-wild with restlessness. The walls of her office started closing in on her, as if she were trapped in a story by Edgar Allan Poe.

She needed air, she needed to move, to burn off anxiety. She changed into her jeans and boots and told Bridget she was going to take a ride.

Bridget's eyes widened. "But if something happens? If they call?"

Mickey patted her cell phone. "They'll call this number first."

"But how will I know?"

"I'll call you first thing, I promise. I'll be back by lunchtime." *But I won't feel like eating*.

She glanced into the living room. "Where's our guest?"

Bridget shrugged. "He just went out to his car. He said he was going to take a drive."

"I hope it's a long one," Mickey said grimly. *Like to the southernmost point of Argentina*. She pushed open the back door and saw Adam standing by his rental car. He had a map spread out on the hood and was studying it.

When he heard the screen door slam, he raised his eyes, looking her up and down. "Going riding again?"

"I can't stay in the house any longer," she muttered.

"Me, either. I thought I'd take a look at the country."

She stopped beside him and threw a glance at the map. It was of Claro County. A line as red as blood marked the boundaries of the lease land. Resentment boiled in her chest. He could pretend to be sensitive, but he wasn't.

"You're going to look for the lease land? At a time like this?"

He frowned. "What's wrong with now?"

"All Carolyn can think about is whether her grandchild's going to live or die. But *you're* going to check out the land you're going to take from her." She made a sound of disgust.

"I have to go somewhere. I have to see it sometime. And once I see it, I'll leave and get out of your hair."

She blinked in surprise. "You're leaving?"

"Yes. I don't like being here any more than you like having me. I'll come another time."

Relief surged through her.

He said, "So I'll look at it. If you don't mind, I'll come back and stay until you hear about the baby. Then I'll go."

She stared at him dubiously. "Why do you want to hear about the baby? You don't even know these people."

He shot her a look of such disdain, that for a moment, in spite of his shabby clothes, he had an almost regal air.

"No. I don't know them. But she's my sister. That makes Beverly my niece. And her baby my great-niece."

"Why this sudden flowering of family feeling?" Mickey challenged.

He frowned. "They're the only blood kin I've got. They sound like good folks. I'm concerned, that's all."

Mickey didn't want to believe him. He was an intruder and a usurper. He couldn't suddenly push himself into being a member of the family.

He saw her doubt and cocked his head. "This thing about the land doesn't have to get ugly, you know. It can be settled to everybody's satisfaction."

"That's not the attitude you had last night. Last night, it was your land, and that was that."

"Last night we both said things we shouldn't have. In ways

we shouldn't have said them. Look, just tell me how to get to Enoch's land. I don't see any main roads."

"There aren't any main roads."

"Then where are the back roads?"

"You couldn't get there by the back roads." She nodded at the compact car. "Not in that."

"What do you mean? I need a truck? A jeep?"

"At the very least."

He lowered his face slightly, looking at her from under his forelock. A sly smile touched the corner of his mouth. "How about a horse?"

"What about a horse?"

"Could I get there on horse?"

"Naturally. That's the way it always used to be done."

"Then you show me the land. Come with me. I told you I can ride."

Mickey was stunned by the suggestion. "I can't do that."

His eyes held hers. "Why not?"

Flustered, Mickey turned away. "I wouldn't feel right. I told you."

"Because of what Carolyn's going through?"

She stared at the stable. "Yes. Exactly."

He paused, then said, "Come with me for her. I'm trying to make a peace offering, Mickey. I started out wrong. Last night, you said you'd talk to me later. It's later. Ride and talk to me."

She kept her gaze on the stable. The pregnant bay mare grazed alone in her paddock. "I wouldn't know what to say. I'd be worried about Caro. And the baby. And Beverly."

"Worry doesn't do them any good."

"It's all I can do."

"No. You can occupy yourself with an unpleasant task—me."

She almost smiled. That's what he was, all right: a highly unpleasant task. If the lease land was really his, he could claim it and never take Carolyn into consideration. Or, Mickey could see if it was possible to build a bridge between him and Carolyn.

She thought harder. Maybe if he learned more about Carolyn, he'd respect her and treat her as the valuable human being she was. Mickey had her misgivings, a shadowy sense of danger, but she made up her mind.

She turned to face him. "All right. I'll take you there. But I'll have to tell Bridget to hold lunch. It'll take us a while by horseback."

The breeze rumpled his hair. His eyes were bluer than the bright May sky behind him.

He nodded. "Good," he said. "Because we've got a lot to talk about."

CHAPTER SIX

MICKEY AND ADAM walked to the stable. She didn't look at him, but instead gazed at the wildflowers when she spoke. "Can you ride Western saddle?"

He almost laughed. "Western. English. Or none."

She slipped him a measuring glance. "Oh?"

"I grew up on a sort of horse farm. In northern Florida. Near Ponte Vedra."

"A *sort* of horse farm?"

He didn't like talking about his past, but if she was going to trust him, he had to be open. "My grandpa bred 'em, trained 'em, bought and sold 'em. Summers he ran a kind of riding camp for kids. Lessons. Trail rides. Beach rides. That kind of stuff."

"Sounds like a good place to grow up."

"It was." Deep within, he still missed it and always would.

"You and your mother lived with him?"

"No. My grandparents raised me."

Mickey looked curious, but reluctant to ask more.

He said, "My mom thought I'd be better off with them. And I was."

That didn't explain it, and he knew it. "She had a career. She was a jockey. A good one."

"A jockey? Really?" Mickey said. "Carolyn's niece was a jockey for a while. Lynn."

"My mother was great," he said. "She won a lot of purses.

She did some commercial work, endorsements and stuff. She had to be on the road a lot."

"Oh." Her voice had a hint of pity that he didn't want or need.

It wasn't that his mother hadn't loved him. She had, and he knew it. But she had to make a living, and she did the best she could. "She came home whenever she was able," he said. "It wasn't like she abandoned me. Don't think that."

He'd adored her. She was little and beautiful and had a bubbling laugh and golden hair. He'd thought she was the best rider in the world. When she was home, he'd followed her around like an adoring puppy and was heartsick when she went away.

He didn't want to mention that part, so was glad that he and Mickey had reached the stable. "Which horse do you want me to take?" he asked.

"Your choice, except for the Arabians. Only Carolyn and I ride the black. And the bay's never been ridden. She's flighty. We're going to need time to train her."

I could ride her, he thought. *If she wasn't pregnant, I could be on her back before sundown.*

He knew it was true, but Mickey would never believe him.

He'd looked the other horses over this morning while talking with that high-and-mighty foreman, and he'd looked them over well.

He said, "I'll take the gray."

She lifted a dubious eyebrow. "He's got a lot of spirit."

"I like that."

"He's used to that saddle with the conchos. And the red blanket."

"Fine. What's his name?"

"Smoky."

He smiled. "How do, there, Smoky. How do, big boy."

He rubbed the gray's neck gently and talked to him in a low voice. He didn't hurry the animal, and when he slid on the headband and put the bit to Smoky's mouth, the horse accepted it calmly.

She chose a palomino gelding that seemed like a parade horse, high-stepping and showy. She handled him expertly and swung the heavy saddle onto his back with ease. Adam watched her out of the corner of his eye and knew she was keeping watch on him, too.

"Whose horse is that?" he asked, nodding at the palomino.

"Beverly's. His name is Dandy." She led him out of the stall.

Adam placed the blanket on Smoky's back and stroked it smooth. "Who's this big guy belong to?"

"Sonny. Beverly's husband. He and Beverly are looking for a little ranch outside Denver. He bought Smoky at an auction in Austin, and he's boarding him here until they find a place."

"He must be a good rider. This boy's full of vinegar, all right."

"Sonny? He's a natural. He was never on a horse before he was twenty, but you'd never know it."

"Some people are like that. They're born with it." He picked up the saddle, folded the girth, put stirrup irons across the saddle's seat, and swung it onto the horse's back. He pulled the girth under Smoky's belly and buckled and tightened it.

"You *do* know what you're doing," she said.

Smoky nuzzled him and playfully lipped the sleeve of his shirt. "I know horses," Adam said. "I know boats. That's about it."

They led the horses from the stable and mounted. She did it smoothly, and he did it even more so. She looked at him with something akin to respect. "Let's ride," she said with a flick of her reins.

He stayed slightly behind her, letting her take the lead. She headed away from the bridal path, across flat ground thick with blooming bluebonnets. It was pretty country, downright beautiful with so much in blossom, and he could understand why people would fight to keep it.

He'd hoped Mickey wouldn't dig any more into his past, but she did. "You said Carolyn and her family were the only kin you had. What's happened to *your* family? Your mother?"

He squared his shoulders. "She died when I was twelve. She'd been in Oregon. She'd gone to talk to a sponsor. She fell. That's all. She fell down the stairs at a motel. You know, those outside concrete and metal stairs they have. It was raining, starting to freeze.

"She slipped and broke her neck. She was a born athlete. She could handle twelve hundred pounds of galloping horse, but she slipped on the ice. And died."

"I'm so sorry," Mickey said with feeling. "It must have been terrible for you."

Twelve years old had been too old to cry, he'd known, but he'd cried in secret every night for weeks. His grandparents had been devastated.

He said, "My grandma and grandpa never got over it. She was their only child. They had her late in life. Grandpa pretty much let everything go. He died two years later.

"Grandma sold the farm and we moved to Panama City. I got a part-time job at a marina. Grandma wasn't well. She died when I was eighteen. I went to work for an old guy who taught me the charter-fishing business. I took to it. I wanted to be away from the horses for a while."

Too many memories, he thought. It was too complicated; she'd never understand.

"Too many memories?" she asked.

Her words jolted him but "I guess so," was all he said. The vista of flowers was changing, the bluebonnets giving way to yellow ones like daisies and the orange-gold of cactus blossoms.

"No other family?"

He shook his head. "Grandpa immigrated from Russia

when he was young. His name was Vladimir Duranovic. He claimed he had Cossack blood, and that's where my mom got her talent. My grandma was an only child. So no. I don't have cousins or aunts or uncles."

"That's why you wanted to find your father?"

He shrugged. "I guess. I started a few years back. There are agencies that do that kind of thing. It was too late. All the detective found was his death certificate and obituary. He'd married, but no kids were mentioned. Only Enoch was. That was it."

The yellow-and-orange flowers were suddenly bisected by a narrow dirt road that was rutted and rocky. Mickey took it, and he stayed abreast of her. She was right. His rental car could never have made it.

She turned to him, her brow furrowed. "I still wonder why you'd want to find your father. I wouldn't go looking for mine."

That's right, he thought, *fathers are a raw subject for you.* "You're bitter about yours. I wasn't."

She said nothing, only nudged the horse to a faster walk. She stared straight ahead at the road.

Adam urged Smoky to keep up. He said, "My father didn't *want* to leave. My mother broke it off. She found out he was already married. She told him to hit the road and not come back—ever."

Mickey looked unconvinced. "That still doesn't seem like much of a character reference for him."

"She said he wasn't a bad guy to have for a father, but she wasn't going to marry him even if he got a divorce. She didn't like being lied to, she wouldn't stand for it. She didn't know she was pregnant when she sent him packing, and after she knew, she never told him."

Mickey frowned. "He'd left his wife and two children in Texas. I wouldn't say he was a *good* guy to have for a father."

"I really don't think my mother knew about the children.

Only the wife. Nobody ever mentioned them to me until Enoch did."

"Your father was over forty when he walked out on his family here. He must have been twice your mother's age."

"More. She was eighteen."

"Good grief!"

"She didn't care. She had a mind of her own. She saw him, she liked what she saw, so she took up with him—until she found out he wasn't divorced like he said."

"But she told you his name?"

"Yeah. But she told me never to look for him. Maybe she thought I'd be disappointed. Maybe she figured he'd done his part, and we didn't need him for anything else."

"Done his part? Just by fathering you?"

"She looked on it more as *siring* me. Like he was basically good stock. She said he was strong, he was smart, he was healthy, he was good-looking, he was skilled, he was charming and he rode well. She said I could have done worse in the father department, so to let it alone."

"You didn't think that was a little, well, strange?"

"I told you. She lived life on her own terms. So do I."

Mickey shook her head, clearly puzzled, maybe disapproving. "All right. You gave up horses for fish. Then what?"

He'd been honest with her, but he didn't like talking about himself. He was tired of it. "Let's give it a rest, okay? You talk for a change. Tell me about my sister."

"Your half sister."

"And my niece."

"Your half niece."

"Yes," he retorted, "and my half brother-in-law and my half nephew-in-law or whatever he is. My whole half family."

Mickey reined in her horse, then swept out her arm. "Look. There it is. The lease land. It starts right there, at that little creek, the eastern border. That's what Enoch left you—or so you say—the next eleven thousand acres. Clear to that far mountain. That's how far it goes."

He'd stopped beside her. The sight stunned him. Beyond the creek was an immensity of land, rough, varied and nearly empty.

Until this moment the lease land had been an abstraction to him, a means to an end. Now that he saw it, awe rose in him.

My father knew this land, he thought. *And so did Enoch.*

He had the strange illusion of coming back to his roots, of coming home. But it was only an illusion. He knew where home was.

And he could not believe this great stretch of Hill Country was his. Its grandeur forced him to ask himself, *Do I deserve this?* He knew the answer was no. But that didn't matter. He needed it.

MICKEY WATCHED his reaction. He seemed struck speechless. Maybe he was overwhelmed by the sweep of the land. Or maybe he merely gloating, computing how much it was worth. She truly could not understand this man.

A herd of cattle, Brangus, grazed in the middle distance. Mickey was struck by the irony. Most of Carolyn's best grazing places were on the lease land and much of the natural water supply. If she lost this acreage, she'd be forced to cut cattle production by half.

"So what do you think of it?" Mickey asked tonelessly.

"I think it's a long way from the ocean."

What does that mean, she wondered. But she said, "Do you want to ride part of the perimeter?"

"Sure," he said, his eyes on the far horizon. "Why not?"

She kneed Dandy to guide him off the road and through the scrub and wildflowers. Adam said, "Carolyn uses this for grazing?"

"It takes a lot of acres to support one head, let alone two thousand."

He nodded. "I can see. Not a lot of forage."

"No. The horse pastures up by the stables are seeded, so they're fairly lush. Out here, it's a lot more hardscrabble."

"But still valuable."

Uneasiness prickled through her. "The value goes up and down. That developer inflated prices—for a while."

He looked somber. "And Carolyn's had use of it for twenty years. She's not going to be happy."

"No. She'll be heartbroken. And hurt. And probably furious at Enoch for breaking his promise."

"It was his land to give. I didn't ask for it. I was as surprised as she'll be."

"But your surprise was pleasant," Mickey returned. "Hers isn't."

"Look. I said maybe we could work this out in a friendly way. Tell me more about her. Please."

Mickey hedged. "You seem to know plenty already. You knew Beverly'd been a beauty queen and married a doctor, didn't you? You knew it when you made that crack in front of her picture."

He looked irritated with himself. "I shouldn't have said it."

"Then why did you?"

He was silent a moment, a breeze rose, rustling the horses' manes, tossing the wildflowers. "I felt…out of my element. Outclassed."

This surprised her. "Outclassed? Did you think we're snobs? That Carolyn's a snob?"

"Enoch thought that she was…overprivileged, I guess."

"That's not true. She worked as hard as any man—especially after her father walked out. She *saved* this ranch."

Adam shrugged irritably. "Look, Enoch and his brothers grew up dirt-poor. He thought Carolyn's mother lorded it over Steven, and that she turned both girls against their father, and Enoch resented it. He resented that, and he probably resented that he had to take his lease money from her family, but they'd made the only offer. He didn't like taking money from a woman, either. It was the way he saw it, that's all."

She put her hand on her hip and looked him in the eye. "There are people—and I suspect Enoch was one of them—who are jealous of anybody that has more than them. They're snobs in reverse. God knows, Caro always paid him and she tried to be polite, and he never gave her a kind word."

"He thought that she was being phony, *pretending* to be polite."

"Carolyn doesn't have a phony bone in her body," Mickey protested.

Adam looked at the sky as if searching it for extra patience. "I'm just telling you his version. He told me she'd write him nicey-nice letters at Christmas and put in snapshots and stuff. He thought Beverly being a beauty queen was the stupidest thing in the world. He laughed about her marrying a doctor because he said that's what all beauty queens do."

This fired Mickey's innate protectiveness. "Beverly's not a stereotype, and neither is Sonny. *Nobody* in this family's stuck-up."

He was silent a moment then said, "You seemed pretty frosty when we met."

"You weren't what I expected." And that, she thought, was the greatest understatement of her life.

"Right. Clothes make the man, eh? I looked like a bum."

"That wasn't it at all." Instantly she regretted the words.

"Then what was it? You stared at me like I was a Martian."

Her mind spun. She couldn't say *You were the handsomest man I've ever seen. It was like having a Greek god appear on the doorstep.*

She had to be careful even now of looking at him. It was addictive. The face wasn't merely handsome, it was interesting. It wasn't a pretty mask hiding a vacuous personality. A sharp but complicated mind worked behind those striking features.

She managed to sputter, "I knew that Enoch was an old— that he was old. I thought you'd be another old geez—that you'd be elderly. And I'd forgotten you were coming."

"I'm not sure that's the whole truth."

"Yes, it is," she lied. "And why would *I* be snooty? I told you—I was a ward of the court. A nobody. Vern and Carolyn took me in."

He lifted one eyebrow, his expression quizzical. "Yeah. Tell me about that. What happened to you?"

"It's a perfect example of how good-hearted they are. There was no foster home available in the county. So Vern brought me to the ranch. And there was still nobody who'd take me in. Then one day Caro said, 'Would you like to stay here, with us?' And by that time, there was nothing I wanted more. I've been here ever since."

There, thought Mickey. *That ought to convince him how generous Vern and Carolyn are, and how kind.*

But he looked at her strangely. "You didn't have any relatives?"

"None who wanted me."

"You said your mother died. What happened to her?"

"She drank." Mickey said the two words sharply, hoping he wouldn't ask more.

But he didn't heed her tone. "That killed her?"

"That. And pills." Her throat tightened, almost choking her.

"Accidental overdose?"

"Suicide," she admitted bitterly. "She tried it half a dozen times. She'd leave these notes about how she wasn't any good and she didn't want to live. It was awful. I'd come home from school, find her and call 9-1-1. The last time, I came too late, and I…and I…"

She'd known her mother was dead as soon as she'd seen

her. She knew, and it was as if her own heart stopped. Stunned, she'd gone outside and sat on the steps of the trailer house and cried. A neighbor, fat old Mrs. Clancy had finally come over and asked what was wrong.

Mickey had managed to say, "She finally did it. Mama did it." She couldn't bring herself to say the words "dead," or "suicide," or "killed herself." She'd just kept crying.

Mrs. Clancy had stood there a long time and finally said, "Well, honey, maybe she's better off. Come to my place. I'll call the police."

But Mickey was so resentful of those words, she'd refused to move. *Honey, maybe she's better off.* The statement had angered her and made her feel a deep and terrible guilt. She'd been ashamed of her mother. But she hadn't wanted her dead. She was still sitting alone on the steps, crying silently, when the police and ambulance had arrived.

The memory made her throat ache harder. "Listen," she said with all the control she could muster, "I don't want to talk about it. This isn't about me. It's about you and Carolyn."

But he got that sympathetic look on his face that always confounded her. "How'd she support you? Your mother?"

"We were on welfare. I said I don't want to talk about it."

"I'm sorry. I'm sorry you went through that. But I see why you're so loyal to them."

She couldn't speak, so only nodded. Her life had been hellish until Carolyn and Vern came into it. Her mother had needed a man, but one man had turned into a string of men. Mickey'd come to despise the weakness, the need, the waste and growing humiliation of it.

She was grateful when Adam changed the subject. "I suppose Carolyn resented Steve Randolph. Her father. Our father."

Mickey sighed. "She's tried to come to terms with his leaving. She says she has. Mostly."

"What's that mean—mostly?"

Mickey guided Dandy around a patch of prickly pear. "Her parents' marriage wasn't happy. Steve Randolph had left before. More than once. The last time he left a letter saying he wasn't coming back. His daughters were both married by then, and he thought nobody needed him—or respected him."

"Did they?" His tone was doubtful.

Mickey frowned in concentration. "He claimed Carolyn took her mother's side. And that Pauline was starting to. Carolyn admits it's true about her—but not Pauline. Their mother ran that marriage. Yes, she tried to turn the girls against him."

Adam said, "But he took it for all those years?"

"That's what Carolyn says. Her mother owned the ranch, and her mother called the shots."

Adam looked disturbed. "Did he cheat on her? Was that part of the problem? Look, that sounds nosey. But he was my father, too. I want to know."

Mickey got off Dandy and led him across a trickling branch of the creek. Adam did the same with Smoky. She thought hard, and she thought of what Carolyn herself would say.

She remounted the palomino. "His problem wasn't women. His problem was places. He said he hadn't found where he belonged. His brothers had. But he hadn't."

Adam had led the gray across the creek, stroking his neck and head, speaking softly to him. He, too, mounted again, a fluid movement that she had to admire.

"So did he find it?" he asked. "The place where he belonged? In Canada?"

Mickey shook her head. "I don't know. Carolyn doesn't know, either. You shouldn't ask me—I really have no right to talk about him."

She nudged the palomino to avoid a strange stretch of pitted limestone, level to the earth. Adam did the same, but he persisted in the subject. "You don't want to talk about him because you never knew him?"

"That's part of it."

"But you know Carolyn as well as anybody does."

He had her there. Over the years, she and Carolyn had talked about everything, including their feelings about their fathers.

"Look," she said unhappily, "You say you're her brother. If you really are, you should talk about these thing with her, not me."

He tossed her a curious glance. "You believe me? That I'm her brother? You don't have to have proof from the FBI?"

She cast an uneasy glance at the sky. Clouds had started to roll in from the south. "You look like you're related," she admitted. "I'd have to be blind not to see it. Your eyes, your hair, your bone structure…"

"This horse feels lightning coming," he said.

She stared at him in spite of her vow not to. "What?"

"This horse," he said. "Smoky. He feels lightning coming. He doesn't like it. He wants to go home. He wants to go now. Let's turn back."

She was amazed. Smoky hated storms. If one was really coming, he would sense it. But how could Adam tell? Could he read the horse as if the creature was a book?

"You haven't seen all the land," she said.

"The horse isn't happy."

With those words, he turned Smoky in the opposite direction and headed back toward the stable. Mickey had no choice but to follow him. She neck-reined Dandy and heeled him to catch up.

"I said you haven't seen all the land," she repeated.

"I've seen enough," he said, urging Smoky to a faster pace.

He paced it just right, she thought. The land was rough; it was unsafe to speed a horse. But he both puzzled and fascinated her. "The land is why you came. What do you mean, you've seen enough?"

"It's land," he said. "It's nice. But it's in the wrong place."

"The wrong place?" She was more bewildered than before.

"I know where I have to be," he said.

"What? Where? What do you mean?"

But there was a rumble of thunder in the distance, and the wind gusted, carrying the faint but unmistakable scent of coming rain. He had followed her to the middle of the lease land. Now he led them back, as if he knew the way better than she did.

ADAM LED SMOKY to his stall. He'd enjoyed the feel of the big gray beneath him, but he knew the horse was glad to be in the safety of the stable. He had understood the animal's first signs of uneasiness, the fine flicker and ripple of fear in the muscles. Werner Blum, the stable man, had herded all the other horses except Jazmeen to pasture. By one o'clock, she'd come in from her paddock and paced restlessly in her special stall.

Restless, pretty lady? Adam thought. *I think you're getting ready to pull a surprise.*

Jazmeen, as if she did indeed have secrets, turned from them, walked to the paddock door and sniffed the outside air nervously.

The first drops of rain drummed on the roof, and Smoky's nostrils flared, his eyes rolled. Adam unfastened the girth and swung the saddle off. "Smoky, you'd never make it in hurricane country," he said softly. He turned to Mickey and said, "What do you do with this poor guy when he's out in the pasture and it starts to rain?"

Mickey, dismounted, was leading Dandy into a neighboring stall. "I go get him. But how did you know that he…"

Her voice trailed off. Adam shrugged. "I just know. That's all. What happened to him? Close to a lightning strike?"

"We have no idea," she said. "Sonny got a bargain on him. He's part Arabian. But he doesn't like storms. We've noticed that. Something must have happened."

"Lightning," Adam said. "Yeah, that's what he's saying. Has—what's his name—Sonny ridden him in the rain?"

"No. He's been able to ride him just a few times on visits."

"Yeah," Adam said, stripping off the saddle blanket. "Well, he should know. Have you told him?"

She put the stirrups in the up position. "Yes. I told him over the phone. I also sent him a note to remind him, and an e-mail, too."

Adam shot her a grin. "Jeez—you are Miss Efficiency."

She smiled and shrugged.

He said, "You don't pasture the full-blood Arabs with the others, do you? Whoa, Smoky, boy. You're safe in here."

"Oh, no," she said as he soothed the gray horse. "The mare has her paddock. The black's in a separate pasture. He gets aggressive."

"He's the sire of Jazmeen's colt?"

"Yes."

"Carolyn going to keep breeding him?" he asked, using a feed sack to start rubbing down the twitchy gray.

"Yes," Mickey answered, but she hesitated to say more. There were things she didn't like revealing about Carolyn. Breeding horses could be expensive, and Carolyn was gambling that she could fight the unstable beef market by breeding and selling fine horses. But it was a costly gamble, and Mickey didn't want to blurt out too much about the Trents' finances.

"The black's a fine horse," he said. "Outstanding. The bay's good, too. She's got prophet's thumb."

Mickey pulled off Dandy's saddle. "Prophet's thumb? What's that?"

"On her neck. An impression, a kind of dent. It looks like a thumbprint. Old-timers say it's a good sign. Truth is, it's caused by pressure from when she was in the womb. Just a quirk of fate."

She eyed him as she put the saddle on its rack. "Is that something you learned from your grandfather?"

"Yep."

"Will she be a good mother?"

"She's anxious. I think she misses a horse she was with. A mare, probably her mother. But she's not cranky. If she's treated right, she should do fine."

Mickey nodded, but said nothing. The two of them worked without speaking. The rain thudded down harder. Adam had forgotten the feel and smell of a stable in a rain. It was like coming home again after years at sea.

He finished grooming Smoky before Mickey was done with Dandy. He moved to her side and began to help her. He didn't ask, but she didn't protest. Their movements fell into a natural, mutual rhythm. Dandy turned his head and nuzzled Adam's sleeve. The animal nickered and softly head-butted his shoulder.

Adam laughed and ruffled the palomino's mane. His eyes met Mickey's. He realized that they worked well together. Almost perfectly. And he liked being with her, being close to her.

And then they were done.

He couldn't think of anything to say. She was silent, so he guessed she couldn't either. Wordlessly they drifted to the stable doors and watched the rain pouring down in crystal sheets.

He became more conscious of her nearness. The day had cooled, but he could feel the heat of her body, as if his own had suddenly become ultrasensitive. The scent of hay and horses tickled him, filling him with odd yearnings.

He glanced at her as she stared into the curtain of the rain. She was not classically beautiful. She was pretty in an understated way that he liked. He liked it a lot.

Her profile had character. Yes, that was the word that came to him: character. Her features were clean-cut and even, her skin flawless. Everything about her seemed orderly and…good. Even though she'd been through so much, too much as a child and young woman.

Good wasn't a word he usually applied to people; he wasn't a people person, he tended to keep to himself. Yet he sensed something in her that impressed and attracted him. Oh, she could be fierce in her defense of Carolyn and Carolyn's family, but Mickey Nightingale was not ferocious by nature.

She murmured, "We could run for the house. Or try to wait it out…."

"Let's wait," he said. He liked being isolated with her like this. The damp in the air made her hair curl more uncontrollably. He was tempted to touch it.

He inched a bit closer to her. She noticed, he could tell, but she did not move away. He edged closer still.

He said, "Do you think of me as a bad guy?"

Her expression seemed to stiffen with control. "I don't know what to think of you. There's a saying: 'The enemy of my friend is my enemy.' If you're Carolyn's enemy, you're mine."

"I don't want to take Carolyn's land away. I've got no use for it. I'll sell it to her. I'll ask a fair price. I'm not greedy."

She glanced at him, doubt in her eyes.

"What's wrong?" he asked.

She looked at the rain again. "Vern said I could talk to you about—this situation. That I could be Carolyn's—"

She didn't seem to be able to find a word so he supplied one. "Proxy?"

She shook her head so her dark hair moved intriguingly. "No. I can't speak for her. But I can listen for her. I can hear what you have to say."

He turned so that she had to look him in the face. "Mickey, I never asked for this land. If I could, I'd give it to Carolyn. But I can't. I need money, and Enoch knew it."

Conflicting emotions crossed her face. "Money isn't what Carolyn's about. Especially not now." She glanced at her watch and a shiver ran through her. "The operation starts in less than an hour. I'm not sure I can talk about money."

"But you said—no. Never mind. It's okay. Maybe we can talk later. Mickey, don't look so sad. Please."

"Yes. Later. Maybe." Her voice sounded choked. "I'm sorry. My emotions are all over the place today."

"I understand," he said. And he did. Under her cool, efficient facade, she was both tender and passionate.

"It's just that I wish I was there with them," she said.

"I understand," he repeated. "It's hard to go through these things alone."

She gave him a glance that seemed grateful. And because he didn't like to see anyone in pain, he slipped his arm around her shoulders. It wasn't meant as a sexual gesture, only a human one intended to comfort.

At first her body tensed, but then she seemed to relax and accept his touch. He thought, *We're a lot alike, the two of us.*

What she thought, he did not know. Together they watched the rain fall in silver streaks.

CHAPTER SEVEN

MICKEY'S EMOTIONS spun so crazily they frightened her. At the same time, Adam's nearness felt good, reassuring and even natural.

She seemed to fit perfectly into the curve of his arm. She thought of what he had said. Perhaps he'd spoken truly, perhaps he didn't have to be an enemy.

But just as the rain began to slow, Leon Vanek's black truck pulled up to the stable. He saw Mickey standing with Adam's arm around her, and he looked both disgusted and offended.

Mickey sprang apart from Adam, and he let his arm fall to his side. Leon got out of the truck, slamming the door hard. The rain dripped off his hat brim and ran down his yellow slicker. He stamped inside the stable and did not speak to Adam.

To Mickey he said, "I thought you'd be inside waiting for Vern or Carolyn to call."

She bristled at his disapproving tone. "I have my phone with me. I always do."

"Hmph. Had any word?"

"No. I'll tell you as soon as I do."

"Please see that you do." He put a belittling twist on the words. Turning from her, he muttered, "I came to set up a cot for Werner. I'm going to start having him sleep here and keep watch on the mare. We got a foal on the way. *Somebody* 'round here needs to tend to business."

Mickey ignored his jibe. "I'm going back to the house." She glanced at Adam. "Do you want to come?"

"Sure." But he turned to Leon. "You should wrap that mare's tail in gauze or flannel. She's closer than you think."

Leon snorted in disgust. "Don't tell me how to do my work."

"Come on," Mickey said in a low voice to Adam.

Gritting her teeth, she headed out of the stable. The rain had dwindled to a sprinkle. Adam stayed by her side.

"Vanek shouldn't talk like that to you. He was insolent."

"He's usually the other way around. So polite he's smarmy."

"He likes you. Has he got a claim on you?"

"No. Absolutely not."

"He thinks he does."

"Then he thinks wrong."

"He's wrong about the mare, too," Adam said.

Mickey looked at him in puzzlement, her eyes squinting against the drizzle. "You think she's due that soon? I've kept all the charts. The foal shouldn't come until next week or later."

"She's a maiden mare, isn't she? They can fool you. I'd say he already should have had somebody in there nights, keeping watch. She'll drop it by this weekend, I'll bet. You have a vet on standby?"

"Not yet. Not until next week."

"Maybe you'll be lucky," he said, but he didn't sound convinced. They hurried up the stairs of the back porch, wiped their feet and entered the kitchen. Bridget looked up from the counter, where she was cutting cooked potatoes for potato salad. "No word?" she asked immediately.

"No." Mickey shook her head. "It's too soon. The surgery starts in half an hour."

Bridget wiped her hands on her apron and put her arm around Mickey. "And who knows when it'll be over? But here, it's past lunchtime, and you need to eat. You'll try to eat, won't you?"

Mickey smiled weakly. "I'll try."

"Goodness," said Bridget, stroking her sleeve. "You're damp. Go shower and change your clothes. You don't want to take a chill. That's the last thing we need, for you to come down sick."

Bridget squinted critically at Adam. "And you, too."

He gave a shy grin. "I live on a boat. I'm used to being wet."

"Well, you smell horsey, the both of you. Clean up, says I. We'll all breathe the better for it." As if to prove her point, she sneezed.

"Bridget's allergic to horses," Mickey told Adam. "And we're giving her a double dose."

Mickey led him down the hall, and they went to their separate rooms. Mickey laid fresh clothes out on her bed, stripped down and took a warm shower. For a few wonderful seconds the water gave her a surge of pure, sensual pleasure, washing away worry and bewilderment.

But the respite was brief. She worried about Carolyn and Beverly and the baby. She worried about Vern and Sonny. She didn't know how or when she'd tell Carolyn about Adam. She was no longer sure what she herself thought of him.

She dressed slowly, trying to sort out the situation. The more she was around Adam, the more he reminded her of Carolyn. It wasn't only his looks: the blond hair, the striking eyes, the high cheekbones. It was his strange combination of independence and kindness. Carolyn was a natural athlete, and so was he, but far more so.

He said he would sell the lease land to Carolyn. Would he be like her in business, fair and honest? Or was he only beguiling Mickey, trying to gain her confidence so he could use her to influence Carolyn?

Last night she'd felt as if he might try to kiss her and that she might have let him. This morning in the barn, if she hadn't been so concerned and overwrought, his putting his arm around her might have led to other things.

This bothered her most of all: she found him attractive, far too attractive. She couldn't let his magnetism overwhelm her common sense just when she needed to keep her wits the most.

And it was the wrong time to have such feelings; it wasn't decent of her to have them. Especially for him. Her emotions were volatile over family matters, and that made her vulnerable.

She must be cautious. Very cautious.

ADAM RETURNED to the kitchen before Mickey. "Ah," said Bridget, "you smell like a person again."

He thought he smelled like Palmolive soap when he was used to smelling like horses or the ocean's brine. The soap he washed with on the boat was homemade. He bought it at the farmers' market from an elderly lady named Aunty Amaya, who had a stand under a palm tree.

"I'll get you a cup of coffee, warm you up inside. Take it into the dining room, I'll start setting out lunch."

"I don't need to eat in the dining room," he said. "The kitchen's fine."

"Kitchen's fine for lunch for family, not company," she said.

But, Bridget, I am family. Whether they want me or not. He said, "Let's ask Mickey if she'd rather eat here."

"Fine." She handed him a mug of coffee. "You really live on a boat?"

"Yes. A sloop."

"Sloop? What a funny word. What's a sloop?"

"A sailboat. But she's got a motor, too."

"My, my. How long you been doing that?"

"About eight years." He paused. "Bridget, can I ask you something?"

She shook her finger at him in mock scolding. "I got in trouble once for talking too much to you."

"Just one question." He leaned to look down the hall. He saw no sign of Mickey. "Does she have a man friend? Somebody special?"

A look of conflict crossed Bridget's ruddy face. She hesitated then whispered, "No. She should, but she doesn't, and I never said a word about it to you. Don't ask me more."

He gave her a conspiratorial grin. Then he heard a door open and close. He looked down the hall again, and saw Mickey walking toward him. She wore jeans, a white shirt and a lightweight blue blazer. She looked tidy and neat, almost severe, except for the curly hair. Yet something about her made his heartbeat skip. His grin stayed in place.

She didn't smile back. He glanced at the kitchen clock and knew she wouldn't smile again until she heard from Vern, and even then she might not. Vern's news might be bad.

His own smile sickened and died. "I was asking Bridget if the three of us couldn't eat in here together?"

"Oh, not me—you're the company," Bridget protested.

"I don't know…" Mickey said.

"Please," he said. "I'd be more comfortable. Or, at least, you two eat together. You probably want to be together. I'll take a plate and go in the den or something."

"There'll be none of that," Bridget said, clearly disapproving.

"Maybe he's right," Mickey mused. "This is hardly an ordinary day. Let's just eat here. Bridget, you, too. Please."

"Well…" said Bridget. But then she shrugged and began to set the kitchen table for three. "We're not fancy at heart, none of us, are we?"

"I'm not," Adam said.

"Me, either," said Mickey. He drew out a chair for her to sit, and waited to seat Bridget, too.

She looked pleased. "You may not be fancy, but you got manners."

He sat, and she passed him a platter of sliced ham and turkey. "So why do they call it a sloop?" She turned to Mickey. "He lives on a sloop boat. Fancy that."

"It's from the old Dutch word, *slupen*. It meant 'to glide.'"

"And is that how you make your living," Bridget asked, "slooping around?"

He speared two pieces of meat and passed the platter to Mickey. "No. I make my living fixing other people's boats."

Bridget passed the potato salad. "Carolyn's uncle had a boat in the Bahamas. Is that how you met?"

Adam saw Mickey throw him a sharp look. He knew she hadn't told Bridget the truth about him and didn't intend to. She meant Carolyn to be the first to know. "We had that in common, yes," he said. It wasn't a real answer, but it passed for one, and it wasn't a lie, either.

He saw Mickey had taken one thin slice of turkey, and now she put only a dab of potato salad on her plate. She toyed with the food, but had yet to take a bite.

Mickey said, "I thought you started out in the charter-fishing business." She clearly wanted to keep the conversation on neutral topics.

He nodded. "I crewed on a deep-sea fishing boat for an old guy. He taught me the ropes. He wanted to sell her to me when he retired. My grandma'd left me some money. I bought the boat and did that for a few years, but I got more interested in sailboats. I bought an old sloop and repaired her. Then I helped a friend build one, and finally I gave up the fishing business. Didn't like it."

"Didn't like it? Why?" Bridget asked, her eyes wide. "I know men who'd fish every day of their lives if they could."

"I didn't like trophy fishing. The guys who wanted to kill a big fish so they could hang it on the wall and brag about it. More and more I realized the ocean's powerful, but it's also fragile. The ecology."

He still hadn't seen Mickey eat. She must have felt his eyes on her. She cut off a tiny slice of meat and chewed as if she had no appetite.

Bridget said, "Eat, Mickey. You'll waste away. Carolyn needs you strong."

Mickey squared her shoulders dutifully and began to obey, but with no gusto. What a soldier, Adam thought, strangely touched.

Bridget turned again to Adam. "And this sloop of yours. She's got a name. All ships have names, don't they?"

"She's a boat, not a ship. A ship's much larger. She has a name. The *Katrina D*."

"Ah. A lovely name," said Bridget. "And why did you call her that?"

He felt a twinge of self-consciousness. "I named her for my mother."

He remembered seeing his mother from the stadium stands, dressed in her racing silks, her golden hair hidden by her cap. Such a small, disciplined woman in perfect control of such a powerful animal. God, he'd been proud of her.

Mickey cast him a searching look. He ignored it and asked Bridget to pass the platter. "This is mighty fine," he said. "I'm not used to home cooking."

Mickey pushed her plate away. "I'm sorry. I really can't eat. I think I'll go to my office. I'd just like to be alone for a while, if nobody minds."

Bridget said, "Mickey, just a little more. Cake? Would you like a piece of cake?"

"No thanks. I'll be fine. I'm sorry."

Adam studied her expression. She looked close to tears. "It's okay," he assured her.

He watched her leave and walk back down the hall. In a low voice, he said, "She's taking this hard. She really cares for those people."

"She loves them," Bridget said, staring after her moodily. "And why shouldn't she? Who'd she ever have before in her life to depend on? Nobody. Nobody at all."

Then she stared at him and frowned. "I didn't say that— even if I did, you didn't hear me."

CAROLYN THOUGHT, *Watching your child suffer is the worst fate in the world.*

Last night Beverly hadn't slept well. She was still in pain from her caesarian. She was allowed to push the button on her morphine drip every ten minutes, but it didn't stop the pain, only dulled it.

Every time Beverly woke up, she asked about the baby. She always said the same thing. "Something's wrong with her. What? Why can't I see her?"

At first they'd taken turns—not lying, but softening the truth. It was Sonny who did it best. He'd stroke Beverly's disheveled hair and talk in a low voice, saying there was a little problem, nothing the doctors hadn't seen before and couldn't fix. They'd fix it tomorrow.

Carolyn, not as calm or articulate, would only say, "Now calm down, love. You were premature yourself. They didn't let me hold you for the first two days."

But by midmorning, Beverly, despite the haze of drugs, sensed things were badly wrong. She became distraught.

So Sonny kissed her and explained. Carolyn sat on the other side of the bed, feeling weak and helpless, while Sonny talked. "Bev, the baby's got a problem with her heart.

"It's called pulmonary aratesia with a ventricular defect. She can't get enough blood flow to her lungs."

Comprehension registered slowly in Beverly's teary eyes. "She can't breathe? Or— Oh, God, Sonny, not enough blood flow! She's a—blue baby?"

Carolyn cringed at the term; her mother and grandmother

had used to whisper about two frail-bodied children of a distant relative: "They couldn't live—blue babies, you know."

Carolyn, a child herself then, had always envisioned two feeble little goblinlike beings, blue as turquoise and not real people.

But little Carrie was heartbreakingly real. Her blueness had no cartoonish brightness; it was the dull, dying color of oxygen starvation. She was nothing at all like a goblin, only a tiny human child in trouble.

Beverly started to cry in earnest, but Sonny quieted her. "Beverly, surgeons solved this problem almost sixty years ago. The operation's been done here too many times to count. Harrun el Zaid's going to be chief surgeon. Carrie couldn't be in better hands."

Beverly gave a little sob, but nodded. Sonny had told Carolyn that el Zaid was the best pediatric heart surgeon in the state.

"They'll put in a shunt," Sonny told her. "You know that, right?"

Beverly nodded again and tried to blink back tears.

"They'll divert blood from the subclavian artery to the pulmonary artery. It's called the blalock-taussig shunt. That'll fix her up. Her lungs will get the oxygen she needs."

Beverly had been around hospitals enough to understand what he meant, but she also knew that was not the whole story. "F-for now. But she's so little. She'll have to have m-more operations."

Sonny wiped her eyes with a tissue. "Harry says probably two. When she's four to six months old, she'll get a Glenn shunt. When she's five or so, a final Fontana surgery. And then, honey, she should be fine, live a perfectly normal life."

She clutched his hand. "Sonny, she's bad off, isn't she? Or they wouldn't be doing it on her this soon."

He kissed her again. "They're doing it to save her. And they will save her. Harry's never lost a child with this procedure. Not one. And he's not going to lose Carrie."

Beverly squeezed his hand more desperately. "But there can be complications."

"They're rare," he assured her.

"She can still have long-term effects."

"She may need more antibiotics than most kids. Maybe blood tests. We'll see. Honey, please take a little morphine again. You're exhausting yourself."

Reluctantly Beverly obeyed and pushed the button. A moment later her eyes fluttered shut. Sonny lifted her hand and kissed it. "I love you," he said.

Beverly, in her half doze, gave a weak smile. When she seemed to sink into a light sleep, Carolyn whispered to Sonny. "Step outside and talk to me a moment, please."

"Sure," he said. He got up and strolled into the hall. Carolyn followed, throwing a worried glance at Beverly. She moved down the hall, out of earshot if Beverly should wake.

Vern had not been with them. He did not deal well with seeing people in pain, so he'd gone to the chapel. Sonny stopped and put his hand on Carolyn's shoulder. "What is it?"

She looked up at him. He was a tall, Eurasian man, black-haired, dark-eyed, who spoke with the slightest of accents. Once Carolyn had seen only his difference from the people of Crystal Creek. She had disapproved of Beverly's attraction to him.

Now she was ashamed of that prejudice. Carolyn no longer saw any difference or strangeness in him. He was one of the finest people she'd ever known, and she adored him and was proud of him and proud that he and Beverly had chosen each other. But she was so troubled at this point that she doubted even Sonny.

"Are you telling us the truth about this?" she asked, her throat tight.

He put his hands on her shoulders and looked her in the eyes. "Yes. I swear it. I wouldn't lie to you. This child belongs to all of us."

"But…" Carolyn managed to keep her head high and get the words out clearly, "this operation *could* fail."

Sonny bent closer, gripping her shoulders more tightly. "The success rate is ninety-nine percent, Carolyn. Those are excellent odds. And Harry is as fine a surgeon as we could ask for. Will you trust me on that?"

Numbly she nodded. "But those aftereffects? What about her—her brain? If she hasn't gotten enough oxygen? Will she be—"

He moved closer. "There's a chance she *might* lose a few IQ points. She *might* develop a learning disability. But even that's less of a risk nowadays. Carolyn, they've been doing this operation since 1944—it's older than you are."

She mused on that, on those decades of experience. And she saw that Sonny believed what he said and was using all his willpower to make her believe, too.

She swallowed and took a deep breath. "Go back to Beverly," she told him. "I'm going to see Carrie. And talk to some of the nurses. I'll be back before the operation."

He kissed her on the forehead. For a long moment they held each other.

DURING THE OPERATION, Carolyn sat at Beverly's bedside, holding her daughter's hand. *This is the longest afternoon of my life,* Carolyn thought.

Vern and Sonny were in the waiting room outside the surgical unit. Poor Vern, Carolyn thought. He was all right in Sonny's presence, because everybody in the family was better when Sonny was near.

But Vern, too tenderhearted for his own good, couldn't bear to see Carolyn's anguish or Beverly's fear.

Beverly stirred drowsily. She struggled to stay awake, but the morphine in combination with her restless night let her sink intermittently to a more merciful place. Beverly's brief naps, never deep, seemed a blessing to Carolyn.

But when awake, Beverly was now calmer than Carolyn. She believed in Sonny with all her being. Carolyn did, too, but she could not truly banish dread. She'd lost too many people in her time, far too many. It shattered her to think this tiny baby, a being so new and precious, might be ripped away without ever knowing life or how much she was loved.

Carolyn shook her head helplessly, hating the power of death. Death robbed and ruined. It broke people with sorrow. It severed connections held most deeply and dearly. And Carolyn had so few of those connections left.

As a child, she'd yearned for a bigger family, a close-knit, vigorous clan of sisters, brothers, aunts, uncles and a score of lively cousins. But, no, her family had always been small. Now it was mostly gone, its one new hope in senseless peril.

Please live, Carrie. Please live for all of us and for your sweet self. Please. Please. Please.

Carolyn held Beverly's hand and stared at her daughter, so drawn, yet still beautiful. How often Carolyn had wished she'd had more children—a house filled with them. But the fates had given her only one—so Carolyn loved Beverly as if she were a whole crowd of children living in a single body.

Carolyn had gone half-mad with loneliness when Beverly married and left Texas. There was such an emptiness in her life, she could scarcely endure it. Only Vern had known how much she missed her faraway child.

Carolyn suspected that was why he'd brought neglected little Mickey Nightingale into their home. Without the girl, Carolyn wondered how she would have survived Beverly being so far away.

Dear Mick. She'd needed mothering, and Carolyn had

plenty to give. Mickey had come to them looking like a waif. She was skinny—not fashionably slim—but downright bony from not having had enough to eat.

She needed reading glasses, but had never had any. She had cavities that had gone unfilled. Never in her life had she had a professional haircut.

Her clothes were a disgrace. Carolyn bought her all new ones and burned the old.

She took her to Dr. Nate Purdy, who said the girl was seriously anemic and put her on a regimen of Vitamin B shots. He told Carolyn that Mickey had been more neglected than physically abused, but she should see a therapist to help her cope with any emotional damage.

Carolyn took Mickey to the best child psychologist in Austin. He said she was a remarkably resilient young woman. She seemed repelled by sex because of her mother's affairs. But she could talk sensibly about her feelings, and he figured in time she'd come around, when she met the right man.

The psychologist also told Carolyn that the girl had an IQ of 137. She was gifted. And she'd proven herself a genius at organization. She'd made herself indispensable to Carolyn and Vern.

Carolyn's jumbled thoughts drifted over everything that Mickey must tend to this week, but she knew the girl would be absolutely dependable and—

Oh good Lord, Carolyn thought with a start. That Duran man from the Caribbean! He'd come to the Circle T! Why, poor Mickey was probably dealing with him at this very second. The whole matter of the lease land…

Beverly tossed and groaned. Her eyes opened groggily. "Mama? Is the operation over? Have you heard anything?"

"No," Carolyn said, stroking Beverly's forehead. "I'm sure we'll hear something soon. Your lips look dry, honey. Do you want some water?"

"Mama, what I would love more than anything is a soft drink. Do you think they'd let me have one? Or orange juice or iced tea?"

"I'll get you something," Carolyn promised. "There's a vending machine just down the hall. I'll be right back."

She took her purse and rose from her chair. She felt creaky, as if her age had doubled since she'd entered this hospital. But she held her head high and forced her gait to be steady as she marched down the hall.

Oh, when would this operation be over? When?

And what weird thought had been galloping through her mind when Beverly had awakened? Carolyn struggled to recover it as she fumbled in her purse for money for the machine.

Then it struck her a second time. She'd completely forgotten about Adam Duran, Enoch's will and the lease lands. "Oh, to hell with the lease lands," she muttered, unable to find the right denomination of bill.

Of what importance was the stupid lease land at a time like this? She would gladly give up every acre if Carrie was all right. What good was land compared to family? May God punish her if she ever thought otherwise.

At last she found a dollar bill and slipped it into the machine. She was about to punch the selection button for orange juice, when she heard her name called.

The voice was Vern's. "Caro! Caro!"

She spun, staring down the hall. She saw Vern and Sonny. They'd just come through the double doors from the waiting room. They had their arms around each other's shoulders and were grinning.

"Vern?" she called, fearful of hoping too much. "Sonny?"

She ran toward them, and Sonny swept her up in his arms and whirled her around. "Carrie's fine," he laughed. "She made it. She came through like a trooper. Your grandbaby's safe."

A bolt of joy flew through Carolyn. She threw her arms

around his neck, laughing and weeping at once. Her purse, still open, spilled its contents clattering to the floor, but she didn't notice.

She hugged her son-in-law and didn't care about anything in the world but this wonderful, wonderful gift of life.

THE PHONE RANG. Mickey tensed as she answered. "Circle T. Mickey Nightingale."

"Mick, it's Vern. The baby's going to be fine. She's a little fighter, she is. They've got her wired up again like she's a computer, but you should see her. She's a beauty."

Mickey wilted, half-faint with relief. "Oh, Vern. I'm so glad."

"I'll let Carolyn tell you all about it," he said. "But I wanted to mention the Duran man. I haven't reminded Carolyn about him. I think she's completely forgotten him. This has smacked everything else out of her mind. How are things going?"

Mickey put her fingertips to her temple. This was a moment of happiness and triumph. It was not, she felt, the time to deliver the troubling news about the lease land.

"It's going as well as can be expected," she said. "He understands. He said he'd wait until there was word about Carrie. Then he'll go. He'll come back when you're home and things are calmer."

Vern paused. "I thought he was staying until Friday."

"His return ticket is for tomorrow afternoon. But he doesn't want to presume on us any longer—"

"Mick, let him presume away. Make him happy. This is a day of celebration for this family. Spread the love."

Mickey winced. "Love" was not a term she needed to hear.

Vern must have read something into her silence. "There's not a problem with him, is there?" He lowered his voice conspiratorially. "Is he an old crab like Enoch?"

"No, no," Mickey said, flustered. "That's not it." *That's not it at all*. "I'll ask him to stay, if that's what you really want."

"It's only one more night," Vern said. "And Caro did invite him. You know her. Now that he's come all that way for nothing, she'd want you to treat him like her long-lost brother."

Oh, God, oh, God, oh, God. Mickey squeezed her eyes shut and put her fist to her forehead.

Vern went on blithely, not realizing the irony. "You might even break out a bottle of that champagne for supper tonight, Mick."

"Vern—you mean your *special* champagne?"

"Heck, yes, Mick. I feel expansive. I'd like to buy champagne for this whole hospital. Friends, enemies, strangers—the whole world. Give him caviar if he wants it. Ah, I see Caro waving at me from the doorway. She wants to talk to you. Don't mention Duran if she doesn't—all right?"

"All right." Mickey knew she was sinking more deeply into a quagmire. But she heard mixed voices in Vern's background, happy, excited, exulting in their good fortune.

Then Carolyn was talking to her, so intense and elated that Mickey had to smile. "Mickey, it was a miracle—a miracle. She was blue when she went into that operating room. Just this terrifying twilight blue, her little mouth dark purple. And now she's pink! Her mouth's like a rosebud! Oh, it's unbelievable. The doctor said he watched her change color right before his eyes!"

Carolyn bubbled on about the baby, about the doctor (a true genius!), about how wonderful everyone was at the hospital, about how wonderful Sonny was, how happy Beverly.

"And I want you to order that pink panda, please, have it sent here express. Right to the hospital. Carrie's going to be here at least another eight to ten days, and so are we.

"And, Mickey, I know it's a lot of work, but could you mail everybody's presents? Oh, and I want you to do something special for me. You know Vern's the churchgoer in the family, not me. But would you go to church for me Sunday? Vern said you told him Reverend Blake and Reverend Casterleigh stopped by and said they'd keep us in their prayers. Would you go and thank them for us, personally?"

Mickey felt a twinge of misery. "I was planning on going." She remembered her discomfiting promise to tell the Sunday school class about loving enemies.

"That's wonderful of you, dear. And oh, all Pauline's children sent flowers, and J.T. brought her a dozen yellow roses. And Tyler sent Beverly's very favorite—pink tulips. So much on his mind, selling that winery, but he remembered her and her pink tulips."

Mickey smiled. Carolyn said, "Wait, honey, Beverly wants me for something. Goodbye, sweetie. We all love you and miss you and wish you were here with us. I'm forgetting something, I know it. Am I? Forgetting something? Never mind. It can't be important. Oh, Mick, just *wait* till you see her."

Mickey shook her head as she hung up. She felt as exhausted as if she'd spent the afternoon in the operating room herself. Her knees were weak when she got up from her desk.

She went to the kitchen to tell Bridget the good news. But the kitchen was empty. She looked out the back window, but there was no sign of her outside.

Mickey made her way through the house, calling Bridget's name, but there was no reply. She knocked on the door of Bridget's room. Only silence answered.

Mickey saw no sign of Adam, either. Had he and Bridget gone somewhere together? Where was everyone? She walked down the other hallway and knocked on the door of the guest room.

A few seconds passed, and she heard movement within. The door swung open and Adam stood there, a worn book in one hand, his other buttoning up his shirt. She saw a vee of muscular chest dusted with golden hair.

"Oh." Her heart jammed in her throat.

He frowned. "Is something wrong?"

"I— No. I was looking for Bridget. I wondered if you'd gone somewhere together."

He looked at her as if she was making no sense. "I don't know where she is. Are you all right? You're pale."

She felt a vein leap in her throat. "Vern called. The baby's going to be fine. The operation was a success."

He grinned, a bright flash that seemed so sincere it jolted her. "That's great. Great. But you look like you're going to pass out."

She made a helpless gesture, throwing out her hands as if in surrender. "I kind of feel like passing out. But I'm so relieved."

He stopped buttoning his shirt and took her by the arm. "Come on. You hardly touched your lunch. Have a glass of milk. Maybe we can find some of Bridget's cake. You could probably use some sugar."

Without protest, she let him lead her to the kitchen. He pulled out a chair for her to sit. She did, and he took the milk from the refrigerator, poured her a glass and set it before her.

Mickey was not used to a man waiting on her, but she was still dazed and wrung-out and high on happiness. "Thanks," she murmured.

"Where would Bridget put that cake?"

She waved her hand in protest. "This is enough for now. Really."

He came and stood at her side. "I promised you I'd go as soon as you got news. I'll keep my promise. And Mick, I'm glad it was good news."

She sipped the milk and it helped. Her head cleared slightly. She took another sip.

She met his eyes, which once again perplexed her because of the sympathy she saw in them. Sympathy that she wanted to believe was real. And yet...if he stayed longer, she might learn what was true and what was not.

Caution, she told herself again. People far wiser than herself had been fooled by the clever, the manipulative and the unscrupulous.

But she took a deep breath. "Don't go yet. Vern doesn't want you to. He was insistent about it."

"I'm already packed."

She shook her head. "No. He's in seventh heaven. He says they invited you to stay, and you came all this way for nothing. He's right. It's the least we can do. Honor the invitation."

His face went solemn. "But they don't know who I am. Do they? You haven't told them?"

"This isn't the time to tell them," she said, and turned her gaze to the checkered tablecloth. She took another drink to fortify herself.

He was silent a moment, then said, "When will you tell them? Or do you want me to do it myself? Which'll be easier on her?"

Mickey bit her lip, wondering which answer was the right one.

At that moment, Bridget came in the back door, carrying a bowl filled with strawberries. As soon as she saw Mickey, her eyes widened in apprehension, and she went stock-still.

"News?" she asked, her free hand flying to her bosom.

"The baby made it with flying colors," Mickey said, suddenly able to smile again. "She's doing fine. Carolyn said it's like a miracle."

"Praise be," Bridget cried and the strawberry bowl began to slip from her grasp. Adam sped to her side and saved it so that only a few berries spilled out and rolled across the floor.

Mickey rose from her chair, she and Bridget sped toward each other and hugged. Adam set the strawberries on the counter and started to bend to pick up the fallen ones.

But Bridget was so swept up in joy and relief that she made a grab for him. A strong woman, she hauled him, too, into her embrace. She gave Mickey and him each a smacking kiss on the cheek. "Tonight," she vowed, "we'll celebrate, and we'll celebrate right!"

CHAPTER EIGHT

BRIDGET, HER ARMS around Adam and Mickey, had pulled them so close that Adam's face was only inches from Mickey's. Her hair tickled his jaw, and he found himself fascinated by the trace of milk on her upper lip.

The upper lip itself fascinated him. So did the lower one. Her mouth was temptingly close to his, and his upper arm pressed against her soft breasts.

He forced himself to draw back from Bridget's embrace, his heart slamming. He grinned at her, a bit sheepishly. She clasped Mickey in an even more bearlike hug.

"I had faith," Bridget said. "But I'll admit, I was still nervous as a cat in the rain. That's why I went down to the strawberry patch. I told myself, 'We'll have fresh strawberry pie tonight. Because that child will be all right. She *will*.'"

She released Mickey and turned to Adam. "Unless you'd like strawberry shortcake better?"

Adam knelt and gathered up the spilled fruit. "I was just telling Mickey I'm going back to Austin. I wanted to hear about the baby, and then I'd be on my way."

"No!" Bridget protested, obviously disappointed. "You've changed your plane ticket?"

"No," he admitted, rising and dropping the berries into the bowl. "I fly out tomorrow afternoon. But I've imposed on you long enough."

He saw a complex mix of emotions cross Mickey's face.

"You're not imposing," she said. "You were *invited* here. I told you. Vern specifically asked you to stay tonight. It's true."

Bridget entered the fray. "We've got a perfectly good guest room. Why should you have to pay for a hotel room?"

"I wouldn't," Adam said. "I'll sleep at the airport."

"The airport?" Bridget cried. "That's a scandal. You'd have to sleep on a bench."

Mickey nodded. "Carolyn would scalp me if I let you sleep in the airport."

Adam couldn't tell if she felt determined that he stay, or merely resigned to the possibility.

Bridget said, "And I took a leg of lamb out of the freezer. Too much for Mickey and me. I counted on having you here. And it's not just a supper. It's a feast of thanksgiving. We won't take no for an answer. Will we, Mickey?"

Mickey swallowed. "No. We won't."

"I'm going out to the garden and pick some fresh lettuce and beans. And I expect you to eat your share." She shook her finger with mock sternness at Adam. Then she beamed. "But first, I'm going to call everybody I know and share the good news."

Still smiling, she strode off toward her room.

Adam and Mickey stood facing each other, awkwardness vibrating between them. She looked away from him. "I have people to phone, too. Lynn. Martin. Kasey. Violet. Nora and Ken Slattery. Reverend Blake—"

But before she could flee him, he said, "You said Vern wanted me to stay."

"Yes," she said, clasping her hands in front of her, fingers locking hard. "He even wants us to open a bottle of his special champagne for you. That's a sign he means it *absolutely*."

He stepped closer to her. "And you? Do you want me to stay?"

She kept staring at the floor. "I—don't mind."

"Would it be better if I left? I can grab my stuff and be gone before Bridget knows. You can explain it any way you want."

She ran her tongue over her upper lip. "It's…okay. When you said we had lots to talk about, you were right. It'll be easier if we know each other. If we can be…"

"Friendly?"

"Amicable," she said. "We can try for amicable. And frank."

Then she unclasped her hands and walked down the hall. She paused, glancing back. "Supper's usually at seven-thirty. You'll be here?"

He took her in, from the long, curling hair to her well-shined boots. His heartbeat speeded again. He said, "I'll be here."

MICKEY MADE her calls to spread the good news. The first call was to Cynthia, J.T.'s second wife, but she already knew. J.T. had called. He was flying home tonight. "I was so happy when I heard about that baby I cried like one myself. And, ooh, it'll be good to have J.T. back."

The McKinneys were officially retired now and had tried to take a long trip to celebrate. But J.T. had pined for his beloved Hill Country, and Cynthia had taken pity on him. They'd been home for less than a week when he'd flown off to Denver.

"It was really generous of him to fly them out there."

"He's a generous man," Cynthia said fondly.

"Yes. He is." Mickey thanked her and rang off.

She called the other people on her list, then phoned Saks and ordered the giant pink-and-white panda to be wrapped and sent express to the hospital.

As for the other presents, Mickey needed to drive to town to buy packing boxes and strapping tape, then come back and get straight to work. Work was what she needed to keep her out of Adam's way until supper. Afterward, she'd excuse herself and go back to packing the mountain of gifts.

On the way out of the house, she met Leon Vanek. "I was looking for you." Irritation rasped in his voice.

"Me?"

He glowered with self-righteous sternness. She remembered the overbearing way he'd acted when he'd seen her in the stable with Adam.

"You," he said in the same tone. "You were supposed to keep me informed on the Trents' grandkid. That the operation went okay. Bridget called her uncle. I had to hear it from him. How come you didn't report to me like I told you?"

Mickey stopped, her fingers on the handle of her car door. She *had* forgotten to tell Leon. He again simmered with resentment that he'd had to learn crucial news from an underling.

For a split second Mickey felt a twinge of guilt for violating protocol. But Werner, the stable man, was Bridget's uncle. He had worked at the Circle T for thirty years and had known the Trents since Beverly was a little girl. Leon Vanek had been with the ranch only a matter of weeks.

"I'm sorry," she said as civilly as she could. "Our first impulse was to call family and close friends. I certainly didn't mean to leave you out."

He crossed his arms. "How does this affect the ranch? How long will Mrs. Trent be gone?"

"I don't know. The baby has to stay in the hospital for at least another eight days. I'm sure Mrs. Trent won't be back before then. I can't tell you any more because I don't know myself."

He lifted his big chin. "Then I'll be the one making the main decisions about running this place. I suppose she'll want me to ship out those yearlings on schedule."

His self-importance grated on Mickey. "I suppose she will. But today, frankly, her mind's on other matters."

"Then I'm going to be mighty busy all weekend. No time to myself. I reckon I'll drive into Austin for the evening. Go see my cousin and his wife. There's a young lady they've been hankering for me to meet. Reckon maybe I ought to give them the courtesy of obliging."

What's that mean? Am I supposed to be jealous? Mickey thought in amazement. "Certainly. Have a nice time," she said, her voice stiff with politeness.

He put on his Stetson and touched the brim as if in a farewell salute, but Mickey saw the gesture's hint of contempt. He turned on his heel and stalked toward the stable where his pickup was parked.

Mickey got in her car thinking that he'd shown none of his usual elaborate politeness. It was as if he'd been wearing a mask the whole time he'd been at the Circle T, but it was starting to slip badly.

He acts as if he owns the place and everything on it, Mickey thought, thrusting the key into the ignition. *Including me.*

She feared again that Carolyn and Vern had made a mistake in hiring Leon Vanek as foreman. But she didn't have time to worry about possible wrong decisions. Her job was to help celebrate what had gone right today—wonderfully right.

LEON VANEK waited until Mickey's car was out of sight before he got into his truck and headed down the lane. He'd told the truth about going to Austin. But he had no cousin there, although he frequently mentioned this mythical relative and his equally mythical wife.

At least once a week, Leon claimed to visit the couple, but instead he went cruising in Austin's red-light district, looking for women who catered to men with special tastes.

Leon knew his urges weren't ordinary, but they didn't strike him as dangerous, at least to himself. He liked dominating, playing rough. Sometimes a man just needed to slap and pinch and punch to get real satisfaction, that was all.

Maybe this was one reason Mickey stirred him. She seemed so in charge of her feelings that he'd like to strip her of control, see her begging for him to satisfy her. But he could also enjoy the image of her totally obeying him, playing the pain game with him.

He'd love to punish her tonight; he'd revel in it. She'd always pretended to be so innocent, but now she was sharing the house with that long-haired pretty boy with his shabby clothes. That's all he was, a pretty boy. He didn't even dress like he had a job.

The sight of Mick cozying up with him in the barn had infuriated Leon, and he wanted to teach her a lesson, a humiliating one. Since he had to restrain himself, he would punish and humiliate somebody else instead.

But while he did it, he would be thinking of Mickey.

IF ANYTHING, Bridget had made the table even more festive than the evening before. A bouquet of white peonies flared out of a silver vase, yellow candles burned in the silver holders.

A bottle of Vern's special champagne sat cooling in a gleaming bucket, and Adam felt even more out of place. Mickey sat at the other end of the table, looking proper and determined. He knew she'd quiz him again as soon as they were alone.

"You aren't going to eat with us?" Adam asked Bridget uneasily.

"I'm eating in with Eva. She's my niece, the one who works over at Mary and Bubba Gibson's. I invited her special. Her husband's in Galveston, and that leg of lamb's big enough for four."

"She could join us," Adam suggested, unwilling to let hope die.

"She wouldn't be comfortable," Bridget said. "Besides, we'd just talk about family. Yack, yack, yack. But I'll tell you what. She won't be here for a few minutes. I'd have just a sip of that champagne. If you'd do the honors and open it."

Adam looked at the champagne, which had a strange uncorklike cork that was caged in a network of small wires. He'd never opened a bottle of champagne in his life.

"I don't know how," he said.

"Perhaps that speaks well of you," Bridget said. She plucked up the bottle, did something to the little wire cage, put her powerful thumbs on the cork and sent it out of the bottle with an explosive pop.

Bridget filled his glass, then Mickey's then took a third from the sideboard and poured herself a small helping. "To little Carrie," she said, "and Beverly and Sonny and Carolyn and Vern."

The three clinked their glasses together and drank. Bridget finished her sampling in one healthy swallow. "I'll be out with the lamb in ten minutes or so," she said and vanished back inside the kitchen.

"This is fancier than I'm used to," Adam said in a low voice. He stared at his salad, which was made of lettuces he had never before seen.

"Me, too," Mickey said. "Well, she wanted to make it special. Have you *really* never opened a bottle of champagne?"

"No," he said. "Why would I? Most of the wine I drink, you just unscrew the cap."

She rewarded him with a small, off-center smile. God, he thought, she had a lovely smile. He'd like to be able to make her use it more often.

She said, "You said you'd built a boat."

"I have. I've helped build a couple."

"Don't you break a bottle of champagne on one when you launch it?"

"That's a ship. Ours, we just shook up a bottle of beer and sprayed it."

"We. You have a partner? More than one?"

He shook his head. He was primarily a loner and always had been. "No. Just when somebody wants to hire me to help."

She suddenly switched to business mode. "You said you'd sell the lease land to Carolyn."

"Yes." He sipped the wine, which seemed to sparkle on his tongue. He realized it was an extremely fine wine, the sort of thing that he didn't want to learn to like too much.

"You said you'd give her a fair offer?"

"I won't ask her for what that billionaire guy, that Fabian, said it was worth."

"Nobody'd expect you to. He started a land boom. The bubble burst, and the whole economy's changed since then."

"I know." Adam had phoned a few Hill Country Realtors before he left Los Eremitas. He figured the land should go for about eight hundred dollars an acre.

Mickey looked at him over the rim of her glass. He knew she was smart and that she'd probably called Realtors, too. She said, "Eleven thousand acres is going to come to a lot of money."

"I know that, too." He'd figured it out—just under nine million dollars.

"I keep Carolyn's books," Mickey said. "Most of her money goes right back into the business."

Adam looked around the dining room. Everything in the house looked expensive to him. "She seems to be doing okay."

"She works hard, and she makes a profit. It's not always a big profit. Cattle prices go up and down. If you think the Arabians are a luxury, they aren't. They're a hedge against what can happen to the beef market. Why couldn't she just go on leasing the land from you? She wouldn't have to pay out a fortune, and you'd have a steady income—just like Enoch."

"I need money in a lump sum."

Mickey toyed with her salad. "May I ask why?"

"I need land in the Isabellas. I can get a good deal if I pay cash."

"How much cash? Carolyn's not going to want to take on a big debt at this point in her life. She can't. Really. She can't."

He set down his glass and met her gaze. "I don't mean to disrespect you. I understand that you know her finances. But when it comes to the price, I think I should talk to her about it."

Mickey sat straighter, her face a masterpiece of control. "Of course. But will you say *why* you want land there? A business investment?"

"No. I'm not a business type. It's more something I want to save."

Bridget came through the door bearing a platter of sliced lamb and a casserole of scalloped potatoes. "These are Carolyn's favorite potatoes," she said. "I wish she was here to have some. But I had her on my mind so I made them. Just think—Carolyn a grandma!"

Mickey smiled weakly, and so did Adam. Bridget turned to Mickey. "And I want you to eat hearty. I swear you worried five pounds off today."

She hustled back into the kitchen, letting the door swing shut behind her. "Bridget thinks a lot of Carolyn," Adam said.

"Everybody thinks a lot of Carolyn," Mickey answered pointedly. She helped herself to the thinnest slice of meat. "Now you were saying you wanted to save something? Like what? The environment? A threatened part of the environment?"

He heaped potatoes on his plate thinking, *I'd better break this to her slowly.*

"I brought some books with me," he said. "One's called *The Fragile Islands*. It's for Carolyn. If I leave it with you, will you give it to her?"

"Of course."

"I'd like you to read it, too. Will you?"

Mickey nodded, but puzzlement shone in her face.

Adam took a deep breath. "It's about the ecology of the Isabella Islands. When the Spanish discovered them, there were great forests, towering trees. The coasts were filled with colonies of seals. Beautiful parrots, so many that a flock in flight could block the sun. There were thousands of a native species of flamingoes. Tens of thousands of whales came to those waters."

Mickey tilted her head like someone who knows bad news is coming. "And then civilization came..."

"They cut down the old forests for logging. They clubbed the seals into extinction. The Isabella sea turtle's extinct. The whale population's decimated. There aren't thousands. Just a couple hundred."

As always, he grew passionate about the subject. "The parrots lost their environment. Those that nested on the ground had their eggs eaten by feral pigs and cats. They're endangered—they may not make it. The flamingoes were slaughtered for their feathers. Feral donkeys trampled their eggs, the pigs ate them. They may not make it either.

"There were giant iguanas. People ate them, or caught and sold them for pets. The feral animals got them, too. So the iguanas are also endangered. The water's overfished. The Isabellas have one of the most beautiful coral reefs in the world. Three hundred acres of it have been destroyed—gone forever."

Adam, not normally talkative, could talk eloquently about the havoc humans had wreaked on the islands. He told her that the Isabellas had some of the most beautiful water in the world. It was being polluted by hotels and cruise ships and oil tankers. The once crystalline beaches were threatened by spills and garbage.

Mickey listened, and she asked questions. He was shocked when he realized he had talked all through supper. Bridget had brought in dessert and coffee, and he was so intent he hardly noticed. He felt a wave of self-consciousness and silenced himself.

Mickey sipped her coffee. "But you haven't said what you're interested in doing. What is it?"

He hesitated. "Maybe you should read the book first. Then it'll be easier for you to understand."

The candlelight flickered, and he couldn't decide if her expression was suspicious or neutral. She said, "I won't have time to read it before you go. Tonight I have to wrap packages. And you leave after lunch tomorrow. I don't know when I could—"

"It's okay," he said. "After you read it, you can write me. I'll explain. I'll send pictures."

Although she seemed reluctant to agree, she nodded. "I'll take down your e-mail address."

"I don't have a computer."

She blinked in disbelief. "Why? Can't you have one on a boat?"

"I could. I just don't."

She gave a little laugh. "But how do you exist without the Internet? Everybody has it."

"I don't. I'm not interested in stuff like that."

"So I'll have to write you a real letter?"

He smiled. "You sound like I'm asking you to step back into the Stone Age. But yeah. Write me a real letter. Put it in a real envelope with a real stamp. And I'll write back the same way." He paused and added, "But I'm not very good at it. Writing about Enoch was hard. I probably said everything wrong."

"Well…" she began.

But the kitchen door flew open and Bridget said, "Mickey. Werner's here. He said he'd just started settling down in the stable for the night, and the mare went into labor. You'll be wanting Dr. Hernandez."

Mickey felt a stab of panic. "Good grief—Leon said it wouldn't happen until at least next week."

I told you different, Adam thought.

Mickey stood, flinging her napkin onto the tabletop. She snatched her cell phone from her belt and punched in a number.

Adam glanced at Bridget, who stood in the doorway, her posture tense and her hands clasped tightly. Then he turned his attention back to Mickey.

"Hello, Tracy? This is Mick. Is Manny there? Jazmeen's gone into labor. She wasn't showing any signs, but it's happening. He's where?" She bit her underlip, then said, "Well, I'll try Dusty, then. Oh, you would? Yes. Thanks a million, Tracy. I appreciate it."

Mickey clicked off the phone and looked uneasily at Adam and Bridget. "Manny Hernandez is tied up. Lynn's yearling got kicked in the knee by another horse. They have to X-ray, and there may be surgery. And Dusty Turner's at a vets' convention in Dallas."

"Oh, dear," said Bridget.

Mickey shoved the phone back into its holder. "Tracy's calling Manny. He'll come as soon as he can. I'm going out to check on Jazzy."

"I'll go with you," said Adam.

"Change your clothes first," Bridget told Mickey.

But Mickey didn't care about her clothes. She was already on her way.

WERNER BLUM stood on the back porch, looking solemn and anxious. He was a wiry little man in his early sixties, with a cowboy's leathery face and bowed legs.

"What's happening?" Mickey asked, heading toward the stable.

"She didn't show no signs today that I could see," Werner said, falling into stride beside her. "No waxing up. No muscle shrinkage. She's bagged up a little, but not near what you'd expect. She's been actin' flighty, but she *always* acts flighty."

"How far along is she?" Mickey asked.

"Gettin' into the second stage, I reckon," Werner answered. "She's layin' down in the paddock, and she's strainin', but I don't see no sign of nothin' comin' yet. I don't know that she's in trouble, but it's her first time, and I reckoned you'd want the vet standin' by."

She was dimly aware of Adam at her side as she told Werner that no local vet could come yet. Worry gnawed her. She had seen foals born a few times, and it had happened quickly and easily. But those mares had been tough little range horses, not highly bred stock like Jazmeen.

She looked hopefully at Werner. "Can you help her if she has trouble?"

"You gotta have a sure, strong hand for that," he answered. He held up his right hand, which had a bandaged wrist and a splinted thumb. The week before he'd had a roping accident with a yearling calf.

"If everything's normal, I can help," Adam said. "But if the foal's breeched or has its head turned, you'll need a vet—from somewhere."

They'd reached the gate of the paddock. Werner opened it and let Mickey enter first. The paddock's soft light shone down on the mare, who lay on her side in the damp grass. When the humans approached, she lifted her head in alarm, the whites of her eyes showing. She struggled to her feet, and backed into the corner farthest from them, swishing her tail.

Mickey started toward her, but Adam put out a hand to stay her. "Let her be. She'll lie back down. She's getting ready for the contractions to start."

Mickey stopped, but looked uncertainly at Werner. Werner nodded. "He's right."

The mare lowered her head, then tossed it and nickered unhappily. Her sides glistened with sweat. She was visibly straining. Mickey said, "If she gets in trouble, and Manny can't make it, I'll see if I can get a vet to come from Fredricksburg."

Adam said, "Let me look at her."

"She don't take easy to strangers," said Werner.

"I'm not a stranger. We got acquainted this morning."

Now Werner threw a questioning glance at Mickey. Mickey nodded. "He grew up on a horse farm. Werner, this is Adam Duran. Adam, Werner Blum. Bridget's uncle."

Werner gave him an awkward, left-handed shake. "You ever helped a mare foal?"

"Many a time."

The mare blew out a noisy breath. She resettled her weight on her feet, then sat. Mickey's eyes widened at the unnatural position.

"They do that sometimes," Adam said in a low voice.

"Yup," said Werner.

Then Jazmeen stretched out, lying down again on her side with her legs stretched straight out. Contractions seized her, mighty ripples that heaved her body. Mickey tensed in sympathy.

"You got antiseptic?" Adam asked. "And a surgical glove?"

"Right inside. I'll get 'em," Werner said and hobbled into the stable.

Jazmeen's contractions ebbed, then stopped, and the mare lay breathing hard. Adam walked to her, talking softly. He spoke in a soothing flow, and the mare's ears twitched as if in recognition. He stroked her side and neck. She lifted her head and nuzzled his elbow, then gave a sort of sigh and lay her head on the ground again.

"Atta girl. That's my nice girl. We're going to check you, you and junior. Or junioretta. We're going to take care of you."

His hands moved over the horse's belly, her flanks, stroked her legs. She accepted his touch without protest, and Mickey thought she seemed calmed by it. She'd always believed that she was good with horses. But not as good as he was. He had a gift.

Werner came back out, but stopped in his tracks, staring at Adam and the mare. Then he spread out a piece of oilcloth by Jazmeen's head, and set out the antiseptic bottles, a towel, a packaged glove and a bucket of water. "I'll get you another bucket for rinsin'," Werner muttered and went back inside.

Again Jazmeen started to rise, but she got only halfway up, assuming her awkward sitting pose again. She strained harder than before. Adam crouched beside her, stroking her neck and flanks, never stopping the stream of low talk. Then, to Mickey's amazement, for a few seconds, the mare lay her forehead against his shoulder.

A shudder ran through the horse, and she lay down again, stretching out her legs. Werner appeared with a second bucket. Just as he set it down, Adam said, "It's starting. Okay, Jazmeen. Okay, baby doll. You're doing it just fine."

The blue-gray membrane that enclosed the placenta emerged from beneath the mare's tail. Mickey held her breath in wonder. She could see, ghostlike in the membrane, the foal's small front feet. Another set of contractions surged through Jazmeen's body.

"Come on, Jazzy," Mickey whispered. "Come on, girl." The mare was struggling to push the foal's head free.

The placenta broke, expelling fluid, and Mickey knew that was normal. She could see the little hooves, freer now, twitching ever so slightly. But although the foal's forelegs should be appearing, they did not. Jazmeen strained harder.

Then contractions ceased again, letting the tired mare rest.

Adam looked up at Werner. "I'll let her go through a few more rounds. Then, if she's not any farther along, I'll examine her."

Werner nodded, then moved to Mickey's side. After three more series of contractions, the foal's legs still hadn't appeared. *Oh, God,* Mickey thought, *something's wrong. No. No.*

Adam rolled his sleeves up farther and tied Jazmeen's tail up with a flannel bandage. He washed her hindquarters with antiseptic, then scrubbed his hands and arms, He slipped on the surgical glove.

Mickey clenched her teeth, praying that he knew what he was doing. Gently Adam gripped the foal's fetlocks and pulled to draw out the forelegs. They slipped out a bit farther, and with another pull, the knees appeared.

But Adam frowned. "I think it's got an elbow hung up on the rim of her pelvis."

Mickey winced. The joint called the elbow was the highest in a horse's front leg—and the largest. Shaped like a triangle, it could become wedged against the mare's pelvic bone, unable to move.

From between his teeth, Adam said, "I'll try to ease it into a better position. Then, if the head's not turned, I think everything'll be fine."

Mickey had spent too many years around horses and cattle to be squeamish. But she was always awed when an animal the size of a horse or cow, torn by the pain of birth, allowed a human to do such invasive things to it. Once again, she held her breath, pressing her lips together.

Adam slid his hand inside Jazmeen and felt for the little horse. "The head's in the right place. Let me get that elbow free. Ah! There."

He pulled again, and now the upper forelegs slid into view, followed by a little black muzzle. Mickey was weak-kneed but found herself grinning in pleasure.

Adam drew his hand free and began to clear the foal's nostrils of any of the membrane that might block its breathing. The black nostrils flared and gave a tiny snort. Adam laughed, and so did Werner and Mickey.

Werner threw an arm around Mickey's shoulders. He leaned close to speak into her ear. "Where'd you find this guy?"

"I didn't find him," she returned. "We were just lucky he was here."

"Look at him," Werner murmured. "You know what he is, don't you?"

She didn't. The more she knew him, the more mysterious he seemed. She shook her head.

"Then I'll tell you." Werner's voice went low with wonder. "He's a horse whisperer, that's what he is. A genuine, by God horse whisperer."

CHAPTER NINE

THE FOAL, a black filly, was born at one minute after nine that night. Werner announced the time, reading it off his ancient army wristwatch.

"Then she's an early bird." Adam grinned up at him.

Mickey, puzzled, said, "An early bird? Why?"

Adam stroked the filly's flank. "'Cause eighty percent of horses are born between 11:00 p.m. and 1:00 a.m. She's two hours early. Aren't you, Early Bird?"

Mickey smiled. "I knew they were usually born at night. I didn't know they kept such a tight schedule."

The foal was struggling to get to her feet, her long legs bending and straightening in vain. But she was game and finally made it, hooves splayed wide apart, legs quivering, yet holding her head at a cocky angle that seemed to say, "Hey, look at me."

"Atta girl," Adam told her. "Werner, could you pick her up and hold her in front of Jazzy here so that mama doesn't get too nervous?"

"That I can do," said Werner. He picked up the little filly and set her in front of Jazmeen. The foal collapsed in a heap and had its attention commandeered by a thorough face-washing from its mother. Then, the mare stood, the foal again struggled to her feet, and Jazmeen began nuzzling and licking her all over.

"Ah," Werner said stepping back and grinning, "it always does your ticker good, that sight."

It was a wonderful sight, Mickey thought. The foal was no beauty now—she was all skinny legs and knobby knees, her ribs showed, her coat was damp and mussed, her tail was short and bristly—but someday she would be a magnificent horse, as beautiful as her father.

Adam had just finished cleaning Jazmeen and was putting antiseptic on the foal's umbilical stump when Manny Hernandez pulled up. Mickey saw the lights of his truck in the drive and waved wildly at him, telling him to come see.

Manny laughed when he saw the little filly poised on her shaky legs. "Well, looky here. How did it go? Tracy said you sounded nervous."

"It went fine, I think," said Adam, "but you decide. You're the doctor."

Manny examined both the mare and filly, asking questions. "Looks like you did fine without me. I'm sorry I didn't make it sooner. Lynn's new Thoroughbred took a bad kick in the knee. Didn't have to operate, thank God. Draining and shots and bandaging. Some stitching up. He should be fine. So should these two, from what it looks like now. Examine the afterbirth when it comes. If it's intact, Jazzy should be in good shape. If it's not, give me a call, and I'll fix her up."

After Manny drove off, Werner said, "You two go back to the house. I'll stay here and keep an eye on things."

"I can wait with you," Adam offered.

"Nah. I got my cot. I'll catch a few winks. I'm a light sleeper. Don't worry. I'll check 'em both every two hours or so."

"You sure?" Adam asked.

Werner clapped his good hand on Adam's shoulder. "Sure as shootin'. Why should I be tired? You done all the work. Carolyn's gonna be mighty proud of this little lady. Mick, you give her my congratulations on *both* baby girls, hear?"

"I hear, Werner," Mickey said. "And thanks for everything."

"Thank him." He nodded toward Adam. "He played stork."

Mickey kissed Werner on the cheek in gratitude anyway. She strolled back to the house, Adam beside her. The moon was a thin crescent, and only a few stars shone, but she could make out the familiar shape of the Big Dipper.

"Werner's right," she said to Adam. "I owe you thanks, big-time. I don't know what we would have done if you hadn't been there. Would the foal have gotten born?"

He was silent a moment. "Well, they both needed help. But your vet would have been here in time. So it's not a big deal."

You're too modest, way too modest. The thought shook her, because only yesterday she'd thought of him as arrogant. They climbed the stairs in silence.

In the kitchen, Bridget sat at the table playing solitaire. She looked up from her cards apprehensively.

"Mother and baby are doing fine," Mickey said. "The foal's a black filly, and she's going to be a beauty."

"That's a load off my mind," Bridget said, sweeping up her cards.

"Here it is, the happiest day of Carolyn's life. I didn't want it spoiled by her horse to go dying on her. What a day we've had!"

As if to emphasize it, she sneezed violently. She looked at Adam and waved him away. "To the shower with you. You smell like a horse yourself. And look at you—you've blood and Lord knows what else on your shirt."

She sneezed again. "And you smell, too," she told Mickey.

"I hardly touched the horses."

"You've been near 'em, and my nose knows. Clean up. You didn't finish your champagne, either. I corked it back up and left it cooling in the bucket. You can drink a toast to the horses."

The idea startled Mickey, but also pleased her. "Will you?" she asked Adam. "Toast Jazmeen and the baby?"

"Sure," he said with a smile that struck her as shy.

"As for me, I'm off to bed," said Bridget. "Babies born too

soon and horses born too fast. I'm worn out entirely. Good night."

She rose, picked up her cards and lumbered down the hall, shaking her head.

Mickey and Adam looked at each other. She felt suddenly self-conscious and wary. He was dirty, sweaty and his hair hung in his eyes.

But never in her life had anyone looked so handsome to her.

This troubled her. Even more troubling, she'd seen that he could be as kind as he was handsome. It was a powerful combination. Too powerful.

ADAM SHOWERED and dressed quickly. Now he wasn't so sure that he should have accepted Mickey's invitation to finish the champagne. His feelings for her were complicated and growing stronger all the time. What kind of mess could *that* lead to?

He pulled on the jeans he'd worn the first day. He had one clean regular shirt left and an old T-shirt. He supposed he should save the regular shirt for traveling tomorrow.

He slipped into the faded T-shirt, which had once been white and now was gray with age. It had an almost equally faded picture of a bearded man on the front. Well, he'd gotten a kick out of it once, but tonight he supposed it made him look like a stupid slob.

Now she's making me worry about what I wear, for God's sake. What's happening to me? What's she turning me into?

But he sat down, pulled on his boots, raked a hand through his damp hair, and went to the dining room. He took the champagne from the bucket, which Bridget must have refilled with ice. The bottle was frosty cold.

He frowned at it. There was quite a bit left. They'd each had only one glass before dinner. He'd forgotten about it, and guessed maybe Mickey had, too. Bridget had brought them red wine with the lamb....

I'm drinking red wine and champagne at the same meal, and eating strawberry shortcake. I'm starting to like the smell of that soap they've got in the shower. I've got to get home. I wasn't meant to live this way.

But all those thoughts fled when Mickey entered the room. She hadn't dressed up either. But the sight of her made his heart pound, and a giddiness filled him that was part happiness and part fear, and he could think of nothing to say to her.

She wore dark jeans and a different kind of blouse than usual. It was dark pink and white and very pretty. The neck was surprisingly low. He swallowed.

She studied his face. "Is something wrong?"

He showed her the champagne bottle. "I, uh, didn't know you could put the cork back in this stuff. I thought maybe the bubbles die—or something."

"I think it's okay for a while. I don't really know much about champagne."

"Me, either."

He hoped he could get that weird cork off and tried to remember how Bridget had done it. By sheer luck he managed, and was relieved that it didn't fly across the room and hit Mickey in the eye or that foam didn't gush out of the bottle and drench the carpet.

Bridget had set out two clean glasses, and he filled them without spilling. They each picked up one, and Mickey clinked hers against his. "To the new foal."

"The new foal."

They sipped, then stood in a silence that felt awkward to Adam. At last Mickey said, "It seems silly standing here. Too formal. Let's go into the den."

"Sure." But he still felt uneasy. It was as if the birth of the foal had forged a bond between them, one too powerful to be denied or ignored. And he had not come here prepared for such a feeling. No, he was a loner.

"BRING THE CHAMPAGNE, will you?" Mickey led the way into the den, switching on the overhead light, then dimming it. She sat on one end of the long, leather sofa and gestured at the other. "Have a seat."

He sat down on the other end, looking as if he didn't know where to place the champagne bucket.

His embarrassment amused Mickey, but also filled her with an odd tenderness. He'd expertly managed a thousand-pound mare in distress, but *now* he was flummoxed by moving a bottle? "Just set the bucket on the floor. It's okay."

He did, then as if to fortify himself, took a longer drink.

She watched him, then said, "Helping the foal get born—you handled that beautifully. Did your grandfather teach you how?"

He nodded. "Him. My grandma, too. They bred their own horses. Not fancy ones like Arabs, though."

"Did you ever think about being a vet?"

"I thought about it." He shrugged. "But I was never one for sitting in school. And then, I got all caught up with the boats."

She wanted to speak the truth and not have it sound like flattery. "It's just that you're so good with horses. It's a gift. I'd think you'd want to use it."

He looked at her sharply. "You really think so?"

His intensity unsettled her. "Yes. Werner said—he said you were a horse whisperer. Are you?"

"Some people call it that. My grandpa could do it, too."

She frowned, trying to puzzle him out. "But you left all that behind. Why'd you go to the Caribbean?"

"I'd never been anywhere but Florida. It was time to move on. I just…felt it. Time for change."

"So now you'll go back to the Isabellas—for a while?"

"Longer than a while."

"You won't be tempted to move on again?"

"No."

He said it with certainty, as if he knew exactly what he wanted from life and where to find it.

She twirled the stem of her glass and pretended to watch the bubbles rising. "What will you do when you go back?"

"Same thing. Fix boats. Build boats."

"And that property you want to buy," she murmured, "Will you live on it?"

He shook his head. "I've got the boat to live on." He cast her a sideways look. "What about you? Won't you ever be tempted to move on? To make a change?"

The question caught her by surprise. "I love it here. Coming here was the best thing that ever happened to me."

He said, "You feel needed here."

He seemed to peer into her soul. Nobody had wanted or needed her before she'd come here. She wasn't worth anything to anyone except herself—and sometimes doubted even that worth.

It unnerved her, this insight of his. She squared her jaw. "What's wrong with feeling needed?" she asked defensively. "Hasn't there ever been someone who needed you?"

His expression turned wary. Had she accidentally hit a nerve?

He went silent a moment, as if in inner conflict. "Not 'someone.' But I'm needed. Not by a who. By a what."

"Adam, that's so cryptic. *What* needs you?"

"It's—hard to explain."

"Is it some cause? Why don't you just tell me?"

He frowned, then shook his head. "It'd be easier to show you. Wait here. Okay?"

She watched in puzzlement as he rose and made his way down the hall. He disappeared into his room.

ADAM'S PROBLEM was how to explain an inexplicable passion.

It would be easier if he could take her to Los Eremitas. If

she saw for herself, she would understand—he knew she would, she was that kind of woman.

Could he put it into words? He doubted it. Pictures were supposed to say more than words. He had pictures, but were they eloquent enough?

He opened the dresser drawer and took out the folder, the envelope of snapshots and the videotape. He set his jaw and strained to summon the power to tell her in the right way, so she could *feel* what was at stake.

He thought of the look in her eyes when she saw the new-born filly stand for the first time.

"Okay," he breathed to himself. "Okay." He could only try. He went back to the den, and she looked at him searchingly, her hazel eyes full of questions.

He stood before her and held up the boxed video. "Have you got a machine that'll play this?" His voice came out gruffer than he'd intended.

"Yes." She nodded at the far corner of the room. It had a pair of smaller sofas and a matching armchair, arranged to face a large television screen.

He offered her the tape.

She rose and took it. It was in a generic white box, its edge hand-labeled "The Wild Horses of Los Fremitas."

Her brow furrowed and she gave him another curious look. "Wild horses? In the *Caribbean?*"

"If you play it, it'll explain," he said, praying it would. To do something, to do anything, he refilled both champagne glasses.

She went to the big screen and slipped the video into a machine on a shelf beneath it. He followed, carrying the glasses. "Sit," she invited, gesturing to the sofa most directly facing the screen.

He sat, his heart thudding against his ribs. She turned on the TV and picked up the remote control for the tape machine. She took her glass from him, then sat beside him. She seemed very close. This was both distracting and exciting, and his heart thudded harder.

The screen went from black to a patternless swarm of colored dots. "This was made by a television crew from the Bahamas," he said. "It was a segment for one of those news shows that are, uh, about all kinds of different stuff."

"A magazine show?"

"I guess." He cursed his own ignorance and watched the dots dance senselessly.

He waited and hoped. He swallowed and hoped harder.

MICKEY WATCHED as the screen filled with an aerial view of an island surrounded by a dazzling blue sea. A strip of white beach ran along the island's edge. Although mostly flat, hills rose near its southernmost tip. Its interior was a dull darkish green.

But buildings were visible along the coast, including big ones that must be resort hotels. Two highways crossed each other near the land's center. Their gray lines formed a clear, but slightly skewed, *X*.

Mickey could only think, *The water's beautiful. But I thought the land would be greener.*

A woman's voice with a plummy British accent began to narrate, "Los Eremitas Cay. Fast becoming a tourist mecca in the Caribbean. But Los Eremitas seems to have a secret...."

The picture changed to show a fat, fiftyish man in red swim trunks. He wore sunglasses and had zinc oxide on his nose.

Off-camera, the woman asked, "Have you ever heard of the wild horses of Los Eremitas?"

He glowered over his sunglasses as if she was trying to trick him. "What?" he demanded. "Wild horses? There ain't no wild horses here."

"People say there are," said the woman. "A herd that's been here centuries."

The man laughed at her. "That's a crock. I know this island. We been coming here ten years. There ain't any horses." He turned his hairy back on her and wallowed into the surf.

Next a blond girl, wearing a tiny orange bikini, put her finger to her lips thoughtfully. "Daddy's been bringing the sailboat here for years. There aren't any horses. No. Absolutely not. I would have heard."

Then an elderly black man was raking his tiny yard. "Used to be many horses. Many, many. Not now." He raised his hand and drew his forefinger across his throat. "Killed. Every one of 'em."

"But some people," said the narrator, "tell a different story. Albert Penndennis, a retired dentist, is one."

A kindly looking man with leathery skin and snow-white hair walked along a rutted road in a forest. "I remember the horses from when I was a boy. I grew up on a citrus plantation near here. Sometimes my brothers and I would see some of them grazing near the orchards.

"The herd was about a hundred then. My grandfather said once there were nearly three hundred. They're still here. Not many. But some.

"They mostly keep to the forests, stay out of sight. But if you know where to look, you'll see them.

"They're not all dead. Not yet."

The shot changed to show a small herd of horses, perhaps seven, grazing in a clearing. They were such beautiful horses that Mickey sat straight up, blinking in surprise.

"Indeed," said the woman's voice, "they're *not* all dead. Albert Penndennis says he believes there are seventeen surviving horses, traveling in several bands. And that these extraordinary animals are probably direct descendents of the horses of the Spanish conquistadors. And they've run wild here since the sixteenth century."

The scene changed to a pristine beach and a sea so beautifully blue it made Mickey's heart ache. She recognized the voice of Albert Penndennis.

"How did the horses get here? The most common theory is they survived a shipwreck and swam ashore."

The picture shifted to another shot of the small herd, with a close-up of a handsome paint horse, rich brown and white. Its size was much like a mustang's, its coat gleamed, and its head, held high, had an elegant shape and luxuriant mane.

"Like Hidalgo," Mickey said in almost childish delight. "The horse in the movie."

Adam nodded. "Almost exactly like Hidalgo. Strong. Great endurance. Fast."

Off-camera, Albert Penndennis said, "Abandoned by humans, the horses thrived. But then the humans came back."

The scene changed, and with a shock Mickey recognized Adam. He stood among the horses, and they seemed comfortable in his presence.

The woman narrator spoke again. "Albert Penndennis may have known about the horses for longer than almost anyone on the island, but boat builder Adam Duran knows them best."

As she spoke, Adam reached his hand to a handsome bay and stroked its neck. The narrator said, "He is the only person that the horses allow to touch them. Adam, can you explain why the horses' numbers have dwindled so dramatically in recent decades?"

Adam wore his faded jeans and shirt. His untrimmed hair stirred in the breeze. He looked more stoic than happy at being on camera. He held his forefingers up to form an X. "The highways," he said. "The horses used to keep mostly to the interior. The highways broke up their territory into quadrants. It gave their enemies ways to get to them more easily."

"And what are their enemies?"

He scowled and stroked the bay again. "Hunters. Years ago,

the only ways into the interior were old logging roads. It was a hard trek. Now it's not. What they killed, they had to lug out. But now they can load up a whole truck."

The scene shifted again to Albert Penndennis and the narrow road in the forest. "How do we know there were really so many more of them?" he asked.

"For one thing, we can look at the bones," he said, answering his own question.

Mickey flinched as the camera panned the ground, and there, strewn among the pine needles, were the scattered bones and crumbling skulls of two horses.

Albert knelt and touched a hole in the forehead of one skull. "Bullet hole," he said sadly. "When my grandfather cleared land for his farm, he found the bones of dozens of horses like these."

The tape shifted to another road, a different part of the forest. Adam walked alone. "The hunters used dogs. We've got a lot more dogs on the island now—they've gone feral. They can take down a lame horse. Or a young one."

He crouched by the savaged body of a small foal, probably only weeks old. Mickey, sickened, had to turn her eyes away.

"Dogs," she heard Adam say on the tape. His voice vibrated with sorrow and futile rage.

ADAM FOUGHT not to writhe with self-consciousness. The tape ended with a shot of him, Albert Penndennis and Albert's wife, Elsie, a small, lively looking woman with freckles and curly gray hair.

Albert did most of the talking. He told how Adam had started a fund to save the horses, and how the three of them formed the original board. The board had now grown to seven and included a minister of parliament, Dandaro Smith.

The tape cut to a close-up of Adam. "Adam," said the woman off-camera, "you've poured a lot of your own money into this fund. And a great deal of your time. Why?"

He frowned unhappily. "If somebody doesn't help, they'll die. And something that can't ever be replaced will vanish from the earth. Something wild and free. I can't stand by and do nothing." He nodded toward Albert and Elsie. "Neither can they."

The end credits rolled over a long shot of five horses galloping across a green, open space. The last words appeared, "Copyright Caribbean Broadcasting Corporation (CBC)."

Adam didn't want to look at Mickey, fearing she might think he'd been showing off. In truth, he'd hated being in front of the camera, but Albert and Elsie had threatened and wheedled him into it.

Still, he stole a glance, and even in the dimmed light, he could see she was upset. Her face was strained, her chin quivered and tears glittered in her eyes.

She squared her shoulders and kept her eyes on the screen, which had gone black. "So that's why you want money? For a preserve?"

"Yes. And I know I look stupid on television, but I wanted you to see the horses. Not just in still pictures, but live, moving things. Real as the horses in your stable."

She bit her lip, then said, "Why did they have to show that poor little foal all torn up? That was—" she didn't finish the sentence. She just shook her head in frustration.

"It's bad, yes," he said. "But it's not as bad on tape as when you really see it. You get sick inside and think, 'Oh, God, another one gone.'"

"The horses are so beautiful," she said. "It's hard to believe they're wild."

"They probably came from the best Spanish stock. Spanish Barbary. It's an old line. With Arab blood. There aren't many pure Spanish Barbs left."

She refused to meet his eyes. "And you brought this to show Carolyn?"

"Yes. If she'll agree to look at it. And other things. The

book." He handed her the envelope. "Snapshots. If you want to see."

He sensed reluctance in the way she took it, but she drew out the photographs and began to go through them. They were mostly of the horses, but there were some Albert had taken of him, doing tasks like treating a wound or helping a foal learn to nurse.

"Do they have names?" Her voice was tight.

"We give them names, yes."

She pointed to a tall bay horse, the one he had touched in the video. "Who's this?"

"A stallion. Goya. He's fine. He's the dominant male."

"And this one?" She indicated the handsomest of the pinto horses.

"That's Dulcinea. She died last year."

She faced him now, her eyes full of shock. "How?"

"Somebody set an illegal wild-pig trap. Rigged with a noose. She choked to death. The more she struggled, the more the rope tightened."

It still nauseated him to think of it. He shook his head, unable to say more about it.

"Tell me their names," she said. "Tell me all about them."

MICKEY LISTENED, seeming fascinated. The more she asked, the easier it was to answer her.

"But how did *you* find them?" she asked. "Some people have lived there all their lives and didn't know they were there."

"I kept hearing stories. So I was determined to find out if they were true. Finally I met Albert. He told me about them. He took me into the interior. And I saw them and—"

He paused, his self-consciousness returning. He'd revealed more of himself than he'd intended.

The first time he'd seen the horses, it was like having a

magic arrow shot into his heart. It didn't hurt him, but it forever changed him. For years he'd been drifting, aimlessly, staying a few weeks at one island, maybe as long as a year at another.

He'd never thought of having a fate or a calling. But when he saw the first small band of horses of Los Eremitas, he knew why he'd been looking for them. They were his destiny. Although he hadn't known it, they were why he'd gone to sea.

But he couldn't say that to her. So he said, "I saw them, and that was that."

He shifted, and his shoulder grazed hers slightly. The touch gave him a sensation of benevolent lightning surging through him.

"That was that," she repeated, her eyes on his. "You mean you'd work to save them?"

"Yes." He gestured at the folder in her lap. "That's got some newspaper stories in it. And some—documentation. Our charter. That we're nonprofit. What money we got and where we got it. What we've spent and where we spent it. But you don't have to look at it now."

She ran her fingers over the battered blue cover. "You started a fund? You and Albert and Elsie started the board? What do you call it?"

He stared at her hand as if hypnotized. It was a small hand, smooth and neat. It looked delicate, but he knew it was full of strength. He wanted to touch it so much that it was like a killing weight on his chest.

He said, "We call it the Wild Horse Organization of Los Eremitas. That's not catchy, but the initials spell W.H.O.L.E. And that was kind of the idea we wanted."

She thought a moment. "That the horses are part of the whole ecosystem, that it would be incomplete without them?"

He smiled. "Right. And not letting the horses be injured or threatened anymore if we could help it, that they be healthy—whole in that sense."

"Restored," she said, nodding.

"But, of course, there are people who think I'm crazy."

"For trying to help?" She sounded indignant on his behalf.

"Yeah. They say if I want to help, why not help people?"

"But you *are* helping people," she protested. "People need nature. We *need* the wild things."

He found that he was touching her arm in agreement. "Yes. That quote's our motto. 'In wilderness is the preservation of the world.'"

She tilted her head in the most beguiling way. "Who said that?"

With his free hand he pressed his fist against the picture on the chest of his T-shirt. "Henry David Thoreau. He also said, 'Preserve life rather than destroy it.'"

She stared at his chest and the corners of her mouth turned up faintly. She barely touched her forefinger to the picture. "Thoreau, the writer. I thought he looked familiar. I read *Walden*."

"So did I." He thought maybe this wasn't the time to tell her he had read it sixteen times. He thought it was time to kiss her.

He put his hand over hers, so that hers rested against his heart. He wondered if she could feel it beating. She raised her eyes to his.

No woman had ever looked at him quite that way before. It had something in it that shook him. It was like recognition, as if she knew him in a way other people didn't.

He lowered his head, his lips hovering above hers.

"We shouldn't…" she whispered.

"Yes," he breathed. "We should."

CHAPTER TEN

TREMBLING INSIDE, Mickey lifted her face to his. He took her mouth in a kiss that began gently, almost hesitantly, as if he might draw back at once. But he did not, and neither did she. A soaring sensation flew through her, a giddy rising of desire.

His mouth became bolder, and so did hers, as if they both knew that this was what they wanted, and they had wanted it from the beginning. *This is so good,* her body told her. *More. More. Much more.*

He put his hand to her hair, lacing his fingers through it, cupping the back of her head so he could increase the pressure of the kiss. She leaned nearer to do the same. He slid his other arm around her waist, pulling her closer still. His chest was hard and muscular against her yielding breasts, making her nipples tingle in a way that was new and wonderful to her.

He was so strong that she couldn't have broken away if she'd tried, but she didn't try. Her arms rose of their own accord and wound around his neck. She felt the dampness of his freshly washed hair and the pulsing beat of a vein in his throat. His skin beneath her fingertips was firm and warm. He smelled of soap and tasted like champagne.

His hands moved to her shoulders, his lips to the hollow of her throat. Her blood drummed, her yearning growing, and when he lowered her to lie back, resting her head on the sofa arm, she did not resist.

He kissed her mouth again, his tongue inviting hers to play and tease, a prelude to greater sensuality. She liked the warmth and moistness, the excitement of exploring each other.

His lips moved to nibble her jaw, the side of her throat, and his hands framed her breasts, which seemed to swell as if wanting to fill his clasp completely.

Her gauzy blouse was tucked into her jeans, but he began to pull it free from her belt. She felt his callused hands under the cloth, under her camisole, moving against the bare skin of her sides.

His thumbs skimmed the smooth, taut flesh of her stomach, and she sighed, settling more deeply beneath him. Then as his lips once again took hers, his fingers moved over her bare breasts.

He cupped them, then stroked them, and then began making love to their throbbing tips. He pushed up her blouse and his head moved down. Warmth surged through her when he kissed her just above her navel, his mouth warm and hungry.

Mickey had been blissfully losing herself in pure pleasure, but now reality struck her like a lightning bolt. In a few seconds, she would be half-naked on Carolyn's love seat, her breasts bare and being kissed by a man she hardly knew. He had already half seduced her.

She seized his hands and pulled them away from her sensitive flesh. She jerked her blouse and camisole back down and sat up with a start.

He drew back, but his hands gripped her shoulders. She pushed him farther away, a blush burning her face. They stared tensely into each other's eyes, and Mickey thought, *I shouldn't have let this happen.*

He seemed to be thinking the same. Regret and desire mingled in his expression. He shook his head in frustration. "Mickey—" he said from between his teeth.

She wanted to tell him to let go of her, but she couldn't. It was as if he'd hypnotized her.

He said, "You're right. If we go any further, I won't want to stop. I don't want to stop now."

She thought, *I can't do this in Carolyn's house, with a man who's going to take what by rights belongs to her. Not after all she's done for me.*

He'll put her in debt for the rest of her life. She'll have to mortgage the Circle T to the hilt to buy that much land. Maybe even sell the Arabians.

This man is Carolyn's worst nightmare. Did he cast a spell on me? Did he make me crazy?

She dropped her gaze from his. She managed to whisper, "It's not right."

"Not yet," he said. "Maybe someday it will be."

He released her and drew away. "You should go to bed. Lock your door. That way I'll know you don't want me to come in. Otherwise…"

She stood, guiltily tucking her shirt back in. She turned and fled down the hall into the sanctuary of her room. She stood, breathing hard and staring at the closed door for a full thirty seconds.

Then, her hand shaking, she reached out and locked it.

She sat on her bed and put her face in her hands, dazed and churning with conflict.

MICKEY TOOK another shower, as if by washing away Adam's touch she could clean herself of wanting that touch.

She put on her most unattractive, boyish pajamas, climbed between the sheets and switched off the bedside lamp.

His muted footsteps sounded in the hall. She tensed as they stopped, pausing outside her door. She held her breath. He tried the doorknob, but gently, only once, and then he walked on.

She exhaled, a sigh that combined relief with frustration.

Adam Duran had set her aflame with passion, just at the stage of her life when she'd convinced herself she was fireproof.

He was gorgeous enough, she supposed, to infatuate the most experienced woman. Mickey was far from experienced.

She was twenty-seven years old and had had sex with only one partner. She had done it when she was sixteen, an act of sheer stupidity. She'd wanted to know what it was like. And why her mother needed it so desperately.

It was terrible. The boy had been clumsy and greedy, and each time he'd pawed and penetrated her, she was more repulsed. By the fourth time, she'd hated it and broken up with him, feeling disappointed and cheap.

She thought that she'd immunized herself against sex. Until now.

She *desired* Adam Duran, and it frightened her. It threatened her certainty of who she was and what she wanted. It betrayed Carolyn.

She had come to the Circle T on Vern and Carolyn's charity. The roof over Mickey's head belonged to Carolyn. Everything came from Carolyn, Mickey's rooms, her bed, her food, her education.

Mickey was Carolyn's friend and employee; her job was to guard the welfare of the ranch as much as Carolyn herself did. So why, tonight, had she forgotten everything Carolyn had taught her? Instead she had acted like her real mother. Shameless. Reckless. Unthinking.

She nearly wept in self-disgust.

Oh, Adam was handsome. He seemed idealistic and sincere, and his cause sounded noble. Yet what did she really know about him? The bottom line was he'd come to lay claim to more than half of Carolyn's land. Land worth nearly nine million dollars—or more.

Mickey knew everything about Carolyn's finances. Caro

and Vern lived well, but they had paid off the second mortgage on the ranch only two years ago. The tornado that had
struck Crystal Creek ten years ago had done far more damage to the Circle T than insurance had covered.

They'd worked hard and were enjoying the first flush of
prosperity again. With the yearly lease payments off her
back, Caro could relax. She and Vern and the ranch should
be secure.

But Enoch had broken his promise—Adam said. If that was
true, he was about to tear apart the fabric of Carolyn's whole
future.

Mickey tossed, pulling the covers closer around her as if
they could protect her from her dilemma.

If Adam was sure to bring Carolyn shock and loss, how could
Mickey feel drawn to him? It wasn't just traitorous, it was stupid and naive. And it was happening far too fast. Last night
she'd thought he was a villain, tonight he seemed too good to
be true.

What did she really know about this man? Was he who and what
he claimed? Was he even related to Enoch? Or, if he was, could
he be pulling a con with a multimillion-dollar payoff? Maybe ro-
mancing the unworldly secretary was just part of his game.

She'd seen it in a dozen films, read it in half a hundred
books. A charming scoundrel, an elaborate scam, a gullible
woman wooed for money or power or both.

Mickey knew this was cynical, but she was trying hard to
think straight. She should be led by cold logic, not the heat
of sexual longing.

But logic kept getting sidetracked. She remembered Adam
with Jazmeen, helping deliver the foal. He might lie about
anything, but he could not fake his gift with horses.

She remembered the videotape, as well. She wanted to believe it. It seemed genuine—but was it?

Couldn't such a thing be faked if someone was clever and

ruthless and determined enough? God knew there was enough money at stake for someone to try.

And did he really have a valid right to the land? Had Enoch actually been cruel enough to change the will without a word to Carolyn?

She twisted in the covers, knowing what she had to do. For the time being, she would tell neither of the Trents anything about Adam Duran. Let Carolyn enjoy, for a little while at least, a respite of happiness.

In the meantime Mickey would check out every fact on this man, taking nothing at face value. It was her honor-bound duty.

And she would have to stay out of Adam Duran's arms. Absolutely.

Yet, when she fell asleep, she dreamed she was in them. And that she loved being there.

MICKEY WOKE shortly after dawn and knew sleep wouldn't come again. She wanted and needed a long ride to clear her head. She dressed quickly and headed for the stables.

She saw Adam at the paddock, sitting on the top rail, stroking Jazmeen's neck. *Oh, of course, he's here,* Mickey thought darkly. What more perfect place for him to be? What could he more irresistible? Keep your head screwed on straight, Mickey. He's probably just using you to get to Carolyn.

Jazmeen rubbed her muzzle affectionately against his knee, as her foal nursed. Adam wore the same clothes he had last night, the ragged jeans and the graying T-shirt with the picture. When he looked up and saw Mickey, he didn't wave or smile. Instead, he looked as self-conscious as she felt.

She couldn't avoid him, and she'd seem like a twit if she snubbed him. So she strolled to the paddock, slowly, to prove she was in no hurry to meet him. "Good morning." She made her voice as neutral as possible.

"Good morning." His tone was as cautious as hers.

She leaned her arms on the top rail and gazed at the filly. "She looks even prettier by day."

"Yeah, she does." He scratched Jazmeen's ears and she nickered with pleasure.

"Where's Werner?"

"I told him I'd spell him until the vet came. For him to go home and sleep in a real bed."

"Hmm." It was the most noncommittal answer she could come up with. "So everything seems okay?"

"With the horses? Yes. Top-notch."

But he frowned, his expression far from pleased. Mickey, wary but curious, said, "Then what's wrong?"

He met her gaze. "What I did last night—with you—was wrong."

She jerked up her chin defensively. "What? That we kissed? We were high about the filly. We had some champagne. It wouldn't have happened otherwise. Forget it."

"Will you forget it?"

"Yes," she lied, trying to shrug it off. "It meant nothing. Maybe it shouldn't have happened. But it won't happen again."

He said, "I have things to settle with Carolyn. Things that are—primal. Land, money, blood. I made a mistake by putting you in the middle. I told you things that I should have told her first."

Once again, he'd thrown her off balance. What he said was true, but she hadn't expected him to admit it.

He turned his attention back to the horses and tousled Jazmeen's thick mane. "Your first loyalty's to Carolyn. It should be. This is your home."

Mickey wanted say, *Yes, it's my home, my only real home. And Carolyn has been better to me than my mother ever was. I owe her and Vern my very life.*

Instead she simply said, "Right."

He lifted his head, squinting toward the far horizon. "I came here with news she won't like. When I found out she was gone, I should have gone back and waited for the time to tell her myself. But I told you, and that puts a burden on you that you don't deserve. I'm sorry."

Her throat tightened. "Then why *did* you tell me?"

He shrugged. "Maybe I wanted to impress you. Make you listen to me."

The answer was too simple and raised her ire. "Well, you certainly got my attention. 'Hi. I'm Carolyn's brother, and I own the lease land.'"

"I said I was sorry. Sorry that I told you and sorry that I stayed."

"Then why *did* you stay?" she demanded, though she knew it wasn't a fair question. Vern had told her to make Adam welcome. She herself had insisted that he remain or Carolyn would be hurt.

He looked at her again, his gaze steady. "At first, I wanted to stay because of Carolyn. You were so passionate about her and Vern. And—I liked hearing that. I liked seeing her house. I could understand her better. It's not a snobbish house. It's a home."

He glanced at the land around him. "She's taken good care of this place. She's responsible. She loves her family. She inspires loyalty. From people like Bridget and Werner and you."

He gave Jazmeen a last caress, then slid from the fence and stood, one hip cocked. He hooked his thumbs in his front pockets. "It was you most of all that made me think I'd like Carolyn if I knew her. That I'd be glad to have her for a sister. Yeah. You did that."

Mickey held out her hands in frustration. "Why are you saying this?"

He swallowed. "Because for a while I wanted you to do the same for me—with her. I wanted you to believe I was okay.

And for you to help her believe it. To help convince *her* that I'd try to handle the matter of the lease land with—honor."

"You mean that you wanted me to be your go-between? Give you a glowing reference? Were you trying to cultivate me for that? I wouldn't exactly call that honorable."

He grimaced and kicked at the dirt. "I just wanted some respect from you. Some acceptance. You said we could try to be 'amicable.' You said to be frank. I tried to be. I thought if I was honest, you might be a sort of peacemaker between us. But then it got…complicated. No. It was complicated from the start. From the moment I saw you…"

What are you trying to say to me? Mickey wondered, her throat constricting more tightly. *That you used me? Or that you care for me? Or both at once? Or that you don't even know yourself?*

Adam seemed to search painfully for words. "I didn't intend for it to happen this way. I got swept up. Thoreau says, 'Things don't change, we change.' And maybe…"

Mickey's phone rang, and she snatched it up. "Yes?"

"Mick, it's Bridget. I can see you from the kitchen window. I'm so glad you're not gone yet. Can you come back to the house? There's an emergency."

A chill shot through Mickey. "Not the baby?"

"No, no," Bridget said, but she sounded distraught. "This is about the ranch. I don't know what to do. Can you come right away?"

"Absolutely. I'll be there in a minute."

She flicked off the phone and said to Adam, "I have to go back to the house. There's a problem."

Adam stepped toward her. "Mickey—"

"I have to go. And I also have to tell you something. I won't be your cheerleader for Carolyn. The thing I'm going to have to do is check out everything you've claimed. Every single thing. Completely."

She turned on her heel, glad to escape him and all the contradictions he made churn inside her.

ADAM WATCHED her go, purposefully striding toward the house and not looking back.

He'd tried to be honest with her. He supposed he hadn't been honest enough. He swore and kicked the dirt again.

And he was an idiot trying to tell her how much he cared for her by quoting Thoreau. But Thoreau said things better than he did. *The heart is forever inexperienced.* Adam hadn't realized how inexperienced his own was until he'd met Mickey. He'd tried to maintain his independence and self-reliance. He thought he'd learned the art of needing no one.

He hadn't. He'd been a long time without family. As long as Carolyn had been a cold abstraction to him, he'd never thought of forming a bond with her. But her house had an aura of intense family love.

He'd gotten caught up in this family's crisis over a baby he'd never seen, whom he hadn't even known existed. But this child had touched him because she was helpless and hurting.

She was also of his own blood. And so was Beverly and so was Carolyn. They had men whom they loved and who loved them. And he felt himself standing at the far edge of their circle, alone, wanting to move inward, become part of it. To be with his own people again.

But if blood joined him to Carolyn, he feared the land estranged them.

Adam cared nothing about this land, but Carolyn loved it. Carolyn had been promised it, he had been granted it.

He could not expect her to accept this fact—or accept him—gracefully. As ugly as it was for both of them, it came down to money. She would have to buy what should have been her rightful gift.

And he had to take this money from her. He would be willing to sacrifice the bonds of kinship for it. Mickey could not change this, no one could.

He hadn't planned to put Mickey at the center of these conflicts, and he hadn't planned on wanting her the way he did. Had he thought the power of sexual desire could overcome all the obstacles between them? If so, he'd been a fool.

The women he'd bedded had always made it clear they wanted sex. Mickey was more innocent. If she'd been close to trusting him, he'd ruined it.

He had set out to live a simple life and found himself mired in complexities that had no solution. He'd struggled this morning to explain himself, and he'd failed.

He watched as she entered the house, slipping out of his sight. He damned himself, and he damned the land and most of all, he damned the money.

MICKEY SAW BRIDGET standing by the counter mixing pancake batter with a vigor that seemed almost desperate. Her face was grave.

"Bridget? What's this about?"

Bridget stopped stirring, but gripped the spoon so tightly that her knuckles whitened. "Did you notice Leon Vanek's not around?"

Mickey hadn't. Her attention had been only on Adam. "I thought he was probably out on the range somewhere."

Bridget shook her head. "No. He never came home last night."

Mickey looked at her questioningly.

Bridget took a deep breath. "He was in the Austin jail. For soliciting an undercover policewoman for sex. And resisting arrest."

Mickey's mouth fell open in disbelief. *"What?"*

"It was one of those—those stings, they call them. My niece Edda just phoned. She's a secretary to the detective division. Two policewomen were posing as prostitutes, 'undercover,' she said. Leon solicited one. And when she said he was under arrest, he swung at her and tried to bolt."

"Good grief," Mickey said. "He hit her?"

"He grazed her chin, then he scuffled with the two men backing her up. One blacked his eye. They found a concealed handgun in the glove box of his truck. He shouldn't have had it. He'd lost his permit to carry a concealed weapon—because of a violation. They released him just now."

Bridget shook her head in consternation. "Edda said she struggled with her conscience about telling us. But she thought we should know."

Mickey sank into a chair and put her head in her hands. "Soliciting sex? Resisting arrest? *And* a weapons charge?"

"Vern and Carolyn won't stand for it," Bridget said. "I know it, and you know it. But you'd better call them, Mick. See what they want you to do."

Mickey clutched her head more tightly. He'd gone too far for mercy. Soliciting a prostitute? He might be forgiven for that. He would plead that he was only human, had the same urges as any man, and had been cruelly set up.

A concealed weapon without a permit? Many people would forgive that, too. This was Texas, where some had strong sentiments about gun rights.

But hitting a police officer—a *woman* police officer? No, that wouldn't be tolerated.

On the other hand, wasn't a person innocent until proven guilty? Would he have to go to court? But how could he possibly plead innocent with at least three undercover police officers testifying against him?

Mickey's temples throbbed. "Bridget, does he have a court date—or what?"

"Oh, Lordy, I didn't think to ask. I suppose. And him always so polite. Who would have thought it? Carolyn will nail his hide to the barn door."

Mickey sighed. She lifted her head and glanced at her watch. "It's nearly eight in Denver. I'll call. She and Vern don't need another problem at this point. But I don't think there's any choice."

"I don't, either. You could wait a few days, though—do you think?"

Mickey squared her jaw. Was it hypocritical to tell the Trents about Leon Vanek, when she hadn't told them about Adam?

No, she decided, the cases were hardly equal. Leon's case was unpleasant, but not earth-shaking. Adam's was another matter.

"I'll call them now," she said. "I'll do it from my office."

CAROLYN WAS BUBBLING with relief and good humor. When she heard Mickey's voice, she launched into a high-spirited account of what was happening.

The baby was recovering splendidly. She was a most beautiful and amazing baby, and this was not just Carolyn's opinion, it was everyone's, even the nurses and orderlies.

So tiny, but such a fighter! Such will to survive! And that beautiful head of black hair, just like Sonny's.

Mickey let Carolyn go on at this ecstatic pace until she finally paused and asked, "But what's happening there?"

Mickey gritted her teeth. "I've got good news. And I've got bad news."

She told the good news, that Jazmeen had foaled a handsome little filly and both were doing well.

"I'll be switched," Carolyn said. "I knew she was nearing her due date, but I swear I hadn't given her a thought. It's just as well. I would have been worrying myself sick over that, too. She didn't have any problems?"

Well, Mickey admitted, yes, there had been tense moments, but the visitor, Adam Duran, had grown up on a horse farm, he'd known what to do.

"That's a blessing," Carolyn said. "And Mickey, I'd forgotten him, too. I apologize. I woke up in the middle of the night. I shook Vern and said, 'Omigod, Enoch's executor was coming.' But Vern said he'd talked to you and you were taking care of it. Thank you, honey. And I'm so sorry for putting you to the trouble."

Mickey fought against wincing. "It hasn't been any trouble."

"Send him my apologies for not being there. I hope he'll understand."

"He understands. He says he'll set up a meeting at another time."

"Ah, good. And give him special thanks for helping with Jazzy. Tell him I'm in his debt. But you said you and Werner and this Duran man were there when Jazzy foaled. Where was Leon Vanek?"

"That's the bad news," said Mickey. She recounted exactly what Bridget had told her.

"Fire him," said Carolyn, her voice firm. "Give him his walking papers, two weeks severance pay and ten minutes to clear out. I won't put up with that kind of behavior from my foreman. I wouldn't put up with it from anyone."

"You want *me* to fire him?"

"No, no. I can't do that to you. I'll fire him myself. As soon as you see him, tell him to phone me. Wait. Oh, this is a fine pickle. Tell Vern, will you? He's the one with the legal mind. He'll know what to do. I swear I can't think straight. But, oh! I'd like to wring Vanek's neck—the brute."

Then Mickey had to explain the situation to Vern. He was more coolly analytical about it than Carolyn.

"Resisting arrest? The *best* he can hope for is a fine and a suspended sentence. He can't stay on with us. Have him call *me*. I'll deal with it."

"You're sure?" Mickey asked, relieved.

"Yes. I'll lay it out for him in a way that leaves him one option—resign now or be fired. It's his choice."

"I'll have him call you. Vern, I'm sorry. I hate to throw a shadow on Carolyn's happiness."

"Don't worry your head about it. All she has to do is go look at that baby and she'll be on cloud nine again. I can't imagine what could really bring her down at this point."

I can, Mickey thought. *And his name is Adam Duran.*

But she didn't say it.

MICKEY TOLD BRIDGET to let her know when Leon Vanek returned to the ranch. A glance out the window showed her that Adam was still at the paddock. He was inside the rails now, stroking the filly, getting her used to human touch.

To avoid Adam, Mickey skipped her morning ride and downed a hurried breakfast. She went to her office to wrap gifts for shipping. At ten o'clock Bridget peered into the office and said, "Leon's back. His truck went by."

Mickey thanked her. She waited five minutes for Leon to reach his house, then grimly dialed his number. He answered with his usual self-important greeting, "Circle T Ranch. Leon Vanek, foreman."

Not for long, she thought grimly. "Leon, it's Mickey. Bridget said you just got in. That you weren't here last night."

"Had a little trouble at my cousin's place. Flat tire when I was leaving. The jack slipped. Blacked my eye. Swelled up pretty bad. Thought I shouldn't drive. Spent the night with a compress on it. But I'm fine now."

He said this so smoothly, with such seeming straightforwardness, that it appalled Mickey. Did he think they would never find out? That he could brazen this out?

Ice in her tone, she said, "You weren't here when Jazmeen went into labor. She foaled last night."

That silenced his glibness for a heartbeat. "She foaled? She gave no sign of it." He sounded as if the horse had schemed to trick him. Quickly, he added, "You should have called me. I'd have gotten there somehow. I hate to say this, Mickey, but you were a little derelict not to contact me."

The nerve! She thought, *the boldfaced, lying nerve of him.*

"When things started happening," she replied, "they happened fast. We got along fine without you."

"I hate to think that's possible," he laughed. "I'm glad nature took its course. What did she have?"

"A filly."

"Well, I'll come up to see her right now. Why don't you meet me at the paddock? We had a date, as I recollect. Don't be alarmed by this shiner I'm sporting. It doesn't hurt much."

His flirtatiousness turned her stomach. "No. I just talked to Vern in Denver. He wants you to call him. Immediately. Here's the number. Take it down." She dictated it to him.

"Fine. I'll call you afterward. Then we can meet. I figured that mare for an easy birth all along. Filly, eh? Little stud would've been more valuable. But I guess a filly'll do."

"Call Vern," she said and hung up.

Time passed with excruciating slowness. She went to the kitchen and poured herself a cup of coffee.

"Well?" asked Bridget.

"He's probably on the phone to Vern right now. Or packing."

"Ooh," said Bridget. "So we'll be looking for a foreman again?"

"I'll write an ad this afternoon." Mickey glanced out the window and saw Adam and Manny Hernandez standing by Manny's truck. The two men were grinning and shaking hands. Then Manny climbed into the cab and pulled away. Adam turned and headed toward the house.

Mickey quickly made her way back to her office. She

didn't want to talk again to Adam. She would have to soon, but not yet. Too much was happening, and she had too little time to sort through it.

ADAM SAT in the kitchen, eating breakfast. Bridget, unnaturally quiet, busied herself with making coleslaw for lunch. She seemed both anxious and glum.

Mickey was elsewhere, keeping to herself. He supposed she was avoiding him, and he couldn't blame her. She probably couldn't wait for him to be gone. He couldn't blame her for that, either.

He heard footsteps thundering up the back stairs and saw Bridget flinch. Someone banged on the door so hard that it rattled. Bridget squared her broad shoulders, went to it and flung it open.

Leon Vanek muscled his way past her. His usually neat clothes were disheveled, and he had a bruised and bloodshot eye, swollen half-shut. "Where's Mickey?" he demanded.

Adam's nerve ends twitched, recognizing trouble. He laid aside his knife and fork.

"Mickey's busy," Bridget said.

"I want to talk to her." Vanek straightened to his full height and bellowed. "Mickey! Get out here!"

Adam eased his chair back from the table. So far the big man hadn't bothered to look at him.

"Mickey!" Vanek's face reddened and the veins in his neck stood out.

"I'll get her," said Bridget, wiping her hands on her apron. She started down the hall, and Adam watched as she met Mickey midway. The women stopped, exchanging worried glances, and Mickey whispered something in Bridget's ear. Bridget nodded and hurried to her room.

Mickey marched to the kitchen door and stood, disdain in every line of her body. "What are you yelling about, Leon?"

He shook his finger at her. "*You* knew what was happening. *You* knew what Vern was going to say. Somebody's been telling lies about me, and I reckon it's you. You or that big, fat cow of a cook."

"Don't talk about her like that," Mickey snapped.

"Somebody slandered me to the Trents."

Adam eased back farther, so he could rise swiftly if he had to. Vanek was six inches taller than he was and outweighed him by a good eighty pounds. He was also edging dangerously close to rage.

Vanek glared at Mickey, and his bruised and bloodshot eye made him look primitive, almost bestial. "You listened to lies about me, and you told lies about me. You betrayed me."

Mickey held her ground. "You lied yourself. You weren't with your 'cousin' last night. You were under arrest."

Arrest? Adam's interest shot up, and his muscles tensed.

"Somebody violated my privacy telling you that," Leon accused. "Violated my rights. Who was it?"

"You were trying to solicit sex. You solicited the wrong woman."

"It was entrapment, dammit. It was a frame-up."

"When she told you that you were under arrest, you tried to hit her. You *did* hit her. "

"I tried to get away from her, that's all. She grabbed at me."

"You fought with her backup men."

"Police brutality," he shot back.

"That's how you got the black eye."

"Police brutality!"

She crossed her arms. "You'd better leave, Leon. You're only making things worse."

He shook his fist again. "I haven't had my day in court. But I'm being treated like a convicted criminal. Vern backed me into a corner. I have to resign. On the basis of gossip and a wrongful arrest—"

"Go, Leon," Mickey said. "Just leave."

Leon took a step toward her.

Adam stood. "She told you to leave."

Leon shot him a contemptuous glance and called him an obscenity.

"She told you to leave," Adam repeated. "Leave."

"Who's going to make me? You, Goldilocks? You going to get in my face, hippie faggot?"

"If that's what it takes." Adam stepped between him and Mickey, clenching his fists.

He knew he could stare down a twelve-hundred pound stallion, and he hoped he could stare down Leon Vanek. Otherwise, he'd fight him. He had no choice.

CHAPTER ELEVEN

MICKEY'S HEART climbed into her throat.

She hated violence, and Vanek was poised on the brink. There was something monstrous in him, a wounded, raging pride that threatened to overpower all reason.

This time he'd dropped his cloak of silky manners completely, his guise of respectability gone, and he stood in a kind of nakedness, all his deformed egoism revealed. Most frightening, he seethed with destructive frenzy.

Don't! she'd wanted to cry out when Adam stepped between her and Vanek. She was terrified he'd trigger the man into attacking.

Vanek was taller and more powerful. His arms were longer, and he could land a punch without being touched himself. Adam could not begin to match him for brute strength. But he showed no fear. He bore himself as if he was unquestionably the man in control.

Vanek looked at him for a long, challenging moment. But then something in Adam made him look away.

"I'm not fighting you," he muttered in disgust. "I'd beat the crap out of you, then get hauled in on assault. I'm not falling for it, fag."

He stalked outside, slamming the door. Mickey ran to lock it and shoot the bolt. She turned and leaned against the door, drained.

Her eyes met Adam's, and for an instant she saw what

Vanek had seen in their depths. She was shaken by that look; it was masculine, territorial and primitive. She'd never imagined he could seem so threatening.

Then she heard Vanek's truck start and pull away with a screech. The ferocity in Adam's gaze faded. "Are you all right?"

"I—yes. I was afraid that he was going to go for you."

"So was I."

"Could you have taken him?"

"I guess we'll never know." His smile was slow and a bit embarrassed.

She looked him up and down, certain now that he would have knocked Vanek cold. "He's a coward. Thank God."

Adam unclenched his fists. "Yeah. Keeps it simpler. And doesn't bloody up the kitchen."

Bridget bustled down the hall. "He's gone? I called the sheriff and then Werner. But, Lord, I was afraid nobody'd get here soon enough. I was in Vern's study, shaking like a leaf and loading the shotgun. I've never seen a man so mad. What happened?"

Adam wouldn't say, so Mickey did. "Adam faced him down."

"Praise heaven, because I'm a lousy shot. I may break out another bottle of Vern's Special for lunch. Oh, here comes Werner—I'll tell him to watch out for Leon."

She undid the door and rushed out to her uncle's parked truck. Werner had come with Craigwell, one of the biggest men on the ranch. Bridget locked her fingers over the base of the open window on the driver's side and leaned toward Werner, talking excitedly.

"I hope he doesn't come back," said Mickey, watching out the window.

Adam stepped behind her, close enough that she prickled with awareness of him. "He won't." His voice was low and sure.

She didn't want to turn and gaze into his eyes again. She kept watching Bridget and Werner and said, "How do you know he won't?"

"A hunch. If he's got a charge against him, I'll bet he'll jump bail and disappear. He doesn't want to be prosecuted. He couldn't stand it."

She nodded. Vanek's pride was his undoing. "I hope you're right."

"He wanted to impress people. He had ambitions. You were one—he wanted you. I told you that, remember?"

She knew it, but it seemed a shameful thing. "I didn't want him."

"Good."

There was a beat of silence, and Mickey felt him move closer still. He said, "You're sure you're okay?"

"Yes. I'm fine."

"Then why are you trembling?"

She looked at her hand resting on the windowpane and realized he was right. A tremor thrummed through her system, almost imperceptibly. But he had noticed. He was learning to read her body, and they both knew it.

"Aftershock, I guess," she said as casually as she could. She lowered her hand so it was out of sight.

She raised her chin. "Now Carolyn has two things to thank you for. The filly. And getting Vanek out of the house. I'll be sure to tell her—that's what you want from me, isn't it?" She knew it was a needlessly mean thing to say, but she felt torn and defenseless. "Well, everything in its time. I'm not going to rush to tell her."

"What I want—" he began.

But then a car from the sheriff's department pulled up. She didn't know how he would have ended that sentence. She wondered if she would ever know, truly, what he wanted.

MICKEY HELPED Bridget set a table on the patio, pleading with her to join them for lunch. Bridget would have none of it. She'd be intruding, she told Mickey.

"You wouldn't at all. He'd like it, I'm sure," Mickey said, trying to hide her growing desperation.

Bridget cast her a sardonic look. "I'm of another opinion of what he'd like—so that's that."

And that *was* that. Bridget had made a centerpiece of flowers from the garden, putting them in a pretty, green-glazed vase. The day was perfect, the sky a tender, cloudless azure, and beyond the garden, the yard was a vivid carpet of bluebonnets.

So Mickey soon found herself sitting across from Adam. He was dressed for travel, which, in his case, meant his jeans were clean, but faded and patched at the knee. His once-blue work shirt had been washed so often it was nearly white.

Putting him in fine clothes would have been gilding the lily, Mickey admitted with chagrin. She wished his hair didn't glint so brightly in the sun and that his eyes didn't so perfectly match the vibrant sky.

Bridget had relented and not raided Vern's private store of champagne. But she had opened a split of a good brand, just enough for two glasses. "You're driving, after all," she said to Adam, then disappeared inside.

Mickey, all business, said, "Let's drink to your having a safe trip."

She raised her glass, and so did he, but he didn't touch it to hers. "No. Let's drink to—harmony."

"Fine. There's been little enough of that lately." She clinked her glass against his, and they each sipped, furtively eyeing the other.

At last he said, "Have you talked to Carolyn again?"

"No. I talked to Vern and told him Vanek was gone. I didn't go into details. Not yet."

She made the underlying message clear: *I didn't mention*

you. I aim to find out the facts about you, just like I told you.
But she knew she'd have to tell the whole truth soon.

He shrugged. "Probably best."

She set down her glass, resting her clenched fist beside her napkin. "What's your next move, if I may ask? How do you intend to break the news to Carolyn?"

He shifted his shoulders as if the question made him uncomfortable.

"I'll need your help."

Her nerves tingled with wariness. Did he mean he needed her complicity? "How?"

"Timing. When do you think she's going to be ready to hear it? I don't want to hit her with it while she's still all frazzled."

For her sake—or yours? she wondered, but said, "The longer you wait, the harder it'll be. Because she'll have spent that much more time in ignorance, thinking things are all right. Not knowing who you really are. Or why you came."

"When should I do it?"

"When she's certain that little Carrie's out of the woods."

"Can I phone you to ask?"

She hesitated, then said, "Yes. But then, how will you tell her?"

He gritted his teeth. "I might not do it so well by phone. I guess I'd better write her."

Mickey shot him an ironic glance. "Excuse me, but you're not so good at that, either. That letter of yours set everybody on edge. Frankly, it was curt to the point of rudeness. We all thought you were a crabby old geezer."

He sat farther back in his seat, looking abashed. "You did?"

"We did." She took another sip of champagne. This was not going to be an easy conversation.

"Then how should I say it?"

"I can't tell you what to say or how to say it." She pressed her hand against her chest and leaned toward him. "When you talk about things you care about, you're very articulate. Say what you feel."

He fell into silence, took another drink of champagne, then said, "There's a line of poetry. It's about this guy's trying to think how to say something. And at the end, it goes, "'Fool!" said my muse to me. "Look in thy heart, and write."' That's what I should do, I guess."

Mickey blinked. "What?"

"'Look in thy heart, and write.' It's in a poem. I could try that. It won't be easy."

She looked at him askance. "You read poetry?"

"Well, yeah. I read a lot. I don't have a television."

Mickey sighed. "I should have guessed that. But poetry?"

"My grandma left me some books. One's a big poetry book. Some things you can read a bunch of times. Poetry's like that."

She was impressed, but once again, she felt a frisson of doubt. Was he a poseur, like Leon Vanek—only much, much better?

"All right," she said, determined to test him. "Recite me a poem."

His brows drew together. "Any poem?"

"Yes. Something you like."

He paused. He looked at the vista of bluebonnets for a moment. Then he said, "There's part of one I think of when one of the horses dies."

The rainbow comes and goes,
And love is the rose,
The moon doth with delight
Look round her when the heavens are bare;
Waters on a starry night
Are beautiful and fair;
The sunshine is a glorious birth;

But yet I know, where'er I go,
That there hath passed away a glory from the earth.

He paused. "It's a long poem. Do you want me to go on?"
She was puzzled and fascinated, and she did want him to go on.

But Bridget came, bearing plates with barbecued chicken, coleslaw, grilled vegetables and her homemade rolls. She also brought word from the sheriff's department that Deputy Clyde Botts had pulled over Leon Vanek and warned him to stay away from the Circle T.

"I thought that'd put your mind to rest a bit," she told Mickey. "And, oh—Reverend Blake just dropped by. I asked him to stay for lunch, but he was on his way to a luncheon. He left a folder for you. He said it's for the Sunday-school class you're going to teach. I put it in your office."

The Sunday-school class. Love thy enemy. Mickey fought against visibly cringing.

When Bridget left, mischief sparked in Adam's eyes. "So what are you going to say Sunday? That the lion should lie down with the lamb?"

"Only if the lamb is smart enough to know that the lion's old, slow, toothless and not hungry."

"You're a skeptic, aren't you?"

I've been able to resist your charms, if that's what you mean. Mostly. Except for some occasional lapses—a thousand or so.

She said, "I just like to know what I'm dealing with."

He held her gaze. "And that's why you're going to check on me?"

"Yes." Why did she feel so petty saying it?

He nodded. "Hire a detective?"

"Yes. A detective at least."

"Fair enough." He reached into his hip pocket and drew out

a battered wallet. He flipped it open. "That's my social security card. That'll make it easier for you to check. Want to write it down?"

He said it so calmly that it startled and embarrassed her. He set the open wallet before her and dug into his pocket again, producing a small, dog-eared notebook and a stub of carpenter's pencil.

"Go ahead," he offered. "Be my guest."

Her cheeks burned, but she tore a page from the little notebook and copied the information. He was right; it would be invaluable to a detective. "You don't seem the type to have a social security number," she muttered.

He ignored the jibe. She pushed the wallet, pad and pencil back toward him. He took them and shoved them into his pocket again. "And what happens if you find out everything I've told you is true?" he challenged. "How will you feel then?"

She pretended to be engrossed in toying with her food. How would she feel? Would she be joyful that he actually was what he seemed to be? Or simply more conflicted?

She said, "It's Carolyn's feelings you should worry about, not mine."

"I suppose that if she resents me, you'd never come to see me."

Mickey jerked her head up in surprise. "Why should I come see you?"

"I'd like to show you the horses. What we're trying to do. For you to see the island. You'd like it, I think. But you wouldn't come, would you? If she didn't approve."

No, she thought, with a sick tightening of her heart. *I wouldn't.* She shook her head no, once again not meeting his eyes.

"The Trents' life will always be your life? Won't you ever make one apart from them?"

She made her face blank and forced the conversation away from the dangerous course it was taking. "What's the difference in time zones between here and the Isabellas? What time will you get home? Tonight? Tomorrow?"

Her tone was brisk because her loyalties had been forged long ago, and to change them was unthinkable.

BRIDGET SAID her goodbyes in the kitchen. Mickey could tell that Bridget wanted to fling her arms around Adam and give him a great, smacking kiss on the cheek. A warning look from Mickey made her confine her farewell to a hearty handshake.

"And I hope we'll meet again," Bridget told him, slipping Mickey a slightly defiant look.

"I hope so, too," Adam said. He turned to Mickey. "Would you walk me to the car? I have something to say to you."

She nodded. She was glad he'd be gone within minutes. But a strange sadness filled her, too, a sensation of enormous loss.

He picked up the duffel bag, pushed open the door and held it for her. She led the way down the steps, then side by side, they walked to his car. She realized they walked slowly, like two people who don't want to part.

He threw the duffel bag into the trunk, but he didn't shut the door. Instead he unzipped the duffel and drew out a small Swiss Army knife and a pale yellow bandanna handkerchief. Puzzled, she frowned.

"I borrowed this knife from Werner," he said. "Will you give it back to him?"

"Yes, but…"

He pulled out a narrow, shining blade and offered it to her. She took it, confused by what he wanted. He held out his hand toward her, palm up, fingers stretched out. "Cut me," he said. "Just enough to draw blood."

"What?" Mickey asked, bewildered.

He stepped nearer. "One of the things we want for the horses is money for DNA testing. To prove they're from the old Spanish line, the original mustang stock. DNA's just about infallible. Carolyn will probably want to know if she and I really share genes. Take a few drops of my blood. She can test it."

Mickey could only stare. He was that certain of his kinship?

"Go on," he said, stepping closer. "You do it. That way you'll be sure I didn't switch something. Though what I'd switch or how, I don't know."

He held out his hand. "Go on. Just stick the point in my finger. I won't mind."

She looked at his fingers, spread out as in offering.

"Do it," he said, his face earnest. "Draw blood."

Her breath caught in her throat. "I—can't."

"Then I will." He took the knife from her before she could protest, and lightly stabbed the point into the tip of his middle finger. Mickey winced as a bright drop of blood welled out.

He wiped it onto the yellow kerchief, then squeezed out another drop, and then a third and fourth. "No more," she said in a shaky voice. He flapped the kerchief a few times, to let the sun and air dry the blood. He was intent on his task, but she could only watch, as if mesmerized, as the breeze played through his hair, the uneven locks of dark gold mixed with light.

He folded the kerchief carefully and handed it to her. It was warm from the sunlight and his touch. He smiled to encourage her.

Slowly she took it. *I'm holding a tiny part of him,* she thought. *Of his heart's blood.*

She accepted it, filled with fresh tumult. He would not dare do such a thing unless he was telling the truth about his father. He snapped the blade back into the knife and offered it to her. He laid it on her palm and closed her fingers over it. "Tell Werner thanks for me, will you?"

"Yes." She looked numbly at his hand clasping hers. "Of course. You're…you're not hurt?"

"No. It's already stopped bleeding."

He squeezed her hand, let go, zipped his bag back up and shut the trunk.

He turned to her.

"I'll send Carolyn a letter as soon as you think she's ready. I'll send it express. I'm sorry I dragged you into this. But I'm not sorry, because—" he glanced about uneasily, shrugged, then looked into her eyes "—because I've gotten to—"

She tensed, waiting for him to finish the sentence.

But he didn't. He said, "I know I've made every mistake in the book with you. I've put you in a rotten situation. But I never lied to you, Mick. May God strike me dead if I did."

She shook her head, and stared off into the distance, fighting tears, unable to speak.

He took her by the shoulders and made her look at him. "I may never see you again. I guess that's up to Carolyn."

He bent nearer, gripping her more tightly. "Last night I kissed you. It wasn't because of Carolyn. It was because of you. If you believe only one thing I've said this whole time, believe that. Please."

His intensity stirred a crazed fluttery feeling deep inside her. His nearness and his words half stunned her. *Please*, she prayed. *Please be the man you seem to be.*

"Can I kiss you goodbye?" he asked.

Mickey felt as helpless as she had the night before. All her vows to be cold-blooded and logical flew away. She did not think of loyalties or debts. She could think only of him and that he was going away.

His hands were on her shoulders, his thumbs grazing the sides of her throat. She raised her face to him, lips parted.

It took a small, sweet eternity for his mouth to lower and take hers, gently at first. But the kiss deepened, as if he and she were trying to tell each other what they could not say any other way.

It was long and bittersweet, and neither of them seemed

able to end it. But then they heard a truck door slam, and they jerked apart guiltily. Mickey saw Ernesto, the assistant foreman, his hat pulled down, hobbling toward the house. He coughed, as if making sure his presence was known.

Adam looked at Mickey, then took her hand. "Goodbye, Mick," he said.

He wanted to kiss her again, she saw it in his eyes. And she wanted him to.

But he let go and stepped away. "Goodbye," he repeated. Then he got into his car, his face tight with control. He glanced at her one more time and gave her a sad smile. But he didn't speak again. He started the engine. He drove away and left her standing, staring after him, until all she could see was a cloud of dust slowly dissolving into nothingness.

From the paddock she heard the healthy nicker of the new foal.

Ernesto stopped before her. "You said to drop by this afternoon?"

Mickey tried to pull herself back to routine. Ernesto would have to take over Leon's duties, and she would have to help ease his load. He was aging, only months from retirement.

There was a ranch to be run, and she had a job to do.

MICKEY TALKED to Ernesto about branding the spring calves, then slowly walked up the stairs and into the deserted kitchen. She wondered where Bridget was and hoped she hadn't seen that long goodbye kiss.

She made her way down the hall to her office and the heaps of packages. Almost all were packed and ready to go now. Only three remained. She'd finish, then drive into town, and send them.

But a strange emptiness haunted her, and she recognized the unfamiliar feeling—loneliness. She'd felt it often as a child and adolescent, but never since coming to the Circle T. Not until now.

"I *wanted* him to go," she told herself. But yet…her lips still tingled from his touch, and she felt hollow and yearning now that he was gone.

For God's sake don't miss him, don't even think about him. She thought of the folder of clippings she hadn't read. It was still in the den on the end table. Although she had an almost irresistible urge to pore over it, she would not. Not now. She'd look at it when her head was clearer and her emotions cooler.

"Get to work," she ordered herself. She wrapped the remaining packages, then carried the whole lot to her car. Taking care of business, that was what she needed to do.

When she reached town, it was quiet for a Friday afternoon. Crystal Creek was as peaceful as if Adam Duran had never come near it. Everyone that Mickey met asked her about the baby and Beverly and Carolyn and Vern. They all said to send their good wishes.

Nobody mentioned Leon Vanek, so that particular nasty piece of news was obviously not yet in circulation. Mickey was grateful. There would be gossip about him, a lot of it, and she didn't want to add to it. If people asked about him, her answers would be discreetly vague.

So she went about her tasks as if nothing at all had changed in Crystal Creek or at the Circle T—or in herself.

WHEN MICKEY got back to the Circle T, she went straight to her office and began to tidy it, putting away all the paraphernalia of wrapping. Then she sat down, opened the telephone book, and dialed the Schumann and Associates Detective Agency in Austin.

She spoke to the founder, Edward Schumann himself. She'd made a list, so she could discuss what she wanted in a cool and organized way.

He was to check on Adam Duran born in Porte Verde, Florida, now living at Los Eremitas in the Isabella Islands. She was particularly interested in his parentage and in an organization on Los Eremitas with the acronym W.H.O.L.E. She gave Schumann Adam's post-office box and social security number.

Also, she wanted to run a check on the last years of Enoch Randolph's life, with whom he associated and the state of his mind. There was the matter of his will, written last year.

She hung up feeling cold, efficient and lousy.

Her heart yearned to believe Adam. But her reason insisted that she could not accept what he said on faith. She *had* to have him investigated, even though some part of her deplored herself for this snooping.

They should have questioned the facts about Leon Vanek more thoroughly, she rationalized. Look at what had happened when they took *him* at his word.

She tried to lose herself in work, by composing an ad for a new foreman.

MICKEY AND BRIDGET ate a quiet supper together. Perhaps the meal was too quiet. They avoided talking about Vanek. He was an unpleasant subject, and Mickey knew talk of him would lead to talk of Adam.

Mickey could tell that Bridget liked Adam and had questions about him. She was probably curious about why Mickey had said he was no friend to the people at the Circle T. But above all, Bridget was circumspect. She didn't mention Adam at all.

Perhaps she could tell that Mickey didn't want to speak of him and perhaps she sensed why. They made small talk, mostly about the assistant foreman, Ernesto. He didn't relish the sudden burden of extra duty. But he would take it on without complaint. Like most of Carolyn's employees, he was fiercely loyal.

Mickey had no appetite for dessert, so she took her mug of coffee and went back to her office. She'd steeled herself. It was time to open Adam's folder.

She clenched her jaw as she laid it on her desk and took her seat. She lifted the faded blue cover.

The first thing she saw was a copy of a newspaper article from *Los Eremitas Herald, The Island Weekly News.*

In bold type the headline said,

One Foal Dead, Another Injured

Last Thursday one foal of the island's herd of wild horses was killed and another injured. Adam Duran, chief defender of the herd, says he believes the horses were attacked by dogs.

Duran said he noticed the colt, Ortega II, had disappeared from the herd and that another foal, the filly, Paloma, had bite marks on her hindquarters and left hind leg. Duran found Ortega's gnawed remains after a two-day search in the forest.

The injured filly, Duran said, should be fine, but he is especially saddened at the other foal's death. Paloma and Ortega were the herd's only twins. They were six months old.

"Even in domestication, twins are rare," said Duran. "The world may never see their like again."

Mickey, feeling numb, stopped, picked up the packet of snapshots and found the picture she remembered, a pair of wobbly legged bay foals, almost identical. She turned it over and read the handwritten words, "Ortega II & Paloma, three days old."

She swore quietly, feeling ill over the colt's senseless death. She fought against imagining the details.

She thought of the cattle out on the range lands of the Circle T. There were fences of barbed and electrical wire to protect them. Men on horseback kept track of them; men in trucks brought them feed when forage was poor.

A platoon of cowboys made sure they had water and defended them from predators, human and otherwise. The cattle were inoculated against disease, given professional care when injured; they were monitored, guarded and chronicled in the ranch's books.

The newspaper article had a fuzzy black-and-white picture of Adam, kneeling to bandage the leg of the surviving foal. Mickey could barely make out his features. But concern showed in every line of his body. Her heart knotted more tightly.

There were copies of other articles:

"Mare Dies: Caught in Pig Trap"

"Hoof-Care Program Desperately Needed"

"Stallion Dies of Infection"

There were articles from other Island papers, the *Barbados Nation*, the *Bahama Journal Daily*, the *Bermuda Gazette*, the *St. Lucia Star*, the *Abaconian*.

Hope stirred deep within her. There were too many articles, too many papers to fake—weren't there? Adam's work with the horses wasn't known in the world at large, but it was in his own region. W.H.O.L.E. was always mentioned. It had to be real, didn't it?

But her hope warred with a growing desperation.

The sale of the lease land might give Adam a chance to save the horses. But it would put Carolyn, kind and generous Carolyn, in debt for the rest of her life. Mickey put her hand to her stomach, feeling queasier than before.

She wanted to believe in Adam, and she wanted him to win his impossible battle. But she loved Carolyn. There was no right side to choose.

CHAPTER TWELVE

CAROLYN CALLED the next morning.

"Oh, Mick—we just came back from looking at the baby. She's gained an ounce! Can you believe it? It's the cutest ounce you ever saw. And she smiled when we were there! Everybody says she just had gas, but I *know* she smiled. And eyelashes? This child's got eyelashes like you never saw."

Mickey smiled and shook her head. Carolyn's euphoria wasn't running down, it was growing greater every day.

Carolyn said Beverly was much better physically, but on an emotional roller coaster. She was giddy with happiness over the baby but having crying spells because she couldn't yet hold or nurse her.

"Still, things are settling down," Carolyn said. "Today, I'm trying to get organized. I've actually written a list of things to ask you. Ready?"

Mickey took a deep breath, knowing somewhere on that list were questions about Adam. "Yes."

Carolyn said, "First question, can you ever forgive us?"

"What?" Mickey asked, startled.

Carolyn sounded chagrinned. "Can you forgive Vern and me for having matchmaking gleams in our eyes? For thinking you and that vile Vanek man might be a pair? I swear, Mickey, it makes me cringe. I wanted to believe I'd found a fine foreman. He fooled me. Maybe I wanted to be fooled."

"He fooled almost everyone."

"That's what Vern said. We're both sorry. Please accept our apology."

"Don't worry about it a bit."

"Which isn't to say that you *shouldn't* find a nice man," Carolyn said, bouncing back into form. "Only a truthful one. Honorable. With ideals."

Mickey winced. Those words might describe Adam. She remembered the easy confidence with which he'd shed his own blood, daring her to test his truthfulness. She remembered the video, the newspaper articles, the way he'd treated Jazmeen.

But Adam could also become a man whom Carolyn resented with all her heart. He would cast her future into such darkness that she'd fight him bitterly. And Mickey couldn't blame her.

Carolyn asked about Ernesto and added, "I need to give him a decent bonus. Then I have to go on an austerity program. I need a sign over my desk—Absolutely No New Debts. I've set a record in splurging. If I keep up at this rate, we'll have to mortgage the place. I never want to go through that again."

This time Mickey's wince was closer to a grimace, and she was grateful Carolyn couldn't see.

"The next item," Carolyn said blithely, "you got the presents sent?"

"They're all on their way. The first wave should arrive today. The jeweler called earlier this morning. Carrie's locket is ready, and I'm driving into Austin to pick it up."

"You're a treasure, my girl. Maybe I don't really want you getting caught up with some man and going off with him. What would we ever do without you? Now, where was I? Oh, yes, Adam Duran? He's left?"

"Yes. He probably got back to the islands late last night."

"Was it a fairly friendly visit?"

"It was—friendly enough." Mickey tried not to remember the feel of his mouth on hers, his strong arms winding round her. *It was too friendly.*

"So what's he like? Does he seem like a nice sort of guy?"

"Uh, he's rough around the edges. But, in my opinion, he seems—" *He seems truthful. Honorable. With ideals. Oh, Carolyn, what do I say to you?* "—he seems better than I'd hoped. He's—not like his letter."

"Thank God. From that letter, he sounded like a perfect pain in the wazoo. Tell me more."

"Really, Caro, you should meet him and make up your own mind. I don't want to influence you one way or the other."

"Oh, fiddle, I trust your opinion. Did he say anything about the will?"

Here it comes, Mickey thought with dread. *Either I lie outright or perform such fancy footwork that I'm almost lying, anyway.* She opted for footwork.

"He knew that he shouldn't talk about it to me." *He knew it, but in the heat of the moment, he had.*

Carolyn sounded puzzled. "But Vern told you it was all right to discuss it with him."

Mickey swallowed. "That business is between you and him, Carolyn. It—it shouldn't go through a third party."

"Did *he* say that?"

"He said, uh, it was best he discuss it with you personally."

"Mickey, you sound odd," said Carolyn. "Is there something wrong? Is there a problem with the will? A complication?"

"That's something that he'd have to tell you." Mickey's footwork no longer seemed fancy to her, it felt merely devious and desperate.

Carolyn was silent a moment. "I hope this doesn't mean trouble."

Mickey was thankful to hear Sonny's voice in the background, commandeering Carolyn. "Hey, Grandma! The biggest panda in the world just arrived. Beverly's so overcome she's having another weepy spell. She wants to hug her mama—right now."

"The panda! Oh, thanks, Mick. You're a doll, just a doll. We'll talk later. Thanks for all you do. You're my rock. Always dependable. Love ya."

They said their goodbyes and hung up.

Mickey changed clothes and set out for Austin. She had told Carolyn the partial truth. She was going to pick up little Carrie's locket.

But late last night, when Mickey had trouble sleeping, she'd made a decision. She would take Adam's blood sample to a DNA testing laboratory.

She would also take a cotton blouse that Carolyn had thrown into the ragbag. Sabur had tossed his head at the wrong moment and given her a nosebleed. The lab would have plenty to work with.

This morning she'd phoned the lab at 9:00 a.m. They told her they could get results in six days, perhaps sooner. It would be a long and excruciating wait. But she had to do it.

CAROLYN WENT into Beverly's room and hugged and petted her and cajoled her until her tears changed to smiles.

"I love you, Mama," Beverly said, when Carolyn and Vern were about to leave for lunch. "I wish you and Vern could stay for weeks and weeks."

"I wish we could, too, sweetie," Carolyn said, stroking her daughter's hair. "But I've got a ranch to run. And Vern's got cases piling up at the courthouse."

She kissed Beverly on the forehead and said they'd see her in an hour. She and Vern walked to a little Mexican restaurant two blocks away. The Colorado sky was clear, the air cool and bracing.

Now that the baby was faring so well, Carolyn felt a wonderful contentment, a sense of near completeness. "I love it," she said. "Our little family's gotten bigger. Somebody new to love."

She linked her arm affectionately with Vern's, and he patted her on the hand. "She's a honey. And so are you. And pretty hot stuff for a grandma."

Carolyn gave him a conspiratorial smile. Last night, for the first time since the crisis, she and Vern had made love. It had been good, so good that she still felt aglow with it.

"You're quite the guy yourself, foxy grandpa."

Yet in spite of her happiness, Carolyn felt a tiny, niggling sense of regret. "I wish we could get here more often. But we do have responsibilities...."

"Maybe you should cut down your responsibilities. Think about getting a manager, like J.T. did. Somebody to take over your duties."

He said this so mildly that she didn't think he was serious. But then he added, "I like being the justice, but my term's up in two years. I don't have to run again."

She blinked in surprise. "Not run? You've never said that before."

"I just started thinking about it this trip. Seeing how happy you are around Beverly and the baby. We ought to be able to take more time off."

Carolyn's forehead creased in a small frown. "A good manager is even harder to find than a good foreman. And he'd cost a fortune."

"It's just something to consider, my sweet. Give you more freedom."

Carolyn thought about it, growing more pensive. Soon all her sister's children would be in Claro County again. She dearly wished Pauline could be there to welcome them home—Tyler especially.

But Beverly and Sonny would never return to live in Texas.

Their careers were here, and they loved Colorado. This filled Carolyn with restless yearning.

She adored Pauline's children and grandchildren. She loved them for themselves and for the link they gave her to her sister. But she hungered to be near her own child more often. She missed her daughter with an anguish she'd never let Beverly know. Only Vern suspected how much.

And as for little Carrie, she weighed only five pounds, ten ounces, but she already took up enormous space in Carolyn's heart. To see them more often would be…heavenly. Yes, very heavenly.

"Have you started to brood?" Vern asked. "There's only one remedy for that. Dr. Vern's enchilada-and-margarita cure."

They'd almost reached the restaurant. Carolyn smiled at Vern, grateful for his kindness and sweet temper. She tried to regain her sense of joyous wholeness.

"At least the ranch is doing well enough that we can afford to visit here," she said. She would no longer have to pay to lease Enoch's land, and that, thank God, would make the Circle T far more profitable.

Vern reached the door and opened it for her. "How are things—back at the ranch?" he asked affably. "You talked to Mick?"

"Fine, just fine," said Caro.

"Let's hope so," he said. "She's sounded kind of odd lately."

"If anything was wrong, she'd tell me," Carolyn said. "That girl couldn't tell a lie if her life depended on it."

THREE DAYS PASSED, and each made Mickey feel worse. Her stint as a Sunday school teacher was less than impressive. Six- and seven-year-olds, she discovered, asked hard questions.

"If you're s'posed to love your enemy, how come there's war?"

"If a guy is going to shoot you dead, do you have to love him?"

"Should cats love dogs?"

"Boxers hit each other and don't turn the other cheek. Do they go to hell?"

"Should Spider-Man love Doc Ock?"

"Does God love Satan?"

"The kid next door beats me up all the time, and my mom says if I don't learn to fight back, I can't go outside anymore. So she's wrong? And I should just *let* him beat me up?"

By the end of the class Mickey felt not only exhausted, she felt battered. "Love thy enemy" consisted of three short words. How could they hold so much complexity and so many paradoxes?

Worse, through the whole morning, she'd thought of Carolyn. How could Caro view Adam as anything except an enemy? How could she love a man laying claim to half her ranch?

Her talks with Carolyn had led her into torturous verbal mazes. Every time Caro brought up Adam Duran or the will, Mickey answered vaguely or sidestepped a straight answer or tried to change the subject. Deception, she decided, consumed her in body and soul, and she wasn't cut out for it.

Luckily, Carolyn was still elated over the baby. She would go into long, bubbling monologues, describing the infant's every wiggle and burp.

But she was also starting to ask more about affairs at the ranch, her questions growing more specific. Carolyn was slowly moving back to normal, and normal meant knowing every detail about the Circle T. It also meant greater curiosity about when she would hear from Adam concerning the will.

The tangled threads of Mickey's life grew more knotted when, on the third afternoon, the detective phoned.

"Miss Nightingale, this is Edward Schumann in Austin. We have some of the information you asked for on Adam Duran. We can fax the documentation or post it by regular mail."

Mickey went numb at his words. She sat down heavily at her desk. "Fax it, please. Also mail me a copy."

"Will do. Do you want a quick rundown over the phone?"

She stiffened her spine, and picked up a pen. "Yes. Please."

"Not your typical past," Schumann said, sounding scientifically detached. "Born in Porte Verde, Florida, father unknown. We're working on getting a birth certificate. He grew up with his grandparents on a combination horse farm and camp. Mother died when he was twelve…"

He went on, confirming everything Adam had told her. He ended, "In Los Eremitas, he's part of a group founded to protect wild horses. There's a fund but not much money. Only $1097. It's his only bank account. No record of any arrests. No credit problems we can see. Can't find anything suspicious. Want us to look harder?"

Mickey's conscience prickled, but she said, "I do. Please dig deep."

"Yes, ma'am. But I have to say he's a hard one to trace through regular channels. Doesn't live like most people. No phone, no credit cards, no car."

"I know," said Mickey. "He marches to a different drummer."

She felt somehow tainted. So far, Adam seemed to have been entirely honest. But to discover that, she had to act as if she had ice in her veins, and remind herself he wasn't a person, merely a suspect.

For Carolyn's sake she wanted him to be a liar and imposter, quickly exposed. But in her own heart, she prayed he was exactly what he seemed, then cursed her own disloyal desires.

Schumann said, "We're working on the matter of Enoch Randolph. We'll have a detective to fly from Nassau to do the interviews. We know Randolph died of emphysema. He may have been of perfectly sound mind."

So does that mean the will is valid? Carolyn loses the land?

But Schumann could give her no certainty. "Or he may

have been crazy as a loon. No evidence either way. We'll
keep after it until we know."

"Yes. Good."

He paused. "One thing about Duran. His group is interested
in buying a large tract of land for a preserve."

"I'm aware of that."

"It'll cost a lot of money."

Mickey found she was holding her breath. "How much?"

"It's on Los Eremitas. Big price tag. Seven and a half million dollars."

Mickey suppressed a groan. "Seven and a half million?"
She could imagine Carolyn's reaction when she heard *that*.
The lease land was worth all that and more. Mickey had hoped
that Adam might offer Carolyn a bargain, but now she knew
he wouldn't. He couldn't afford to.

She hung up and, torn, looked again through the snapshots.

Paloma and Ortega II. The horses running along the beach,
and beyond them the sea stretching, jewel-blue and bright.
Adam, his bare chest being nuzzled by the beautiful bay.

A FULL MOON SHONE over the harbor at Tomcat Cay. Adam
watched its light—broken into fragments—dancing on the
wavelets.

Tomcat Cay was a small island with fewer than sixty per-
manent residents, a scattering of vacation homes and one
quiet hotel. The roads were all dirt, and hardly anyone owned
a car. Mail came and went by ferry.

There was one grocery store, a tiny liquor store, a church,
an elementary school and a cluster of small houses on the road
that led from the harbor. These buildings were the closest
Tomcat Cay came to having a "town." Between the church and
the school was a small square park.

The island's one public telephone was mounted on an iron
pole at the edge of the park. Most of the people on the island

didn't have phones. They communicated with each other by shortwave.

Adam was lucky. Tonight the park phone was working— often it wasn't. He used one of the newfangled phone cards he'd bought on Los Eremitas and dialed Mickey's number.

The fronds of palm trees rustled overhead in the night breeze, and a hundred yards away, the sea mumbled and rumbled. He heard, across thousands of miles of ocean and land, a phone ring in Texas. And then he heard her voice.

"Hello?" His heart seemed to gather itself then bound like a stallion breaking into a gallop.

"Mickey, it's Adam. Can you talk?"

"Yes. Are you back in Los Eremitas?"

He took a deep breath. The air was sweet with the scent of flowers and tangy with salt, but suddenly it didn't seem to have enough oxygen.

"I've been there. Tonight I'm at a place called Tomcat Cay. It's one of the Isabellas. I go back home tomorrow."

"Tomcat Cay?"

She sounded amused, and he remembered her smile when it was wry, one edge of her full mouth quirked. He remembered the shape of her lips, and the feel and the taste of them.

"I came over to talk to a guy who knows an equine vet who might consider retiring in Los Eremitas. We need one. We need one badly."

Her voice softened. "Have you seen the horses?"

"I've seen one band of them. They split into bands."

"Were they all right?"

"The ones I saw were. The others, nobody's seen for a while. Sometimes they move deep into the forest. They're not like plains horses. They like the cover."

He wondered which room she was in. He wanted to picture her as clearly as he could. He wondered if she was sitting in the lamplight. He remembered how it brightened the tips of her dark hair, how it made her skin look golden. Golden and soft.

She said, "I read the articles you left. I read the book. I was looking at the snapshots again today."

Hope and apprehension mixed in him. His muscles tautened. "And?"

"And they're—wonderful. But I can't go on keeping the truth from Carolyn. She's starting to suspect that I'm holding something back. Vern said he *knew* I was. He came out and told me this afternoon that I should warn her if there's going to be trouble."

His body tensed even more. "There doesn't have to be trouble—"

"Adam, *I've* had time to digest the news, and it still boggles me. It's one thing for her to find out she's got a brother she never knew about. It's another thing altogether to find you've inherited what she'd been promised for years. She's a gracious woman, but only a saint could be gracious about *that*."

He knew she spoke the truth. His own first impulse had been to think of Carolyn not as a kinswoman, but an opponent. There were eleven thousand acres of the Hill Country at stake. She'd been promised them free and clear, and she would fight for her right to have them. In her place he'd do the same.

He shifted his weight and stared out at the moonlight, shattered and playing on the sea. He said, "You're telling me it's time to get in touch with her. Does that mean the baby's better?"

"Much better. She can go home in six days. And then Carolyn and Vern are coming home. So yes. It's time for you to get in touch."

"I've been working on a letter." He had. He had scratched out so many words he couldn't count them. His wastebasket was full of crumpled papers.

Mickey said, "Then send it."

He closed his eyes in resignation and listened for a moment to the sea.

"I will. How do you think she'll take it?"

This time it was Mickey who hesitated. "Frankly? I think she'll be furious with Enoch. She'll be hurt. And her instinct will be to lash out. Carolyn's not a passive person. She loves this land."

He set his jaw. "She'll take it to court?"

"That'll be her first impulse."

He scrubbed his hand across his forehead. Court was the last place he wanted to be. Courts could take years to resolve conflicts. He didn't have years. There were too few horses left and they were dying too fast.

He said, "And if she chooses to fight me to the end, you'll take her side?"

"I'd have to. You know that."

"Yeah." He looked up through the palm fronds at the stars. "I know."

"Adam?"

He found the North Star and stared at it, as if for guidance. "Yes?"

"The horses that you saw? Was Paloma one of them?"

So, he thought, she cared, maybe just a little. "Yeah. She's a big girl now. A yearling. How's Jazmeen? And the foal?"

"They're fine. They're just beautiful."

"I sent you a letter. I told you I would. It doesn't say much."

It doesn't say what I feel for you. I don't know how to put things like that into my own words.

They both went silent. He could think of no more to say. The breeze swelled, and he watched the moonlit bougainvillea blossoms stir. Their perfume wafted more strongly on the mellow air.

She said, "No matter how Carolyn reacts to you, remember that she's a good person at heart. It's just that Enoch promised thirty-five years ago that the lease land would go to the ranch. For thirty-five years she's believed it. That's a long time, Adam."

He gave a sickly smile at the irony of it. "That's before you and I were born. It all started before we even existed."

"Yes. I wish it hadn't gotten all tangled up like this."

"So do I." *Because I don't want us to be on opposite sides. It's the last thing I want.*

She said, "You've seen how Carolyn lives. You've seen the land and know what's at stake for her. I hope she'll look at what's at stake for you. I'll give her the book. And the folder and photos. Everything you left."

"She could come here and see," Adam said, then stood amazed at the words he'd just spoken. They seemed to have sprung from nowhere.

"What?" Mickey asked, sounding as astonished as he was.

"She could come to Los Eremitas and see the horses herself. She and Vern. Maybe then she'd understand I don't want the land or the money for myself." He tightened his grip on the phone. "You could come, too. I'd find a place for you to stay. What do you think?"

"I—I don't know."

Hope surged again. "Would Carolyn come? Would she consider it?"

"I don't know," Mickey repeated. "Ask her."

"If she came, would you?" His heart beat fast and hard, pounding like the sea.

"Yes," she whispered. "Oh, yes."

TWO DAYS LATER, Carolyn and Vern stayed home from the hospital in the morning. Beverly had been released, and she and Sonny had gone back to visit Carrie.

Carolyn knew that Beverly and Sonny and the baby needed time alone together. She'd been guilty of hovering over her daughter and didn't want Sonny to think he had been cursed with a mother-in-law who clung like a possessive octopus.

Carrie would leave the hospital in three days. Carolyn wanted to share in this triumphant homecoming, but then she would go home herself. She liked Denver, but she wasn't meant for city life. She missed the Hill Country, and she worried about the ranch.

Mickey was left all alone to run the considerable business affairs of the Circle T. And although Carolyn trusted her implicitly, Mickey sounded strange whenever she was asked about Adam Duran's visit; she sounded—and this was most unlike Mickey—evasive.

Vern told her not to worry, but she sensed Vern, too, suspected there might be unpleasant news about the will. She told herself it didn't matter; she had a good lawyer and Martin could undo any hitch.

No, what troubled her most about the ranch was finding a new foreman. That was her main worry about things back home.

Until 10:47 a.m. That's when the FedEx deliveryman rang the bell and had Carolyn sign for a letter package. At first she thought Mickey must be sending something, but then she saw the return address was Los Eremitas, the Isabella Islands. And the sender was Adam Duran.

Slightly apprehensive, Carolyn drifted back to the living room and sat on the pale blue velvet couch. She opened the package. It contained a folded letter and a square white envelope that looked as if it held snapshots.

She unfolded the message, unable to shake her sense of foreboding. The letter was dated yesterday.

Dear Carolyn Trent,
First, I want to apologize for the tone of my previous letter. I didn't mean to sound curt and overbearing. It was a difficult letter to write.

Carolyn shrugged. An apology? Well, that was nice of him.
So far, so good. She read on.

There are situations that aren't easy to explain. You and
I are in this kind of situation, and I wish I had the power
to express it plainly. I probably don't. Perhaps it's better I do it by letter, rather than face-to-face, as planned.
I went to the Circle T, as Enoch asked. Fate took you
elsewhere, and we didn't meet.
    But having spent time at your ranch, I no longer feel
as if I'm approaching a stranger.

She raised an eyebrow. Something hard to explain? Well,
at least he was being polite this time. And that was a pleasant touch, that he no longer thought of her as a stranger. She
read on.

The truth is that, without knowing each other, we shared
Enoch as an uncle. We shared him because you and I
have the same father, Steven Randolph. I was born at
Porte Verde, Florida, in...

Carolyn's mouth fell open in shock. A half brother? Her
father hadn't been content just to run off and leave his family? He had the gall to bring another child into the world? She
felt as stunned as if she'd been struck.

Adam Duran said that his parents hadn't married. *My God,
I've got a half brother who's illegitimate?*

She'd thought that she'd come to terms with her father
years ago. Now she knew she hadn't. Resentment rose in her,
a hot, choking wave. Even from his grave her father was in-
flicting pain, complication and sorrow.

Her brother—her unwanted brother, because he brought
old angers and sorrows flashing back—had written more.

He'd learned that Steve Randolph had died in Canada, but that Enoch was alive. Moreover, this "brother" of hers lived only a few hundred miles from Enoch. They'd met last year. They'd spent time together. Enoch came to Los Eremitas to see Adam's project. Adam claimed he was working to help preserve a herd of wild horses.

None of this made sense to Carolyn. It was like an elaborate prank, a disconnected bad dream. What was this man getting at?

Carolyn, I'm sorry to be the bearer of this news. It dumbfounded me, and I'm sure you'll feel the same way. After Enoch died, I learned that although he'd promised the lease land to you, he left it to me....

Carolyn's vision swam and she felt faint. For a long, suffocating moment she couldn't breathe. Finally she took a ragged gasp of breath and cried out, "Vern! Vern! Vern!"

Vern bolted out of Sonny's study, his expression alarmed. "Caro—what's wrong?"

Tears of pain and betrayal burned her eyes. She rattled the letter as if she was trying to kill a poisonous creature by shaking it. She looked at Vern in despair. "This Duran man—he says he's my half brother. He—he insinuated himself into some sort of 'friendship' with Enoch. And he's cheated me out of the lease land—he's as good as stolen it!"

Vern stared at her blankly. "What?"

"He claims Enoch changed his will," she said, barely able to speak. "And left the land to him—this—this bastard brother. If he really is a brother. How many times can my father hurt me? How many? And Enoch? It's like he's slapped my face just for—meanness."

She crumpled the letter and threw it across the room. She threw the envelope and cardboard letter packet with even more vehemence. Her chin trembled at the anguish of such treachery, but she clenched her fists. "Well, I'll take Adam Duran to court," she vowed. "By God, he's picked on the wrong woman. He'll wish he'd never crossed my path. I fought Brian Fabian, and I can fight him."

But then she began to cry as helplessly as a child.

CHAPTER THIRTEEN

THE CELL PHONE CHIRPED, and the caller ID displayed Carolyn's name. A nervous tremor rippled through Mickey.

If Adam was true to his word, his letter to Carolyn must have arrived in Denver. The bomb had dropped.

She answered, hoping to disguise her apprehension. She couldn't. "Yes?" she squeaked.

"Mickey, I got a letter from Adam Duran this morning." Carolyn's voice shook with emotion. "Did you know he was sending it?"

"Yes." Another squeak.

"Do you know *what* it says? Do you know what he *claims?*"

Mickey squirmed. "Er…more or less."

Carolyn's tried to make her tone harder, but her voice still trembled. "He says he's my half brother. And that Enoch left the lease land to *him.* You *knew?*"

"It—it came out," Mickey said miserably. "I wish it hadn't."

"You didn't *warn* me? Mickey, how could you *do* such a thing? You let this man blindside me, catch me completely off guard."

"Caro, I didn't want to be the one to break the news. I thought that something this important, he needed to tell you himself. He did, too."

Mickey could see Carolyn in her mind's eye, pacing like

a suddenly trapped prisoner. Her chin would be high, held at a combative angle, but she would be feeling as much panic as anger.

"You kept this from me—something this important. For the first time in my life, I'm disappointed in you."

The words cut Mickey to the core of her heart, but she would take responsibility for her actions. "You were under duress. It was my decision not to let you know until the baby was better. And I believed he should be the one to tell you."

"*You* should have told me immediately. This man has shaken my life down to its very foundation."

Mickey squared her jaw. "I'm sorry. I did what I thought was best for you at the time."

"And Mr. Adam Duran—" Carolyn's voice almost broke when she had to say his name "—is a…a coward. He doesn't even come to tell me face-to-face. He sends a…a damned letter."

"He did come to tell you face-to-face. He had to go back."

"A *coward*. He didn't even give me a real phone number so I could call him up and ask him to clarify this—this mess. Just that stupid marina number again. Not even an e-mail address."

"He doesn't have a phone. He doesn't have e-mail."

"*Everybody* has a phone and e-mail," Carolyn almost wailed. "It's irresponsible not to. The only personal thing he sent is his post office box number. Does he think I'm going to try to resolve this by snail mail?"

Mickey chose her words with care. "He could make arrangements for a phone call, if that's what you want. Didn't he write you that?"

"How do you know so much?" Carolyn asked, suddenly suspicious. "Did the two of you get chummy? Did he woo you over to his side?"

This was the charge that Mickey most wanted to avoid. "He was here two and a half days. Vern insisted he stay. So did you.

Yes, I talked to him. I had to. There's obviously an immense problem here—"

"You bet your boots there's a problem. And I'll solve it. I'll sic a whole pack of lawyers on him, snapping like hounds at his heels."

Mickey wished Carolyn had picked another image. It made her think of dogs running down the wild foals, swarming over them and tearing at them.

"I don't know if this will he claims he's got is genuine," Carolyn muttered. "Even if it is, it can be broken. Enoch couldn't have been in his right mind to change it. He *couldn't*." She paused, then sounding suspicious again, "Have you seen the will?"

"No. He left a copy. It's sealed. I haven't opened it."

"Open it now. Get a copy into Martin Avery's hands immediately. And fax a copy to me. You've got Sonny's home fax number. Do it as soon as you hang up."

"Yes. Immediately."

"I don't even know if this man is really my brother," Carolyn said with despair. "If he's some kind of—a con man, I'll have him behind bars so fast his head will spin. Anybody could come along and *say* he's my brother. People try scams like that all the time."

Mickey held her tongue.

Carolyn's tone became one of weary bewilderment. "I don't know if a word he says is true. There's this—this rigmarole about wanting money to save wild horses. Wild horses in the Caribbean? I never heard of such a thing. But why make up such a story? Couldn't he do any better than that?"

"The wild horses are real," Mickey said. "I've had a detective check out Duran. Everything he says about himself and the horses is true. I have a file of newspaper articles on the horses. And his work with them."

There was a long silence at the other end of the line. Then

Carolyn said, "Good God. You think it could be true? That he's my half brother?"

Mickey took a deep breath. "He's left another envelope he says has some documents. It's addressed to you. I haven't opened it, either. Carolyn, maybe I'm out of line, but I've taken steps. He gave me a blood sample. I watched him bleed on a handkerchief. I took it to a lab, along with that pink blouse that got ruined."

"From when Sabur gave me the nosebleed? You're having a DNA check run?"

Mickey sat very straight at her desk, every muscle taut, praying she hadn't been too presumptuous. "I thought you'd want to know as soon as possible."

Carolyn seemed struck dumb.

"I did that," Mickey continued desperately, "and I hired the detective because I thought that's what you'd want. You have to know the truth."

"The truth," Carolyn said, "doesn't always set you free." Another long silence. "How long does it take, the DNA testing?"

"Another three days," Mickey said. "I hope I wasn't out of line—"

"No, no. You did absolutely the right thing. But what if he's really my father's son? My God—no, I won't believe that. I can't believe it. I don't want to."

Caro had doubts, but Mickey sensed that she was wavering.

Carolyn said, "He left all those things, but you didn't look at them?"

"Carolyn, this is so *personal*. I didn't think I had the right to look. But I'll get it to you right away, and you can send it all to the detective to check out."

"Yes…yes…that's what I can do." Then more uncertainty crept into her voice. "Mick—what was he like? You never said. How old is he?"

"Thirty-three."

"Good grief, younger than Beverly."

Mickey took a deep breath. "Caro, for what it's worth, there's a family resemblance. He looks a bit like you. Even more like Pauline."

"That could be a coincidence." Carolyn hesitated again. "Looks mean nothing, anyway. What kind of man did he seem to be?"

This was the hardest question Carolyn could have asked. Mickey cast about for an answer. "He's very good with horses. He's—gifted, in fact."

"A man can be good with animals but lousy with people," Carolyn returned. "What about his character?"

Mickey did not want to utter her true feeling. *If he's what he says he is, he's the most extraordinary man I've ever met.*

She said, "To me, he seemed—genuine. A kind and decent person."

"Well," Carolyn said with a bitter little laugh, "we all thought that Leon Vanek was just swell, too—didn't we?"

Mickey wanted to counter that she'd never liked Vanek. That he was too slick, too ingratiating. Adam seemed just the opposite. But she answered, "Maybe you should meet him and judge for yourself."

Carolyn hesitated again. "This would-be 'brother' has invited Vern and me to Los Eremitas. As if we could have a little chat and—*poof!*—this ghastly mess would resolve itself."

"Well?"

"I just might take him up on it," Carolyn said. "If he's bluffing, he's going to be very, very sorry."

Carolyn said she had to get off the phone, that Sonny and Beverly would be home soon, and she needed to regain her composure. She wanted to stay as calm about this as possible in front of Beverly, who already had enough on her mind.

"I'm sorry I've been hard on you, Mick," Carolyn said, chagrin in her voice. "It's been a terrible shock. A terrible, terrible shock."

"I understand." They said their goodbyes and hung up. Mickey rose from her desk and moved to the window, staring out toward the lease land. It lay in the far distance, vast and hazy in the day's growing heat.

Then she turned back to her desk. On it, the folder lay open, showing the fuzzy news photo of Adam bandaging the injured filly's leg. Beside it was the stack of snapshots. On top was the one of Adam and the bay.

Next to it lay the message he had sent her by mail. As he'd told her, it was short.

Dear Mickey,
Thank you for everything. I've thought of you often since I left Texas. They were good thoughts.

Tell Bridget and Werner hello. I'd like to hear how the little filly and Jazmeen are, but not if it goes against your loyalties to write.

I suppose our loyalties decided our fates before we ever met. We'll have to abide by what those loyalties and fates imposed on us. Like the poet says, it's useless "to resist both wind and tide."

There's more to say, but I don't know if I should say it.

Yours,
Adam

It was a letter that she found both straightforward yet mysterious, much like the man who had written it.

MALACHI PENNYWORTH came with a message for Adam. Malachi was second shift manager at the South Harbor Marina. A stocky black man, he had shoulders as wide as an ox-yoke, but a merry twinkle danced in the dark eyes behind his thick glasses.

"Adam," he called. "Hey, Adam."

Adam was on the deck of his sloop, mending a casting rod. "Malachi, my man. What's up?"

"I took a very interesting call for you," Malachi said, crossing his arms across his broad chest. "From a lady in the States. She sound like maybe she's got a twist in her knickers. She wants you to call her right back."

Adam put aside the rod and leaned both arms on the rail. Only two women in the States might phone him, Mickey or Carolyn Trent. His heart flew up, hoping it was Mickey.

"Her name be Carolyn Something," Malachi said. "In Denver. I wrote it down, back in the office. She wants you to call so much she left *two* numbers. She said call right away. She didn't sound happy. What you done now, boy? You done some woman wrong?"

I hope not, Adam thought, wild hope dying. The moment of confrontation had come, and Carolyn could be hotly furious or coldly combative. He had no idea what she would say to him.

"I'll be right in." He made his way down the dock and into the marina. He was barefoot, shirtless and wearing ancient cutoffs.

The office was open on the side toward the sea. He leaned against the counter and used the unfamiliar phone card again. He waited for the connection to go through, thinking of the hills of Texas, a place so unlike this, his home.

He stared off across the harbor, past the sloops, the fishing boats, the little catamarans and the big yachts. The sun had nearly set, and the sky, rose-colored, was deepening into purple, turning the water dark.

The tide was coming in, its crash and murmur growing louder. Gulls circled and screamed in the fading sky. He heard the phone ring in another country. Then he heard a man's slightly accented voice. "Dekker residence. Dr. Dekker speaking."

Carolyn's son-in-law. "This is Adam Duran in the Isabella Islands. I got word to call Carolyn Trent at this number."

"Hold, please. I'll get her."

A long moment of silence. Adam thought of the dozens of snapshots he'd seen of Carolyn. *I've seen my sister's image.* He thought, *I'm going to hear my sister's voice.* An odd feeling tingled deep in his chest and churned the pit of his stomach.

"Hello? This is Carolyn Trent." Her low voice was clipped and businesslike.

He stood straighter, as if coming to attention. "Yes, ma'am. This is Adam. You got my letter?"

"Indeed, I did. You make some disturbing claims, Mr. Duran. You can hardly expect me to accept them at face value."

He watched the sun suddenly slip out of sight. It did that on an ocean horizon. One moment it was there, a mere orange sliver where the sea met the sky. Then it was gone. Darkness.

"No, ma'am. I don't expect you to believe any of it at this point. But I'll do whatever you want to convince you."

"I've talked to Mickey. I have a copy of this so-called will in my hand right now. My attorney in Texas is already looking it over. You have a lawyer where you are, I suppose?"

Her tone was imperious, but he sensed a quiver of vulnerability behind it. "Yes, ma'am. I've showed it to a lawyer."

"And *your* lawyer, of course, would say it looks perfectly fine. Mine may say differently. If so, I'll be seeing you in court. I warn you, I don't welcome a fight, but I don't back away from one, either."

"I hope it won't come to that," he said. "There are better ways."

"I'm sorry, but I really have to question whether you're my half brother or any relation whatsoever. I'll soon have your 'documentation,' too. I'll have it examined *very* carefully. Mickey has a detective agency investigating you, by the way. And she's having the DNA testing done."

Adam took a deep breath. Carolyn talked to him as if he was a cheap con man, but that was no surprise. "A detective? Fine. DNA test? I'm the one who suggested it. I understand your position."

"Good," she said. "My attorneys will be talking to yours."

"Okay, Mrs. Trent, if that's what you want. But I hope you'll talk to me, too. I think we could work this—"

"I've talked to you quite enough for the present, thank you. Goodbye."

She hung up. Glumly Adam put the phone back on the receiver. Her reaction was what he'd always expected. It was why he'd gone to Texas with a chip on his shoulder. Then he'd embraced Enoch's low opinion of Carolyn and had been willing to fight. Now it was the last thing he wanted.

Because of Mickey Nightingale.

CAROLYN PUT DOWN the phone in Sonny's office. For a moment she sat, staring at nothing, stunned to the center of her soul.

Then she put her face in her hands and once again began weeping helplessly.

She heard Vern's voice behind her. "Caro? What's wrong?"

She couldn't stop crying, and she didn't want Vern to see her like this, so she kept her back to him. "Leave me alone," she managed to choke out. "Just—leave me alone."

But Vern would never turn from her when she was unhappy or in pain. She felt his hands gripping her upper arms. He drew her to her feet, making her face him, and when she wouldn't look at him, he enfolded her in his arms, so she could lay her wet cheek against his chest.

Good, dear, loving Vern. She wrapped her arms around his waist and held tightly to him. But her sobs didn't stop.

"Caro," he said in concern, "my dear, my darling. Tell me what's wrong. What? What did he say to you?"

How could she explain? It wasn't *what* Adam Duran had said to her. It was *how* he'd said it.

She drew back, her eyes brimming, and took a long, quavering breath. "Oh, Vern," she said, her voice choked, "It was like talking to a ghost. It was like talking to my father when he was young. This man sounds exactly like my father did. My God, what if he really *is* my brother? I don't want a brother. I don't need any more reminders of my father or what he did to us. I don't need *any* of this."

BY THE NEXT MORNING, Carolyn had convinced herself that she had overreacted to Adam's voice, tricked by her own imagination and frayed emotions.

In front of Beverly and Sonny, she managed to put up a front of false cheer. "A little problem with the lease land," she said. "Just like Enoch, being a pain even from the Great Beyond. Nothing that can't be ironed out."

But in private, she suffered three setbacks.

The first came from her attorney, Martin Avery. "Caro, to put it bluntly, the will seems valid. I've talked to the attorney in Nassau who drew it up for Enoch, and both the men who witnessed it. All three say Enoch was frail, but he seemed perfectly sane. The witnesses are respectable men. A former judge and an Episcopal priest. Now, I intend to—"

Carolyn bristled defensively, not wanting to believe him. "Martin, it can't be valid. Adam Duran must have somehow tricked Enoch. And, for that matter, who *is* Duran? He may just be a slick hustler who convinced Enoch they were kin."

"That, Caro, will take more investigating than I can do, frankly. You'll need a detective—"

"Mickey's already hired one. And why would Enoch disinherit me without a single word? It's cruel and unfair. I never treated him badly—never."

Martin sighed. His voice sounded weary. "Caro, listen,

please. Winslow, the attorney in Nassau said that Enoch considered you rich in your own right. That you didn't need the money, and that Duran did."

"I'm not a wealthy woman," Carolyn fairly wailed. "And to keep the ranch in the black, I *have* to have use of the lease land. I'm fifty-six years old. I'll have to remortgage my ranch, and I can't face it again, Martin. We worked like dogs to be in the clear. I was promised that lease land, and I more than kept up my end of the bargain."

"Carolyn, I'm only reporting what Winslow said."

She apologized, ashamed for fussing at Martin who was not only a good lawyer, but a good friend, as well. She said goodbye and took two aspirins, because her head was pounding.

The aspirins were just taking hold when the second blow fell. A FedEx mailer came from Mickey. "Ah, Mick," she breathed. "You're such a good girl. I hope you sent something to make me happy."

Vern came to her side, bringing her a cup of tea. "The stuff you expected from Mickey?"

"Yes," Carolyn said, tearing into the package. It contained a large yellow envelope, a packet of photos and a blue folder. Vern put the cup on the coffee table and sat beside her on the couch.

She opened the envelope and found a dozen pages clipped together. The top page was the copy of a birth certificate from the Florida Office of Vital Statistics. It gave Adam's full name, Adam Mikhail Duran, his sex and date of birth.

His mother was listed as Katherine Ann Duran, birthplace, Porte Verde, Florida, her age at her last birthday was nineteen.

But none of this registered for Carolyn. What leaped from the page was the name, birthplace and age of Adam's father: Steven Osgood Randolph, birthplace Claro County, Texas, forty-nine.

"Oh, my God," Carolyn gasped, her hand flying to her throat. Immediately she looked at Vernon, pleading with him to agree. "It could be a forgery, couldn't it?"

"It's possible," Vern said. But she knew he said it more out of concern for her than conviction.

Fingers trembling, Carolyn lifted that page and looked at the next. It was a copy of a letter written on stationery with a letterhead. It was addressed to Adam Duran of Los Eremitas, the Isabella Islands.

UK PeopleTrace
10 Bostwick Lane
London W8 5TZ England

Dear Mr. Duran:
We are pleased to report that we have found a match for the person you are seeking, Steven Osgood Randolph, born 1920, Claro County, Texas, U.S.A.

Unfortunately, Mr. Randolph passed away in 1989 in Perth County, Ontario. Our Canadian bureau located his name in the National Death Records (see attached) and thence found his obituary in the Byronville weekly news (see attached).

His employer was Ewan Burns, Jr. of Burns and Sons Farm, Perth County (see attached).

Locating Mr. Randolph was complicated by his emigration in approximately 1972 (see attached), but we are confident that this person is, indeed, the object of your search.

Please contact us if we may be of further service.

Carolyn felt hope withering within her as she read the words. "Oh, God," she said. "It's him. This is my father, they're writing about. Enoch said he'd died in Canada."

It was the only time Enoch had ever written anything more than his standard receipt message. "P.S. Steve died in Ontario last August." The blunt message had stunned her, then numbed her. She'd told herself she felt no grief, no sense of loss, nothing.

"In this place? Byronville?" Vern asked, putting his arm around her shoulders.

Carolyn blinked back tears of frustration. "Enoch never said. I never asked. I told myself I didn't care. That to me, he'd been dead for years."

She set her jaw and turned to the next page, the obituary.

RANDOLPH—Steven Osgood, age 67, died August 17 at his home in Byronville. He was born December 14, 1920, in Claro County, Texas, to Osgood K. Randolph and Emily Lanstaff Randolph. He grew up in the Texas Hill Country, and worked as a horse trainer and foreman. He worked for some years as a trainer in the southern Atlantic states of the U.S.A. In the early 1970s he moved to Ontario. He was preceded in death by his brother Thom Kenneth Randolph.

Survivors include his wife, Clotilda Anna Sandoz Randolph and his brother, Enoch James Randolph of Little Exuma, Bahamas.

There will be no services.

Carolyn's lips parted, and a small war flared in her breast, astonishment battling resentment. "He married again? My mother was still alive then! He never divorced her. How could he do such a thing?"

"Easy, hon." Vern rubbed her shoulder. "It's a long time over now."

"And what about Pauline and me? We survived him—and it wasn't easy surviving what he did to us. We're not even mentioned. Didn't he even tell his second wife that he had children? It's like he's rejected us all over again."

"Caro, you told me once that you'd made your peace with him."

"I was wrong," she said, her lower lip trembling. "Deep down, it hurt more than I ever let show. He caused so much pain—so much—and now *this*."

Numbly she looked at copies of her father's death certificate, his citizenship papers, the curt letter from his employer.

Steve Randolph worked for four years for me as a horse trainer. He was dependable, but kept to himself. I did not know him well, and I did not know his wife at all. She passed away three years after he did.

Sincerely,
Ewan Burns, Jr.

Carolyn sagged against Vern's shoulder. She held the sheaf of papers pensively. "This is the most I've known about him since he left us. And it's so little. I don't even know if it's true about—about Adam Duran."

She set the papers aside and opened the battered blue folder in her lap. "More horse pictures," she said, picking up the snapshots and flicking through them "I tell you these don't look like wild horses, to me. That part certainly doesn't ring true. To me, they look—"

Then she came to the picture of Adam with the big bay horse. Her mind seemed to split into two numbed halves, and her heart felt as if a crack suddenly jagged through it. From deep in her memory surged the image of another man, young, blond, strongly built, impossibly handsome.

She sat straight up, staring at the picture. "Oh, no," Carolyn said with gasping sob. "Oh, Vern. This could be a picture of my father. It *could*. And he's so like Pauline. So like."

She stared at the photo and tears welled in her eyes. There were legalities to go through. There were challenges to be made.

But Carolyn knew in her heart that Adam Duran might well be who he said he was. She didn't know how this would change her life—or the destiny of Circle T. But both would change. Of that she was certain.

IT WAS MICKEY who delivered the last blow. She went out for an hour and rode Sabur, bracing herself to be the one to break the news to Carolyn.

As she rubbed the big horse down, she also tried to sort out the tumult of her own feelings, and found it impossible. At last she threw down the curry comb and raked her hand through her hair, which was as tangled as her thoughts.

She could wait no longer. She took her phone from her belt and sat on a bale of hay. Mechanically she punched Carolyn's number into the phone. She held it to her ear, waiting, and while she waited, she watched dust motes dance in an errant sunbeam.

"Hello?" said Carolyn.

"Caro, it's Mick. Can you talk?"

"Mick, is this about the results from the lab?" Carolyn's voice sounded tired and sad.

"Yes."

"Then let me sit down. All right. Vern's here with me. Tell me."

Mickey drew a deep breath. There was no gentle way to say it. "There's a match. You share a parent."

"Oh, my God," Carolyn said with a catch in her voice. "I was afraid it was true, but I kept hoping…"

"Yes. I'm sorry to upset you, Carolyn. So sorry."

"This is pretty late in the game to find out I have a brother. *And* I've been disinherited because of him," Carolyn quavered. "Oh, *damn* my father. And damn Enoch. I—I can't talk. I just can't. I—I'm sorry."

Carolyn choked off a sob, and Mickey felt terrible for her. "Goodbye," she said softly. "We'll talk later."

She clicked off the phone and sat staring at the shifting dust motes in the sunlight. The people she loved most in the world were shocked and suffering.

Carolyn and Vern had planned carefully for their senior years and financial security. Those plans would be blown to hell. She'd tried not to think of Carolyn weeping, desolate, on Vern's shoulder, and Vern, too, stunned but trying to comfort her.

Mickey put her face in her hands, wanting to cry herself. Part of her was devastated by Carolyn's misfortune. But part of her was glad for Adam. He could follow his dream.

And he was who he'd said he was.

He was really the man he'd seemed.

She lifted her face and blinked back the tears. She must force herself to ignore the conflict that would overwhelm her if she let it.

She squared her shoulders and got back to work.

THE NEXT DAY Mickey was delighted to hear that Vern and Caro had also had some very *good* news: the baby was coming home earlier than predicted—tomorrow.

Vern called to say they would be back at the Circle T the day after that. J.T. was in California and was flying back with Tyler's two daughters, Pauline and Grace, while Tyler and Ruth packed up to move home. J.T. would stop in Denver, see the new baby and pick up the Trents.

Vern said that Carolyn still didn't want to talk about Adam Duran, and she wasn't going to tell Beverly and Sonny yet. But she'd probably talk to J.T. She trusted his opinion and his discretion.

Mickey, of course, was to tell no one. She and Martin Avery were the only two people in Claro County who knew about the trouble.

The ranch, oblivious of the crisis, buzzed with excitement: Vern and Carolyn—coming back at last. Bridget cleaned and polished and baked and made Vern's favorite fudge. Mickey picked wildflowers and arranged them in bouquets throughout the house.

Ernesto had finished with the spring branding, and had everything on schedule. Mickey curried and brushed Sabur until he gleamed like jet. She had groomed Jazmeen and the newborn filly that everyone still called only by the nickname Early Bird.

Mickey showered and changed into gray slacks and a simple white blouse. She was excited and eager to see Carolyn and Vern, yet she was also apprehensive.

Carolyn's manner on the phone had become strange. She always asked if the detective had discovered anything new, and she always had another set of questions she wanted the agency to answer. When she was on the subject of the detective, she sounded like the no-nonsense businesswoman she was, determined to know the hard facts of the matter.

But she had also grilled Mickey about Adam in a different way. So many questions: how he looked, how he handled himself, what did Mickey think of him?

The trouble was that Mickey thought of him fondly—and constantly. He haunted her like a phantom lover. She pored over memories of him lovingly, like a miser delighting in his treasure.

She told herself again and again what she had said to him: *The enemy of my friend is my enemy*.

But he still came to her in dreams, unbidden but welcome; they talked and walked and rode together. They smiled and gazed into each other's eyes. They embraced. They kissed. And more. She awoke from these dreams feeling guilty—yet wonderful.

Now she heard Bridget's cry, "Here they come!"

Mickey stood up from her desk, looking out the window. J.T.'s car was drawing up in the drive bringing Caro and Trent to their doorstep.

Joy flooded Mickey as she ran outside to greet them. But another emotion cast a shadow on her happiness. The shadow was shaped like Adam.

But then, they were all hugging and kissing and exclaiming: Carolyn, Vern, Bridget and Mickey. How good it was to be home! How good it was to have them home!

"Did you get the pictures of Carric I sent by e-mail?" Carolyn asked, squeezing Mickey and rumpling her hair.

"She's gorgeous. You're right—such eyelashes."

"Am I an ace photographer or what?" Vern laughed, hugging Bridget.

"A genius." Bridget kissed his cheek. "The child's beautiful."

"Of course, she's beautiful. She's related to Caro," Vern said. "Good looks run in the family."

Mickey thought of Adam, the sun bright on his tossing hair, and felt small and disloyal.

As if Caro read her mind, she drew back from Mickey and looked, unsmiling, into her eyes. "We have a great deal to talk about, you and I."

Mickey's heart took a long, awkward skip.

"Later," Carolyn said. "After lunch. You can show me the new filly. And we'll talk."

"Ah," said Bridget with a naive laugh. "So many new additions to the family!"

Mickey looked Carolyn in the eyes and thought Bridget had no idea how right she was. *Caro, Adam's your brother. Can you accept him? Is it possible?*

But Carolyn's green gaze told her nothing.

MICKEY AND CAROLYN leaned their arms on the top rail of the paddock and stared in admiration at Jazmeen and the new foal.

The little filly was steady on her feet now, although her legs still seemed comically long. Her mane was filling out, and she had learned to eloquently flick her little whisk broom of a tail.

Carolyn said, "Is there anything more exciting than new life in this old world?"

"I guess not." Mickey remembered how Adam had handled the foal.

"Seeing my grandbaby was almost a mystical experience," Carolyn said. "There she was—one of a kind, unique, a tiny, new individual. She's the future. But she's also a creation of the past. Beverly and Sonny are in her. And Sonny's parents and grandparents—it goes back and back. Beverly's father, Frank, is there in her. And so am I."

She turned to Mickey. "Part of my mother is in that baby. And—my father. My father left us. Like yours left you. So how do you feel about your father these days?"

Uneasiness rippled through Mickey. "I don't feel much anymore," she admitted. "I don't let myself, if I can help it."

Carolyn nodded. "That was my strategy, too. I could feel terrible about it. Or I could just try to cut off my emotions. I thought I'd done a fairly good job. And then, this business came up."

This business meant Adam. Mickey swallowed and kept staring at Jazmeen and the foal.

Carolyn said, "How would you feel if you suddenly found out that you had a brother? A half brother?"

Mickey faced Carolyn, looking into her eyes. "My first reaction would be that I wouldn't want to meet him. That he had nothing to do with me. But, I guess it really should depend on what kind of a man he is."

Carolyn nodded. "That was my first response. Why *should* I want to know him? But you're right—it depends on the sort he is. So, you've met him—my half brother. What kind of man is he?"

Mickey's heartbeat skittered. Torn between loyalty and honesty, she said, "I think he's a good man." She hated the quaver in her voice.

"Do you?" Carolyn lifted an eyebrow. "The 'good man' is in a position to cost me either millions of dollars, or half my ranch. Do you know how hard I've worked to make this ranch prosper?"

"Yes."

"I've lived my whole life here. So did my mother. And my grandparents. And their grandparents. I started helping my mother run this place when I was nineteen years old. She couldn't depend on my father. So she depended on Frank and me."

Mickey bit her lip. She knew the land was not merely Carolyn's heritage, but her identity.

Carolyn said, "When my mother died, I ran it with Frank. Beverly's father. When he died, I ran it alone. It's been my life. Now I may have to hand half of it over to a brother I've never seen. Well, I certainly can't expect him to say, 'Oh, no, *you* keep it. It's no big deal.'"

"He knows he's put you in a terrible position," Mickey said. "He feels bad about it. I can tell."

Carolyn's smile was ironic. "How nice of him. And I understand his position. If someone left me eleven thousand acres, *I'd* want them. And it doesn't matter what Enoch wrote in a will years and years ago. What matters is the last will he signed."

Carolyn sighed. "I've seen close families ripped apart over bequests. Bequests far smaller than this. People who'd grown up together became enemies. Their love turned to hate, they stopped speaking, they said rotten things about each other. I swore I'd never be that way. Well, little did I know."

Mickey felt hollow and cold. "You hate him?"

Carolyn looked pensive and shook her head. "When I

thought Carrie might die, the lease land seemed the least important thing in the world to me. I would have traded it for her in a second."

Mickey, puzzled, frowned slightly.

Carolyn said, "Something like that—a sick child, a child in danger—puts things in perspective. Would I have given the lease land to save her? Yes. The entire ranch? Yes. And yet I love it. My instinct is to fight for it."

"I understand," Mickey said, her voice tight.

"I talked to Bridget about Adam Duran. She was careful about what she said. You warned her something was up, didn't you?"

"Yes. I didn't say what."

"Ah, that's my Mickey. Always sensible. Always discreet and dependable."

I wasn't sensible and discreet when I was in his arms. Or when he kissed me.

Carolyn smoothed a fluttering strand of blond hair back into place. "Bridget couldn't disguise that she liked him. She, too, said he was kind. And brave. That he stood up to Vanek. Even though Vanek was much bigger and nearly out of control. And that's true?"

"Yes. It is."

"I talked to Werner, too. He didn't know why I was asking. He had nothing but respect for the man. He said he probably saved this filly's life. And Jazzy's ability to have more foals. Did he?"

"I think he did."

"Werner thinks he's a horse whisperer. Do you?"

"Yes. It was amazing."

"I talked to Manny, too. I phoned him. He said the same thing. That the man knew horses and he loved them. Manny liked him, too."

Carolyn smiled, almost sadly to herself. "You know, it's occurred to me over the years that Enoch could have lost the land the same way he got it, in a card game. He might have married and left it to a wife, a child. He could have gambled it away or sold it without asking me. A dozen things might have happened to it."

"I suppose," said Mickey.

"But what did happen is that he left it to a man who seems to be my half brother." She looked at Mickey, her expression sardonic. "My half brother who has a crazy idea about wild horses. And do you believe him—about the horses?"

Mickey squared her shoulders. "Yes."

"You don't think his motivation is just greed?"

Mickey raised her chin. "I don't think he's got a materialistic bone in his body."

"Then," Carolyn said, turning to look at the filly again, "I think Vern and I should go to the Caribbean and see for ourselves. I want you to come, too. You're the link between us. It'll be less awkward. Will you do it?"

"Yes," Mickey said. She said it solemnly, but her heart soared.

CHAPTER FOURTEEN

ADAM CLIMBED into the rigging to replace a fraying halyard. The morning was bright, and a small school of dolphins played in the harbor. He stopped to watch them, smiling to himself as they rose almost in unison, showing their sleek backs before diving again.

Then Chauncy, the day manager at the marina, appeared on the dock, yelling at him to come phone somebody named Carolyn Trent in Texas.

The message darkened Adam's day like a storm cloud. He scrambled down, strode barefoot into the marina and went to the phone. Chauncy, who was tall and handsome, was flirting with two teenaged girls and paid him no mind. Adam was grateful for that.

Adam expected Carolyn to be so cold he'd get frostbite. She'd announce that she was unleashing an army of lawyers on him who would chain and fetter him in court and strip him of every cent he had.

But when she answered, she wasn't cold. Neither was she warm, but she was civil, no longer combative, almost subdued. "I looked over the material you left. I also had a detective check you out. I admit the evidence seems convincing. We may be—related."

What? he thought, jolted.

Weariness crept into her voice. "And the will *may* be valid. I think I should meet you. So if the offer to visit Los

Eremitas is still open, my husband and I would like to come."

And Mickey, he thought, his heart bounding. *Will Mickey be with you?*

"The invitation's still open, ma'am," he said. "My sloop wouldn't be too comfortable for you, but I'll find you a place."

"No, we'll stay at a hotel. There *is* a hotel, isn't there?"

There were hotels and guesthouses and resorts. He didn't like them. He considered them an eruption of carbuncles festering along the coast. "Friends of mine have a house you can use. You'll have more privacy."

"I don't intend to impose on anyone." Aloofness had crept into her tone.

"You wouldn't be imposing. The folks who own it work with me on the wild-horse project. They'd want you to use it."

"It's not just Vern and I. We're bringing Mickey. Unless you object."

His heart took another leap, and he was glad Chauncy wasn't looking, because he couldn't keep the grin from his face. "No objection, at all."

"I might even," Carolyn's voice grew chillier, "have her look at your bookkeeping."

He swallowed. W.H.O.L.E. didn't have a real bookkeeper. It had only him, and he wasn't good at it. "She'd probably be a big help."

"Is there room at this house for Mickey, too?"

"Yes, ma'am. There are two bedrooms downstairs and a third in the loft. It's got a screened-in deck and an ocean view."

"I hate leaving the ranch so soon after just getting back. But this is a serious matter." She said she intended to arrive the following weekend and stay not more than four days, if that.

Four days to win her over, he thought. *Four days to settle this peacefully. Or four days to screw it up and watch it all go to hell.*

He hung up the phone feeling daunted. So much was at stake. The horses. Any relationship to what was left of his father's family.

And Mickey—lovely, loyal, honest Mickey.

THE FLIGHT FROM Miami was in a small, cramped plane that made its progress by pitching and bounding. Yet in spite of the jolting dips and lurches, Mickey felt exhilarated.

Through the small window she saw a sea of such improbable colors, she couldn't believe it was real. It was vivid jewel-like blue in places, and for the first time she understood the real meaning of the words "aqua blue."

But aqua darkened to sapphire in some places and brightened to brilliant crystal green in others. It went on and on, changing and inventing and reinventing colors and patterns of color like a great kaleidoscope.

Carolyn sat in her cramped seat across the aisle. She stared out at the ocean without awe or any kind of emotion on her face. She seemed lost in thought. A fearless flyer, she didn't seem to notice the plane's swoops and thumps.

Vern, however, was a white-knuckled passenger on the most placid flights. He sat in the seat before Caro's, and Mickey could see enough of his face to tell he was fighting a bad case of the collywobbles. The plane's five other passengers acted as if nothing was unusual, and took each plunge or shake with something akin to boredom.

Then the plane began to descend, and Mickey saw islands ahead. She stared at them in disbelief—they looked as flat as sugar cookies to her. She had expected great, rolling hills and looming mountain peaks. The first islands were small and stony, almost bare.

Larger ones eased into view, nearly as flat, but wooded. Now the plane was so low that she could see the landing strip beneath them, a narrow gray ribbon. The trees on either side were mostly pines. The soil looked as thin and bare as that of the Hill Country.

The plane's wheels hit the tarmac so hard that Mickey's teeth rattled, and Vern emitted an unhappy cry that sounded like "Whup! Whup!" A few more jounces and jolts, and the plane rolled to a stop and was mercifully still.

The other passengers began gathering up their carry-ons and parcels, and Carolyn did the same with a businesslike air. She kept her face perfectly blank. Vern had turned in his seat and was checking out his wife apprehensively, as if assuring himself she was still in one piece.

But this was Mickey's first time in the Caribbean, and she practically had her nose pressed against the window. The airport was small—almost comically small. It didn't seem much larger than the Long Horn Coffee Shop back home.

Carolyn had said that Adam was meeting them. She hadn't sounded happy about it. In spite of her controlled expression, she must be filled with turmoil at the thought of meeting her brother.

But Mickey looked for him eagerly, too excited to disguise her emotion. Was he really inside that strange little pink-and-green building? Would she walk through the door and see him? Would she feel even more excitement? And if so, how would she hide it?

ADAM WAITED outside the airport on the sidewalk. He knew the drill. The Trents and Mickey would have to go through the crowded little customs room, open their luggage, show their passports and make their declarations. They would then be released into the tiny lobby, which would be crammed with people waiting to take the next plane out.

But then, he looked in the open door and saw her—Mickey. She looked dazed and lost, and he knew she was searching for a familiar face, his. He couldn't help himself. He called her name and stepped inside.

He couldn't help the next thing that happened, either. They moved toward each other, and he reached for her, putting his hands on her shoulders. She gazed up at him with smiling lips and shining eyes.

He'd never seen her so pretty. She wore a yellow sundress that looked sensational with her brown cascade of hair. He bent toward her. She raised herself to meet him. He would have kissed her and kept on kissing her until the world fell away and he saw stars and moons and comets whirling behind his closed eyes.

But then a man Adam recognized from photographs— Vern—came through the door from customs, wrestling with his roll-on bag, which seemed to be losing a wheel. Mickey came back to herself with a start, and sprang away from Adam. Had Vern noticed? Or had he been too harried by his flight and his rebellious roll-on?

One glimpse of Mickey had made Adam lose control. What if Carolyn had seen? She would have known instantly that there was something between them. And she would have felt not only stunned, but betrayed and hurt.

"That's Vern," Mickey breathed.

Adam nodded. "I'll go help him."

She nodded, and he edged through the crowd. He was dressed as usual, faded jeans and a work shirt limp from many washings. This was the first time he'd seen Mickey in a dress, and she looked so lovely that he could barely take his eyes from her.

He shook Vern's hand, then knelt to fix the offending wheel.

Vern stepped back inside customs, and Adam knew he was going to help Carolyn. Mickey made her way to Adam's side. He stood, spanking his hands clean, just as Vern led Carolyn through the door, her garment bag over his arm.

Carolyn stopped before Adam, standing completely motionless.

Her face, so carefully expressionless before, suddenly looked as vulnerable as a child's.

She stared at Adam, and he stared at her. *My God,* Adam thought. *She's like a queen.*

Vern, seeing her bewilderment, slipped his free arm around her. Mickey said, "Carolyn, this is Adam Duran. Adam, Carolyn Trent."

Adam extended his hand. Carolyn stared down at it, her lips parted as if words failed her.

CAROLYN KNEW that she was standing in the lobby of the Los Eremitas airport at three o'clock in the afternoon, and that she was fifty-six years old.

But her mind cartwheeled through time and space, and she was back in Texas again, and it was forty-four years ago. Although she knew perfectly well she was an adult, she was also a twelve-year-old child.

She flashed back to just after her eighth-grade graduation. She was staring down at her father's hand as he extended it to congratulate her. It was the first time he'd ever shaken her hand as if she was a real grown-up.

His hand had been exactly the size, shape and color of the one Adam Duran offered. Adam's had the same long fingers and strong knuckles. It was bronzed by the sun and toughened by work. The veins stood out on the back of the hand, and the wrist was chiseled.

She'd been proud of her father at graduation. He was handsomer than anyone else's father. He wore his hair longer than was fashionable at the time. It was dark blond with sun-colored streaks, and it set off his tanned face and the startling blue eyes that Pauline had inherited, but Carolyn hadn't.

She looked again at Adam's face, and felt the sense of dislocation in reality even more strongly. She was two people at once, and he was even more. She was both a grandmother and a young girl. But he was her father, her sister in young, masculine guise, and he was…her brother, who was mysterious and possibly dangerous to her home and security.

Gingerly she took his hand in hers, and they exchanged a handshake that she found awkward, yet charged with meaning. He smiled as if in embarrassment. She saw he had a slight gap between his front teeth, as her father had had. Exactly as Pauline had had.

Even the way he stood was familiar, wearing jeans and cowboy boots, one hip cocked. "You look like your pictures," he said in a voice that sounded slightly awed.

"So do you," she said, and realized her tone was the same.

Self-consciously they released each other's hands. "Welcome to Los Eremitas," he murmured. "Thanks for coming."

Carolyn nodded, falling numbly back into the present. "I'm sorry that you had to waste that trip to Texas."

"It wasn't wasted," Adam said with a sidelong look at Mickey. "It was a good trip. Very good."

ADAM, FEELING deeply unsettled, led them to a white Range Rover. He couldn't stop looking at Carolyn because he was certain now that she was his sister. She even had a passing resemblance to Enoch, with those green eyes.

But neither could he stop stealing glances at Mickey. Her presence hit him even harder than Carolyn's did. He was aware of her with every atom of his being. His head buzzed from her nearness, his heart thudded, and his senses spun dizzily.

"This isn't my car," he said. "I borrowed it. You'll be staying at a house that belongs to Albert and Elsie Penndennis."

Vern opened the door for Carolyn. "Get in, honey."

"Let Mickey sit there. I'll sit in back with you." Adam hadn't thought Carolyn had any bashfulness in her, but now she acted downright shy.

Mickey slipped into the passenger seat, and Adam had an intriguing glimpse of a tanned thigh beneath the yellow sundress. She said nothing except a whispered "Thank you" to Vern.

An uncomfortable silence settled as he started the car.

"So," Vern said with too much enthusiasm, "this was a British possession once, wasn't it?"

"Yes sir," Adam said, "but the Spanish discovered it. In the sixteenth century."

"Is that so?" Vern said. Adam blessed the man. It was too soon and too awkward to speak of all that had brought Carolyn here. It was not private enough to talk to Mickey. *What am I going to say to her? What?*

So he was grateful to babble about Spanish explorers and British colonists and twentieth-century independence. And he was deeply grateful that Vern was kind enough to keep asking questions.

MICKEY WATCHED Adam turn the car from the highway and steer it down a rutted road. She had been shaken by her first sight of him and Carolyn together. The resemblance between them was stronger than she'd realized. They had the same deep-set eyes, the same square jaw and stubborn chin.

But something subtler linked them, a likeness that transcended the differences of age and sex. Their bone structure was similar, the color and texture of their skin, the athletic way they carried themselves.

But Mickey was afraid to be caught studying Adam, so she gazed out at the countryside. Away from the highway, the landscape quickly grew rural with a touch of wildness.

Scrub and weeds flanked short, twisted trees. There were cacti and scraggy vines and an occasional tall tree that looked lonely among its low-crouching neighbors.

The few houses, widely separated, were painted in lively

colors: pink, turquoise, and lilac. Their yards were cleared and planted with flowers that hugged the earth.

Then the ground grew more barren, showing patches of gray stone and sweeps of sand. The wild vegetation thinned out to cacti, weeds and a few gnarled trees. Mickey sensed they were near the sea.

Adam slowed to point out a neat yellow house ahead of them. It stood beside the road atop a gentle rise. "That's where you're staying. It's furnished. Al and Elsie live about a mile north. You'll meet them later."

He pulled up in the narrow, gravel-covered drive. There were flowers planted at its edge, ordinary flowers, little red begonias. Mickey realized she'd expected orchids and masses of exotic blooms.

She looked with curiosity at the yellow house, so neat, compact and solitary. Just beyond it, the edge of the sea was visible, the same peacock-blue she'd seen from the sky.

Adam got out and opened first Carolyn's door, then Mickey's. Mickey, as if mesmerized, strolled to the highest part of the yard. She saw a stretch of ocean and white beach so perfect it looked man-made. But she could smell the sharpness of the salt air and hear the low rumble of the surf.

Vern, his arm around Carolyn, moved to stand next to Mickey. Adam came to her other side and stood, folding his arms across his chest.

"The beach is *empty*," Vern said. There was not a soul to be seen on its whole dazzling stretch.

"The resorts are on the other side of the island—mostly," Adam said. "One's going up near soon, though." He nodded his head toward the south.

He didn't look or sound happy about it, Mickey thought, and no wonder. How many beaches as fine as this could still exist? What would happen when a resort seized a chunk of these immaculate sands?

"We went to Honolulu," Vern said. "Beautiful beach. But so many people you could hardly put down a towel."

"Yeah," Adam said, crossing his arms more tightly.

It was then that Mickey tore her eyes from the sea long enough to notice a lovely white house farther off and to the north, on one last rise before the beach began. "Ooh," she said.

Adam followed her gaze. "That's the Penndennis's house. He and his wife were born and raised here. He was a dentist in Nassau, and she was a teacher. They retired back here about five years ago."

He handed Mickey the car keys. "These are for whoever wants to drive. Just remember you drive on the left side of the road here."

Mickey took them. Her fingers brushed his, and a tremor of excitement spun through her. They keys were still warm from his grasp.

He said, "There are some groceries and supplies in the house. And beer and wine and rum and stuff. Anything else you need, you can go back to the highway, turn south. There's a little store about four miles down. If you want more choice, there's a supermarket in town, about nine miles."

Mickey fingered the keys and looked into his eyes, which seemed an identical blue to the sea beyond them.

Vern drew Carolyn closer to him. To Adam he said, "If we take the car, how do you get back?"

Adam gestured to an ancient motorcycle propped against the side of the house. "That's mine. The car belongs to a friend. He went to Miami. He said you could borrow it."

Mickey marveled at the generosity of Adam's friends.

He drew another set of keys from his pocket. "Come on," he said. "I'll show you the house."

"And then?" Carolyn spoke for almost the first time since they'd left the airport.

He looked her up and down solemnly. "Then I guess we should try to get acquainted."

FROM THE OUTSIDE, the yellow house was tidy, but seemed an ordinary little house tucked into an extraordinary setting.

But houses could fool people, and this one had fooled Mickey. Inside it was so airy, it didn't seem small at all. It was decorated with a simplicity and spareness that seemed Japanese inspired, and this gave it an air of spaciousness and tranquility.

Mickey loved it the minute she walked in the back door. There was a small kitchen, orderly without being fussy. A teakettle sat on one burner of the stove, and there was a bouquet of fresh flowers on the counter. "Hmm," Adam murmured, glancing at them. "Elsie's been here."

He sniffed the air, and Mickey did, too, smelling something fresh-baked and fragrant. Adam lifted the aluminum foil from an oval platter heaped with chocolate-chip cookies. "Yup. Elsie's definitely been here."

There was a combination living room and dining room, with a simple pine table that could seat six. There was a sofa and armchair, and a CD player, but no television. But Mickey found it hard to concentrate on the decor because her eyes kept traveling to the window to gaze hungrily at the beautiful sea.

The living room led to the deck, and Adam pulled open the glass doors. He gestured for the others to step through, then followed. Mickey thought, *If this was my house, I'd never leave it. Ever.*

She realized for the first time the house stood on a small peninsula. From the deck, she could see the ocean on three sides, all rimmed by sparkling beach. As she watched the waves drive toward the shore, she saw how they curved like the necks of horses, maned with foam.

Vern said, "Why are you smiling, Mickey. What are you thinking?"

"Of Neptune's horses," she said softly.

Vern tossed her a puzzled glance, but Adam nodded. "Yes." His eyes met hers. He understood. He saw the same thing she did.

But quickly they both looked away. Adam gestured at the white wicker furniture arranged in a semicircle facing the view. "Have a seat. Would you like a drink?"

A bottle of white wine was chilling in a silvery bucket. Four stemmed glasses were set out next to a plate of cheese biscuits covered with cellophane. Another vase of flowers stood beside the wine.

"I could use a drink after that flight," Vern said, sinking onto the cushioned sofa. "Your friend Elsie went all out to make us feel at home,"

"Indeed, she did," said Carolyn, settling beside him. But she looked more worried than comfortable.

"Elsie's a good soul," Adam said, wielding the corkscrew. He turned to Mickey. "Don't you want to sit?"

Startled, Mickey realized she could have stood all day watching the waves gallop toward the shore, then transform themselves to lacy foam and retreat again. This was the first time she'd ever seen an ocean this close.

With a nervous smile she went to sit beside Carolyn. Adam poured the wine and handed out the glasses. He took one himself and sat in a wicker rocker.

This seems symbolic, Mickey thought, she and Vern protectively flanking Carolyn, as if the three of them were ranged against him.

Adam wasn't a natural host, but gamely he lifted his glass. "To you," he said. "In thanks for your hospitality to me."

His eyes lingered longer on Mickey than Vern or Carolyn.

"Did my Mickey treat you well?" Carolyn asked, a bit stiffly.

"Your Mickey did," Adam said. "She's a credit to you."

"The ranch couldn't function without Mick," Vern said, resting his arm lightly on Carolyn's shoulder. "Could it, Caro?"

"No." Carolyn took a meager sip of wine, then trained her gaze on Adam. "I want to thank you in person. For your help with the mare and foal. My vet said you did a fine job."

Adam seemed embarrassed by praise. "They're doing all right?"

Carolyn looked at Mickey, as if to say, *You tell him.*

"They're doing beautifully," Mickey said. "Jazzy's a good mother. We think the foal's calmed her down. And the foal's beautiful. Her coat's smoothing out, and she just shines. And she knows she's pretty. She's got attitude. And mischief in her. Not malicious. But she's already got a sense of humor."

He nodded, pleased. "Has she got a name?"

"We're in the process of registering her. Officially, she'll be Jazzdancer al Akmar. But everybody calls her Early Bird. Early for short."

He gave her a small, private smile that made her heart flutter, then turned to Carolyn again. "And how's your family?"

Mickey felt Carolyn tense slightly at the word *family.* "Our granddaughter's doing quite well. No complications, and she doesn't need anticoagulants, which is a blessing. My daughter's in seventh heaven now that she's got her home. And the new daddy's very proud."

"That's good," said Adam. "And how are things at the ranch?"

Carolyn threw Mickey another you-tell-him glance.

Mickey said, "We think we've found another foreman. He's young, but he's good. And this time we know his background firsthand."

Adam gave Mickey a concerned look. "Vanek hasn't been back?"

She shook her head. "You were right. He's disappeared. He's dodging that court date."

"I want to thank you for your help in that matter, too," Carolyn said. "Bridget said she was worried about Mickey trying to handle him alone. But you made him turn tail."

Adam shrugged and made a helpless gesture, as if he hadn't really done anything. "She was doing fine. I just shortened the process, that's all."

Carolyn said, "You haven't mentioned your work. Your horses."

Mickey knew it pained Carolyn to bring up the topic of the wild horses, because it would lead to other, more difficult subjects.

Adam met her gaze. "They're not my horses, ma'am."

"Then whose are they?"

"Everybody's. I guess they belong officially to the government of the Isabellas."

"But the government's done nothing to insure their survival? It's up to individuals?"

"So far. The Isabellas aren't rich. The main income comes from the tourist industry. Which is growing. That's good for the economy, but bad for the horses. We've got someone trying to get help from parliament. So far, the horses aren't high in parliament's priorities."

"And why are they so high on *your* list?" Carolyn asked. "What do they have to do with you? Why do you have so much concern?"

"I guess it's in my blood," he said.

"Your blood," Carolyn repeated. "Which you say is the same as my blood. That my father is also your father."

"I truly hope that doesn't upset you too much, ma'am."

"It upsets the very hell out of me," said Carolyn. "At my age, it's not easy to adjust to suddenly having a little brother. So I suggest that you stop calling me 'ma'am,' which is really getting on my nerves because it makes me feel even older. Call me Carolyn. And I also suggest we get to know each other. Take me for a walk on the beach—just you and me."

She rose and offered him her hand, an almost regal gesture. He stood and took it, lacing his fingers with hers.

"Let's go for a walk," he said. "Carolyn."

CHAPTER FIFTEEN

THEY HAD REACHED the edge of the sea.

Carolyn knelt to undo her sandals by a clump of sea grapes. Adam stepped out of his deck shoes. Carolyn kept stealing glances at him. *This beautiful young man is my brother,* she thought, lost in the strangeness of it. *He's so like Daddy. So like Pauline.*

It was surreal to see him in such a spectacular setting. The water was so perfectly blue and the sand so brightly white, they seemed the stuff of dreams. Adam himself might be illusory.

But he offered her his hand to help her rise, and when she clasped it, it was warm and human and full of strength.

She gave him a hesitant smile, and dropped his hand. They began to walk along the shore. *It's real, all of it,* she told herself. *Him, too.*

The sand was hard and hot beneath her soles, but cool and smooth when freshly washed by a wave. The sea itself was almost cold when it surged over her feet, tickling her arches and lapping at her ankles.

The sun in that mystic sky was also real. She felt its heat and saw how it sparkled on the waves and threw shadows of her and Adam on the beach, sometimes the two shapes merging into one.

Now she could look back and see the trail of their footprints, disappearing here and there, where the surge of the water washed over them and smoothed them out of existence.

All those footsteps, she thought, led to this instant and this place. Her feeling of unreality grew. It was as if every step of her life had brought her to this moment. Why?

For a long time, neither of them spoke. Adam truly did seem to have a streak of shyness in him. At last, just to say something, Carolyn said, "We're here because of a turn of a card, you know."

She shot him a questioning glance and wiped a blowing strand of hair from her face. "Did Enoch tell you that? How he won the lease land? Playing poker?"

Adam nodded, his lips curving in a wry smile. "Five card draw. He had a pair of aces, a pair of threes and a one-eyed jack. He threw away the jack and drew the ace of hearts. Full house, ace high."

"And that's what brings you and me here," Carolyn said. "That ace."

"He called it his ticket to freedom."

She gazed out at the sea. "It was. He was set for life. I can see why he chose to spend it in a place like this."

"He didn't live fancy," Adam said. "He liked nature. He hated it when he had to go into the hospital in Nassau. He was in and out, four or five times. He had to stay close to it, so he took a room in a boarding house."

She thought of the strong young Enoch she'd known years ago, and tried to picture him, weakened and aged, transformed into a dying man. She couldn't.

She said, "He won that land the year before my father left us. We always figured Dad went down and spent time with Enoch." She gave Adam an oblique glance. "But it looks as if he got sidetracked in Florida. With your mother."

He cleared his throat. "Yeah. That he did. I suppose you missed him when he was gone."

"You suppose wrongly. I resented him. Not so much his leaving as the *way* he left. Going off, never sending back word. As if we all stopped existing."

She paused, watching a flock of gulls settle, bobbing, onto the sea. "He never looked back," she said softly. "Pauline and I used to wonder if he'd met another woman, had other children. It's not as if we never imagined someone like you might exist. We did. We couldn't ever really quite *believe* it. Yet here you are."

Adam acted as if he didn't know what to reply. She added, rather tartly, "And you lay claim to half of what I *liked* to think of as my ranch."

He looped his thumbs in his belt and shrugged. Whatever he was, he wasn't glib, Carolyn thought, which was a point in his favor.

She studied his profile and again was struck by the family resemblance. She said, "I'd also thought of Enoch changing his mind about the land. There was always the possibility it wouldn't come to me. After all, he didn't like me much, did he?"

Adam stopped and faced her. "He said your mother turned you and your sister against your father."

Carolyn raised her chin, trying not to let it tremble. "That's not right. Pauline never turned against him. She was wrapped up in her own family, that's all, she had three small children. It broke Pauline's heart, his leaving."

"But not yours?"

"No. Not at first. At first, I was just glad that the fighting and sniping and quibbling had stopped. Deep down, I thought he'd come back. He always had before. But this time, he didn't. My mother thought to her dying day he'd come back to her. Only Pauline knew that he wouldn't. She knew him best."

"Enoch told me that Pauline was dead. I was sorry to hear it."

"She died too young. She didn't live to see her children's weddings. Or any of her grandchildren. I looked at little Carrie in Denver and thought how lucky I am. How very lucky."

He swallowed and said, "I need to explain something. When I came to Texas, I had a chip on my shoulder. I thought you'd resent me and fight me, and I was ready to square off against you. But then, my mind got changed."

She'd guessed as much. "Mickey changed it?"

She looked ahead at the empty beach before them, like a blank page waiting to be written. The sea mumbled and whispered, regular as a great heartbeat.

"Yes. Mickey. She made me see you as a person, not a— a—"

"An obstacle? An opponent? A contentious rich woman who'd fight tooth and nail over money?"

"Well," he admitted, "yes. She's like your champion."

"She's like a lot of things. Like a daughter—she filled a huge void when Beverly got married and went away. And like a sister. I'd lost mine. Mickey helped fill some of that emptiness, too. She's my friend, as well, a good friend."

"She stood up for you."

"She's a stand-up gal." She smiled at him. "She defended you, too, you know."

He frowned in surprise. "She did?"

"Oh, she was careful about it." Carolyn tilted her head and nodded. "Scrupulous. She didn't entreat me on your behalf or anything like that. I had to drag an opinion out of her. But her opinion of you is higher than she'll admit. That's one reason I'm here. To see what she liked in you."

She could swear that under his tan he blushed. He took a deep breath. "I'm grateful to her for that."

"You should be grateful to her for a lot. She took it upon herself to check up on you. She found out you seemed honest. Of course, she would have found out if you were dishonest, too."

He gave half a smile. "She's quite a woman."

Carolyn changed the subject. "Now, when do I see these precious horses of yours? Do they ever come here, down to the sea?"

"Not often. They like to stay in the forest. We don't always know where they are. We take turns, week by week, keeping track of them. This week one band's at the edge of the woods. They're near the orange groves of the old Penndennis farm. I'll take you there tomorrow morning."

"Good. And this evening?"

This question seemed to stymie him. Clearly he wasn't used to entertaining people. "I—I thought I'd just let you alone to enjoy the house and the beach."

"Why waste the evening? Let's get to know each other better. What's the best restaurant in town?"

For a second he looked as if he wanted to grin, but then his face went serious. "The Mango Tree. Carolyn?"

It still sounded strange, hearing a voice so like her father's say her name. "Yes?"

"You accept it? That I'm your half brother?"

She sighed, suddenly weary, but held his gaze. "I'd be a fool to deny it, I'm afraid."

Then she looked out at the sea and tears rose in her eyes. "I told you the truth. I always thought that someone like you might come along. My father had a way with women. I knew that this was possible. I knew it was even—probable."

He stepped closer to her, as if he might touch her to express his sympathy, his concern. But something in her didn't want that yet. She had made a long, long journey today, both in distance and emotion. She realized she didn't have the strength to go farther.

She blinked back her tears and straightened her back. "Let's go back to the house," she said.

"Sure," he said, as if he understood, as if he, too, was making the same journey.

ADAM HAD BEEN drunk only twice in his life and had sworn not to do it a third time. But tonight, sitting in the restaurant, he felt half-intoxicated. Mickey made his head spin one way, Carolyn another.

Mickey somehow looked more beautiful still. The yellow sundress became her, and it showed more of her body than he'd ever before seen. She had lovely shoulders and smooth, firm arms, toned but still feminine.

The dress was not cut daringly low, but when she moved a certain way, he could glimpse the beginning of the velvety cleft between her breasts. He kept hoping she'd move that way again and again.

Her dark hair fell in a rich tumble to her shoulders, and he remembered how it felt when he laced his fingers through it. Secretly he studied the gentle curves of her lips and remembered how they tasted, how soft they were beneath his own, and how they could be both shy and eager.

She made him ache with desire, yet he could not let these feelings show. He wasn't sure how she felt about him, and the day had been complicated enough. Besides, he was also growing besotted with Carolyn.

I have a sister, he thought. She was funny and ballsy and said what she thought. She asked bold questions, lots of them.

"So your mother told our father to hit the road and not come back?"

He nodded, embarrassed because he didn't like to talk about himself this way. "Yes. She was a strong-minded lady."

"So was my mother," Carolyn mused. "How odd. Daddy's weakness was strong women. And your mother never told him she was pregnant?"

"No. She was too mad at him."

Carolyn hooted. "Amazing. My mother sent him packing once, and he stayed away four months. When he came back, she was five months pregnant with me. He was *shocked.*"

They all laughed, and Adam thought, *That's pretty amazing. Our father gave us things in common, all right.*

"Tell him about Pauline," coaxed Mickey. Did Adam imagine it, or was she truly caught up in this exchange? She seemed fascinated.

Carolyn smiled ruefully. "Pauline was the sweet one. I was the one full of piss and vinegar. I was headstrong, like Mother. Pauline was a throwback to our Aunt Elena. Elena was a gentle soul and softhearted."

She smiled in remembrance. "But Pauline was an excellent rider. She got that from Daddy. She got his blue eyes and his singing voice. And she got his double-jointed thumb. I did, too. See?"

Carolyn held up her hand and wriggled her thumb in and out of a position that made it look broken.

"Ewww," said Vern. "I get queasy when you do that."

But Adam grinned, feeling drunker than before. "I got it, too." He held up his own hand and made the same motion. They began to do it in synchronization.

"Oh, Lord," Vern moaned. "Two of you."

"Beverly has it, too," Carolyn said. "Maybe Carrie will be the same. Wouldn't that be something? Four generations of freaky thumb tricks."

Mickey laughed, which filled Adam with a sensation of dizzy happiness. She said, "Tell him about Pauline's children."

Carolyn rattled on affectionately about her sister's children. "I was so happy when Tyler decided to come back to Texas. His roots are in the Hill Country. There are some people who just belong to a certain place. It's imprinted on their souls."

I know, he thought. *I'm one of those people.*

He looked at Mickey wondering what was imprinted on her soul.

She didn't meet his eyes.

THE NEXT MORNING, Mickey awakened to the sound of the sea. What a wonderful sound it was, she thought, great and primal like the heartbeat of the planet.

She left the bed and went to the window, throwing back the curtains. The sunlight flowed in, drenching her in its warm, gold light. She could just see the water, an even more vivid blue in the newness of morning.

She wanted to throw on her clothes and run down to the beach, to walk at its foaming edge and, for the first time in her life touch and be touched by the sea.

She glanced at her watch. It was not quite 7:00 a.m. Adam wouldn't come to guide them to the horses until nine. She had enough time for a short exploratory walk.

The house was so quiet that she knew she must be the first one up. Quickly she slipped out of her nightgown and donned dark blue shorts and a white camisole and oversize white shirt.

She gathered her hair, curlier than ever in the sea air, into a simple ponytail and tied it with a white scarf. She didn't bother with makeup. She scribbled a note to Vern and Carolyn, left it on the kitchen counter and set off down the path that curled toward the shore.

She felt a surge of freedom and exhilaration. The air was fresh at the Circle T, but it wasn't as zingy and cleansing as this air. The sky was wide in Claro County, but not as wide as here. And even the vastness of Texas was dwarfed by the immensity of the sea.

The closer the path wound to the water, the more squat and wizened the trees became. But she admired the strength and vigor it took to take root in this increasingly barren ground. Even the gulls' harsh cries were exotic to Mickey's ears.

She was glorying in all this newness and almost ready to throw out her arms in celebration at beholding such a fresh world and having it all to herself.

And she was glorying in her solitude. Then she rounded a curve and almost ran smack into Carolyn. "Oh!" she cried, startled.

Carolyn grinned. The breeze had tossed her hair and pinkened her cheeks. She said, "I saw you starting down the path."

"I didn't see you. You took me by surprise."

"I was in a little cove down that way—" she pointed to the north "—with Adam."

Mickey felt her own cheeks grow pink. "Adam? How'd that happen?"

"We agreed to meet and watch the sun come up. Last night at the restaurant. You'd gone to powder your nose, as we used to say when dinosaurs roamed the earth. I wanted to talk to him in private some more."

"Oh. Of course."

"He rode his motorcycle, parked near the house and was waiting for me when I stepped out the back door." Carolyn leaned toward her, scrutinizing her. "Why do you look guilty? Do you *feel* guilty about something?"

"No," lied Mickey. "Not at all. It's just that if he's down there, maybe I should go back with you."

"Nonsense," Carolyn said with a laugh. "He's waiting for you."

"Why? How could he know I was coming?"

Carolyn reached out and adjusted Mickey's collar. "He said, 'I bet she'll be here. She seems the kind of woman who'd go for a walk on the beach in the early morning.' And I said, 'You've got that right, kiddo. That's my Mick.' Go on. I'll have coffee waiting for you both when you get back."

She patted Mickey's shoulder and went on her way up the rise. Mickey's heart felt like a pendulum swinging in her chest. *Should I go to him? Yes. No. Yes. No. Yes. No.*

She wasn't prepared to meet him. Should she turn around and catch up with Carolyn? *Yes. No. Yes. No. Yes. No.*

Her heart would knock too hard. She'd let her eyes linger on him too long. She'd be tongue-tied and awkward and uncertain with him. But the chance to see him—just for a little while—alone?

Yes. Yes. Yes.

HE WATCHED HER stroll toward him with her usual perfect confidence. His pulse quickened and his breath locked in his lungs.

She had that efficient, cool aura about her that had so put him off the first time they'd met. For God's sake, how could she be so aloof and businesslike on a *beach?* The answer was she couldn't. It was a pose, her defense mechanism. She probably felt as uncertain as he did.

He stuck his thumbs in his back pockets and started walking to meet her. He tried to affect a certain air, casual but jaunty. He would probably trip over a hermit crab and fall on his face.

But the closer he got to her, the better he felt. She looked perfect against this beautiful backdrop. She looked as if she belonged here, even if she didn't know it yet.

He took in her autumnal hair, already coming undone and waving in the high breeze. He'd never seen her bare legs before. They were long and shapely, the ankles trim.

The wind pasted her white shirt against her body so that her small breasts stood out with sculpted clarity. She carried her sandals dangling from the fingers of her left hand. She and he came face-to-face beside an outcropping of weathered coral.

"Hello," he said. "I thought you might come along."

"I didn't know you were here—until I met Caro on the path. I was going to explore."

"Ah," he said, "you'll need a lifetime for that."

She looked at him questioningly.

"It changes all the time. Never exactly the same beach twice. Each tide takes thing away. And brings new ones in."

"Is the tide coming in or going out?"

God, he could get lost and stay lost in those gold-flecked brown eyes of hers. "It's low tide. It'll turn soon and come back in. Can I explore with you?"

She nodded and began walking toward a large formation of dark rock. It jutted out into the sea, forming a kind of barrier between this stretch of beach and the next.

He fell into step beside her. Like her, he was barefoot. He wore cutoffs and his Henry David Thoreau T-shirt. He'd donned Henry because he was going to be with ladies today. He usually went shirtless.

He said, "I owe you thanks. Great thanks."

"Me? Why?"

"For speaking to Carolyn on my behalf."

Mickey kept her eyes straight ahead, watching the waves break against the rocks. "I hardly said anything. When she asked questions, I answered, that's all."

"You also checked me out. Thoroughly. Even the DNA."

"I did what I thought I should do. Oop—"

A gust of wind loosened the white scarf around her hair, plucking it away like a conjuror. Adam sprinted, leaped and caught it before it was blown out to sea. He offered it to her. "Better put it in your pocket. It'll never stay on. Wind's brisk today."

She shook her head. "I don't have any pockets."

"I'll keep it for you then." He folded the silk into a small square and slipped it into his hip pocket.

She gave a rueful laugh. "I look like Medusa."

He watched her long hair stream and dance. "No," he said. "You look like a mermaid." He imagined her with a bra made of two starfishes and smiled to himself.

She sighed, ran her hand through her hair to smooth it, then gave up.

He said, "You made this meeting possible between Caro-

lyn and me. She wouldn't have come if you hadn't done all
that research. You didn't lose time. You went digging straight
after the facts."

"She had to know them. The sooner I got them, the better
for her."

He studied her clean-cut profile and her locks streaming
out behind her. She would have made a lovely figurehead for
a sailing ship.

He said, "You proved that I was telling the truth."

"I might just as well have found out you were lying. I
wanted her to know the truth, no matter what it was. Not to
spend time agonizing over it."

"Did you think I was lying?" he asked, still studying her.

"I was doing my job, that's all. What I thought doesn't
matter."

"It matters to me."

She stopped and faced him. "I didn't know what the detective would find. I didn't know what the DNA would prove.
I had to be prepared for anything. You might have been an es-
caped ax murderer from Cleveland for all I knew."

He smiled. "Are you disappointed I'm so dull?"

She glanced away and started walking again. "You're
hardly dull. Have you and Caro talked about the lease land?"

"Ah, Mick, that's you. Sticking to business. No, we
haven't. She wants to wait until she's seen the horses. But I
think we can—negotiate. And make it friendly. I hope so.
She's quite a woman."

"Yes. She is. And no matter how friendly negotiations
are, buying the land is going to be a big financial setback
for her."

He shoved his hands into his pockets. "Yeah. That's the
bad part."

They had almost reached the rock formation. She tried to
push her hair from her eyes and said, "Give me back my

scarf, please. My hair is blinding me. The prettiest beach in the world, and I keep getting swatted in the eyes so I can't see anything."

He said, "Sit down and I'll braid it for you."

"What?"

They were on the leeward side of the formation, so he led her to a niche well protected from the wind. "Sit," he said, gesturing toward a flat slab of rock. "I'll braid it."

She looked at him in disbelief. "What do you know about braiding hair?"

"Nothing about ladies' hair. But I've done plenty of horse's manes and tails in my time. Come on, sit. I'll do your mane."

She laughed but sat. He sat behind her and began to comb his fingers through her tangled curls. They were silky and thick, and they shone brown-gold in the sunlight.

She kept her back as straight as a little girl behaving very well in school. He divided her hair into three equal strands and began to plait it. He saw her velvety-looking nape and couldn't help that he touched it as he worked. He fought the desire to lean forward and kiss it.

"You know one reason to braid a horse's mane?" he asked.

"It helps train the mane to lie on the right side of its neck," she answered primly.

"It also shows off a pretty neck to advantage."

She did have a pretty neck, and again he was tempted to nuzzle it, right behind her ear. But his words must have made her self-conscious, for she sat up straighter.

"Do you really think this is the prettiest beach in the world?" he asked.

"Yes. But it's also the first one I've seen. And the first time I've been this close to the sea. Is the water always this blue?"

"Mostly. It used to be even clearer. But the hotels and cruise ships are taking their toll. This is still a fine stretch of beach, though." He'd almost finished the plait. "Okay, this is crude," he warned her. "I'll tie your scarf around the end so it'll hold till we get back to the path."

"You said it couldn't hold in the wind."

"Not if you tied it. I can do it."

She turned, glancing at him almost teasingly. "What makes you so good?"

He drew the scarf from his pocket. "Because I'm a sailor, me feisty wench. Knots is me business."

He wove one end of the scarf into the braid so it would be more secure, then bound the plait with the rest of the scarf in a modified clove hitch. He gave her braid a playful tug. "Now you can see the beach to your heart's content."

She stared out to sea. "That might also take a lifetime." She said it almost sadly.

He edged nearer to her, wanting to put his hands on her. "You can always come back here again. Will you?"

"That depends on how things work out between you and Caro," she said in the same tone. "The hard part's not over yet."

The money, he thought. *It always came down to the damn money.*

She was right. He had no right to caress her again until he truly had settled things with Carolyn. Gruffly he said, "Come on. We'll find you some seashells."

And although he ached to, he didn't touch her again.

VERN INSISTED that Carolyn sit in the front of the Range Rover with Adam. He and Mickey sat in back.

She'd brushed out her hair and rebraided it in case the ride would be windy, and dressed in another sundress, a bright pink one. Carolyn looked stylish in a pale yellow pantsuit with a matching visor, white sandals and shoulder bag.

They went down the long brownish gray rutted side road to the highway again, and all the way to the Penndennis family farm, Carolyn peppered Adam with questions about the horses. And all the way, Mickey wondered when Carolyn would broach the subject of the land.

Although Caro seemed to feel genuine friendliness toward Adam, both she and Vern had been closemouthed about what they were actually going to *do* about the land.

The gate to the farm was open, and Mickey saw the orderly lines of citrus trees, more richly green than the grass. There were a few men tinkering with a tractor by a barn. Adam stopped and asked if they'd seen the horses today, and one said yes, down the road about a kilometer, grazing near the south orange orchard.

"Was that part of the Penndennis family?" Carolyn asked, after they drove on.

"No. They're workers. Jake Penndennis, Albert's brother, runs this outfit. He's in the Bahamas on business right now."

Vern was squinting at the trees, as if trying to figure out if they grew lemons or limes or oranges or grapefruits or kumquats. "A kumquat's a citrus isn't it?" he mused, almost to himself. "But what do you do with them, anyway?"

It was at that moment that Mickey glimpsed a horse in the distance, a white shape that appeared for a moment, then slipped away like a ghost and disappeared into the grove. "Ohh," she breathed.

Adam slowed. "They're up ahead. Did you see them?"

But Mickey was the only one who had. Carolyn had been fiddling with her sunglasses, and Vern had been pondering kumquats.

"I saw a white one," Mickey said. "It went west."

"Right," Adam said. "That's Camila. She's one of the younger mares, and the only white in the herd."

Mickey's heart thumped, and she shaded her eyes with her hand, hoping to catch another glimpse. The horse *had* been ghostly, a creature that had come from another century, a living symbol of men long dead and quests long over.

"I didn't see it," Carolyn said, disappointment in her voice.

But then another horse moved ahead among the trees, perceptible for only a moment, a flash of white mixed with brown. Then it, too, vanished, simply faded away.

Adam stopped the Range Rover. "I'll stop here. We can walk the rest of the way."

"Won't we scare them off?" Carolyn asked.

"Not as long as you're with me. They'll let you get within a range of about twelve feet."

He got out of the Range Rover quietly, and so did the others. Mickey was first, and she moved just behind Adam on his left side. Carolyn, holding Vern's hand, stepped to Adam's right.

Mickey knew instinctively to be quiet, and so did Carolyn and Vern. Adam walked a few feet in front of them, his hair tossing in the breeze. He moved quietly, but confidently, and Mickey felt as if he were guiding them into a different reality.

When he reached the spot where she'd seen the first horse, he stopped, looked among the trees and saw something she could not. But he smiled, and gestured for them to follow. He led them through the first line of trees to a wide marge of grass, then through a second line and a second marge.

He pointed. "There. The wild horses of Los Eremitas."

They were beautiful horses, well formed and glossy-coated, with long, lush manes and tails. Mickey suppressed a gasp. They were like creatures of myth to her.

There were eight of them Two foals lay on the ground, a third foal and five adults stood. All eight horses stared at the humans. Their ears twitched forward, and their tails swished slowly. But none moved away.

"My God," Carolyn whispered. She touched Adam's sleeve. "I think you're right. The very picture of a Spanish Barbary. The horse that changed the world. The ancestor of the American mustang."

Mickey and Carolyn had both pored over reference books

and searched the Internet. Spanish Barbs were one of the oldest pure-blooded breeds in the world. Only the Arabians rivaled them.

Yet domestically the breed had been close to endangered for almost a century, crossbred nearly out of existence. In the wild, only a few small herds survived with their blood undiluted.

Carolyn said, "These are the same as the horses of the Spanish Golden Age. They made the conquest of the New World possible."

"Look at that one," Vern said with a smile. "He looks just like that horse in *Hidalgo*."

"He should," Adam said. "They're kin."

Mickey studied them. They were deep-chested with sturdy legs, built for speed and endurance. They had a distinctive Roman curve to their noses. They were smaller than Arabians, about fifteen hands high, but their relationship to Arabs showed in their manes and tails, their fine hooves and small muzzles.

Many Barbarys were solid colored, but this band had four pintos of brown and white, the milk-colored mare, a bay mare and a bay stallion with a star on his forehead.

"Adam," Carolyn said, "if these are true Barbarys and go back to the conquest, they're a genetic treasure-house."

He nodded. He knew. He stared at the horses, his face full of emotion.

He gestured for the others to stay back. Then he walked slowly into the midst of the horses. The bay stallion rolled his eyes and shifted his front feet. He tossed his head, but held his ground.

Adam held out his hand, and the stallion sniffed it, then nudged it with his nose. Adam stepped closer, and placed his hand on the horse's neck. He began to stroke it. The stallion nickered softly, then began to graze again.

Mickey watched as he moved among the mares. All tolerated his presence and his touch. He was talking softly to them. She couldn't understand what he was saying, but the horses seemed to.

"Can I take pictures?" Carolyn asked, a quaver in her voice.

"Go ahead," Adam said, scratching a pinto colt behind the ears.

"I thought there were eighteen of them," Vern said.

"They break into bands. Because of the stallions." He nodded at the bay. "This is Goya. He's the dominant stallion. They can do each other damage. If we had a preserve, we could try to prevent it."

"What's wrong with this place?" Vern asked, sounding truly puzzled. "The Penndennis family tolerates them, right? They don't do damage to the trees, do they? They seem comfortable here."

"They're too comfortable. Years ago this was a cattle ranch. The ground was improved, grasses sown. There's too much to eat here. They can founder, go lame, even lose a hoof."

Carolyn nodded and Mickey winced. She'd seen the pain of a horse with founder, barely able to stand.

"These guys," said Adam, "have evolved to live in the forest where forage is rough. Their digestive systems can't take too much richness. They need to be in the woods. With electric fence to keep them in. And the dogs out."

Suddenly the stallion sensed something and turned. He neighed and began to trot off. The other horses followed, the foals following the mares.

"I guess the visit's over," Adam said, affectionately slapping the smallest foal on the withers as it passed him. Once again the horses disappeared into the trees with eerie swiftness.

Mickey, who'd been enchanted by them, wanted to cry, "Don't go! Don't go!"

"Let's go back to the house," Carolyn said. "Let's have some coffee. We'll talk there."

Adam eyed her warily, and Mickey saw that he knew Carolyn held his—and the horses'—fates in her hands.

BACK AT THE YELLOW HOUSE, Carolyn brewed another pot of coffee. Mickey tried to help, but Carolyn shooed her away with something close to impatience. "Just let me be alone a minute," she said, not meeting Mickey's eyes. "Go sit on the deck with the men."

When the coffee was ready, Carolyn brought mugs, spoons, sugar and creamer on a painted tray. She put it down on the low table and took one of the wicker chairs. One by one, she filled the cups, and Mickey thought she perceived the slightest tremor in Carolyn's hand.

Mickey stole a look at Adam. His face was tense. He didn't reach for a mug. He sat stiffly in the chair, waiting.

Vern looked uncomfortable, and a sudden wave of foreboding swept Mickey.

Carolyn stared at Adam. Her expression was guardedly sympathetic, but there was conflict in it as well. She was obviously going to say something that pained her.

She took a sip of coffee, as if to fortify herself.

Then she placed her cup on the arm of her chair and looked at Adam, her jaw set. "Vern and I have talked. We've talked a great deal. We think at this stage in our lives, it's impossible for us to buy Enoch's land. And so—we won't."

CHAPTER SIXTEEN

MICKEY'S HEART PLUMMETED. The blue day seemed to dissolve into a meaningless gray haze. Adam's face went blank with shock.

Vern watched Carolyn in concern for her. She looked close to tears. She leaned forward and rested her hand on Adam's knee.

She said, "We could mortgage everything and buy Enoch's land. We talked about it a good deal in Denver. We talked about—other things, as well. Downsizing the ranch. Even retirement."

No! Mickey thought. *Downsize the Circle T? Carolyn and Vern retire this early? Impossible!*

"We were in a quandary when J.T. flew us home. He's family, and we told him about the—problem—with the lease land. He said he had an idea, and he'd work on it."

She patted Adam's knee reassuringly. "I won't buy the lease land. But Tyler will. He can. He's just sold the winery in California. He's got the money. And I'll keep leasing the land from him."

Mickey's mouth fell open in amazement. "Tyler?"

Vern nodded. Carolyn leaned forward, staring into Adam's eyes. "Tyler McKinney. Your nephew. Pauline's oldest boy. Selling the winery gave him a big capital gain. He's going to pay off his debts on the Texas winery, but the rest he needs to invest—for tax purposes. He's interested in buying the land that—that's yours now."

"But why does he want it?" Mickey burst out. "Tyler's not

a rancher. He's a vintner. He has enough land over by the Double C."

Mickey shouldn't have asked, it wasn't her business, and her cheeks flamed in embarrassment. But Carolyn gave her a look of wry affection.

"Sweetie, a true Texan *always* wants more land. This is Claro County land we're talking. And Tyler's a McKinney. He wants to keep it in the family. Someday maybe he'll expand the winery into a park and vacation spot. And you know, I think he can do it. Cal's not the only ambitious one in the family. I think Tyler can be every bit as successful."

Carolyn reached into her blouse pocket and pulled out a small envelope. She offered it to Adam. "This is it," she said. "Tyler's offer. He said he thinks it's fair. See what you think."

Confounded, Mickey stared as if she were watching a play, not reality. Adam, too, looked uncomprehending. He opened the envelope and for once his sure hands didn't look so steady.

He drew out a slip of paper and gazed at it in disbelief. He looked at Carolyn. "Eight million dollars?"

"Yes," Carolyn said, drawing back and taking her hand from his knee. "It *is* a fair offer. Vern used to be in real estate. You could ask more, but you might not get it. Do it between yourselves and avoid Realtor fees. It's a good deal, Adam. Truly."

Adam held her gaze. "And he'll lease it to you? Like Enoch did?"

"Yes," Carolyn answered. "My situation stays exactly the same. I don't go into debt. You get your money. Tyler finally gets a large piece of the Hill Country. He's doing me a great, great favor. And he says it will give him pleasure to do it."

"I—I don't know what to say," Adam stammered.

"Don't say anything. Think it over. In the meantime, this

has worn me out. Tyler told me to get acquainted with you, to see the horses. I was to give you the offer if you seemed a decent sort. Vern and I think you are."

Vern, his jaw squared, nodded. "Mick checked you out mighty thoroughly, young man. She could work for the FBI."

Adam shot her a shy smile of thanks. Carolyn said, "Mull it over, Adam. If you have any questions about Tyler, ask Mickey. Vern, get your swimming trunks. I want to go down the beach and see it that water feels as good as it looks. Then I want to lie in the sun and think about nothing at all."

She finished her coffee and stood, and Mickey realized that Carolyn truly was emotionally exhausted. Vern got to his feet and took her arm. "Come on, honey. Let's change clothes."

Carolyn nodded and swallowed hard. "I have a strange feeling. Like I'm seeing the end of one thing. And the beginning of another. Maybe Tyler will own the whole Circle T someday. That would be good. I could live with that."

She paused. "My mother made that ranch her whole life. But her family was all around her. Mine's not. I want to spend lots of time in Denver. I want to enjoy my grandbaby. It's time I slowed down a bit."

Again she looked near tears, and Vern led her back into the house and down the hall to the bedroom.

Mickey and Adam were alone on the deck. He seemed too stunned to speak. He kept staring at the slip of paper that bore Tyler McKinney's offer.

Mickey got up and stood by one of the deck's large screened windows. She was still standing there, her back to Adam, when she saw Carolyn and Vern start down the path toward the sea. Mickey's throat tightened with emotion.

She understood what Carolyn meant by "the end of one thing, the beginning of another." Caro, a grandmother now, had moved into the elder generation. She foresaw the day when she would have to leave the ranch to someone. That someone would be Beverly.

But Beverly would never come back to Texas to live, she would probably sell the ranch, and if Tyler wanted it, she would sell it to him, with sadness at giving it up, but relief that it stayed in the family.

Mickey watched as Vern paused on the path and took Carolyn in his arms. She wound her arms around his neck and laid her face against his chest, as if she needed to draw strength from him.

Mickey's eyes grew misty. But Carolyn, being Carolyn, clung to him for only a moment or so. Then she drew back, patted his cheek, took his hand, and together they walked around a bend in the path and out of sight.

ADAM SAID he would take the offer. Carolyn phoned Tyler. Adam phoned Elsie and Albert Penndennis, who invited them to supper to celebrate.

Mickey didn't really want to go; her mind was too filled with the startling thoughts of Carolyn slowing down and the Circle T being owned by someone else someday. But Caro, with surprising firmness, said Mickey should meet the Penndennis couple.

So Mickey went and was glad. Once she met the pair, she found them irresistible.

Albert Penndennis was a large, jolly man with such a friendly, generous air, that Carolyn was smiling at him almost immediately.

His wife, Elsie O'Neil Penndennis, had also been born and raised on Los Emeritas. She was petite, quick-moving, and elegant, with upswept snow-white hair. She had been a kindergarten teacher.

They ushered Mickey and the Trents into their home and

took them to their screened-in porch. It was large and lovely, overlooking a perfect view of the sea.

After a round of drinks, Elsie Penndennis set out a supper of coconut-mango shrimp with fruit chutney, crab claws in mustard sauce, fresh green salad and seafood-and-pasta primavera. To please anyone who might not like fish, she also had a platter of jerked chicken with fried plantains.

Carolyn was her usual, genial self once more, and Vern seemed relaxed again, although he watched Carolyn through the evening, as if reassuring himself she was truly as satisfied with events as she seemed.

Still, the party broke up early, with Carolyn pleading fatigue.

Carolyn insisted on sitting in the back seat of the Range Rover so she could lean her head on Vern's shoulder. "I can't stop yawning," she apologized. "You've got to admit, it hasn't been an average day."

But when Adam drew up to the yellow house, she said, "You know, it's still early. You two are lots younger than Vern and I. Why should you call it quits so soon? Adam, you could show Mickey the nightlife in town. She's been hanging around us old folks all day."

Mickey stiffened in surprise, but her blood sped. All evening she'd yearned to be alone with Adam. So when he asked her, rather shyly, if she'd like to go, she answered, rather shyly, that she would. As they drove back to the highway, she searched for something friendly and neutral to say.

"Albert and Elsie Penndennis are wonderful," she said. "Truly lovely people. They impressed Carolyn—and Vern."

"Carolyn and Vern impressed them. So did you."

"How do you know?"

"Because Elsie's face is like glass. She can never hide what she's thinking. It shows right through. Besides, she told me so when I was helping take the dishes back to the kitchen."

"Well, she clearly thinks the world of you. And he does, too."

"They're the best friends I've got. I couldn't have accomplished anything without their help. Elsie's great at organizing. I had the idea for the fund but I didn't know how to—how to—"

He couldn't find the word so Mickey supplied it. "Implement it?"

"Right. So we did the homework together. Contacting the right foundation to register, filling out forms and agreements, filing papers—getting the seed money. We needed five thousand to start."

Mickey blinked in surprise. "Five thousand? That's a lot of money."

"I had three and a half in savings. Albert and Elsie put in the rest. There was a lot of red tape. Not my style, but we had to do it right."

Mickey stared at his darkened profile. "You really love those horses, don't you?"

"Yes. I do."

"What would you have done if Tyler hadn't shown up? And Carolyn decided she wouldn't buy the land?"

"I don't know. Whatever I had to, I guess."

Mickey said, "I think it's wonderful that it was Tyler who came to the rescue. For the last ten years, he's been the one who's had to ask for favors. When anyone was in a jam, it was his younger brother, Cal, they turned to. Tyler's luck has never been as good as Cal's. He's needed Cal's help more than once, and that's been hard on his pride. Now he can be the one lending the helping hand."

Adam sighed. "First I inherit money from an uncle I just found out I had. Now I sell it to a nephew I've never met. I've got two nephews and two nieces, and *they've* got kids. That makes me a great-uncle, and that makes me feel I should be about a hundred years old."

She laughed.

He said, "Old Uncle Adam. But when you laugh, you make me feel young again."

He reached over and took her hand. He didn't say anything else. He didn't have to.

St. Joseph was more of a village than town, but its bars and restaurants were still lively. Adam parked, and when they were on the sidewalk, he took her hand again.

The little shops, though closed, still had their display windows lit, showing their wares. Live music with a Caribbean beat drifted from one of the bars, and there was chattering and laughter in the air.

People crowded the small supermarket that was still open. On its cement porch stood bins of fruits that gleamed with color: oranges, lemons, limes, bananas and mangoes.

People hailed Adam, grinned at him, and clapped him on the shoulder. They looked at Mickey with frank curiosity. Adam smiled and nodded back, but didn't stop. He pointed out the sights to her and told her local legends.

They strolled slowly, and the buildings grew fewer, the crowd thinned out, and Mickey could hear the lap and splash of the sea. They'd reached the marina, the farthest building, and its bar was starting to close down.

"Well, that was the north side of the main street," he smiled. "Now I'll show you the south side. Or you could see my boat. If you'd like to."

She hesitated. She could feel the attraction between them starting to sizzle dangerously. "I could look at her. But then go home. They'll be expecting me."

"Come on. I'll walk you to the harbor."

His hand tightened around hers. "I should've stopped and introduced you to people, I guess. I know they're curious about you. It's just—"

He didn't finish and she looked at him quizzically. "It's just what?"

"I didn't want to share you tonight. I wanted to talk to you alone."

He gave her a sideways glance. "Things might not have turned out this way, except for you. I appreciate that. I appreciate you."

"I tried to do my job, that's all. I'm glad it worked out."

The awning over the end of the dock was hung with colored paper lanterns, casting jeweled light on the boards. A group of boats bobbed along a pier that stretched far into the darkness. Most were yachts, some with sails, some not.

"You were right about Carolyn," he said. "I like her. She *seems* like kin. I've got a sister. It's a funny feeling."

Mickey looked at the moonlight dancing on the wavelets in the harbor.

"It's odd seeing you together. You're alike in many ways."

"Yes. We are. It feels…" He seemed to search for the right word and settled for "nice. It feels nice."

Mickey said, "I think it does for her, too. Her sister's been gone for almost seventeen years. She's missed her terribly."

He stopped and turned to her. The moonlight streaked his hair with platinum. He pointed to a sailboat rising and falling in its slip. "That's it. My boat."

Mickey smiled with pleasure. She knew little about boats, but this one was sleekly trim. Its sails were furled, and its polished wood gleamed.

"She's lovely," she breathed.

"Want to come aboard?"

She should have refused, but she had never before been on a seagoing boat before. "Just for a minute."

He helped her onto the deck, and she looked up with wonder at the complexity of the cordage running between deck and mast. "It's like a big spiderweb. And the stars are like decorations caught in it. How do you keep track of what's what?"

"You just learn. The standing rigging and shrouds and stays keep the mast upright. The halyards hoist the sail and running rigging. I could have you sailing her in two weeks."

"Me?" She shook her head in disbelief. "I'm a landlubber."

"You'd love it. It's kind of like a horse. It's a live thing. You learn its ways, its rhythms, how to give it its head and how to hold it in."

She looked about the deck. There seemed little space, with all the ropes and rails and things for which she had no names. "And you live here? All the time?"

"Just about. When the weather's good, I sleep on deck. But I've got a bunk and galley and a head—a bathroom to you. Come on. I'll show you."

He took her by the hand and led her inside, switching on a small sconce light. The living space was so compact that it seemed almost like a playhouse to Mickey. But it was so cleverly constructed, without an inch wasted, that she was enchanted. It was paneled in teak, and had a built-in leather settee and a table of matching teak.

He pointed to different doors. "Galley. Head. Aft cabin. That's where I bunk. This is the forward bunk. He led her toward it and opened the door, switching on another sconce light. "This is where Enoch stayed when he came to see me. But I hardly ever have company. I use it for kind of an office."

The compartment was even tinier than the aft cabin. It held a narrow bunk, as well as a small built-in desk with overhanging glassed-in shelves crammed with books. An enlarged photograph of two horses, framed, hung on the wall.

"Wild horses?" she asked.

He nodded and pointed to the larger horse. "That's Goya. And Dulcinea, his favorite mare. She was the first to let me touch her."

He pulled out a file drawer in the desk. It was packed with folders. "These are the records I've compiled on the horses.

Lineage, health notes, movements, field notes—it's a mess. I need to learn to file...."

He closed it and pointed to the other file drawer. "That's mostly financial. What we have, what we need, estimates—"

The boat, which had been dancing gently with the rhythm of the waves, suddenly swayed, almost lurched, and she struggled to keep her footing.

He seized her by the shoulders to steady her. Outside, she heard the roar of a motor and the churning of water, and the floor rocked beneath her.

"Somebody's out there speeding," Adam said, "and he's going to be in big trouble...."

His voice trailed away. Mickey was no longer conscious of outside sounds. She was barely conscious of the boat's rolling motion. The room suddenly seemed even smaller than it was.

She was aware of his callused hands against her bare arms, of how close they stood, braced not so much for balance but as if ready for something inevitable to happen. He leaned nearer. "All day I've thought of doing this."

Perhaps she should have drawn away, but she could not. He lowered his mouth to hers, his hands moving up to frame her face. Desire rose up within her like a great, sweeping surge. She pressed herself closer to him, and her lips parted beneath his.

His kiss had a desperation in it, and so did hers. Emotions too long held in check broke free, and when he wrapped his arms around her, she gasped in pleasure. Her breasts, nipples throbbing, pressed against the hardness of his chest.

His tongue teased hers in growing intimacy. She traced hers across his upper and lower lips, then tasted him more boldly, more completely. Her daring fueled his, and he kissed her more hungrily still. Mickey, dazed with yearning, thought,

I've wanted you so much. And for so long. Don't stop. Please don't stop.

He lowered his face, pressing his mouth against the hollow of her throat, and she threw her head back in reckless craving, winding her fingers in his hair. His lips moved farther down still, as his hands cupped her breasts, fondling and caressing, his thumbs stroking the tips until they ached for more.

Then he opened the buttons of her sundress so that he could part the halves of the bodice, and her bosom was half-bared to him, swelling up from her bra.

He drew back and stared down at her. He whispered, "You're beautiful. Beautiful."

He slid the straps of the sundress down, so that it fell to her waist. Gently he pushed her bra out of the way and bent to kiss and suckle her.

Mickey, who had spent so much of her life controlling her emotions, was on the edge of losing control.

It felt wonderful.

ADAM HADN'T meant for this to happen. He had thought of it, of course; he had hoped for it, but he hadn't planned it.

Now that desire was set in motion, he couldn't stop himself, and neither, it seemed, could Mickey. She, who had once seemed so cool, was heated and passionate. Had she fantasized about this as much as he had?

He unbuttoned his shirt to the waist and flung it away, so he could feel his naked flesh against hers, completely savor the softness of her femininity. Her hands traveled over the nakedness of his shoulders and chest, making him crazier still.

"How do I get the rest of this dress off you?" he panted. She smiled up at him, a lovely smile, conspiratorial with sensuality. She took a step backward and undid another two buttons at her waist.

The dress slid down to lie like a pink cloud around her sandaled feet. She unfastened her strapless bra and let it, too, fall to the floor. She was bare except for a pale pink silky half slip.

He looked her up and down in happy disbelief. His hands slid around her waist. "Mickey," he said, half-choked with needing her, "do you want this? Really? Are you sure?"

"I'm sure," she said.

He drew her down onto the bunk. He reached beneath the slip and began to touch her most secret places.

MICKEY LAY on the bunk beside Adam. Both were naked. He had pulled a sheet over the two of them, and she nestled in the crook of his arm.

"I should go," she said reluctantly.

He turned and kissed her on the forehead. "I don't want you to. I want you to stay."

"I can't. They may wait up for me. It must be late already. It's going to be hard to explain."

He smoothed her hair with the back of his hand. "Why do you have to explain? You're an adult."

Mickey drew back from him, suddenly feeling moody. "I know. It's just that Caro's had enough shocks for a while. We didn't time this well."

But he stroked her hair again. "I don't think we timed it, Mick. It happened because we wanted it to happen. Since that first night in Texas."

"Still…" her voice trailed off.

In part, he was right. As soon as she'd agreed to go into the village with him tonight, she'd felt the inevitability of making love to him. As soon as she stepped on the boat, she'd known, in her heart what they were going to do. They were consenting adults, they'd had safe sex. It was their business—who could be hurt by it?

But she knew the answer. "I've deceived Vern and Carolyn. Especially Carolyn. First I didn't tell her the facts about you."

He raised himself on one elbow. "That was to protect her, and you know it, love." He kissed her lips.

Love. He'd never said that word to her before, it gave her a shivery feeling deep inside, an unexpected happiness. But she was sad, too. "I didn't tell her how I felt about you. That was to protect me."

"From what?" He kissed her bare shoulder.

"From admitting it to myself. From being on your side, when I owe my loyalty to her."

"But you didn't speak against me. She told me so."

"No. Yet I did my best to find that you weren't the way you seem."

"For her sake?" He kissed her between her breasts. "Or your own?"

She drew away from him. "For hers and mine. We both had to know who you really were. We couldn't afford to be mistaken."

This time he made no move to stop her. "You mean fooled. You didn't want her taken in by a con artist. Who'd take her land dishonestly."

She sat on the edge of the bed, clutching the sheet to hide her nakedness, and gathered her bra, panties and half slip.

He watched. "And if I fooled you, what would I have taken from you?"

"My pride." She stood, slipped into the shadows, turned her back on him and began to dress. "My self-respect. I—I never wanted to be like my mother was. Her judgment about men was terrible. Disastrous. I swore to be different."

He stood and came to her, putting his hands on her upper arms. "And how are they now? Your pride and self-respect?"

She paused, feeling the warmth and strength of his nearness. A fresh tingle of desire flowed through her. "I feel a little compromised. But if we hadn't done this, I think I would have regretted it my whole life. Still, if it was going to happen, it shouldn't have happened this soon."

"We couldn't wait." He moved aside her hair and kissed the nape of her neck. "You know that."

Mickey closed her eyes and shivered. If he kept after her this way, she'd be unable to resist him. She'd turn, kiss him as hungrily as before and end up in his bed again.

"Stop," she ordered, even though her blood was pounding. Again she stepped away. She picked up her dress and tried to shake the wrinkles out of it. "Who knows? The lease land problem's over. We won't see much of each other after this— Texas is a long way from here."

He moved to her, this time standing before her, unashamed of his nakedness. "We will see each other. I'll come to Texas for you. And someday, I want you to come back here with me. For good."

She'd been buttoning the front of her sundress, but she stopped and stared at him. In the dim light, his face looked completely serious. "What?" she said, uncomprehending.

"I want you to marry me," he said. "I love you."

She gave a small disbelieving laugh. "I can't marry you."

"Why not?" He put his hands on her half-covered breasts. "You love me, too. I know because you're here with me now."

"I belong in Texas," she said. But she thought, *Do I? Really? I always thought I did. But it feels so good to be here with you. And so right. Yet...*

She shook her head. "My place is in Claro County."

"No," he said. "It's here. With me. We'll live and work together."

Could they do such a thing? No. It was impossible. The gap between his world and hers was too great. The Isabella Islands were a foreign country, beautiful—but unknown.

Carolyn and Vern were her family. She couldn't leave them.

The Circle T was both her home and haven, where she fit in and did the work she rejoiced in.

Adam's hands moved to her face, his thumbs brushing the curves of her cheekbones. He bent nearer. "Mickey, I know what's going through your mind. You're thinking of how different we are, how different Los Eremitas is from the Hill Country, and how far you'll be from Texas."

"You're right," she said unhappily. "We're not—alike."

"Yes, we are. We're alike here—" he laid his finger against her forehead "—in our minds. And here—" his hand moved to rest over her pounding heart. "In our feelings. In our souls."

His words made her resistance waver, and his touch weakened her.

He took her hand and laid it against his bare chest. "In the deepest parts of us, we're the same."

She shook her head, struggling to overpower her emotions with reason.

He drew even nearer, the warmth of his flesh making hers tingle. "Mick, I'll do anything to make you happy here. I wouldn't ask you to live on this boat. I know Albert and Elsie would rent us the house where you're staying. Maybe we could even buy it someday. A home of our own. Would you like that?"

A knot formed in her throat. Only yesterday she had thought if she had such a house, she'd never leave it. But again she forced herself to stay on the safe and logical side. "It's not just a matter of real estate. Carolyn needs me—"

"I need you more. And the horses need you. The *work* needs you. Elsie's handled all the organizational details from the beginning. But she's elderly, Mick. The job's starting to wear on her. But you—you're a natural. You'd never be bored. And you could do as much or as little as you wanted. But together, who knows what we might accomplish."

He groaned and smacked his forehead. "God, I sound like

I'm trying to hire you or use you or—that's not how I meant it." He clasped her shoulders and peered into her eyes. "The bottom line is that I love you. Do you love me?"

She could not stop herself. She put her arms around his neck, raising her lips to his again. "I do love you," she whispered. "Yes. But love doesn't solve everything."

"It's a great start," he murmured. "You've got tears in your eyes. Don't cry, please. I didn't mean to push. Take your time to decide, Mickey. Take as long as you want. You're worth waiting for."

Confusion tore her. Despite his kindness or perhaps because of it, her tears welled over.

He kissed them away. He undressed her and they made love again. And for a time, her confusion fled. Instead there was joy and desire and a sense of completeness.

WHEN ADAM DROVE Mickey back, the hour was late. The little house was nearly dark, with only the porch, entry and hall lights left on so Mickey would be able to see her way to her room.

But she didn't go inside immediately. She and Adam stood on the back porch, kissing and embracing until she was reeling with pleasure. At last they managed to say good-night.

Mickey slipped inside, still warm from the intimacies they'd shared. In bed, she snuggled against her pillow, remembering the feel of his powerful arms around her, of his lips and hands moving over her. She sighed in gratification and promised herself that she would feel guilty in the morning, but not now. Not yet.

But morning came soon and bright sunlight woke her, streaming through the partially opened blinds. Mickey sat up in bed as if electrified and stared and stared at her watch in horror.

Good grief, it's 10:00 a.m. I never sleep this late. Do Vern and Caro know what time I got in?

She thought of making love with Adam and blushed hotly. She could still imagine the feel of his skin next to hers, the taste and scent of him, the motion of the boat, seemingly in rhythm with their bodies.

Oh, Mickey thought in bewilderment, *the things we did with each other were shameless. And lovely. But how do you look people in the eye the next day?*

"I need a cold shower," she muttered to herself. "A very cold shower."

She took one, but she couldn't wash the memory of his touch away. She put on the primmest outfit she'd brought, white slacks, a short-sleeved white pullover with a mock turtleneck, sensible white flats. She brushed her hair back and subdued it with a white clip.

The only makeup she allowed herself was a touch of pink lipstick. When she looked in the mirror, she saw the image of someone who didn't seem to have a carnal bone in her body.

She squared her shoulders and went out to face Carolyn and Vern.

Carolyn stood in the kitchen, her damp hair heaped atop her head. She wore a short robe printed with a pattern of bright flowers. She poured coffee into one of a pair of mugs.

"Good morning," Mickey said as brightly as she could.

Carolyn gave her a knowing look. "It must have been a good night, too. An *excellent* one."

"Oh," said Mickey, flustered, "We did stay out kind of late."

"Hmm," Carolyn murmured. "Yes. Four in the morning. I heard you on the porch. And his motorcycle—when he finally left."

Mickey bit her lip and said nothing.

"Well, come out on the deck and have a cup of coffee with me. I trust you want coffee. I need it. Albert Penndennis invited us to go snorkeling this morning. And that water's *cold*."

Mickey accepted the filled mug. "Thanks."

Carolyn picked up her own mug and headed for the deck. "I heard you getting into the shower just after I got out. The water pressure on this island is low. I like a bracing shower. One that just blasts you. Oh, well, I suppose a person could learn to live with it."

Carolyn settled into a deck chair and Mickey took the one beside her. "I don't think I was meant to snorkel," Carolyn said, staring out at the sea. "I felt claustrophobic. And I kept expecting to come face-to-face with an octopus or some awful thing. I'm a landlubber."

Mickey gave a dutiful nod. "Where's Vern?"

Carolyn rolled her eyes. "Still snorkeling. He loves it. He's getting in touch with his inner sea lion or something." She shrugged. "We've been married all these years, and I never knew the briny deep called out to him." She smiled. "He's kind of cute in those big fins and the mask, though."

Mickey could think of nothing to say.

Carolyn sipped at her coffee. "We go home tomorrow. Are you ready?"

"Yes." As soon as Mickey said the word, she knew it was a lie. She listened to the low roar of the surf and looked at the blue water foaming to white as the waves broke on the sand. Again she thought of Neptune's horses with their manes of froth, the horses that Adam, too, could see.

"I've been gone so much," Carolyn mused. "It's time to get back to business."

"Yes." But sadness filled Mickey and a sense of loss, as well. *I don't want to go. I don't want to leave him.*

"I wish," Carolyn said pensively, "that I could stay. Have time to get to know my brother better. But there'll be other visits. Many, I hope. The idea's still strange to me, you know. My brother. Amazing."

She paused, then said softly, "Still, it'll be good to get

back. I wasn't cut out for island life. I want to see the hills again. The hills of home."

Mickey stayed silent. She watched the sea, as if she could memorize it and in some small way keep it always.

"Home is a strange concept," Carolyn said, still gazing out at the water. "The Circle T has always been my home. The Hill Country is in my soul. I belong there."

She turned to face Mickey. "But not everyone feels like that about where they grew up. Beverly didn't. When I asked her how she could go to Denver, so far from home, she said, 'Mama, wherever Sonny is, that's *home*.'"

Mickey's muscles tensed. Carolyn nodded. "Vern never dreamed he'd live on a ranch. He does because he fell in love with me—and I with him. Cynthia left New England and everything she knew there when she married J.T. She never thought her home would be in Texas. Until she met him. Then everything changed for her."

Carolyn paused and cocked her head thoughtfully. "People say home is where the heart is. That's a cliché—but like many clichés there's truth in it. Adam's heart is here. Because of the horses."

"I know," said Mickey, trying not to show her uneasiness. Caro was steering the conversation in a strange direction, and Mickey couldn't tell where it was leading.

Setting her mug aside, Carolyn leaned toward Mickey, her face earnest, solemn. "Adam loves you, Mickey. It's clear from the way he acts around you. Vern agrees. I'm sure that Albert and Elsie Penndennis know it, too."

"I— I—" Mickey stammered. She made a helpless gesture.

Carolyn's expression grew more serious. "You're harder to read than Adam is. But I think you love him, too."

Mickey took a deep breath. "I tried not to," she said almost desperately.

Carolyn smiled and shook her head as if in pity. She took

Mickey's hand between both of hers. "Oh, sweetie, I'm not saying it's wrong. He's a fine young man. I'm pleased and proud to have him in the family. And if he's in love, I couldn't be happier that it's with you."

Mickey blinked in astonishment.

"Mick," said Carolyn, squeezing her hand, "my life has been yanked this way and that since Carrie was born. Her sickness changed everything, including me. So did finding out that I have a brother. So did coming here and finding out he's a very good man. Last night I couldn't sleep. I was thinking of you and him. Everything has been so topsy-turvy, and now you might go away from us, too. More change. But I think I'm finally catching on. Life *is* change. To everything there is a season…"

She looked Mickey up and down. "All in white? Like some virgin priestess? Or a bride?"

"I'm afraid I've lost my qualification as a virgin," Mickey said ruefully. "But…"

"Not so sure about the bride part?"

Mickey's throat tightened. She nodded. "There's so much to think about."

"Does that include leaving us?"

"Of course," Mickey said with passion. "You've done so much for me."

"Mick, we'd love to keep you close to us. But that would be selfish. Beverly followed her heart and went to Sonny. Now your turn has come. Change, sweetie. A woman your age needs to be brave enough to take it on. A woman my age needs to learn to accept it. Be free to change, Mick. Follow your heart."

Carolyn kissed her on the forehead. "Just get married at the Circle T, all right? Let me plan and fuss, the way I like to. You're our girl. We want to send you off well when you step into a new life."

Mickey blinked back tears. "You mean—"

"I'm trying to be philosophical about you," Carolyn said, her voice growing gruff. "The task's not easy for me. In fact, it would be easier if you weren't here. I'm starting to feel distinctly less philosophical the longer I look at you."

She kissed Mickey again, this time on the cheek. "The car keys are on the counter. There's just a little time before we leave. Spend it with him. Go to him, Mick."

Mickey didn't have time to think twice. She stood, seized Carolyn by the shoulders and hugged her hard. Then she snatched up the keys. Carolyn followed her to the back porch and stood watching as Mickey unlocked the car.

"Perhaps we could meet for supper again tonight," Carolyn said.

"Yes. Oh, yes."

"But after that, the two of you are on your own."

Mickey grinned and thrust the key into the ignition.

Carolyn waved as Mickey drove off. Glancing in her rearview mirror, Mickey saw her standing tall, but then the other woman rubbed her hand across her face, as if wiping away a tear.

Mickey felt misty, too. As much as she loved Vern and Caro, she loved Adam in a different, life-changing way.

MICKEY DIDN'T FIND ADAM at the marina. The man behind its counter said he had gone to the citrus groves to check on the horses. There'd been the report of another dog attack. Not serious this time, but a colt did need a shot and bandaging.

At the citrus farm, one of the workers told her which road Adam had taken and about how far away he was. She drove slowly and parked about a quarter of a mile from where the man had said. She hoped that if she walked, she wouldn't frighten the horses.

The day was warm, but a cooling breeze blew. The grove

was green, secluded and peaceful. Songbirds warbled, hidden among the leaves.

Mickey saw Adam just as he turned and caught sight of her. Shirtless, he knelt between the rows of orange trees, packing up his first-aid box. A brown-and-white spotted mare stood by him, grazing. The colt, brown and white like its dam, nosed Adam's bare arm then nibbled tentatively at the bandage on its foreleg.

Adam stood, his gaze locked with Mickey's. "I knew from the way the horses were acting that somebody was coming," he said. "I didn't think it'd be you."

"Will they let me come near?" she asked, her heart beating so hard that her chest hurt.

"I'll come to you." He picked up the box and moved toward her. She felt a mixture of shyness and happiness. He acted as if he did, too.

He looked marvelously handsome. His skin was bronzed, and his hair was wind-tossed. He hadn't shaved yet. The sun glinted on his golden stubble. He stopped in front of her and set down the box, but he made no move closer. "I'm glad you're here."

"I am, too." Her heart beat harder. "I came to say—to ask—if you really want to marry me. Do you?"

He stepped closer, seizing her by her upper arms. "Mick, I told you. More than anything. Are you saying…"

"Yes," she said, throwing her arms around his neck. "I'm saying yes. I love you. I want to be with you. Forever."

"Mick," he said with a slow, almost hesitant smile. "Do you mean that?"

"We go back tomorrow. I'll put my affairs in order there, help Carolyn find a new secretary, and, and then—"

"I'll come for you."

"And there's a lot to plan," she said, her lips almost touching his. "I was thinking on the way here. That loft in the house.

You could make that into an office. We could run the fund out of there. You have to get a computer, though. And a phone, definitely a phone. Let's face it, a fax machine wouldn't hurt. I have some new ideas for your Web site, and— Oh!"

She'd been aware of the two horses staring at them with mild interest. But a third, a bay, had joined them, and now a fourth, the white one, appeared.

"More horses," she breathed.

"Yes." He undid her hair clip and let it fall to the grass. He ran his fingers through her hair, tousling it. "Don't worry. They're discreet. They never repeat what they see."

She laughed. "Well, I thought that one thing that might help them would be—"

"Leave the details for later," Adam murmured. He covered her mouth with his and put his arms around her. He kissed her and she kissed him until they were both dizzy. Adam whispered, "Welcome home, Miss Nightingale."

In the background, the little colt nickered. The breeze fluttered, filling the air with the scent of ripening oranges. The leaves rustled, the birds sang, and from the distance came the sound of the sea.

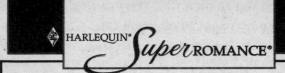

If you enjoyed what you just read,
then we've got an offer you can't resist!

Take 2 bestselling love stories FREE!

Plus get a FREE surprise gift!

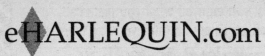

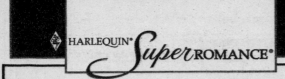

HARLEQUIN *Super*ROMANCE

Single FATHER

The Trick to Getting a Mom
by Amy Frazier
(Superromance #1269)

Alex McCabe and her dad, Sean, have read every
seafaring book Cecil ever published. Who'd have
believed they were written by Kit Darling? Alex wouldn't
have, if Kit hadn't come to town and told them so.

Alex doesn't want to be too pushy and scare Kit off.
She wants the famous travel writer to stick around.
Kit is not only way cool, she actually listens to
Alex—and makes her dad smile a whole lot.

But how is she going to make freedom-loving Kit
stay with them in Pritchard's Neck?

Available in April 2005 wherever Harlequin books are sold.

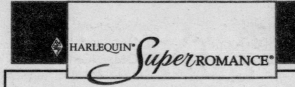